CW00590027

Cold From the North

An Onyxborn Chronicle
by
D.W. Ross

ISBN - 9798555450845

Editing by Kathryn Farmer @ Twenty Six
Cover art by Cherie Chapman

Printed and bound in the United Kingdom
First printing December 2020

Published by D.W. Ross
Contact me at d.w.ross89@gmail.com

Website - www.swordscastleswords.com

For my wife - thank you for making sure I didn't give up.

Chapter 1

The mud was as hard as stone. Ogulf Harlsbane cursed as he tried in vain to break through the glistening top layer with his shovel. He looked along the field, where once there had been row upon row of carrots, cabbages and turnips. Now there was only barren, frozen soil.

He thrust the shovel down again, feeling his braid flip round and brush his face. The rest of his wavy locks followed, tickling at his sore skin.

His latest strike with the shovel proved just as futile as the one before it. Ogulf's eyes wandered from the frustrating grey of the soil and scanned around him again. He could see his hometown, where he would live and die if the cold had its way.

Keltbran had always been cold, but this particular winter had lasted two whole years, completely shattering the traditional running of the four seasons as spring, summer or autumn had been nowhere to be seen for some time.

Ogulf and his people relied on hunting for survival, the deer and boar were harder to find now. And so he missed the hunt. Not so much because he missed the food but more that he missed the thrill of it. Out in the woods and lands that surrounded his hometown it was him against the elements, him against the game he hunted, and– most of all– him against himself. Now the elements always won, the cold subdued him and made the fight against himself even harder.

Life in Keltbran was simple – too simple, perhaps, for Ogulf. He missed the life he had become used to, one that didn't see him constrained by the invisible walls that wrapped the town that he called home; he missed scouring the land with Wildar, trading in the citadels, drinking the wines of foreign lands and occasionally fighting. The last three years had broadened his shoulders and toughened his skin, but if he had known it was to prepare him for this new frigid existence he found himself in, he would have set off for the Far Isles when he had the chance.

That was before the cold. Now he was just another citizen of Broadheim, trapped by the biting cold that was sucking the very life from the land that previously gave so much. In all of his twenty-three years he had never known such un-friendly, bitter weather as this. He would cast his mind back to the last real warmth he could remember, a time when his bones didn't ache, and a time he took for granted.

'Bastard,' Ogulf said as the point of the shovel ricocheted off the solidified, sparkling earth. He may as well have been striking a stone. Beside him, offering Ogulf only his company, was his dear friend Melcun, who was blowing air into his cupped hands. Ogulf felt the fur from his cloak tickle the nape of his neck as a chilly gust of wind swept by. Melcun's cropped hair was frozen at the tips. Cold vapours trailed up from every breath and the sun shone brightly overhead without giving off a hint of warmth, taunting them.

'It's useless. The old lot are going to have us here until we die,' Melcun said, shivering as he spoke. 'Hunger or the cold... which would you prefer to take you?'

'That's a horrible thought,' Ogulf said with one final strike of the spade, he looked at Melcun. His friend's handsome face and pointed features were brushed red and looked sore and they hadn't even been outside that long. Melcun's vibrant grey eyes looked like flint next to the colour of his rosy skin. 'Cold, because at least then I would be numb. Come on, let's go back.'

They walked through the formerly lush fields, the ground crunched beneath their feet with every step they took towards Keltbran.

'Can't you do the fire thing?' Ogulf asked Melcun. 'Seems like it could be quite handy just now.'

'If I could, I would. You know how it works as well as I do – plus imagine the look on the face of old Grolan if I were to magically produce fire from my hands,' Melcun chuckled. 'He'd put me to the rope before I could make any difference.'

Melcun had a point. Magic had disappeared in Broadheim years ago. Rarer still, there had never been anyone with magic abilities born among the people in Keltbran until Melcun came along. His magical talent was the ability to produce fire, and though he never quite understood it or managed to control it despite a near constant barrage of questions about it from Ogulf. The ability came and went as it pleased, and Ogulf hated that it didn't seem to work now, when it would be most advantageous. On the other hand, he was glad it didn't; no mercy was shown to those who practiced magic in their country.

'I know. I'm just getting desperate.' Ogulf stopped short of his home and faced Melcun. 'I thought it would be over by now. This has been well over a year.'

'Closer to two,' Melcun said, blowing into his hands again. 'You must be itching to get away from here. Can't remember you being here this long since we were just boys.'

'Funny you should say that. Wildar was talking about leaving, saying he can get us on a boat at Port Saker and head for the Shingal before heading to Esselonia and the Far Isles and coming back. I was reluctant at first, but the idea is tempting. The only issue is he expects my father to be difficult. Can't imagine he will be happy with his son and his chieftain leaving at a time like this.' Ogulf hushed his tone slightly even though there was no one around them. 'He wants to wait for word from the capital on what we should do next.'

'Esselonia? Oh, not again,' Melcun said and Ogulf looked at his friend just in time to see his eyes rolling. 'He's obsessed with that bloody island.'

'You would be too if you knew more about it. The cold can't touch Esselonia, it's so far south that it is permanently basking in the warm glory of all the gods. Not a frostbitten finger or a pair of rosy red cheeks to be seen there,' Ogulf said, reaching up to pinch Melcun's skin just under the eye.

'You would follow him to the ends of the earth, wouldn't you?' Melcun said.

'Twice and back again.'

'Rowden will never let you leave Keltbran,' Melcun said, 'You're his heir, and at a time like this, he needs you more than ever.' Ogulf felt a sour taste fill his mouth. He loved his father dearly, and he respected him as a leader and as a warrior, but Rowden Harlsbane had been so caught up in grief and responsibility for the last ten years that he had played little part in Ogulf's journey from boy to man. Wildar had stepped into that role, ensuring Ogulf knew how to hunt, scout, fight, and be a man of Broadheim. 'Has your father spoken to the council in Jargmire?'

'All he gets is silence from the capital. The last rider he sent returned saying the gates were barred. Who bars the gates to their own people? Some of the travellers in the inn had a few stories – they say Jargmire and Tran are running out of provisions, haven't got enough to share or even keep their own citizens properly fed,' Ogulf said. 'My father has all but accused them of abandonment.'

'Officially?' Melcun said.

'Of course not, he's not a fool.'

'You think they'll hunker down and wait until it passes?' Melcun's hands dropped.

'Without official word it's hard to know what they'll do,' Ogulf said. 'Look around us, Melcun.' He opened his arms and circled around. 'Tran and Jargmire have closed their gates, we can't rely on them for anything, and we don't know how long this will last. We can't make it over the Sea of Blades without a fleet,' Ogulf said. 'Soon this will all be just as barren as the Throws and I won't wait here until it gets that bad.'

'What would I do if you left?'

'You would be coming with me.'

'You expect Wildar to want the orphan boy on his journey?'

'He was the one who told me to ask you,' Ogulf said, turning to his friend to offer a reassuring smile. 'Might be good for you to get out and see the world. Maybe even learn some more about whatever this talent of yours is.' He motioned to his friend's hands. 'You'll think about it?'

Melcun nodded and the two men wandered towards the border of Keltbran across the bitter, lifeless black dirt. The main road was all but deserted. In normal times, this road would have been bustling: people would be setting up carts, travellers would be using the road as a pass between the east and the west, most likely heading for Tran, Jargmire, or the coast; children would be playing, wives would be chattering and every fibre of the town would be alive.

Empty streets replaced that – gone was the life, now there was quiet. Smoke rose from each chimney as the people of Keltbran huddled in their homes trying to keep warm, many of them believing they could wait out the cold, some foolishly believing they would be saved or supported by the capital.

Ogulf pulled his fur-lined cloak tighter around his neck as they walked towards the sparring yard just past the main square. Every day since the cold had come, the House of the Guided had held a ceremony outside their temple, and today was no different. Ogulf presumed it was their way of praying for help or repenting but he could never tell because they just stood there with their eyes closed and their arms stretched up to the sky. He had seen them do it for minutes or even hours at a time, their robes dancing eerily in the wind while they stood in the abandoned street.

The temple was unlike any other structure in Keltbran. Four stairs led up from the street to a wide doorway, the bricks that held the sanctuary together painted were black, and a sharp spire rose from the thatched roof that towered over the town, coming to an acute point like an arrowhead.

Today as he passed, he pitied them and their ritual. Grolan, Keltbran's resident priest stood above his followers at the top of the steps. The old man's heavily lidded eyes were skyward, his frail arms shook slightly as they reached upwards to the Gods. In front of him were the acolytes of his faith, ten women of varying ages all mimicking his position, facing one another in rows just beyond the temple stairs. Their numbers had grown since the last time Ogulf noticed them.

'Do you think the gods listen to them?' Melcun whispered.

'I hope so,' Ogulf said.

The pair made their way past the tavern. The alley next to it reeked of stale piss like always. Soon the quiet was replaced by the sound of wooden swords colliding as they turned into the sparring yard.

Standing at the fence next to the pit was a burly man with shoulder length hair, his grey beard perfectly straight, flowing down to rest on his chest. Blue eyes of steel and promise sat above chiselled cheekbones, and below them shone an honest smile. His leathers were thick, the strands that bound them woven carefully to create a crossing pattern on each shoulder. He had shoulders so wide he looked like two men across, and a great, rounded gut thanks to his penchant for long mugs of ale. From his hip dangled a single golden hand axe, gleaming in the morning light. It was the most fearsome weapon Ogulf had ever seen.

The broad man was watching two younger men battle with training swords in the circular pit. The dull crack of the wooden weapons took Ogulf to his youth, to times spent under the same tutoring eyes of the man with the axe. A time he cherished.

'Good, right, yes- that's it,' Wildar said. 'Next time, step to the left and strike down at the knee joint to bring him down, then finish him. You'll be a fighter in no time, lad.'

'When can I get an axe like yours, Wildar?' one of the boys said.

'When you get a serious pouch of gold, young Crian,' Wildar said with a slight chuckle, before turning to see Ogulf and Melcun approaching. 'Now, same time tomorrow, lads, okay?' The two young men exited the sparring square, smiling at Ogulf as they passed him. 'Do you miss it?' Wildar said.

'Always,' Ogulf said.

'Well, the things you learnt in here made you the man you are today. We can only hope that the next few turn out to be as able as you, even if we're not here to see it.' Wildar turned to Melcun, 'And you, will you be joining us?'

'I'm thinking about it,' Melcun said, cracking his knuckles, a nervous trait Ogulf had observed in him for years.

'Well, don't take too long to decide, we need to be in Port Saker in a week. Runa won't be joining us so it would be good to have some more familiar faces around.'

'Runa is staying?' Ogulf said, unable to hide the shock from his tone.

'Yes. She's not willing to leave Keltbran when it's like this. She's a good lass, too good. It might make it a bit easier for your father to support you going if he knows someone like her will be staying, though.'

Wildar had a point, but Ogulf knew it pained Wildar to leave Runa here – she was practically his daughter. They always journeyed together, the three of them. Her not being with them wouldn't feel right, but if anyone could fill the void it would be Melcun.

'I'll speak with him tonight,' Ogulf said.

Footsteps crunched from behind drawing Ogulf's attention. Runa was walking down the narrow path, hugged by the climbing walls of the buildings that lined the way.

'We were just speaking about you,' Wildar said.

'Good things, I hope?' Runa said. Her smile was crooked, left that way by a scar she obtained when she fought alongside Ogulf and Wildar in the battles of the Summer of Rebellion. She was beautiful, Ogulf thought, the scar only made her more so; the way she wore it told you so much about her. Well, that and the sword she always carried on her hip. Auburn hair tied in tight braids sat like a crown on her head, and her heavy furs flowed free and long, hiding her body from the cold.

'Always good things,' Wildar said, smiling at the woman.

'Are you here to spar, Runa?' Ogulf said. 'I could do with warming up.'

'You haven't beaten me since before the Rebellion.'

'I guess I'll have to stop letting you win.'

'Ha, the gods know it's me and my spear that leave you on your back in the dirt, you're at my mercy when we're in there,' Runa said, flashing the wicked, pretty smile at Ogulf. 'Actually, I was sent to fetch you; your father has received a scroll from the capital. He has requested all four captains and his chieftain to go to his home so he can update us all.'

'Now?' Ogulf said. Runa nodded. The smile Ogulf loved to see was nowhere to be found. Her eyes were serious now.

'Very well, let's be off then.' Wildar said, walking to-wards Runa up the path.

'Are you coming?' Ogulf said, turning back briefly as he began to follow when he realised Melcun had stayed still. His short hair had begun to thaw since they left the fields; the ends of it danced in the wind.

'I'm not a captain, and Prundan Marsk won't want the pitied little orphan boy hanging around serious meetings. You go on ahead, I have some things I need to do anyway.'

Ogulf nodded and turned back to catch up with Wildar and Runa, his stomach tightening more and more with each step; word from the capital had never felt so crucial.

Chapter 2

The living quarters in the Harlsbane homestead were colder than ever before, the lack of cloud cover in the previous night's sky meant for a night of shivering and a cold home in the morning. You would need ten fires to bring heat to this room.

The upholstery gave off a damp, musty smell that had grown more pungent since the last time Ogulf was in the house. As he walked through the open door of his father's study, with Wildar and Runa in tow, he went straight to the fire pit and let the warmth take the stinging bite of outside out of his hands.

Ogulf's father was sitting silently behind his table. Stress had turned most of his hair grey and his beard looked like a rough collection of dry straw. Ogulf couldn't bear to look at his sunken eyes for too long; they were windows into Rowden's grief and only caused pain whenever he lingered on them. Despite his weathered facial features, Rowden Harlsbane was still well-built, owing to his years of fighting for the King before Ogulf's birth, the muscles he developed then had stayed with him through all the years since like they were some kind of reward for the harrowing experiences he had faced and would go on to endure. On his right shoulder, he wore a steel bracer. On the shoulder panel, there was a craving of a tall tree. It was the only thing he cherished.

In front of him, sprawled across the rough wooden top was a partially rolled scroll, a flattened piece of parchment, next to that a quill with wet ink on its tip and a glass of a dark brown liquid which Ogulf assumed was whisky. The sight of the whisky was enough to make Ogulf nervous; his father only drank it if the pressure and stress was getting too much. The whole way through the winter, the stopper had always been on his whisky bottle, the seal remaining tight and true, waiting to be opened in Rowden's time of need. The fact he had opened it suggested that the contents of the letter from the capital were dire or worse.

In front of him, sitting slouched in the only other chair in the study, was Prundan Marsk, a Captain of Keltbran, and the man responsible for hunting and scouting. His skin was pockmarked and he wore a scowl like a badge of honour, only showing his malicious smile if he was mocking someone. If he hadn't been from Keltbran, Ogulf would not have been fond of the man. In truth, he probably would have wanted to kill him for some of his views, most of which were centred around making Melcun's life difficult.

'You're looking a bit podgy there, Wildar. You've been managing to get more of that ale, I see.' Prundan said. His tone was jovial but there was a seriousness to his question, as there always was.

'I am not sure what you mean,' Wildar replied confidently. He glanced down at his gut, which was more round than usual. 'Ale, and for that matter, any other fermented spirits, work wonders in keeping some of the cold away. You should try it, Prundan; you're looking a bit skinny.'

'Easier for me to hide when I'm this size,' Prundan said. 'I could spot you a mile off, and probably hit you with an arrow from the same distance, with that gut.'

'Feel free to pour a whisky for yourselves,' Rowden said, disregarding what Prundan and Wildar were speaking about. Ogulf, Runa, and Wildar perched where they could. 'The North Hold has fallen.' Silence followed, lingering long enough to make Ogulf's skin crawl.

'What do you mean fallen?' Prundan asked Rowden, sitting up from his slouched position. His trademark scowl had broken to reveal genuine worry.

'A swarm of fighting men are making their way south from beyond the Chasm in the Throws. The fact they took the North Hold rather than just passing through, out of its reach, to raid tells us everything we need to know about their intentions. Either they see us weak or they're also running from the cold and want our fortresses to shelter themselves.'

The flames in the firepit crackled and jumped as Rowden moved from his seat behind the table and threw some dry logs onto the pile. Ashes shot up from the flames as the fresh fuel popped to life.

'How do we know this?' Ogulf asked.

'A letter from the king himself. His advisors expect the horde to move south towards Tran and then on to Jargmire.'

'They'll be crushed on the first day of the siege if they do that. The prince commands a force of ten thousand men at Tran, and Jargmire is impenetrable, how would a horde of raiders ever scale those walls? And if, by some miracle, they did, they'd soon be slaughtered and flung into the moat to rot in the hot springs.'

'The king believes this army moving south dwarfs our numbers. If the scouting reports are true, they took the North Hold, slaughtered everyone stationed there, and are in the process of moving over fifty thousand men further into Broadheim.'

'Reports can be inaccurate,' Wildar said.

'It's all we have to go by. If they have taken the North Hold and they keep moving south, they could be at the walls of the capital within a week.'

'A horde of raiders wouldn't come south in those numbers. Gods, there can't be that many raiders in The Throws,' Wildar said.

'What are you saying, chieftain?' Prundan turned to ask.

'An invasion?' Ogulf interjected.

'I can't see it being anything else. And, if it is, then we're being attacked by Visser.'

'Ha, the Old North?' Prundan said, 'Rising from the ashes of their fallen empire to come and attack us? Don't make me laugh.'

'It's the only thing that makes sense,' Ogulf said.

'None of this makes sense,' said Runa.

'So, what are we to do?' Ogulf asked.

'The letter says we're to wait on further reports from the king. He will be deciding whether or not he needs to call his banners,' Wildar said, stroking his beard.

'The old fool will be reluctant to overreact after doing so during the Rebellion. Won't want to piss off the rich earls if he doesn't have to,' Prundan said.

'Seems more reasonable to do it now. With that many men, this won't be easy to overcome. He should be calling the banners now and meeting them in the field,' Ogulf said.

'That's easy for you to say. Might be the case, too, if you had accepted the post as his advisor. You could have had a knighthood, but instead, you chose to stay here. The gods probably sent the cold our way as thanks for your stupidity,' Prundan said. 'Never in my life have I heard of a man turning down a knighthood, and then we have Ogulf Harlsbane, the man too proud to serve his king.'

'Enough,' Wildar said. Ogulf would have given anything for Prundan to continue; the man had goaded Ogulf like this before, one time it would be too much and Ogulf would reach his limit. But not today. He had his own reasons for turning down the knighthood, and that was all that mattered. 'Rowden, what will we do?'

'Wait on the word from the king. If he calls the banners, we will answer,' Rowden said.

'And if he doesn't?' Runa asked.

'Then we wait here until we're instructed otherwise.'

'Supposing this army takes the capital and comes further south, what would we do then?' Ogulf asked. When he looked at his father, he saw the muscles around the earl's jaw flex.

'That won't happen. The capital will not fall to a horde.'

Ogulf appreciated his father's optimism but his brain worked differently; the king was clearly worried, and if the numbers were to be believed, then this would not be the kind of attack that could be quashed and forgotten about so easily.

'I will call for you all tomorrow so that we can start making arrangements,' Rowden said. 'That will be all for now.'

With a scrape of wood against the stone floor, Prundan pushed his chair back and walked out of the study. Ogulf turned to do the same with Wildar beside him and Runa behind him. He pulled his furs tighter around his neck as he prepared to venture out into the freezing streets once more.

'Well, I guess our trip is on hold for now,' Wildar said.

'I would have to agree with you,' Ogulf said. The sharp, biting wind caught at the back of his throat, causing him to

cough as he wandered out onto the bleak streets of his hometown.

Chapter 3

Ogulf rose the next morning, and as usual, he felt stiff from the cold. Even under multiple blankets, the chill managed to seep through and plunge into his bones, making them throb in a way that was now far too familiar for his liking. There was no doubt that it was getting brisker by the week. He thought about Jargmire and Tran and how helpless the people there must feel. Would they even know an army was coming their way? The walls would surely keep them out, though, Ogulf thought.

The citadels wouldn't fall. They couldn't fall. Tran commanded the biggest force in the whole country, and Jargmire was the most fortified city in all of Broadheim; they would suppress the attacking forces and restore order to the North Hold.

Ogulf made his way outside and began walking down the main stretch of road in Keltbran. He was to meet Wildar in his home, where they would discuss the trip they had planned. If he had any luck, he would also see Runa there.

He was keen to know her feelings now that she had had time to sleep on yesterday's revelations, and he hoped she would be pleased to hear that Wildar and Ogulf planned to stay a little longer.

Runa was five years older than Ogulf and had always been like a sister to him and Melcun.

She was most unlike the other warriors of the clan. She was hardy, determined, strong, and most of all, reliable. She had come from the city of Shingal to Broadheim when she was just a girl. Almost fifteen years had passed since then. Her father was an emissary for the Kingdom of Shingal and he'd frequented Keltbran to discuss trade relations at a time when the town produced enough crops to barter with. A sickness took him during a spell in Keltbran, leaving Runa orphaned in a foreign land. She was well liked by the people of Keltbran, especially Wildar. He took Runa in when she was twelve. Her family in Shingal agreed that she could stay for the winter that year, but she never ended up leaving, even when men came to collect her and take her to her homeland. She refused to leave Wildar or her friends, and eventually, her wishes were respected by her family.

As Ogulf walked on, he noticed a man coming out of Wildar's home, a man he had never seen before. He was smaller than Ogulf, a muscular shape sculpted his thick furs, and he walked fast and light across Ogulf's path and into one of the side streets that wound its way towards the outskirts of Keltbran. The furs he wore were black, as was the large hood that hid most of his face. His mouth and stubble-coated chin were the only visible features jutting out from the shadow of his dark hood. The man wore only one glove. A leather one on his right hand. His left palm jutted from his sleeve and on his wrist was an angry red wound.

Ogulf started and hurried off towards Wildar's home. As he pushed the door open, he was met by Wildar immediately in front of him, and the two men clashed shoulders. 'I suppose you should come in, then,' Wildar said, a vein in his forehead bulging, suggested his annoyance.

'Who was that that just left?'

'A messenger, bringing word of a death in the family,' Wildar said, moving sideways to let Ogulf into his home. It was only slightly smaller than Ogulf's own home, but Wildar's abode was much better suited to Ogulf's liking; it was practical, and because of its size, it was much easier to keep warm. The comforting warmth of the place took over Ogulf's body and he felt the same calm he always did when he entered.

'Someone on the Paleways?' Ogulf asked.

'No, more distant than that. A relative of mine died in Esselonia,' Wildar said. Ogulf watched the chieftain as his shoulders slumped and his voice went flat, almost monotone.

'I had no idea you had family over there.'

'Haven't seen them for decades, but we were close at a time, so it still stings to know they're not with us anymore,' Wildar said. The life had gone from his eyes; they were dull, and he kept blinking to try and suppress the tears that were building up behind them. 'Anyway, I sent a letter back to my family there, offering condolences. Hopefully, we can get moving once this army is defeated at the capital and I can pay my respects in person.'

'I was hoping I would catch Runa this morning as well,' Ogulf said, keen to take Wildar's lead and change the subject to save the chieftain from becoming more upset.

'She's in the sparring yard with two of her underlings. I think she wants to make sure they're ready if the banners are called,' Wildar said with a sigh. He walked over to a hanging pot and poured tea into two delicate cups with markings around the rim, handing one to Ogulf. He looked into the cup as steam flowed up from his tea, taking a deep breath in through his nose and basking in the aroma of the drink. 'I do hope she's able to fight like she used to. She's not been tested since the rebellion, and she's lucky she made it out alive with just that scar as a reminder.' Wildar sighed, then he took a deep breath as he began to stir the tea. He looked like he was trying to stay busy.

'She will be fine, Wildar. You've taught her well,' Ogulf said, trying to reassure the chieftain. 'And, if I know Runa, she will be as ready as anyone else to fight if she has to.'

The large man gave Ogulf a strained smile and sipped his tea. As Ogulf sipped the warm tea, the brittle chill in his bones he had since waking seemed to dissipate slightly as the hot liquid flowed down the back of his throat. Ogulf allowed himself to be comforted by it for only a moment before pushing the pleasant sensations aside.

'If the banners are called, do you think we can win?' Ogulf said, noticing the older man's jaw tense slightly. He knew Wildar liked a straightforward question as much as he did, so he chose not to creep around the subject.

'I'm not sure. I would think we've got a good chance, but this far away from it all it would be hard to say.' Something about Wildar's eyes told Ogulf that he was too distracted for real conversation.

'You're right, here's hoping the king does his best and we get to go back to our travels and get away from this cold,' Ogulf said.

'If only it were that simple. The journey is going to be a bit more complicated now, and I don't mean because of the invasion.'

'What are you talking about, Wildar?'

'It's complicated.' Finally, Ogulf felt like he was getting somewhere but just then, he heard a loud thud, followed by the screeching of a door hinge as someone burst into Wildar's home. The hot air was cruelly sucked from the space and was replaced by the cutting breeze of cool air, and the tranquillity of Wildar's humble dwelling was gone. It was Melcun. His hair looked like a bird's nest and he was panting, trying to catch his breath.

'With me, *now*.'

Each heavy step Ogulf took crunched on the glistening path as he ran. He was still trailing behind Melcun, heading north through the streets of Keltbran. Whatever commotion had sent Melcun sprinting for Wildar's was great enough to draw people away from their hearths and out into the bitter streets. Ogulf tried to pay them no mind as he ran to the main square. He was now only a few steps behind Melcun, but Wildar had fallen slightly behind, unable to keep up with the sprint pace of his younger companions. Ogulf noticed a group huddled around something in the square. Men and women tiptoed to see more, and the ones closest to the middle of the group gasped or covered their mouths.

As they reached the square, Ogulf noticed there was a gap in the group near the communal well, the contents of which had long since frozen. On the edges of the group, a citizen was trying to calm a saddled horse as it reared violently back onto its hind legs. Ogulf knew the horse did not belong to the man trying to subdue it. The steed was huge. It's perfectly kept mane was matted with a spattering of dried blood, and its harness was fashioned from hardened leather with well-polished fastenings and sturdy bronze stirrups. No one in Keltbran had a horse like it; this animal was owned by someone wealthy.

Moving forward, Ogulf gently pushed through the crowds of people and found his father crouched next to a young man, whose eyes were glazed but whose lips were moving. Ogulf moved closer, noticing the man's blood-stained clothes. There were dried red flecks on his pink cheeks, and his jaw was puffy.

'What happened? Were you injured on the road?' Rowden asked the young man. He was motionless other than shivering and Rowden supported the wounded man's head with his hand.

'Ja ... Jarg ... Jargmi–' The man's words were faint.

'You came from Jargmire. What happened?'

'Jargmire has ... fallen,' he said.

'Fallen?' Rowden asked. 'Impossible. The invaders have taken Jargmire?'

The young man's eyes came alive at the last word. He gave a brief nod. 'They slau- slaughtered ever- everyone.' The vigour in his eyes started to fade again. 'You ... must ...' Rowden listened closer as the man faded, as did Ogulf. '... Run.' The last part was said like a whisper. There was a slight commotion as Wildar pushed through the crowd, breathing heavily. As the man's body went limp, Ogulf noticed there was a large gash on the back of his head where Rowden's hand had been.

A chattering grew behind Ogulf as the people gathered realised the young man was dead. Ogulf rose as the murmuring grew to a panic. He felt his chest start to tingle and not because of the cold. Jargmire had fallen. Quickly. The North Hold had fallen only a few days before. Jargmire couldn't have fallen. Not that fast. Its walls could hold a siege at bay for years.

Ogulf's usually undisturbed inner peace was now completely at odds with something he hadn't felt in years–complete and utter terror. Over and over in his head, he played out the worst possible scenario; he saw Jargmire in his mind, and it was burning. He couldn't shake the sight. He knew it wasn't real, but he felt it, so much so that he could swear his cheeks began to get warmer when he thought about it. The sounds of the people's panic were drowned out, replaced by the heavy thuds of his own heartbeat inside his ears.

Aggressively, his father had risen and was making his way to the House of the Guided. Ogulf stumbled to his feet and pushed through the crowd to follow. The people seemed to part for Rowden like water, but as they turned to see where the earl was headed, they blocked Ogulf's path, meaning he had to wade through limbs as if they were a heavy current pushing against him.

He finally managed to push through the multitude of bodies and saw his father climbing the steps to enter the House of the Guided. Shivers crawled up Ogulf's spine as Rowden disappeared into the dark mouth of the doorway. Black smoke rose from a single chimney which jutted out of the intimidating, cone-shaped roof. From the outside, this did not look like a place where those closest to the gods would choose to live or worship; it looked more like something out of a nightmare. Ogulf took the stairs at a rapid clip and followed his father into the temple.

Ogulf knew from experience that, just beyond the door to the House of the Guided, was a tunnel which led down to their main lair. It was vast and cavernous. In the past, the path to the room had been illuminated by glowing plants draped along the walls. They were called Sanlarta roots. In the two years since the ice had taken hold, roots like that had become hard to find, so now the open space just beyond the door and the tunnel were in almost complete darkness, lit only by the flickering glow of a few dying candles.

'No, you should not come down here, Ogulf.' Rowden stopped as the door shut. 'Wait outside, this is no place for you.'

'I'm going with you. They need to understand how bad this is, and you know how difficult they can be.'

Rowden flexed his hand and then stroked his beard. 'Fine, come with me.' They made their way down a winding tunnel which went on for much longer than Ogulf remembered. Roots sprang from the wall where the illuminating plants once hung. They were withered and dead now, and the ends of the branches did not produce light. The stale air made Ogulf feel like he was surrounded by something thick and sinister.

As the father and son continued, a slightly brighter light flickered ahead of them. When they reached the end of the tunnel, they were met with a wide room, vastly different to how Ogulf remembered it. Before, this place had been a shrine to the gods, full of light and life, whereas now it was dark and stank of old, dead leaves. The effigies of the gods were hidden in the shadows of the sparsely lit room.

In the centre of the space was an altar. Behind it was Grolan, the priest, flanked by his female disciples, who stood in perfect symmetry as if they had been waiting for this moment. He wore a dirt marked robe and his hair was matted down, stuck to his forehead in places. His pupils were only just visible through the narrow slits between his heavy eyelids. Black stains crept across his teeth like veins.

Rowden took a step closer to the altar. 'Jargmire has–'

'–Fallen, yes, I am aware,' Grolan said. 'Or perhaps you were going to mention the North Hold. Or even the pending invasion of the whole of Broadheim. The gods had already chosen to bestow such knowledge on The Guided.'

Rowden looked to the dirt floor and stroked his beard. Ogulf had seen his father do this many times so he knew what was coming; Rowden was getting frustrated, the visible parts of his hairy cheeks were flushed red, and most of all, his eyes were dark, quietly contradicting the calm demeanour he tried to show. The sorrow was gone from them for now.

'What do you mean you know?' Rowden asked, his tone tense like his shoulders.

'The gods have told us that the time has come for darkness to reign.'

'Stop talking in riddles, Grolan,' Ogulf said.

'If you knew of these things, then why would you not warn us?' Rowden said to Grolan.

'The gods had not permitted me to tell you. It was not the time. The words had to come from the rider; his blood will lead them here, and the power of the ones who watch over us will protect us.' Rowden's eyes changed as Grolan replied. The acolytes on either side of Grolan stared blankly ahead. They all looked frozen in place, so pale and still.

'They come for Keltbran?' Rowden said.

'Yes, they come with might and purpose as they seek the one that was promised. But they will be struck down by the power of the gods and cast into the void of the Plains of Agony forever. We must wait and be the final stand, the hands and blades of the gods.'

'You mean we are to wait and be slaughtered?' Ogulf said. 'Father, why did we come here? We have no time for nonsense.'

'Because if we have to leave, I need his blessing. Otherwise, half the town will stay and believe that his word is that of the gods. Grolan, give me your blessing to leave Keltbran and take our people to safety.'

Grolan grumbled. 'The will of the go–'

'–The will of the gods should not be to let people who worship them die. Your inaction will be the catalyst of those deaths,' Rowden shouted, cutting Grolan off. 'A boy has just died in our square. He came from Jargmire. They've taken *Jargmire*. Why didn't the gods stop them? Are those in the citadels exempt from the mercy of our gods? At most, this force is a three-day ride from here. We can only hope they take time to regroup before they advance to give us more time to make for the Trail.'

'We will not support your journey south, Rowden,' Grolan said, his voice echoing throughout the chamber.

'If you don't, then those faithful to you will remain here. This is not about power or influence. There will be no Keltbran to have power over once this army gets here. If the gods didn't save the capital, what can they do here? I just want to give the people a chance. Why would you stand in the way of this?'

Grolan's eyes were usually at least half closed. Now, though, they opened wide as if unlocked by a key, the whites of them glowing dully in the darkness of the room. The air behind Ogulf felt like it was being dragged away.

'We can see all, Rowden Harlsbane. What we see is another will going against that of the gods. You are free to leave Keltbran and take those who wish to follow, but the Guided and the faithful will remain to receive our blessings from the ones we pray to. May the gods have mercy on you for your sacrilege and bless your journey so that one day you will recognise the error of your ways.' His voice sounded much more powerful now, as if every word was amplified tenfold. Each word rumbled around Ogulf's ears like war drums, and dirt tumbled from the cavern ceiling in response.

Rowden said nothing, he only grunted. Grolan's eyes returned to their heavily lidded, half-closed norm. The ancient stuffiness returned to the room.

Rowden turned to Ogulf. 'There is nothing more we can do. Come on.' Ogulf and Rowden made their way back up the tunnel towards the entrance. Rowden's steps were filled with anger. 'You make sure that when it is your time to lead our people, you don't rely on the bastard Guided for anything. Bloody heretics. Make sure to always keep your own interpretation of the gods in your heart and follow that, let it take you where it pleases and don't follow any path that doesn't feel right.'

Ogulf's father hadn't said anything like this to him for a long time. He knew his father was a man of the gods, but he also understood how conflicted Rowden had been in recent years, especially since Ogulf's mother had died. He was seeing flashes of the father he remembered and the man he would need to be if they were to survive whatever came next.

As they passed through the door and into the square of the town, they were greeted by the faces of the townspeople. Some looked on concerned, women clutched scarves to their mouths, sharp whispers hid amongst the swarm of gathered people.

Ogulf walked down the steps and into the light of the main square. The bright sunshine made him squint as his eyes adjusted, and the fresh air filling his lungs took away the acrid smell from the lair of The Guided. Rowden came into focus in front of him, bounding ahead through the crowd towards his home, cursing under his breath as every step thumped down. Some of the people reached out to Rowden as he passed them, they asked him questions that Ogulf couldn't make out, but the Earl of Keltbran didn't break a stride.

There was a small gap in the crowd. The lifeless body of the young rider from Jargmire was being tended to by some of the townspeople. They carefully and respectfully laid him on a sheet almost as pale as his dead skin. Nausea coursed through Ogulf like a wave, forcing him to look away from the corpse. The same fate could be waiting for people in Keltbran if they didn't act soon. Who would be there to bathe and burn the dead if everyone was slaughtered? Their flesh and bones would be left to rot in the dirt, their final horrified expressions would be frozen for eternity on their faces, perfectly preserved by the biting cold as a reminder for all of the agony that death brought them.

How could anyone wish to give chance to such a fate? The Guided had always claimed to act in a way that was best for their people, but as far as Ogulf was concerned, it seemed they no longer cared.

Rowden was almost past the crowds when Ogulf felt the urge to call out. 'People of Keltbran,' he said, as loud as he could. The words caught in the back of his throat as the cold wind tried to sweep the words away. His voice wasn't loud enough; he had to repeat himself a few times to cut through the droning noise of panicked conversation. With ease, he vaulted onto an empty cart next to him and scanned the crowd. They began to turn towards him as he shouted, his voice clear this time, and he even noticed his father turn as he reached the edge of the assembled group of townspeople.

'This,' Ogulf said, extending a finger in the direction of the people moving the boy's body, 'Is what you can expect if you stay here.' People tiptoed and turned their heads toward those tending to the dead rider. His skin was translucent; his wide eyes, staring skyward, were still full of horror. 'An army is invading Broadheim.' The people looked at Ogulf, and then at one another, clearly confused. 'The North Hold fell a week ago. This rider came from Jargmire, where he said an army took the citadel and left no one alive. That means Tran will be next, and then there is nothing stopping this army from getting to us. We might not be a citadel, but it doesn't mean we won't be targeted. And if you think we stand a chance when the fight comes... Well, then I call you Brait's Fools.'

'If we stay here, we will die. We cannot wait this out. It won't be slow or something we can put up with like the cold. We will be butchered, so in simple terms, if we wait... we die,' Ogulf continued. 'Grolan and The Guided know this. And yet, he will not tell you to leave, because that would be against the so-called will of the gods. If that is the case, well then, the gods will be Brait's Fools also.' Gasps circulated from the crowd as Ogulf said this. He knew it was blasphemy, but he also knew it was true. The gods who led Ogulf on his path would never leave him to be slaughtered, nor would they allow him to succumb to the cold; they would want him to fight for his survival.

Some of the crowd shouted out, and although Ogulf couldn't understand them, he felt sure that they were countering his comments with insults of their own.

'You may not want to leave Broadheim. I understand this. I don't want to leave our homeland either, my very roots are here, but it's our only chance if we mean to survive.'

'How will we get South when we have no boats?' a voice called out from just in front of Ogulf.

'We take the Widow's Trail.'

A sea of voices crashed upon Ogulf. He made out only a few shouts. 'You lead us to our death on that mountain.'

'How will my children make it round the pass?'

'We would be better off dying freezing and starving in our own beds!' All of these among a verbal peppering of shouts, including, 'lunatic,' 'heretic,' and, 'Brait's Fool.'

'This will be suicide!' One final shout cut through the rest.

'It would be suicide to stay!' Ogulf shouted back, no longer able to mask his frustrations. He took a deep breath in before releasing it to alleviate some of the tightness in his chest.

Ogulf noticed Rowden starting to wade back through the crowd towards him. With a nimble hop up onto the cart, he stood shoulder to shoulder with Ogulf. The wooden slats creaked under the weight of them both.

'My son is right. Now that you know what is truly coming for us, you should understand our predicament. If you wish to join us as we head South, we will be leaving at high sun tomorrow.' Rowden's words left some people in a frenzy, moving towards their homes. Others pushed past them and began to pound on the door to the House of the Guided. 'Ogulf, with me.' Rowden motioned to his son to follow him, and together, they made their back way to his home.

Chapter 4

The evening was young, but already, it was proving itself to be an unpleasant one. So far, it had been filled with heated discussions, half-hearted plans and two separate instances where Ogulf thought a fist fight might break out in his father's home. Tensions were calmed slightly when Yadlin, the town's former priest, showed up to offer his own thoughts on the plans.

Now Ogulf, Runa, Prundan, Wildar, Rowden, and Yadlin were all crammed into Rowden's study. The hermit priest was hunched in an uncomfortable-looking position. His spine was like the wood of a bow, his bald head was a patchwork of discoloured skin, and the only hair on his body seemed to be the grey wisps that sprouted above his eyes. When he spoke, his voice wobbled slightly with age.

'And he said they seek the one who was promised?' Yadlin said, his fore and middle fingers tapping lightly on the table next to him as he talked. 'What else did he say?'

'That the power of the gods would protect us,' Ogulf said.

'He talks in riddles that man,' Yadlin said. 'One of the main reasons I left the temple and never returned. It was like talking to a child, and for someone who says so much, in fact, he says nothing at all. That being said, if you want my interpretation of what he said, there are a few lines which may be of interest.'

Everyone in the room looked on. Wildar was fidgeting, Runa leaned closer to the old former priest, Rowden and Prundan exchanged a glance, while Ogulf found it impossible to concentrate on anything other than the rhythmic tapping of Yadlin's fingers.

'If they come from Visser, they may seek to fulfil the prophecy linked to the ways they followed for years; it's one based on the foundations of the darkest magic known. If fulfilled, it will bring them back to prominence.' Yadlin said, 'The text is very, very old. And it is likely that Grolan has read it too. Rather than being an insight from the gods, it is most likely his own prophecy, one he uses to keep his flock close by in the hope that, by taking their souls to the afterlife with him, he is granted better favour with the gods. If only he knew, our gods don't work like that. Regardless, I fully support your choice to leave. It's no use waiting to die by a blade you can escape. If this is the case, they won't stop at our borders, the prophecy will lead them to attack all Gelenea. They will be headed for–'

'–Enough of this bull about prophecies. Where would we go?' Prundan asked, cutting Yadlin off and leaving the old priest with a bemused smile, his thin eyebrows raised. 'Supposing we make it round the Trail, then what? Just wait at the border and hope they don't make it any further South?'

'We could go to Luefmort,' Runa said.

'Ha, and do you suppose the Shingally's will just welcome us in, then?' Prundan said.

'My uncle is a lord there. I haven't seen him in years, but I am sure he would help us,' Runa said.

'That sounds like a good idea,' Ogulf said.

'I could ride ahead with a few of my scouts and warn them that you're coming.'

'Wildar, what do you think?' Rowden asked. 'Wildar?'

Ogulf looked round to see the chieftain staring out the window, in his own world far away from the conversation. His hands wouldn't stay still.

'Eh?' Wildar said.

'Runa is going to ride ahead to Luefmort and see if her uncle will give us shelter.'

'Oh, right, yes. Good idea.'

Wildar's response caused Ogulf to shiver. Something was bothering the chieftain, something more than these problems they all discussed. Ogulf had never seen the man this unnerved, and he had expected Wildar to put up at least some resistance to the plan to send Runa ahead with only a small group.

But, with Wildar's absent blessing, the plan was agreed, and the group spent the rest of the night discussing their next steps in detail.

**

The next morning when Ogulf was packing his bag, he noticed the light from the sunrise shorten his shadow. He wasn't planning on taking much on the journey South; the things he wanted to take weren't practical or small enough to carry without being a nuisance. So, he decided to take only his axe, his bedroll, a bunch of berries he picked a few days before, a skin for water, and an overshirt to wear while he slept.

His father tasked some of his captains with going around the doors of all those in the town to tell them to travel light and pack smart. Ogulf was one of them and he took Melcun with him, getting him up to speed with all that he had been told at the captains' meeting. He hurried from door to door, met with a mixture of responses; some rubbed their necks anxiously as Ogulf told them what to do, others spat green phlegm at his feet and called him a coward before placing curses on the journey.

Rowden had told his captains that he was troubled by the need to move so quickly. He was forcing people who had spent most or all of their lives here to leave behind their whole existence in search of something new. In the process, he was turning the stagnant town of Keltbran into a flourishing pool of activity as the risks outweighed the comfort that came with staying.

The mood in the town was sombre given the circumstances, but it gave Ogulf a little hope to see his people getting ready to leave. The people here had always strived to prosper, not just survive, and this was no different. Ogulf's people were good people, even in their coldest, darkest hour, they would come through. *Well, some of them at least*, Ogulf thought.

A sudden jolt of panic rushed through Ogulf as he stuffed his crumpled overshirt into his pack. He searched for the trigger or cause. Leaving Keltbran. It wasn't like the times he had left before, knowing he was coming back. Leaving in those instances was easy. This was different. He would leave his home, the memories, the comfort, the roots of his very existence, and in almost all scenarios he played through in his head, he would never be able to return.

Now he wouldn't have a home to return to and had to allow his journey to take him to whatever the gods had fated for him next. As he strapped his bag shut, he tried to quell the emotion inside him. It was the roots he couldn't bear to leave, not the proverbial roots, but the literal ones.

Behind his home stood a huge oak tree, planted in memory of his mother, a place of solace and comfort that he relied on. The relief of knowing it was nearby had been enough to quell even his darkest worries in times gone by.

Now it couldn't do that. If anything, it being static and vulnerable just made it worse.

He hadn't been ready for his mother to leave them when she did. Though, in truth, he doubted he would ever have been ready. His mother had been an incredible woman, not just an earl's wife, not just a trophy of beauty for the people to gaze at, she was a formidable woman with more flair and courage than half of Rowden's captains, old or new. Had she been alive, she would have supported the plans to leave, Ogulf just knew it.

His hands lingered on the harsh blade of his axe as he patted himself down. It was icy to touch and could do with being sharpened–something he would do on the journey to pass the time. Next, he reached into his bedside cabinet and retrieved a necklace, which he placed on his bed. It was made with a small, smooth, jet-black stone, its ridged corners gave it shape, and it was no bigger than a thumb. Symbols were carved around it, these same symbols which Ogulf had stared at on many long cold nights in flickering candlelight as he struggled to find sleep.

The necklace had been his mother's. He still didn't know what it was or what the carvings meant, but in a way, he liked not knowing because it kept part of his mother alive, as if she still had things to teach him. It helped him wonder about his mother, about the things he might have learned if she stayed alive. Along with the tree, the stone kept a piece of her spirit with Ogulf, and having the necklace made leaving the tree behind easier, if only very slightly.

He always kept the necklace in his cabinet, but now he had decided to wear it. He had crafted a new leather strap for it, as the original had not fit around his neck.

For such a slight woman, there was no man who would feel confident if they were to face her with a blade in hand, those were Rowden's words. Ogulf wondered if his father had ever been faced by his mother wielding a weapon. The gods knew there would have been times he might have. Rowden once had a reputation for getting so inebriated that, when he returned home, he would wobble and fall into everything that could make a racket. Ogulf remembered being young and hearing pots clatter and plates shatter as his father returned from the inn. His mother would then storm from their bedchamber to meet him and ask what in the name of the gods did he think he was doing, and why was he making more noise than there was during the world's creation at such a late hour. This would lead to grovelling from his father, then tempered footsteps from his mother, and finally, snoring as his father put his head down wherever he lay to sleep, banished from his own bed by his wife all in thanks to his stupidity.

Tying the knot tight and giving the strap a few tugs to make sure it was secure, he smiled and pictured his mother wearing it. This had been a long time ago, but the image of her in his mind was still as clear.

As he walked along the frozen ground towards the tree, his eyes traced upwards from the roots, higher through the rigid bark and finally to the tallest tips of the highest branches. The tree had grown to be the largest anyone in Keltbran had ever seen, some even said it was among the largest in all of Broadheim. It shot from the ground over fifty feet high and grew quicker than any tree Ogulf had ever seen, dwarfing some of the oldest ones in Keltbran despite being much younger. Its long, smooth roots still seemed to suck plenty of life from the earth, and the tree looked healthy despite the lack of rain or real sun to nourish it. The cold had caused the branches and ends at the top of the tree to wither, but they did so in a way that still captured their grace.

Some people thought privately, and even whispered amongst themselves, that it would be great for firewood, especially with this weather, but no one was stupid enough to say such a thing in front of Rowden or Ogulf.

With the cold so prevalent now, many of the townspeople looked at the tree like it was a beacon of hope, saying while it was strong the people would be strong also. Standing in front of it, Ogulf felt panic flood him again; he didn't want this to be the last time he sought the comfort of the spirit of his mother. Whenever he was troubled and needed to find his way, he spent time at his mother's tree. He wasn't the type to think that trees could talk to people, and it had been years since he truly sought counsel here or even sucked in the calming aroma from the bark. It was just that, when he did, he always seemed to find a solution when he needed it most, all just by sitting and resting his body and mind against the now familiar runs of its roots.

Time was short, so he focused on trying to find the solace he was looking for. As he always did when he came to the tree, he ran his hands down the rough edges of bark, breathed in its familiar scent, and began to think of his mother. Ogulf always chose to rest his back against the tree as if he was leaning on his mother like he had done when he was a child. He never spoke when he was here; he just sat in silence and tried his best to think of his mother.

This time, he was also trying to justify his want to leave. He was a fighter, a proud man, and to leave felt like cowardice. The tactician knew that the odds were against him, though. That staying was tantamount to giving up. For the first time since his first fight, he was faced with a fight he knew he couldn't win. So, there was no other choice but to search for safety and then work out a new plan. The only issue he had was not knowing what that plan was. Usually, he had Wildar to rely on for his next steps or, at the very least, the directions of them. But now, all he knew was that they were headed South, and to get South they would have to make their way around a trail which had claimed the lives of so many men.

It was the same trail that Wildar had attempted before and turned back from. Something Wildar never did, but whatever he had experienced on that trail had been enough to make him vow never to try again.

Seeking the calm reassurance he always looked for from the tree, Ogulf closed his eyes and took a deep breath, adjusting his shoulders to find comfort as the freezing ground began to chill his backside.

His eyes opened as he felt something disrupting his peace. His father's home was ten paces away, but it looked more like a mile, and the solid ground had begun to look more like flowing water. He tried to think of his mother, but he couldn't clear his mind. A dull ache quickly spread to a sharp pain in his temples and his eyes burned, making them feel as if they were balls of fire embedded in his skull and cooking his brain like a roast hog. He tried to call out, but the words never came. The world in front of him disappeared into a black void of nothing, and then suddenly he could see again.

This world was different from his. He was seeing it, but he knew he was not there. He saw a huge mountain with a city built into its walls and sprawled all around it. A huge waterfall spewed out of the mountainside, landing in a pool near the city gate below and trickling through the city limits, giving life to a flowing river of winding blue.

He looked down to realise he was suspended in mid-air. He couldn't see what was stopping him from falling.

By the time he looked back at the cavernous city, he noticed that from every opening, window, or balcony, flames crept out angrily as if they were trying to burn the rest of the world. The entire citadel was ablaze. The waterfall no longer produced water; pouring from the crevice now was a wash of crimson. Blood. The longer he stared at the blaze, the clearer the row of voices became inside his head.

'Death comes for you with the might of fifty thousand swords and more. The power will leave no one but the wicked alive. The world will fall to eternal darkness if it is not stopped.'

The voice was female. It was filled with panic and urgency. 'Do whatever you can. You must not let them have it,' the voice continued, this time it sounded sterner. 'Death is among you. They seek the one born to the call of the black gem. It is near you. They seek it. They seek the one. The one who lures them. They follow her power; they can sense it.'

The voice filled his whole mind, but from his right, he heard the mighty crash of wood being destroyed.

'It must be stopped. Let the gods flight your feet to find your saviour. Be wary of even those closest to you, trust in your will. Only light can stop the Onyxborn and the cold from the north. See this, this death is what awaits if you do not hurry. Stones are cast and motion is underway, this is only the beginning, but you can stop it if you find haste.' More crashes and then footsteps. Ogulf couldn't take his eyes from the blaze of the citadel as he hung in the air. Suddenly, there was a gap in the blaze from a large opening.

From the smoke, an apparition flew towards him, going as fast as anything he had ever seen move. As it got closer to him, it shrieked. The noise was evil and thundered through Ogulf's ears. They ached to the point he thought his head would explode. The apparition got close enough for Ogulf to be sure it was the human form of a woman wearing a head-dress of spikes. The pain from the creature's shriek became too much and Ogulf felt himself begin to fall.

He plummeted fast and felt the cool air rushing past him, causing his clothes to flap and his hair to wrap around his face. The shrieking sound began to dissipate. Ogulf couldn't turn fast enough to see if the apparition was following him. His body spun violently as he dropped, and he noticed the blaze was spread right across the mountainous walls of the huge citadel. Outside the walls was a band of dark figures dressed in dark red robes, all watching the destruction unfold.

When he finally stabilised, he saw the ground rushing towards him. He felt his bones crack upon impact. The crushing feeling accompanied by a sickening pop and a chorus of snaps. With a whimper and a bloodcurdling cough, he was in the darkness once again.

Chapter 5

Ogulf's eyes burned in the brightness. His back was freezing from where he lay, no longer leaning against his mother's tree, but rather on the earth a few paces from its roots. The ground was solid, gritty, and uncomfortable. He groaned and noticed how the upper branches were hanging over him, peering over him, as if checking on his condition.

'What are you doing down there?' Melcun asked as he rushed towards Ogulf. 'I've been looking for you. Everyone is in the square, they're all ready to leave – there are hundreds of them,' he said, helping Ogulf to his feet. Ogulf leaned closer to his friend as his legs began to come back to life, his mind racing in its search for answers as to what he had just experienced. 'Far more than I thought there would be, that's for sure.'

Ogulf felt slightly disoriented as he took his first few steps free from the support of Melcun's arm. A wincing burn lingered in his temples. He dusted himself off as best he could and tucked his mother's necklace under the collar of his shirt. Only half of Ogulf's body seemed to be working, so Melcun grabbed his arm again, dragging him forward. Ogulf accepted the help and let his feet flop on the hard ground one after the other in a thudding, but oddly calming, cadence.

Ogulf started to remember parts of the vision he just had. He assumed he got overwhelmed and then he collapsed. That dream was the most vivid one he had ever experienced. Nothing like that had ever happened to him before. His head was still throbbing as Melcun heaved him along, but his feet were beginning to feel more like they belonged to his body again.

The grogginess wore off as they rushed through his father's home, Ogulf taking a second to glance at it for what he was sure would be the very last time. 'How many people, Melcun?' he asked.

'At least eight hundred want to make the journey South,' Melcun said. 'Maybe more. Some of them seem to have taken a liking to your speech the other day.'

'As good as that is, the Trail will be deadly with that amount of people trying to pass. I guess we need to make sure as many people get through as safely as possible.' As they passed through the other side and out the door into the main street of Keltbran, Ogulf felt that ever more familiar feeling of his stomach turning upside down – the number of people waiting to depart was almost as many as when they celebrated a new year – far too many to make a pass around the Trail. This was a development that would undoubtedly complicate things.

One thing Ogulf noticed as they approached the gathered group was that the mood was different to before. The people who were willing to leave had an eagerness about them, one that was dashed with anxiety and impatience. They wanted to put as much land between them and the invading army as possible. Keltbran felt alive again, only it was for all the wrong reasons.

The two made their way through the people to the main square where Rowden was waiting alongside Wildar and his other captains. As Ogulf approached, he thought he heard a mention of Runa's name, though nothing specific made it through the collective murmurings of the crowd.

'Ogulf, why were you lying in the dirt back there?' Melcun asked.

'I was sitting by my mother's tree when everything just wen–'

'–There he is. Ogulf! Come on, we have leave.' It was Rowden who bellowed from the front of the crowd. 'Grolan is trying to convince people to stay; we can't linger.' Ogulf followed his father's gaze to see Grolan and his disciples on platforms above the crowd. Grolan was particularly animated in a way Ogulf had never seen before.

With the signal of a horn, the group began to move to the path that led south of Keltbran. Ogulf marched at the front with Wildar and Melcun, his father and Prundan just behind them.

On the outskirts of Keltbran, Ogulf noticed a familiar figure in the road ahead. Yadlin was standing there with a thick cloak on. The wise old man wore a pleasant smile as Ogulf approached.

'You won't come with us then?' Ogulf asked the old man.

'I doubt I would even make it to the Trail, never mind around it, my young friend,' Yadlin replied with a chuckle. 'Fear not, I won't be staying in Keltbran.'

'Then where will you go, Yadlin?' Ogulf asked, stopping along with Melcun and Rowden as the rest of the group plodded past them. Ogulf noticed Wildar was still preoccupied by whatever it was that was plaguing him as he moved by, his shoulders were high and full of stress.

'Of that I am unsure. I may make for Saker, and from there, try to find a boat to the Shingal and start a new life. Perhaps incorporate a vice or two here or there this time around,' he said with a wicked smile.

Despite his position as a man of the gods, Yadlin had always hinted that he regretted not taking part in some of the frowned upon but pleasurable experiences the world had to offer. Rowden let out a hearty laugh at his comment while Ogulf looked at the ground.

'If that's the case, then I pray to the gods you get to enjoy your debauchery,' Rowden said. 'We will meet again, I feel it. Stay safe, Yadlin.'

The priest's smile crept a little wider and he nodded at Rowden. 'One day. Some place. Yes, you're right,' Yadlin replied. 'Follow your will, all of you, for that is the true will of the gods. And know in your souls that the gods you and I follow would never want for a person to give up, so keep fighting, striving, and believing until your last breath. Only then can you overcome the darkness. And you–' He motioned to Ogulf. '–I was eager to see you at the helm, I have no doubt you will do great things, young man.'

Ogulf felt the corners of his mouth curl upwards in reaction to Yadlin's words. It wasn't forced; it was a sincere reaction to a sincere compliment. Power or influence were never accolades that Ogulf had ever sought, but a statement like this, coming from a man of the stature of Yadlin, was one of the greatest pieces of praise he had ever received.

Yadlin turned, placed his hands in the pockets of his hooded robe, and began to walk across a rock-peppered brush away from the path. He moved methodically as if every step had a purpose, eyes down and forward without so much as a glance at the people moving behind him. Rowden sighed and re-joined those walking, while Ogulf's gaze lingered for some time on Yadlin as he walked off across the rugged field towards the treeline of the forest. He had wanted to ask the old priest about the vision he'd had, but that would have to wait until the next time they saw one another.

'Let's get moving, Ogulf,' said Melcun, removing Ogulf from his daze. He turned to Melcun before stealing one glance back at Yadlin, who had disappeared past the boundary into the dark of the forest.

The beginnings of the journey south passed without much notice. Ogulf and Melcun were given the responsibility of making sure the pace was kept at the rear of the fleeing group. Prundan sent a group of his best scouts ahead to make sure the path they took was clear. He didn't expect trouble, but there was no harm in employing some extra caution.

They passed a few abandoned villages between Keltbran and the Widow's Trail. The citizens of those villages were the first to head for the citadels and they passed through Keltbran to get to them, telling stories of the cold and despair and how all of the fish in the Blades had died off.

Some of the fleeing townsfolk were naturally slower than others. As Ogulf grew frustrated at keeping the rear, he had an urge to push ahead, but his responsibility was clear, so he had to be as slow as the slowest man. He had seen snails move faster than some of these people as they trudged through the desolate frozen landscape. Before long, some became disheartened, and turned back towards Keltbran. At first, Ogulf and Melcun tried to stop them, but after the first few instances, realised their efforts were futile. The people had made their decisions to turn back, so they pressed ahead with those willing to do the same.

On the second day of their journey, the trekking band of townspeople trailed along a wide path which used to be used for transporting goods from the eastern shores to the citadels. It was a flat expanse of grey dirt which made Ogulf think of death. Broadheim was dead, there was no reason to stay if this was all that there was. The flat plain rose up to a small hill, and at the top of it, he finally got a glimpse of the Widow's Trail. He had seen it before when he used this road, but never like this.

*Do these invader*s *know that they are taking a land that is ripe only with despair?* he thought as he let his eyes run up the dead crop lines to his right.

The Widow's Trail was a formidable beacon of terror which people knew not to attempt. They looked at it as the journey to death itself, and so most people avoided it, instead seeking passage by ship if they had to journey to other parts of the Gelenea. The Trail was seen as a hopeless option, and now the bleakness of the mountain seemed to have enveloped the entire country. Everything looked like it had been kissed by death. Hopeless mud, hopeless people, and a hopeless country.

The path disappeared, going from clear and carved to lost in a grey stretch of dirt as Ogulf came over the brow of a hill. The people traversing down the other side had lost the uniform lines of their marching order and now looked like a disjointed swarm as they carefully placed their feet in the icy mud of the steep slopes in front of them.

'I knew it would be bleak,' Melcun said, placing his feet meticulously as he navigated the sharp side of the hill. 'But I at least hoped we would be able to feel a bit of warmth by now. Wishful thinking is for Brait, I suppose.'

'Hope is good. Hope only exists on the other side of that mountain.'

'Aye, you're right,' Melcun said, stopping for a moment to squint at the mountain in the distance. Ogulf did the same as some of the slower travellers moved past them, stumbling on the uneven surface of the hillside.

Ogulf had never seen the Widow's Trail this close. There were bigger mountains in Broadheim, that was for sure, but there were none quite as daunting as this one, which was their only viable path to safety.

The mountain looked steeper than anything he could comprehend. Somehow smooth and rugged at the same time. The peak climbed to a dizzying height before descending harshly to meet the rise of another smaller mountain behind it, and the land around it was sucked in at the base, making the flat path around it incredibly narrow. Waves crashed along what looked like a jagged bed of rocks where the mountain met the water. It was clear why people died trying to pass this mountain. Ogulf felt his stomach drop, and for a brief moment, he considered swimming across the Blades, feeling it might be less terrifying than the Trail.

The two friends made their way across and down the hills, carefully placing each step on the ground before bearing weight down on it, and in this fashion, they edged towards the foot of the trail. As they did, the group in front began to congregate atop a long, flat ledge ahead.

The wind began to howl. It was much colder on the hilltops than it had been on the low ground. *And this is probably warm compared to what it's like up there,* he thought as he looked up at the mountain pass again, shivering as he bundled his cloak tighter around his neck, pressing on towards the group.

The people of Keltbran set up a makeshift camp in a lightly forested area. The dead trees offered no shelter, but Prundan said that was better than sleeping in the open and Ogulf agreed, as much as it pained him. It was late afternoon by the time the camp was set up. By now the sun was setting, and the light of the day was fading. The biting wind swept through fiercely, an enemy to those trying to light fires, snuffing out every spark that almost caught in the flint and dried bark with ridiculing gusts. Some people resorted to huddling together for warmth, entire families were clustered under blankets and all linked at the arm, staring on as the unlucky member of their brood tried in vain to start a fire.

At least one, maybe even two, hundred had turned back towards Keltbran. Ogulf was glad in a way; the ones less willing would be the ones who could make the Trail harder. When they got onto the Trail, there was no going back.

Eventually the wind calmed slightly, and fires were lit, just in time to counter the darkness that was beginning to take over. The hopes of a warmer air to the south had not yet come to fruition. Ogulf found this disheartening but tried his best not to show it. Spirits were lifted slightly when the scouts came back to the forest camp with three deer and a brace of rabbits. There wasn't much, but the meat was shared as much as it could be among those without sufficient rations. Ogulf refused his share and stuck to the berries he had. They were frozen solid, bitter, and had a chance of giving him stomach cramps, but it wouldn't feel right taking rations from people who had nothing.

Once people had had the chance to rest, to let the warmth from the fire take the ache from their bones and have something to eat, Rowden called a meeting of his captains.

'We go in groups tomorrow. The scouts have said the Trail won't take all of us going at once and we can't take that risk. I'll be leading the first group, Prundan you lead the second, I'll ask Melcun to take the third, and Ogulf and Wildar take the fourth group.'

'You are going to let the orphan boy lead a group?' Prundan asked.

'Yes. Without Runa, Zemin, and Pelta, I need to try and find some new leaders among us. Think of this as a test for him.'

'Brave time for you to try such a thing, Rowden,' Prundan said.

'Well, if this doesn't show us what he's capable of then I don't know what will. What else could challenge him like this?' Rowden said. 'Ogulf and Wildar, you go together as the path will likely be degraded by the time you set off. I need my two best, my very best, to get that group around the Trail to safety.' There was annoyance in Prundan's eyes as Rowden spoke. 'Getting groups of ten around this trail would have been hard enough, but we're taking at least a hundred each. It sounds impossible, I know, but it's better than dying by cold, blade, or bellyache.'

Ogulf hadn't heard his father speak like this in a long time. It was almost as if being away from the decay of Keltbran, now in search of hope or prosperity, he was becoming the Rowden that his people needed him to be, the Rowden that Ogulf remembered. There was a collective nod from the group of captains. Wildar gave Ogulf a reassuring smile, the first notable expression change since his mood had dropped the day before.

Having Wildar with him would instil a level of confidence in his group; they were two of the most experienced scouts and fighters in Keltbran and they both knew how to lead.

Rowden continued. 'Is it as bad as they say, Wildar?'

'It could be worse. There are two ways you can go up the mountain, one is the Hard Way and the other is the Long Way. The Long Way around is the only way we can consider. The Trail we take will run up the hard side of the mountain at first, then it wraps around the face and then spirals down from the peak. It's deceptive; some parts look like a leisurely walk, others you've got about an inch of rock between life and death, so… be warned and tread with as much caution as you can,' Wildar said. 'The peak was as far as I made it last time. You could see the South Hold from there it was so clear.'

'Why didn't you keep going?' Ogulf asked. He tried to make the question sound as innocent as he could.

'Fear. The slope to the peak was hard, but I was younger, fitter, then, and I knew I had more in me. But when we passed the peak and saw what was below, the sight rattled me in a way I have never quite got over.' Wildar's voice sounded uncharacteristically unsteady as he ran a hand through his beard. The group around him leant in closer, listening intently, even Prundan.

'The whole path down was littered with bones and ragged garments. The bones stood out the worst; the rock on the mountain is so dark, except for the peak with the snow covering, so the frozen white bone was unmistakable. I didn't try to count, but the whole face leading down that slope was peppered with jutting joints. So, we turned back.'

Prundan laughed. 'And you lot expect us to make it through this Trail with all these people.' He threw a wood chip into the fire aggressively. 'Should have stayed in Keltbran with The Guided and avoided this Brait's quest.'

Wildar attempted to respond but was cut off by Ogulf. 'It would be a Brait's quest to stay in Keltbran and be slaughtered, Prundan. We have to take the risk.'

'Well, I should expect that kind of talk from a man of your stature, but make no mistake, young Harlsbane, this isn't a battle, not in the sense of the ones you've fought and won before. Even the ones when you were outnumbered five to one had better odds than this,' Prundan said.

Melcun arrived just as Ogulf was about to reply. 'You sent for me, Earl Harlsbane?'

'Yes, I need you to lead a group around the Trail tomorrow, can you do that?' Rowden said.

Ogulf watched Melcun's eyes widen and his shoulders pull back.

'I'd be honoured, I'll do my best,' Melcun said, letting a proud smile pull over his face.

'Heh, your best probably won't be good enough, orphan boy,' Prundan said. He walked over to Melcun and gave him a soft, open-handed slap to the face. The sound of skin hitting skin was quiet, but the mocking intent of it was clear for all to see.

Melcun's eyes went wild with fury but his body remained placid. Ogulf swore he saw a spark jolt from Melcun's hand, but as he did, the group were distracted by the whinnying of a horse drawing closer to them. People began to shout, and all of the captains reached for the weapons at their hips as they spun to face the noise. The horse drew closer. It was a Keltbran scout, returning to camp. When they saw this the captains began to sheath their weapons, but they continued to scan the tree lines for some minutes afterwards. Ogulf let out a sigh of relief as his breathing began to settle again.

'Earl Harlsbane–' The rider dismounted and approached the captains. He was out of breath, despite having been on horseback. '–I got here as quickly as I could.'

Prundan went to the man and motioned for him to sit down. He handed him his skin of water. 'I've rode a full day from Port Saker.' The rider gulped water.

'Saker? I thought it was abandoned,' Prundan said.

'So did I,' the rider said. 'You said to go to Skargholm.' He looked at Prundan. 'The road was unpassable, the ice was too much, so I made to go around Yales Lake and turn back toward Skargholm at The Split, but when I got to Port Saker…' The rider's demeanour changed and fear crept into his eyes. He gulped more water and stared at the fire. Prundan was looking on at him, concerned.

'What did you see, lad?' Rowden asked.

'An army.' The rider was staring into the dancing flames as if reliving the memory in the shapes that they made. 'Countless soldiers. Droves. Thousands. They were all dressed in plated armour, dark red and evil looking. They had horrible weapons – not normal blades or axes – brutal ones like I've never seen.' His gaze broke and he looked at Rowden. 'They must be the horde.'

Wildar was stroking his beard as he glanced sideways at Ogulf. The once deflating feeling of alarm coursed through Ogulf again. He'd never felt fear like this. He searched his mind for more worrisome situations, and in truth, there were none. If the invaders were at Saker, they had come across the border at multiple points. The old East Hold had to have fallen. 'If they're in Saker, they must have come around the Long Peaks,' Ogulf said, loud enough for all to hear but directing the words at his father. 'That can't be possible.'

'Unless they split their force before attacking the citadels?' Wildar said.

'Perhaps,' Rowden said. 'I wouldn't say much sounds impossible anymore given what's happened over the last week.'

Ogulf knew his father was right; it was absolutely possible for all of these things to happen, it was just that no one imagined they would come to pass or that an army or anyone would actually manage feats like this. It was cold, Broadheim was fortified, and the world was at peace.

'If the East Hold has fallen there is no doubt that this is an invasion,' Prundan said. 'But from where? Surely it cannot be from beyond the Chasm?'

Frigid weather and winters in the continent of Gelenea tended to spread from the worst hit parts in the north before tapering off in severity in the warmer climates of the South. For the past two years, almost everyone in Broadheim had assumed anyone situated to the north of their border must have had the cold a lot worse than they did.

'Were there ships in the port?' Ogulf asked. 'Could they have come from Shingal?'

If this was the case then the most peaceful realm in all of the known world had decided to change their focus, so Ogulf thought it unlikely. The Kingdom of Shingal had always prided itself on being an ally to all, and it prospered like no other country could, but a change of tactics may have meant that the Shingally's had noticed the weakness in Broadheim – the cold would have presented a ripe opportunity for a force to invade. They would have to cross the Sea of Blades to reach the East Hold – a treacherous task, even for the most advanced fleet. Not only that, but the invasion came from the north and the Shingally Empire only bordered Broadheim from the South. Furthermore, for a wealthy and powerful kingdom like the Shingal, an invasion of Broadheim would be a fruitless endeavour, unless they had an interest in taking the barren, dying land or their goal was simply to enslave the population. As the stories went, the horde were slaughtering all who stood in their way, so this couldn't be the case either. Ogulf didn't give the idea more than a glancing thought.

'No boats. Only men on foot and some on horseback.'

'We haven't heard from Prath or Ridmir in over five years, and even then, that was an unofficial word – they must have got the cold worse than us. And when we did hear from them, we were on peaceful terms,' Wildar said.

Prath and Ridmir were the twin capitals of Visser, a country that was sometimes called The Old North. It was a vast and formerly populous land which used to rival the Shingally Empire for power, but was now effectively cut off from the rest of the world. Visser lay beyond The Chasm and The Throws to the north of Broadheim. They had been placed in the annals of history as a country constantly struggling to regain their past successes. It was widely accepted the country collapsed before the cold came. No proof of the breakdown ever came, and when the cold didn't go away, the news became unimportant anyway. Ogulf longed to go there if he ever got the chance, to see the fallen empire with his own eyes.

'Terms change,' Wildar said. 'Speculation takes time. We don't have that luxury. We now know this is an invasion; it cannot be anything else. If the citadels and the Holds have fallen, then six hundred Keltbran people aren't going to stop an invading army. The sooner we can get around that pass to the South, the better.'

'Agreed,' Rowden said, supporting his chieftain's theory. 'We go on as planned. The further South we get, the better, and we will know soon enough if this is the Shingal, though I can't see that being the case.'

'The lack of ships makes me agree with you. It won't have been the Shingal. They would gain nothing taking Broadheim. We don't even have grain anymore,' Wildar said to the group, trying to quash the theory once and for all.

'Did you notice anything else, lad?' Prundan asked.

'Their standards. I've never seen them before, not in any texts or in all the time I've travelled. Dark red like fresh blood with black gemstones in the middle, no words, no house names, all the flags were the same.'

Rowden helped the rider to his feet and called on one of his men to make sure he was fed and given somewhere to rest. Prundan followed Rowden and his scout. Ogulf, Wildar, and Melcun remained at the fire.

'Better hope the south is safe. What if this army follows us there?' Melcun said.

'Don't worry. If we make it where I want to go, we will be safe,' Wildar said, his eyes steely and full of resolve as he stared into the fire.

'Esselonia?' Ogulf said.

'Yes, we need to get there. We need to put as much land and sea between us and this army as we can.'

'I've never seen you this worried, Wildar.'

'If I could put into words how my gut feels right now, it would give you nightmares. This prophecy that Yadlin mentioned, if it's what I think it is, worry is only the beginning; soon it will be dread, then it will be terror, and then death. We need to be fast.'

'I didn't take you for one to believe in tales, Wildar.'

'Just because you were told fables as children to tire your eyes and your minds, it doesn't mean there isn't some truth in them. And I know this one has more weight than others. One can only hope that the worst parts are myth and the best parts never come to fulfilment. No use dwelling on it, both of you try to get some sleep before tomorrow,' Wildar said before rising up and walking into the dark of the forests, away from the fire.

Ogulf untucked the leather necklace and began looking at his mother's black gemstone, rolling it from side to side in his hand as light from the fire danced in the dark body of the gem, filling the carvings with brilliance.

By now he was used to the sting of the wind. He resigned himself to the fact he wouldn't get much sleep, so he would try to get as much rest as he could, even if it was just to take the throbbing from his feet for as long as possible. Ogulf bid Melcun goodnight and reluctantly walked away from the dwindling fire towards his pack. By the time he was five paces from its warmth, he was shivering.

Just as he set his thoughts on the south and getting away from the cold, his mind rushed back to what happened at his mother's tree as he willed the stone to give him the answers he sought now. But it wasn't the same and it never would be.

Eventually his mind became overwhelmed and sleep began to creep over him like a calm embrace. He tried to repeat the words he heard in the dream. It must have meant something. He began to say them, but the words tapered off, his aches dulled, and he rested.

Chapter 6

Ogulf woke, shivering from his restless sleep. It was plagued by the jarring sounds of howling animals, constant snoring, and dull aches that made his body tingle whenever he tried to find comfort.

When he did find brief bouts of sleep, his mind rushed between the different parts of the vision he'd had at his mother's tree. The apparition, the huge, cavernous structure in the mountains, and the words spoken by the disembodied voice. His mind was like a chest full of questions, each one trying desperately to escape and find the answers it craved. He still struggled to make sense of it all and spent most of his night staring at the dead, black branches above him, willing them with all of his being to give him some insights or answers even as he cursed himself, for those were not wise trees and their roots could not give him answers.

It was just a vision, a dream, nothing more; it was purely coincidental that it had happened at his mother's tree. Nevertheless, he couldn't keep it from claiming his thoughts, no matter how hard he tried to stave them off. If it had happened anywhere else other than that tree, then he may have been able to discard it. It hadn't, though, it had happened in a place which historically gave him guidance when he sought it most, so he could not dismiss this vision yet. His mind raced as he scoured for answers; this didn't seem like the guidance the tree had offered before, it felt more like a warning. One he couldn't yet understand.

'Today's the day, then,' Melcun said. He was lighting a fire between their two bedrolls. Ogulf had been focused so much on the workings of his mind that he had shut off the sounds of what was going on around him. Scattered around the pair in the forest, people were preparing their packs and eating breakfast.

'I suppose it is. How are you feeling?' Ogulf asked, rolling onto his elbow and propping himself up with an uncomfortable groan. He had gotten so used to sleeping in a bed that the last two nights with just the cold ground to lie on had been some of the most uncomfortable nights of his life.

'Does it matter?' Melcun said, focusing on the fire.

'Of course it matters.' Ogulf pushed himself up more, rolling his neck, trying to loosen the stiffness that clung to it from the failed attempts at sleep. 'I, for one, am shitting myself. And you're leading a group today.'

'Fine, I am scared. And I am angry. That Prundan is always getting at me, Ogulf. He knows how to press me – for the life of me I don't know why he does, though. What have I done to him?'

'I know. But you did almost... How do I put it?' Ogulf said.

'I almost set his beard on fire. I know. It was rash,' Melcun said. 'The further south I am going the more I can feel this ... energy.' He continued in a whisper. 'You saw how it used to be; it would take me hours to conjure so much as a spark sometimes. And now, for some reason, I have *it* right at the ends of my fingertips. I can feel it.' Melcun looked at his hand as he tried to have a spark from two striking stones catch on some tinder. Ogulf looked at his friend getting frustrated as he clattered the rocks together. Melcun dropped them and then looked up at Ogulf, as if he was waiting for permission to do something he had every intention of doing anyway.

'Don't,' Ogulf said, his eyes wide with worry.

Melcun made the slightest circular movement with his hand towards the tinder and dried sticks in the fuel pile, and from nowhere, a flame began to flicker underneath and a few thin wisps of smoke trickled up as it came to life. Melcun gave an awkward, surprised smile when he realised what he'd done. Ogulf had seen Melcun do things like this when he had to, or occasionally when he was angry, but he had never seen him do it this easily. The flames grew, consuming the branches to form a hearty fire. Ogulf was still dumbstruck. He let his hands trail near to the edge of the flame.

The warmth sunk in his fingertips and crept up his arms. It was a feeling he loved, the cold loosening its grip, bit by bit. Giving way to the soothing comfort from the fire made him remember what hope felt like.

'You need to be careful, Melcun,' he said, sitting up and letting the rest of his body feel the comforting heat from the fire. His eyes scanned the people nearby to check if anyone had noticed what had just happened. Since everyone around them seemed too busy focusing on their own tasks, Ogulf let go of the unpleasant worry in his chest. 'No use getting labelled a spellbinder by your own people; they won't accept it, circumstances be damned.'

Melcun was still gazing at his hand. He looked like he was about to try and create another flame so Ogulf reached out and struck him on the thigh. 'I mean it, Melcun.' His friend recoiled when he was hit and nodded nervously. 'We have to prioritise getting south. You throwing hexes or spells around or whatever it is you're doing will only cause problems, especially if one of *them* sees you do it.' He gestured with a nod of his head towards the group of travellers nearby, tone still somewhat hushed so that the crackles of the fire were louder than the words.

Ogulf didn't know much about magic and Melcun was the only person he knew who could wield it. Melcun knew next to nothing about magic either, other than that he could use it sometimes. In Broadheim, the majority of the population took a severe disliking to mages, but that hadn't stopped

Ogulf's curiosity about the arcane, especially given the fact that his closest friend was able to call on the powers of magicka. Abilities like that scared Ogulf in a way, because using them was nothing like brandishing a weapon, but at the same time, that's exactly what they were, weapons of death and destruction according to the old stories. These stories were tall tales of great heroes, the kinds that fathers told their sons at bedtime to prepare their minds for a peaceful night's sleep. *Melcun wouldn't want to wield death in his hands*, Ogulf thought.

'You're right, I'm sorry, Ogulf,' Melcun said.

As the two friends sat by the fire, they saw some of the people start to move towards the edge of the forest with bags slung over their shoulders and determination in their eyes.

'Looks like the first group will be leaving soon,' Melcun said. Ogulf noticed his father approaching them, passing sideways between the people in the crowd heading for the treeline.

'Thirty or so left in the night. Some of those on watch tried to stop them but they wouldn't listen. They said a vision told them to come home,' Rowden said. 'Prundan calls them cowards,' he said to Ogulf.

'I suppose they are cowards in a way. Then again, they have courage by going back to what is surely an inevitable death, which must amount to something, but I'm not sure if it's stupidity or cowardice.'

Rowden was smiling at Ogulf. 'If we run into any problems on the southern side of the Trail, we will be going back to the old ways, sticking to the trees and the dark, just like you've both been taught. We're not cowards, we fight smart, smart people live, stupid people die, and always remember, there is no need for us to fight unless we absolutely have to.'

It pleased Ogulf to hear his father talking this way again. Beyond the Trail, they didn't know what awaited them, so they had to be more cautious; anyone could and should be considered an enemy. Even though the land past there was still technically Broadheim, it was not inhabited the way the main body of the country was. It was all but abandoned after the cold came and the citizens there were shut off from the citadels. Other than a few villages and the old South Hold, there wasn't much between the Widow's Trail and the border with the Shingally Empire.

'Have we heard anything of Runa?' Melcun said.

'Nothing. I expected that would be the case,' Rowden said. 'Not even a trace of her group on the track as far as the scouts could see, which means they never made it this far or …'

'Or Runa covered her tracks?' Melcun said.

'Unlikely, but yes,' Rowden said with a sigh. 'My group is about to leave. Prundan's will leave in two hours' time, Melcun at high sun, and you with Wildar two hours later. That should give us enough time to clear the narrow parts and take our time. We'll wait at the foot of the mountain on the south side; don't worry, you will spot us.'

Rowden walked closer to his son and embraced him. Ogulf was taken aback. His father was a loving man but displays of affection like this were not something he'd offered easily in recent years. As they parted, Ogulf noticed a coating of tears in his father's eyes. They looked ready to spill onto his face at any second. Just as he was about to leave, Ogulf stopped him.

'It's good to see you like this again.' The statement clearly threw Rowden off and he looked on at his son, puzzled. 'You seem like you again.'

With a final squeeze of his son's shoulder and a nod to Melcun, Rowden Harlsbane turned and made his way back through the scattered crowd on the edge of the forest.

Chapter 7

Assembled on the edge of the tree line with the treacherous mountain in front of him, Ogulf glanced at the group he was to lead around the Trail. He recognised most of them. Among the group was Evy, the blacksmith; Cohl, the butcher; Marcas and Manas, the twin brothers of Bharra farm; Sadie, the innkeeper; and a man Ogulf recognised only because he played the lute in the tavern. The majority of his group looked able-bodied, and while their most recent lines of work might not have prepared them for a journey like this, they had all suffered the same hardships in Keltbran. They were hardy people, and if they had come this far, then they wouldn't turn back now.

The previous groups had left a line of heavy footsteps, making it easy for Ogulf, Wildar, and their group to follow their route to the base of the mountain where the path began to narrow. The wind was kind to them as they set off; the bitterness eased off slightly, and wisps of warmth touched Ogulf's skin as he marched in the sunlight. There was plenty of daylight left to make their trip before nightfall. Wildar had guessed it would take them around five hours to get around, if they kept a steady pace, and if the Trail was good to them. Ogulf was not in a place to argue.

The closer they got, the more daunting the Widow's Trail became. Ogulf looked at his group as they came to a path up the side of the ridge, their eyes went wide, their necks craned, and jaws dropped. On either side was a sheer, deathly drop down to the sea below, with jagged rock ridges shooting from the slopes like the teeth of a dark beast. The cragged edges of the cliff face went down for hundreds of feet, their rocks as black as the night, and the white foam of the water danced around the base of the mountain as the waves of the Sea of Blades crashed into it.

On a particularly narrow part of the path, Ogulf noticed severe degradation in the dirt where the other groups had walked. When he placed his feet even very lightly on the path, the dirt crumbled under his boot, a combination of frozen slush and loose rock causing him to slip. He managed to steady himself, then warned the group to take care. This was the kind of obstruction he had worried about; all those boots that had already stomped around the Trail meant that the final group would be met with severely deteriorated walkways, already battered by the fists of time and the weather.

'If the rest of the Trail is like this, it will take more than five hours to get 'round, even with a good pace,' Wildar said in a hushed tone, for only Ogulf to hear. 'We'll be making a descent at nightfall.'

Ogulf didn't protest; he knew that Wildar was right. But what choice did they have? Ogulf had to keep the group moving forward. 'Like you said before, speculation costs time. We keep moving.'

'Aye,' Wildar said with a playful smile and a nod. Despite the fact that he outranked him, Wildar had given Ogulf command of this journey. While they were in the forest, waiting to set off, he told him this was because a fresh pair of eyes would look at the Trail differently; he had seen it before and turned back and he did not want his past experience to get in the way of his judgement now. Ogulf would have liked to decline, but then what kind of man would he be? *I need to do it, for them and not for me*, he told himself, thinking of his people. Wildar was also still preoccupied with something that he would not disclose to Ogulf. Every so often, Ogulf would look at the chieftain and see him fidgeting, shaking his head, or frowning as if he was at odds with a question in his mind. This in turn sent a quiver of unrest down Ogulf's spine; he had never seen Wildar so uneasy in all his life.

Ogulf looked back at the line of people all carefully making their way across the narrow path, which was no wider than a doorway, with a precipitous drop on either side. The next person who wanted to attempt the Trail after the Keltbran people would have a very difficult time getting past as every step seemed to knock a spec of dirt down towards the raging waves, making the track taper even further.

The higher up the mountain the group climbed, the more biting the wind became. The path they were following was steep. It climbed the mountainside at a punishing angle, occasionally turning back on itself, but always, always heading up. Ogulf's thighs burned and stretched more with every step as he pushed forward on the constant incline.

Ogulf could see the remains of what must have been the old footpath as they trudged on. It had once been a well-maintained road which connected North and South Broadheim, and despite the years of decay, the well-trekked road was still partially visible. At the same time the deterioration of the old path was substantial. At some points, stone edges jutted from the ground where there used to be carved steps. Ogulf could see the centre of each was worn away to a dip, showing him where the boots of long-dead travellers had once climbed.

The constant elevation of the mountain meant that the group's progress slowed, and Ogulf reckoned that the ones who passed before them must have struggled here too as he'd noticed marks in the dirt where boots had slid free from the solid ground. Even with footholds becoming harder to access, the group proved resilient under Ogulf's encouragement, and they powered on as the sun began its descent for the day. The winding path led them up and around the peak of the highest mountain on the Trail. Wind stung Ogulf's eyes as he tried to catch a glimpse of the world below. It was like looking at the world through the eyes of the gods. Such a sight should be appreciated. Before he got the chance, the cold became too much. It was almost unbearable for Ogulf. The blue sky and shining sun taunted him again. This time, he thought they were luring him towards warmth. Ogulf grunted, tucked his chin to his chest, fixed his eyes back on the path, and began to move again.

He worked his legs cautiously through the dirt ahead as he began to make the slow, gradual descent down the other face of the mountain, glancing back occasionally to make sure the group were still following behind him.

Now a little further down and away from the harsh torment of the cold, he finally got a view of the lands to the south, and he was struck by the incredible clarity of it. From here, he could see for miles and miles in front of him, and to his amazement, much of the land looked clear of frost and ice. Fields of greens, yellows, browns – fields full of life – were clearly visible. He could see the South Hold far in the distance, its grey hue looming like a shadow beside the vibrant colours all around it.

A smile crept over Ogulf's face. He made no efforts to contain it, just let the tingle of warmth it brought ignite in his chest. *This is what hope looks like,* he thought. Just as he was getting used to the serenity in front of him, he was bumped in the back by one of the people in his group who was still pressing ahead with their eyes focused on the uneven ground in front of them.

Ogulf forced his eyes back to the path and refocused. *Hope was still quite a few paces away yet,* he thought. Something moved on the slope to his left. It was only a flicker but it was enough to catch Ogulf's well-trained eyes. He remembered Wildar's story of the bones littered on the mountainside, but bones didn't move. Ogulf looked properly and noticed no bones, instead he could see the dead bodies of his people scattered down the side of the rock face. Some still had red in their cheeks, others had the grey-white coating of frost on their clothes, and some looked unrecognisable as their mangled bodies lay in horrendous, unnatural shapes in the snow. He counted at least twenty of them, his countrymen, his friends all now wrecked and lifeless.

A scream cut from behind drew his attention. It was louder than the baying cry of the wind. Ogulf turned to see that more of the group were making their way around the bend he had just passed. All of their eyes were lured to the source of the scream, and then to what the woman was looking at; the horrors of the slope were now clear for them all to see. Some began to sob as they looked on. Given that Keltbran was a small place, they must have recognised at least some of the glazed eyes staring back at them. Ogulf hoped they didn't linger too long; they had to keep moving.

The hysterical reactions caused a number of people to lose their footing and stumble. They clung on to those around them, desperately trying to stop themselves from joining the array of empty vessels scattered below them. Ogulf, Wildar, and others near the front called out for the group to calm down, but the panic spread quicker than their shouts could ever have hoped to. Before Ogulf could cry out a second time, he saw a rock at the edge of the cliffside break away and two members plummet down the side of the mountain. As their bodies tumbled down the decline, blood sprayed from newly opened wounds as the sharp rocks punctured their skin. Their souls departed after the first impact, and their bodies became fresh additions to the barbaric collage of death on the side of the Widow's Trail.

'We must be careful!' Ogulf shouted to the group. He couldn't let them slow down, not over two deaths. He couldn't even justify slowing down if they all died. They had to keep moving, and they had to be heedful, if they were to get to their people on the other side. Ogulf had to lead. He looked to Wildar. The chieftain's face was flushed and red, but his eyes were filled with determination. He gave Ogulf an assuring nod.

At the front of the group, Ogulf began to make slow, steady movements onto the next part of the Trail, but his eyes kept betraying him as he stole glances at the south. It was so captivating that was it really any wonder so many people fell off of the edge here? They were lured by a land that looked like the land they used to prosper in, but it was a land they would never reach because they were too entranced by what could be to keep an eye on their footing. *Here is the world that awaits you, it will steal you from the minute you lay eyes on it*, Ogulf thought. He had to calm himself. He could hear people behind him hyperventilating and crying and he ached to give them strength, but it was all he could do to move forward and hope his path was tempting enough for the others to follow. Breathing deeply and studying the rocks in front of him, he took another few steps, each more mindful than the one before.

The path had narrowed significantly. In some places, he had to shuffle sideways with his back against the rough rock. Ogulf noticed the chunks of rock below him on some of the short, flat outlays of the mountainside. This pathway was decaying with every step and they had no other choice but to use it. The fact there were only a few dozen bodies now scattered down the side of the cliff meant that others had made it past this treacherous part of the Trail. Ogulf assumed the path must have been shoulder width wide just this morning and now it was half that at a push, worn away by fleeing feet with heavy hearts.

He felt along the wall to find handholds. The rugged rock felt harsh in Ogulf's palms, their shape made them difficult and uncomfortable to grip. He tested his weight against them and they seemed firm enough to allow some support

The sun began to approach its last phase before setting, letting Ogulf know that time was running out.

Wildar was just behind Ogulf, navigating his way along the ledge in a similarly careful manner. 'We must press ahead, Ogulf,' Wildar said calmly, as if they were not on the edge of a sheer drop down the side of a mountain. 'No matter what.'

Ogulf nodded, pressing his back to the rock face and beginning to shimmy sideways along the narrow path again, this time with more pace. The part he reached now was a foot wide at most. When a pang of bravery filled him, he looked down and noticed that his boots jutted out beyond the ledge at some points. As he stared at his feet, a bead of sweat rolled off his forehead, his clammy hands felt unsure as they gripped at the rocks and he tried to swallow what felt like a brick in his throat.

Another piercing scream came from his left. This time, he didn't look. He didn't have to. Thuds rang out as the falling body rattled against the side of the mountain, with a final, distant crack letting Ogulf know whoever had fallen had landed far below. He edged himself further along the narrow pathway. It felt as though it was going on for miles.

The ledge finally ended and welcomed those who passed it to a flat clearing which looked more like the previous parts of the path on the way up the mountain. The familiar steps with the worn dips in the middle were an encouraging sight. Ogulf and Wildar waited at the edge where the ledge met the clearing and helped others around on to it. Some people stopped before they reached the end, frozen with fear or suddenly looking down and realising the reality of their situation, but a few reassuring words from Ogulf and Wildar seemed to be enough to entice them to move forward.

As the last five travellers were making their way across, the man closest to the clearing stopped. He closed his eyes and refused to move. The others still on the ledge began to shout at the man as he stalled, but he did not move, despite how frantic the people behind him were. Ogulf watched helplessly, then tried to be as encouraging as he could, willing the man to move slowly towards the clearing, but his pleas fell on deaf ears. The others on the ledge behind the frightened man became louder and more agitated as he remained still. Ogulf could hear Wildar's soothing voice trying to calm them as he watched the man on the ledge. His eyes were pursed tightly, and he was uttering something, the same four words over and over again.

A loud crack cut through the commotion as part of the narrow rock ledge gave way. Ogulf watched as the person furthest from him began to plummet from the protrusion, the falling man's body becoming one with a mess of shattered rock from the side of the mountain, which for a brief instant, made it look like he had extra limbs. Letting out a yell as his body dropped, he'd instinctively grabbed onto the person who had been next to him on the ledge. His weight dragged her down as she plummeted too. *They were so close to the doorway to hope*, Ogulf thought.

As if seeing this and hearing the screams of the fallen had given him a rush of adrenaline, the man at the front began to move along the ledge at pace. Ogulf was sure the man had his eyes closed even as he made the last few steps. An angered squabble broke out as the man finally made it to the clearing.

'Enough!' Wildar roared, cutting through the noise. 'We cannot waste any time.'

'Wildar is right,' Ogulf said. 'Come.' He moved through the clearing and back onto the Trail. There were visible foot-steps in the slushy mud leading down a more manageable section of the path, which for the most part, looked sturdy and wide enough for two people to make it down at a time.

As he began to move on the path, he heard the familiar whirr of an arrow getting closer. He felt it flow straight past him and watched a spark fly from a rock in front of him as it ricocheted off the side of the mountain. Instinctively, Ogulf clambered for the cover of the rock face that sloped down the Trail away from the clearing. Others did the same and landed on Ogulf as he crashed into the safety of the space.

'Where is it coming from?' Ogulf cried out to anyone who would listen. He edged to the corner of the turn they had just taken; bodies were still darting around the edge and behind Ogulf for cover. He watched as some of those trying to make it from the clearing were struck in the back, shoulders, and legs with arrows. As he frantically scanned the unforgiving mountainside, he noticed where the arrows were coming from; on an impossibly tight, rugged platform just beyond the ledge stood two soldiers dressed in dark red armour. Their faces were covered by incredibly intricate helmets with only the narrowest of eye slits. They fired and then knocked again as quickly as they could. To the left of them, Ogulf could see some other movement, more men in the same armour attempting to work their way along the ledge, paying particular attention to the crude gap left where the last of his group had fallen.

'We must move,' Wildar said to Ogulf. The older man had shimmied along to hide next to him. 'They mean to pin us here. Trap us.' Wildar's eyes darted around and so did Ogulf's. The arrows were still coming, most never struck anything other than the side of the mountain, but as the frightened people moved to make more room in the sheltered corner, some of them exposed themselves to the attackers. Like sharpshooters, they would loose arrows at their targets, hitting anyone that slipped out of cover with precise strikes.

'This way,' Ogulf said, pointing further down the path in front of them at a gap in the clearing that led back to what resembled a path. 'All of you, with me.' Ogulf began to run towards the space, thinking it should offer enough cover and let them begin their descent away from the arrows. In doing so, those running for the new cover would expose themselves to a chance encounter with an arrow for a few seconds.

Ogulf was sprinting as fast as he could. His feet were light, so he didn't notice if the ground was firm or not. Whistles flew by his ears and yelps and screams came from behind him as he ran. A sharp burning sensation ripped at his left shoulder; he knew what it was, but it wasn't sure if the arrow was still lodged inside him. Diving forwards, he came to a crash on the hard floor and found himself in cover around a bend from the clearing. There would be plenty of room for his people, and to his right was another path down the Trail, one out of the line of the sight of their attackers.

It had only been fifteen feet away, but he felt he'd been running for minutes as he choked to catch his breath. Blood thumped in his ears and he was sure his heart had never beat so fast. Wildar came crashing towards Ogulf, landing hard on his knees and sliding along the rock surface into the safety of their position. Ogulf and the chieftain huddled tight to the wall again to make room for others.

Ogulf could not count fast enough as the bodies blurred past him and 'round the corner, but it looked like there were about seventy or so people huddled around in the space. Ogulf's heart sank. He couldn't be sure exactly how many had been caught by the arrows, but he felt like a failure as he realised that under half of his group had made it this far and they still had a ways to go before they could reach safety. That was if there even was such a thing anymore, now that they were being pursued by these assailants.

His shoulder burned again. Looking round, Ogulf saw that Wildar was wrapping a makeshift bandage around his arm. Blood was trickling from a deep slash where an arrow must have caught him as he ran, passing through the flesh.

As the commotion began to settle and people caught their breaths, the moans of their wounded companions came to them from the exposed area of the clearing.

'Crian!' someone shouted out from the clearing. 'Crian, help me.'

A young boy, he was perhaps fifteen, made to run back to the clearing from the safety of their position, but Wildar grabbed him around the waist and held on tight. The boy flailed to get free but to no avail. 'That's my father … Let me ... I must help him.'

'No, lad, they'll get you too,' Wildar said, trying to restrain the boy as his father's groans continued. A familiar whistle came through the air, followed by a sickening thud, then the groans stopped. The young boy began to shout obscenities in the direction of his father's attackers; he was filled with pure rage and trying to wrestle out of Wildar's grasp.

'If they make it round that ledge we are finished,' Ogulf said. 'We need to keep going.' He began to run. Wildar followed with the young boy, Crian, still screaming and pounding on his shoulder. The cadence of the steps of the others let Ogulf know they were behind him. The thud of boots against stone became their marching song.

Chapter 8

Thankfully, the path around the other side of the Trail was less difficult to traverse. It was not easy by any means, but it was wider, and the footing seemed firmer, meaning Ogulf was able to run at a comfortable pace now, taking the confidence in his steps and letting them push him as far and as fast as they could, safe in the knowledge that his group was not far behind. Most ran at a similar pace, but others lagged further behind. As much as Ogulf wanted to protect the ones at the rear, it would make no sense to rally with the slowest in the group; now was the time in which Ogulf had to move quickly and decisively to get to the other side of the Trail.

He could only hope the progress of their attackers would be marred by the damage to the ledge. Then he remembered what he recently realised about hope: it had meant nothing.

Part of the path wound down at a sharp angle near the base of the highest peak and flowing from a crevice in the side of the mountain, Ogulf saw a huge waterfall. It was so powerful that mist started to gather in damp patches on his face, even though the gaping exit of the cascade was at least ten feet below him. The water fell for what looked like an eternity before meeting the choppy waters of the Sea of Blades in a perfect ripple of foam. The roar of the fall was thunderous as the frothy water spewed over the edge. Ogulf slowed and started to stare at it; the way the water spewed from the mountain like that reminded him of the vision he'd had, only without the fire. Wildar nudged him to keep moving.

The winding path eventually came to a long flat of land which was peppered with snow. He checked behind him again, and to his relief, the group had congregated so they were now running as a pack only a few paces behind him. Even with their dwindled numbers they looked focused, a mixture of fear and determination keeping them going. With a final check of the path above them for their attackers, he called out to the group that they must sprint the rest of the way if they could. No one protested. Instead, they dug the balls of their feet into the ground and opened their strides.

'If we make it that far, the Eternal Overpass is just over this ridge,' Wildar said, panting slightly as he tried to keep up with Ogulf. The Overpass was an incredible structure. Ogulf had heard of it countless times from Yadlin, who occasionally daydreamed about its design and structure out loud during his lessons. The old priest said it was a bridge of wood, steel, and iron chains, and if the stories were to be believed, it was kept in place by magic. The kind of magic that was wound into its very foundations and made it strong enough to stand the test of time; it would not allow the iron or steel to rust nor the wood to wither. Ogulf remembered how Yadlin would peer out of his window during those seminars. His eyes would glaze and his head and hands would move as if he were dissecting the very smallest parts of the bridge in his mind, trying in vain to understand it.

Ogulf could still recall the lecture even though it had been delivered over ten years ago now. The Eternal Overpass had been built one thousand years ago by Fryzer The Red – an adventurer, one of the first people to ever pass the Widow's Trail. Before Fryzer, no one had succeeded in passing the Trail, so the adventurer made it his life's ambition to make the journey easy enough that even the town fool could traverse its steep paths with relative ease. A key cog in his efforts was building a bridge that would let people pass over the Banespit, a gaping hole in the ground with an infinite plunge into the very depths of the earth. So he set about building one which would stand the test of time. Fryzer called upon some of the finest Shingally builders, engineers, and mages to help him build the bridge, they all worked tirelessly for months to construct it, and since its creation, the Eternal Overpass had been true to its purpose without a hint of falter.

Ogulf remembered a time when the Banespit had haunted his dreams night after night. There wasn't much to see according to the books, just a dark void where no life could possibly ever come back from. Fryzer himself always said the Banespit was the most difficult and terrifying part of his journey, and even on his deathbed, he wouldn't reveal how he got over it before the bridge existed. Many theories existed but none held any more weight than the others.

'You're right, and if we haven't seen any other groups, they must have made it across,' Ogulf said, coming out of his daydream. *Or they've fallen into the Banespit,* he thought to himself.

They continued running for a few minutes until Ogulf could just about make out the spine of the ridge in the distance. Just as he felt comforted by the sight, he heard a scream from behind, followed almost instantly by another.

'Those shits have made it down the Trail, Ogulf,' Wildar said, turning to glance behind him but trying not to break stride. As Ogulf turned to look, he saw an arrow slam into the ground between two members of his group, their pace quickened by the terror in the screams behind them. When he glanced over his other shoulder, he saw three armour-clad soldiers with their weapons drawn closing in upon the fleeing group. Despite their heavy armour, they moved with ease and kept to a near sprint the whole time as they bounded forward. Ogulf could see one of the men's eyes through the slit in his helmet and they were wide, white, and full of hatred.

'Over the ridge, quickly,' Ogulf said as he reached the brow of the hill. He stopped and let the others stream past him. Wildar did the same as arrows fell short of them, sinking into the hard mud only feet away. The three chasing soldiers were gaining ground fast. 'We might have to fight them,' Ogulf said, turning to follow the group across the ridge. He looked at the faces of his people, who were pale and panting for breath. Fighting wouldn't work this time, even with the clear advantage in numbers.

The way down to the bridge was steep but passable and the quickest among the group were already approaching the bridge, which to Ogulf's amazement, looked as robust as the stories had said it would be.

Weaved from metal chains, it was wide enough for three men to pass abreast, and when the first runners made their way onto it, a clanging, metallic thud echoed underneath their boots. Their pursuers were now close enough that Ogulf could hear them speaking. Pushing through the burning sensation in his muscles, he kept running as fast as he could.

'Kill the boy. Take the old bastard,' one of them said. Just as he was about to reach the bridge, he noticed Wildar draw his gleaming, golden axe from its sheath. It glistened in the dusky sun, and the reflection glinted in Ogulf's eyes as he looked upon it. For the first time in almost a year, he thumbed the fastening hook off the sheath for his own axe. His right hand and arm felt as if they were independent of the rest of his body as he calmly took the weapon from its holder and gripped its familiar hilt, while his legs were racing, his lungs were on fire, and sweat was pouring down his temples.

As Ogulf's thundering steps finally thudded down on the bridge, he spared a quick glance behind him. 'Once we get to the other side we turn and fight,' Ogulf said, Wildar nodded in agreement. He was panting more heavily now, but Ogulf could see the determination of a chieftain in his eyes.

An unpleasant tinny sound close behind him let Ogulf know that the dark red men were on the bridge and gaining fast. Preparing to make his stand, Ogulf began to look at the ground on the other side of the bridge; it was flat and looked dry, as good a place as any to fight. Becoming aware of his breathing, he sent the last of his energy into his legs to make a final sprint to hopefully gain some ground and give them an advantage on the other side. As Ogulf planted his foot hard for the final few steps on the bridge, an immense light appeared in front of him.

A deafening, crash that seemed to be an entity in itself flew past his head. It gave off more heat than Ogulf could truly comprehend. It was like being trapped in a furnace. Each breath burnt his lungs, his skin prickled, the earth smelt like it was on fire, and his eyes were enveloped by a wall of pure white.

He tried to keep his focus on running as the noise went past, but then he heard a huge crash behind him that disorientated him further. The bridge began to shake just as Ogulf neared the other side. Wildar was a pace or two behind him when the bridge started to disappear from beneath his feet. Ogulf used this last sturdy step to leap and managed to catch onto the solid edge where the bridge met the other side of the Banespit, slamming chest first on the rocky cliffside with a winding thud.

'Ogulf... Ogulf...' Ogulf's eyes were drawn to the source of the sound coming from below him. It was Wildar. The older man was clinging onto the steel slats of the collapsed bridge as it draped its broken walkway into the Banespit. The chieftain was dangling a few feet below Ogulf, his body wavering over the huge black hole. It looked like the beginning of the end of the world. A hopeless place.

Wildar was gripping onto the bridge with one hand, and in the other, he held his prized axe. The slats Ogulf hung onto began to shake. When he looked down, he saw that one of the soldiers in the crimson armour was holding on to Wildar's leg with both hands, thrashing wildly in an attempt to pull the chieftain's grasp loose. Wildar's face was a picture of pain as he fought desperately to cling on, swinging his axe at the man dangling from his leg so hard that it seemed like he would lose his grip trying to strike him, but somehow, the chieftain managed to cling on by his fingertips.

'Take it, please take it.' Wildar was extending his axe towards Ogulf, blade first. The dangling soldier was now trying with all of his might to pull Wildar down into the darkness. He flailed and twisted his body, but to Ogulf's amazement, Wildar hung on. Wildar called out to Ogulf and jabbed the axe closer. 'Take it, boy!'

Just as Ogulf's fingers grasped the cold edge of the axe, he felt a grip on his other arm. Melcun had appeared out of nowhere and was trying to hoist Ogulf over the ledge. Ogulf wanted to be saved, but he didn't want to leave Wildar. Their eyes met as Ogulf took control of the axe, flipping it with one hand to catch a proper grip on the hilt. Wildar's expression grew frustrated but he looked determined to survive. It was as if he was funnelling every ounce of strength into his fingers just to keep a grasp on the dangling metal slats of the broken bridge. Wildar swung his other hand, trying to reach a higher gap and pull himself up, but the attempts were fruitless because he was compromising the strength of what little grip he did have with every one of these small efforts. Ogulf looked down as Wildar's fingertips began to slide and his grip finally started to falter.

Ogulf had all but forgotten the dangling man until he caught glimpses of his armour jutting out from behind Wildar's shape. Wildar was still clinging on. He had tried to wrestle the red soldier off of his leg, but it was not working, and now only the tips of three of his fingers were clinging to the edge. Wildar looked up at Ogulf, his eyes protruding slightly from their sockets as he fought to hold himself up.

'Get it to Feda. The axe, get it to her. She will know what to do. She can stop the prophecy,' Wildar said through gritted teeth as his grip fell to just the top knuckles of two fingers.

'No, hold on, Wildar,' Ogulf said, not paying attention to what the old chieftain said. He just wanted to help him to safety. 'Reach out, take my hand.'

'Gods be with you, Ogulf,' Wildar said. 'Gods be with all of us.'

Ogulf's hand was outstretched towards Wildar, his weight being supported by Melcun, whose body was half-draped over the edge of the pit.

Then Wildar's grip gave in, plunging him into the Banespit. Ogulf cried out as he watched Wildar's body falling. It was eventually swallowed by the darkness of the deep cavern. Body all but limp, Ogulf made no attempt to stop Melcun from hoisting him over the edge with the help of a few others. Shock took over every fibre of his body. He began to pant and grew breathless as his mind became clouded with panic. He was still clutching Wildar's axe when he felt a slap on his face to bring him back to reality.

'Come on,' Melcun said, pulling Ogulf to his feet. 'We need to get to the forest.' As they both rose, arrows began whirring past them from the other side of the bridge, thudding into the trees around them, miraculously, none hit their mark as Ogulf, Melcun, and a few others hurried down the hill and into the forest.

Everything flew past Ogulf in a blur. *Hope obviously doesn't bring clarity*, he thought as he sprinted. He wasn't sure who was in control of his body, but it certainly wasn't him. His legs moved him swiftly towards safety, the will of each movement entirely their own.

As he slowed and the panting intensified, Ogulf realised that, even in the weak light of dusk, there was colour all around him in this forest; the trees were green with life and leaves, the ground was firm and forgiving to run on, birds chirped nearby, and even the wind had softened to a calming rustle. They came to a halt as Melcun called out into the darkness.

'Ogulf's group returns!' Melcun shouted. Ogulf tried to normalise his breathing but his chest opened and closed rapidly. He could hear his own helpless gasps for air, like he was choking on something, but his throat was clear. After a few deep breaths, he dropped to one knee near a small fire, the warmth of which calmed him. He let his eyes wander and found a number of lit fire pits around the forest, their bright light casting the people around them into shadow. One familiar shape was advancing towards him quickly, and even from the outline, Ogulf could tell it was his father.

With a wail, Ogulf fell to his knees, still clutching the golden weapon that Wildar had passed him. As he cried and his father embraced him, Ogulf's thoughts ran uncontrolled. If this was what life looked like in a place of hope and safety, he would take the cold and have Wildar back instead.

The shock of it all became too much. The shock of it all became too much. Breathing hard but unable to take in any oxygen, Ogulf's body fell limply into Rowden's arms.

Chapter 9

A racket of warring voices woke Ogulf. Their tones were loud and angry. Rolling over to see where the noise was coming from caused a harsh pain to flow through his side. It felt like his ribs were being pried apart. He vaguely remembered thudding into the edge of the Banespit when he leapt as the bridge fell, but until now, he hadn't given the pain a single thought. That wasn't the only part of him that ached; his feet were raw and stinging, his knees were skinned bloody, and the gash in his shoulder caused him to feel every single beat of his heart. He looked down at the improvised bandage Wildar had fashioned. It had stayed in place, but it was now caked in dark, dried blood.

The voices he could hear were coming from close by. He focused on a group of silhouettes to his left, standing around a fire. They were moving aggressively in a dance of puffed chests and pointed fingers, the shadows keeping their faces hidden.

Inching to his feet with a wince for every moved muscle, the memories started flooding back. Wildar had fallen into the Banespit, so he was gone. He had asked Ogulf to seek a woman named Feda. Wildar believed that Feda could stop a prophecy and he was to give her an axe. Wildar's axe. His mind was fighting a losing battle as he tried to push away the pain while moving forward to the arguing group. He kicked something with his second step. Looking down, Wildar's axe was placed next to his. The thing had always been an item of amazement for Ogulf, something he stared at with wonder, and now it was there, in the dirt beside his own axe. It was lifeless without Wildar. Just an axe. And it couldn't be his; he was to take it to Feda. *Who in the gods is Feda*? Ogulf thought.

The maze of his mind was twisting and turning through memories at breakneck speed when he remembered something else: the fireball which had destroyed the bridge. Melcun had helped him over the edge. The fireball. Melcun.

'You're a sorcerer!' Prundan's gravelly shouts stood out among the dark figures. As Ogulf squinted, the silhouettes became blurry shapes, and then clear human outlines. Someone was holding Prundan back. A few paces in front of Prundan, another man was being held back. The setting came to full clarity as Ogulf noticed more people beginning to congregate around the argument. He took timid steps forward, closer to the feuding captains.

'I am not!' Melcun said, trying to push toward Prundan while Rowden held him back by the arms. Prundan, on the other side, was being subdued by Evy, the blacksmith. Despite their grievances, and the obvious commotion, Ogulf was relieved to see those familiar faces alive and well.

'Shooting balls of fire from your hands tells me a different story. Enchanter!' Prundan said, and he spat a ball of green grog at Melcun's feet.

'I did what I had to do,' Melcun said. 'Those bastards were about to kill Ogulf and Wildar.'

'And yet your magic seemed to do the trick for them,' Prundan said. 'Wildar's body is lost in the Banespit because of you. Rowden, he is cut from Cormag. He will be the end of us all.'

A jibe like that stung Ogulf worse than his injuries, and it hadn't even been aimed at him. To liken someone to Cormag was the only thing worse than calling someone a Brait's fool. Cormag was the god of all things dark, who had swept the old world away with a deadly plague of evil sorcery before the gods of the new ways confined him to The Pastures of Agony for all eternity. They had then gone on to create the known world, or so the story went.

For years, people in Broadheim who had been suspected of having the ability to use magic had been shunned and told they were descended from Cormag himself, treated as a class below the lowest of the low. Magic and the arcane was not the way of the people of Broadheim - it was a power that should've been reserved only for the gods, not passed on to lesser beings who didn't know how to control it. Sometimes shunning only involved tuts, cautious glances, and the occasional beatings, but other times it meant banishment from the country on pain of death. Those lucky enough to hide their abilities usually fled before they could be banished, typically heading for places where prowess with magic was welcomed – places like the Shingally Empire or the fabled Islands of Brantaga in the far south. Melcun had never expressed an interest in doing this, though, much to Ogulf's relief. Instead, he'd kept his powers concealed for as long as he could, fearing that he would be sent away if anyone caught him.

Only now it wasn't a simple slip up that had exposed his abilities. A small spark or setting fire to a pile of wood could be explained but he had thrown a huge fireball across a fifty-foot bridge, completely destroying the supposedly eternal structure in the process.

Not to mention, Melcun had also inadvertently caused the death of the chieftain of his people. *There's no explaining this one,* Ogulf thought. *It is what it is.*

'You meant to kill Wildar, didn't ya?' Prundan said accusingly. Melcun stopped trying to push past Rowden. His shoulders hunched forward, and his chest deflated; it was like Prundan's words were an arrow that had struck right through Melcun's heart. Prundan shook Evy's restraining grasp from his shoulders as he stopped pushing forward, clearly noticing his words had taken the fight out of Melcun.

'For all we know, he's a spy for these bastards in red,' Prundan said to the people of Keltbran, who had gathered round to watch this exchange. He spread his arms out wide as if to welcome their thoughts.

Ogulf was incensed as he watched Prundan rile up the crowd. Melcun would never do anything like this to harm any of his people, and certainly not Wildar.

With all of his strength, he pushed the grogginess in his gut aside and lunged from the shadows of the gathered crowd towards Prundan, hitting him with a closed fist in the temple. When Ogulf's hand connected, he wondered where the strength for such a blow had come from, then he immediately added aching knuckles to the growing list of things causing him pain. He watched Prundan fall to the floor after the blindside strike as Melcun and Rowden rushed forwards to stop him from attempting another attack. Their hands closed around his upper arms and Ogulf let them hold on to him; he had no desire to throw any more punches.

The rabble went silent, waiting for Ogulf to speak. 'He saved us, you *fool,'* Ogulf shouted at the downed man. People in the gathered crowd began to gasp and mutter. 'If he hadn't done that, Wildar and I *both* would have perished, and there is no way of telling what those bastards would have done if they made it over that bridge.' Prundan looked up at Ogulf with malice. 'There could have been hundreds more of them right behind us. They would have slaughtered us. You should be grateful, because magic or not, Melcun saved us.'

Ogulf stopped pushing towards Prundan and turned away from the group. Prundan rose from the floor and dusted himself off before disappearing into the shadows in the opposite direction, uttering curses.

Rowden and Melcun walked behind Ogulf as he meandered away from the crowd. He swore under his breath at the pain in his ribs. He placed his hand on the trunk of a tree and hunched over; the pain had become unbearable all of a sudden. Ogulf was doubled over, staring at the odd angle the tree shadows created as the bright half-moon illuminated the skies when he heard their two sets of footsteps approaching through the undergrowth behind him.

'You've complicated things, Ogulf,' Rowden said. 'And you, using magic?' Melcun raised his hands as if he were trying to protest the statement. 'No. Let me finish,' Rowden shot back with authority. 'I am thankful. You saved my son. You did what you thought was best. But only a Brait's fool would do such a thing.'

Melcun looked at the dirt but let a scowl take over his face. Before he could respond, Rowden cut him off. 'Now there are people, your own people, who will want you dead if they think like Prundan does – and the gods know that some of them do. I'll do what I can to put them at ease, but no one from Broadheim will be comfortable with having a mage in their ranks. Even–' Rowden raised his hand as Mel-

103

cun tried to interrupt him again. '–Even if your actions did save lives.

'Now, from where I stand, I see this as an advantage. I've known you were – capable, shall we say? – for years. Wildar and I watched from the window of my home while you showed Ogulf how you could spark a fire with your bare hands when you were ten years old, Melcun. How have you kept such a power hidden from everyone else until now?'

Ogulf remembered the very day his father spoke of; it had been only the third or fourth time Melcun had used his abilities in front of Ogulf. Instead of responding straight away, Melcun paused. He was likely waiting for Rowden to start talking again, but Rowden didn't say another word. Ogulf looked at his friend as he let out a long sigh. Ogulf always knew that this moment would come, and given the circumstances, it was actually a blessing that Melcun's powers came to light when they did. A further blessing was the sheer force he'd managed to produce; anything less would have been pointless. Ogulf only wished that Wildar had survived, then this wouldn't be anywhere near as severe as it had been.

Again, a wave of nausea crawled over Ogulf like a spider as he remembered that Wildar was dead. Every time he tried to process the loss, something else demanded his attention. First it had been the argument, then the punch, always the pain, and now this. He could mourn later, for now he had to get his mind right and ensure Melcun was safe.

'Rowden, it- this- whatever I call it, it has never been like this before now,' Melcun said. 'The further south we get, the stronger I can feel it becoming. It's like there is something inside me storing energy or something.' Melcun let out a short breath through puffed cheeks. 'Before, I had to pull so much energy from myself just to create a spark, whereas now–' He looked at his open hand, which began to pulse with an orange glow. '–Now, I can call upon it whenever I want. And by the gods, it scares me.'

Ogulf's eyes were wide as Melcun's hand glowed. The area immediately surrounding them got warmer, there was no doubt in Ogulf's mind that the heat was radiating from Melcun's palm. Just as a small flame flickered to life, hovered, and morphed into a ball over Melcun's palm, he quickly closed his hand into a tight fist, causing the glow, the fire, and the heat to disappear.

'I can feel myself getting stronger, but I'm not even doing anything, Rowden,' Melcun said, tears beginning to well up in his eyes. 'I don't want this. I didn't mean for it to happen. It's a burden. I only meant to protect my friends.' The tears began to flow as Melcun opened up. 'Wildar … I didn't mean for him to die. I tried to save them, both of them. The ones chasing them were so close to them and I didn't know what else to do, all I could do was ... try.' He broke down and the rest of his words fell into a whimper as the sobs took hold.

Rowden embraced Melcun and Ogulf let himself slide to the floor, down the trunk of a tree. The uneven bark massaged his back as he lowered himself, causing the kind of pain that relieves tension. He let himself enjoy the sensation for a brief moment.

Melcun's weeping was loud enough to drown out most of the other sounds. The wind didn't howl here, it just lightly swept by, soothing the burning of Ogulf's skin. With the trunk of the tree propping him up, Ogulf let out a deep breath, one he felt like he had been holding in since before he'd first stepped out onto the Widow's Trail. The South was meant to be where hope was – it was meant to be prosperous – but such things seemed another world away from where he sat. They weren't even a mile past the Banespit and this was already proving to be a Brait's quest, which along with a number of other events in the last day, wasn't exactly what he'd had in mind when they'd all set off from Keltbran what seemed like a lifetime ago now.

Chapter 10

When Ogulf awoke the following morning, he was still perched against the same tree, only now he was covered by a heavy blanket. There was a cold breeze in the air, but it was not the type that sapped your energy, not the type he was used to, it just felt like a natural morning breeze – one that, on any normal day, would be refreshing to wake to. The crisp fresh air was thick with the scents of the forest. Some rays of sunshine penetrated through the ceiling of the trees. Ogulf let his fingers trail through their beams of light, the warm sensation right next to the cold as the shadow created a line in his palm.

For the first time in as long as he could remember, a slight smile curled onto his face as he felt the type of comfort that had long become a memory to him – waking up and not being cold, sources of warmth that were not just fires, the scents and sounds of life.

He looked around and saw most of his belongings nearby. The only thing he couldn't see was Wildar's axe. His untroubled aura was disrupted as he scurried around the tree trunk, ignoring the aches from his battered body as he hunted desperately for the axe.

'Looking for this?' Rowden asked as he extended Wildar's golden axe towards Ogulf. 'Thought I would keep it safe for you. Some weapon that is, sharp as the teeth of the demon gods. Wildar would have wanted you to have it.' Ogulf took the axe from his father. 'I'll take my blanket back when you're finished with it, but I felt you would be in more need of it than me after what you came up against. How are you feeling?'

'Sore.' Ogulf tried to stand, his eyes shut tight and his free hand clutching his ribs. 'Everywhere is sore. How did you get on?'

'Better than I expected; we only lost five people near the peak,' Rowden said. 'The ledge, you know the one I mean, it was bloody terrifying, part of the rock gave way underneath me and I swear by the gods I heard them calling me to the afterlife,' Rowden said in a precise way without much emotion, except when explaining his own near-death experience.

'We saw the bodies. We lost some there as well, not sure how many we lost between that ledge and the arrows.'

'Aye, those who made it back have been sure to tell all who will listen about the arrows. Saying you conducted yourself well,' Rowden said as he rolled up the blanket Ogulf handed him. 'I'm glad you're okay, my lad. I can't be sure how I would have reacted in that situation, but I don't think it would have been the way you did.'

'Wildar–' Ogulf began, hoping to tell his father what Wildar had said.

'–Is gone Ogulf,' Rowden said, cutting him off. 'We've been taught since birth that death is not the end, so treat the passing of these people just like any other, Wildar included. Now is not the time to mourn – we're not safe yet. There will be plenty of time to sink some ales and drown every sorrow you've ever had when we get to Luefmort. I just hope the gods have favoured Runa on her journey. Thankfully, there are no signs to say she didn't make it this far, and that gives me hope.'

That word again, *hope*. All people seemed to be doing right now was chasing an aspiration that might as well have been a mirage for all its substance, and Ogulf was sick of it. He wanted something more, something he could feel, something that would satisfy him enough to keep him from this constant yearning.

Rowden turned and walked back towards a large portion of the group who had gathered near a large, central firepit about twenty paces away. Between them and Ogulf was the open dirt of the forest, sprawling trees with trunks of different widths all with white flowers sprouted around them, and the slumbering bodies of those people who were still enjoying a sleep without trembling.

Those near him looked broken but not defeated. Most organised their things or ate, but they all had the same sorrow filled expression in their eyes. Others wept openly, cursing the gods for taking their loved ones.

The Keltbran were strong people, but an incident like this could shatter anyone's resolve. No one would question their heart or bravery after what they had been through and who they had lost, so the people were given their chance to weep without judgement or disturbance.

Around the central firepit, there were several different groups all huddled and talking separately. Prundan stood at the centre of one of the groups. He tucked his chin into his neck and covered his mouth as he spoke to those around him. Ogulf sheathed Wildar's axe in his belt opposite his own, which hung ready on his left hip. It was too valuable to lie in the Banespit for all eternity, so he decided to give it to Runa; if anyone deserved it, it was her.

As Ogulf made his way closer to what had become the central gathering point, he noticed his father was now perched beside Melcun on a fallen branch, blanket still tucked untidily under his arm. Ogulf watched as his friend's eyes darted nervously around, lingering a split second longer on Prundan and his inaudible council than they had on anyone else. Ogulf knew Prundan would be speculating about Melcun; he would be rallying people to his way of thinking and most likely pointing out that their own earl didn't seem to have a problem with the fact they had a sorcerer in their ranks. Ogulf could only hope those listening were sympathetic and smart enough to know that now was not the time for a banishment or a one-sided trial in a forest. As he got closer to Prundan's group, Ogulf noticed the angry red mark on the side of Prundan's head where he had punched him. Prundan met Ogulf's gaze, and he sneered and spat at the floor as Ogulf passed. Ogulf gave a slight, mocking smile and continued towards his father and Melcun on the fallen log.

'Melcun was just telling me about how Wildar fell,' Rowden said as Ogulf took a seat across from them. Melcun poked at a small fire smouldering in the ground between them, causing the smell of charred wood to fill the air. 'Trust that old sod to leave us now, eh?' the earl said jokingly with a sniff. 'I reckon he would have made it if it wasn't for that bastard who grabbed him. Sure, he was slow in his old age, but he was strong as an ox. Melcun said he spoke to you before he fell, what did he say?'

Rowden looked devastated as he continued speaking about Wildar. He sniffed back hard, the snot gargling in his throat. The only time Ogulf had seen his father like this was when his mother had died, and even then, just a moment before now, Rowden had seemed fine when he spoke with Ogulf on his own. The joking comments were a shield to help him protect himself against his real hurt, which Ogulf knew was brewing like a storm inside him. This was a different tactic for Rowden to employ; usually, he had enough to keep his mind occupied, but in the calming quiet of the forest, the death of his chieftain was the only thing that really seemed to matter.

Ogulf looked over at Prundan's group again. They were still talking in their huddle. He moved closer to Rowden and Melcun and leaned in to create a huddle of his own, and even then, he glanced each way before he began to speak.

'He said that we had to find a woman named Feda. He said she would need the axe so that she could stop a prophecy and save us all.'

Even saying it out loud made Ogulf feel ridiculous, it made no sense, but then nothing had made sense for the last two years – the cold, the invasion, having to seek refuge in another country, dreams of a mountainous citadel on fire, Wildar dying – so this new development was not any more bizarre than what had already transpired. But it was not clear how this could be achieved. For starters, Ogulf wasn't sure who Feda was, how she would be able to save them, or how Wildar's axe could stop a prophecy. And this presented another question which Ogulf found himself pondering as he sat there by the fire: *save us from what exactly?* He wondered if he had heard Wildar wrong. Perhaps he had said a different name or that she could do something else. He ran through the memory in his mind again and again and every time it was the same. Take the axe to Feda. She can stop the prophecy. She can save us.

Rowden and Melcun exchanged glances, both looking as puzzled as each other and about as confused as Ogulf felt.

Ogulf made a point of studying both men's reactions when he mentioned the name Feda, but neither man gave him even the slightest indication that they recognised it.

'I don't know anyone by that name, never heard Wildar speaking of anyone by it either. And what in the name of all gods did he mean about the axe and the prophecy?' Rowden said, glancing back at his son. Melcun shrugged his shoulders towards Ogulf.

'I don't have any idea. Could it be the same thing Yadlin spoke about before we left, the Onyx prophecy?'

'I don't know. But we need to find out.'

'Perhaps Runa will know, she was as close to Wildar as anyone,' Melcun said, then he looked at the smouldering ashes of the fire, his complexion went pale, and the stick in his hand fell to the ground. 'Who is going to tell Runa what happened?'

'Don't worry, I will tell her,' Rowden said. 'And I will explain everything.' He looked at Melcun. 'Everything. You need not worry; she will understand that you did what you had to do to protect your friends, and by the gods, Runa herself will say she would have done the same thing.'

Melcun nodded and Ogulf gave his father a slight smile. He wouldn't wish such a task on anyone, but there was no better candidate for it than Rowden; he had a way with words that helped drain the tension or anger from even the most explosive of situations. Rowden returned the smile but followed it with an index finger pointed first at Ogulf and then at Melcun, and his look turned to a stern one.

'You both listen to me. What Wildar said is not something that we are going to understand any time soon. Right now, we must focus on the last part of our journey, whether that's settling near the border or getting to Luefmort. It will do no one any good if we let this play on our minds, so until we get somewhere that we can talk about this and make some sense of it, we shall not discuss it outside the three of us, understood? Especially with how Prundan is handling himself.'

Both younger men nodded in agreement, then an awkward silence lingered between them all until Melcun asked, 'Couldn't you just remove Prundan as a captain?'

'That wouldn't be wise. Those loyal to him would not be best pleased, and like it or not, they make up a good chunk of our numbers right now, and we cannot afford to splinter more than we already have,' Rowden said. 'And for all his faults, you would be hard pressed to find a man who knows the wilds better than him. He's not quite your ally right now, Melcun, that I understand, but he is closer to a friend than an enemy. You are both Keltbran.'

Rowden had not spoken like this in years. It calmed Ogulf to hear his father's tone change. He had always known what to say, and he saw sense where others failed to – it was one of the long list of traits that Ogulf felt led his father to founding Keltbran in the first place, and becoming the only leader their people had ever known. That part of him had died when Ogulf's mother died, but it seemed to be coming back now, right when they needed it most.

'At last count there are just over five hundred who made it around the Trail. We expected heavy losses on the peak, but the attack has caused the number of dead to soar,' Rowden said. 'We need to press ahead as one, and when we get to Luefmort, we can regroup and make decisions about what we do next.'

'That's just over half,' Melcun said, astounded.

'So, we won't settle near the South Hold?' Ogulf asked.

'No, we make for the Shingal. At least there we might have some form of safety to allow us to regroup properly. If they'll have us.'

Rowden smiled sympathetically at the two younger men and rose to leave his perch – there was nothing else that needed saying. Ogulf looked around the forest and at the Keltbran scattered across the area. Prundan was nowhere to be seen.

'Thank you,' Ogulf said.

'What?' Melcun said.

'Thank you. For saving me.'

'I killed Wildar in the process, Ogulf,' Melcun said, confusion contorting his face. 'You shouldn't be thanking me.'

'You saved *me*, Melcun. Did you expect me not to thank you for that? I know you didn't mean to harm Wildar. But my father is right, we need to move forward. I need you and you need to be strong,' Ogulf said. He reached out to touch

Melcun's shoulder. 'We need to stay strong. Prundan can have his theories, but the truth is, you did what you had to do, and that is all that matters.' Melcun looked up at Ogulf. 'Wildar would say the same thing. And if we're both being honest, I am basically the only friend you have now,' Ogulf finished, trying to tease Melcun. He stood and put his hand out to help Melcun up from the log. Melcun stood tall with Ogulf's help and gave him a smirk. 'Now, let's get ready to leave. The South Hold isn't far from here.'

***

Within the hour, the group had organised themselves to leave the forest and make for Luefmort. They were aided by the faint remainder of what appeared to be an old road. It was uneven, sloped to one side, and was full of holes which were as wide and as deep as two large buckets, but it at least gave them a sense of direction. The divots carved into the ground were the kind that would render a cart and its wheels useless within minutes of a journey starting. On either side were the remnants of an old stone wall. The rocks that made up the wall created a collection of various shades of grey which were the only neutral colours in sight amid the canvas of greens, browns, yellows, and occasional blues in the fields around them.

By mid-afternoon they had made it to the South Hold, and upon inspection from the road, they could tell it was abandoned. It had two great towers which rose symmetrically from a bold keep in between. The battlements wrapped around them in a perfect square and looked almost small when compared to the towers and the keep.

'If it were manned there would be a Broadheim flag flying. Those are the rules. Always have been.' Cohl, the butcher, said to Ogulf and Melcun as they walked together.

'Deserters?' Melcun asked.

'Or they all died from being cut off. Their job is to protect our southern border. They were under order not to leave the Hold so maybe the hunger got them.'

'Surely there is enough to live off around here, though. Plenty for hunting,' Ogulf suggested. He scanned their surroundings; the scenery around them was vibrant. It was a different world to the one he left – it reminded him of how things used to be. 'Or they could have sought some help from the Shingal?'

'Aye, that's true. But I can't see the protectors of a proud nation seeking help from their neighbour, although … that is exactly what we're doing,' Cohl said. Ogulf took this as a jibe at his father, something Cohl would never dare say in Rowden's presence. 'Maybe they deserted after all. Either way, it does not fill me with much hope if that bloody horde gets any further south. Nothing now between here and the Shingal to slow them.'

Ogulf knew Cohl was right. If the invading army got any further south, either by the Trail or by the sea, then there was nothing stopping them occupying all of Broadheim. In Ogulf's opinion, the country was already lost, given that all of the Holds, Jargmire, Tran, and Port Saker had been sacked.

'Do you think they know there is nothing down here?' Cohl said. He spun in a circle as he walked, eyeing the sky and the fields as he did so. 'Well, I hope they feel like fools when they bask in the glory of the empty soil they've taken, and I hope the cold back home turns their balls to ice. We'll get Broadheim back one day, won't we?'

Ogulf thought it best not to respond, and let the crunch of their steps in the muck and on the stone fill the silence instead.

No effort was made to inspect the South Hold. Instead, Rowden made the decision that the group would press forward to the Shingally border and to Luefmort without stopping for the day – a conclusion which drew ire from Prundan.

Cohl continued to walk with Ogulf and Melcun as they trotted along the potholed path. He was a sturdy young man, his hair was fair and always cropped short, a rare style to behold in Broadheim. His gut was round but solid, and a blonde beard sat on his youthful cheeks. His eyes were always open, like he never blinked. On a scabbard on his back, his sword rocked slightly from side to side, the sheath too wide for the blade. Like always, his parrying knife was in a

leather-wrapped sheath on his hip. It was his prized possession.

Ogulf enjoyed the silence among the trees as they
walked. He had nothing to say, and the walk was pleasant
enough to keep his senses occupied and divert his attention
from the throbbing intrusion of all of the questions he sought
the answers to. *Answers cannot be rushed,* he told himself,
remembering one of Yadlin's prized sayings.

The sun was not taunting him on this side of the Trail;
now, even as it began to lower, it still kept the air warm and
the skies bright. Ogulf felt that, with each step away from the
Widow's Trail, the spirits in the group were lifted, and
people even smiled as they walked, letting their eyes wander
across the endless fields of life around them. Eventually
Cohl broke the silence with a chuckle.

'So, Melcun, a fireball?' he asked.

'I'd rather not talk about it,' Melcun said.

Ogulf wanted to interject and warn the butcher off, but
before he could, Cohl spoke again.

'It's nothing to be ashamed of. These old sods might be
fearful, but this could be helpful,' Cohl said.

'This *could* get me killed, Cohl,' Melcun said.

'Maybe. But not if you're willing to use it to protect
yourself,' Cohl said, tapping his temple, his eyes wide and
mischievous.

'What do you mean by that?' Melcun asked.

'Well, if you're too thick to understand, Melcun, what I mean is, if we are attacked again, you can use your powers to protect us. Even with the great military mind of Ogulf here, there is no doubt such an ability could be advantageous.' The butcher cleared his throat. 'I see your swords, spears, and bows, oh villainous challengers, and I shall raise ye one fireball!' Cohl said this in a ridiculous accent, and Ogulf's ribs ached as he laughed. 'No more problems. Only fear. The good kind of fear at that, the fear that makes you untouchable.'

Melcun opened up his strides and walked faster away from Ogulf and Cohl.

'I think he's still a bit down about what happened at the bridge yesterday,' Ogulf said.

'Makes sense, poor lad. I was only trying to cheer him up some. I wasn't joking around for most of what I said, though; powers like that at a time like this, they could make all the difference.'

Ogulf nodded. The butcher had a point.

The part of the road they found themselves on now was closely wrapped on either side by high, overgrown hedges, the leaves and branches of which poked out from the main body of the hedge in an uneven sprawl of joints that caused the growths to bend and twist under their weight. Ogulf was staring at their haunting shapes; the way the branches turned and bent reminded him of the broken bodies on the mountainside. Just as the visions of the dead began to push through, Ogulf heard something coming from the road ahead. The unmistakable sound of a rider on horseback coming closer at speed, the thumping of hooves against dry dirt, was a noise Ogulf would recognise quicker than even the most popular of tavern songs. From his position he knew that, if he heard it, those nearer the front of the group would have heard it also – especially Prundan.

He looked up to see those in front of him scattering into the heavy bushes and the clearing to conceal themselves. Ogulf and those around him followed suit and he landed with a thud in the dry dirt, just about managing to pull himself into a shaded part of the brush. The sounds of riders on horseback speeding towards them from the other direction on the road grew louder; they were heading straight at the group from Keltbran. Ogulf had heard of the bandits who supposedly roamed here, and he felt his heart begin to pulse in the familiar way it always did before a fight as his hand edged towards his axe.

Chapter 11

There were three riders all donned in heavy armour. At first, Ogulf was alarmed when he saw the cut of the thick, steel plate coverings, but when he saw the emblem emblazoned on their chests, the tightness in his chest calmed slightly. The emblem was one of the most well known in all the world: a hawk with wings outspread, reaching from one shoulder to the other, clutching a crown in its sharp, bronze talons. These were not bandits or enemies; they were knights of the Shingally Empire.

'Rowden Harlsbane,' the front rider called out. Ogulf suddenly felt cold at the unexpected mention of his father's name. 'We mean you no harm. We have been sent to escort you to Luefmort.'

No one moved from the brush. It didn't appear that the ride had spotted any of their hiding places at the side of the road. The rider knew they had been there seconds ago, that much was clear given the way he studied the plumes of dust left in the wake of their movement, but he couldn't actually y eyes on any of them. It showed, at least, that the Keltbran could still do things the old way if they had to. Hiding in plain sight was something his people were good at, ingrained through years of practice and tutelage from Wildar, Prundan, and Rowden. Ogulf remembered one of Wildar's rules to live by, one that helped him on more than one occasion during the Summer of Rebellion. Wildar would say, *they can't fight what they can't see.* Those were words all of the Keltbran lived by.

Rowden walked into the pathway with his chest lifted high, despite Prundan's cries of protest.

'Lord Hanrik Vranton has sent us. His niece, Runa, your kin, arrived yesterday.'

'Runa is alive?' Rowden said with a smile. Some more heads poked out from the messy shrubbery. The riders accompanying the main knight stiffened as they realised just how many people there were, and their heads spun wildly as they tried to keep track of how many more were emerging with every second. Ogulf also pushed himself out of the ditch, grunting in pain as his ribs burned in agony.

'Alive, yes, though only just,' the rider said. 'She was injured on the road. When we found her outside Luefmort she was barely conscious, but she told us to expect you before she collapsed. The physician said she is stabilising, but she has yet to awaken.'

'What of her companions?' Prundan asked.

'She arrived alone,' the rider said, his horse trotting impatiently on the path. 'We must make for Luefmort. We have made space for you and your people to rest.' He scanned the group again. 'I can't imagine what you've been through, but you'll be safe from here.'

Ogulf watched his father nod and encourage people to start moving behind the Shingally warriors. Rowden was scanning down the line as they filed behind one another, and his eyes lit up when he saw his son. He waved Ogulf forward with a swing of his arm. As they moved down the road, the track became barely visible, but the three riders didn't seem to mind; they knew where they were going without its help. Even from Ogulf's position near the back of the group, he could tell that Prundan was in deep conversation with his father. As the group walked on, Melcun found Ogulf in the swarm.

'People have been staring at me, Ogulf. People who would smile or wave at me in Keltbran look at me like I am scum.'

'Of course they do. You just produced fire from your hands, Melcun,' Ogulf said. 'If you had lit a small fire or morphed the weather, then perhaps it would be different, but you didn't. Not only that, but knowing the way stories go, I wouldn't be surprised if some fresh elements had been added by now – perhaps you morphed into a demon before it happened or drank the blood of one of your enemies to celebrate. No matter what you say or do now, people will look at you like you're strange. I know that's not what you want to hear, but we cannot change it. What's done is done.'

Melcun nodded. 'You're right.' He wiped tears from the corners of his eyes. 'I just- I'm scared. I never wanted this. Whatever *this* is.'

Ogulf hadn't seen Melcun show emotion like this often. He wasn't a cold or shut off person, but it took a lot to get him to this point. It also distressed Ogulf knowing that his words wounded his best friend, though at a time like this, the truth was the only course to follow.

'I know, but it will get easier. Things will calm down, and my father will keep everyone at bay,' Ogulf said.

'Do you think your father can handle all of this? Without Wildar, I mean?' Melcun said.

'We're going to find out. He seems wounded by it, but there is something in his eyes that is making me think he knows he has to take the reins again. He can do it; he's done it before. And if he doesn't do it now, then what?'

'Then you lead?'

Ogulf laughed nervously at the comment, but the smile died on his lips when he looked over at Melcun and saw that his expression was serious. It wasn't something he wanted to give much thought to, so he would just have to pray to the gods that his father could cope.

The two friends trudged on with the rest of the people of Keltbran, edging closer, step by step, to some kind of safety in the Kingdom of Shingal. The fields that ran alongside the path were getting more and more colourful. Ogulf saw trees full of life, bushes ripe with berries he had never seen before, and stretches of flowing green fields all lounging in the heat of the afternoon sun. Ogulf wiped a layer of sweat from above his brow, thinking how this place reminded him of the way the plains around Keltbran used to look.

The rider at the front shouted to the group behind him that Luefmort was just up ahead.

The city came into view just as the group came over a small hill. Ogulf was surprised by the layout of the city. Luefmort turned out to be a vast town, almost a citadel. It was constructed on a flat outlay, encased in thick, squared-off battlements that were only slightly taller than the largest buildings inside its walls, and it had a broad, grand building at its centre which in Ogulf's opinion, was little more than a huge eyesore. Everything about the town was rigid, uniform, and complimentary to its surroundings, until you looked at the curved, flowing architecture of the central palace.

Ogulf didn't know much about Luefmort; all he had been taught was that it was the gateway to Shingal, and that it had once been a part of Broadheim, before the ancient rulers of Ogulf's homeland had gifted it the Shingal as part of a peace offering meant to end the war they had caused by trying to invade the western front of the Shingally Empire.

The Shingally's had ridden out to meet the invading force in the field of battle, bringing with them numbers so vast that the commander of the forces of Broadheim offered an immediate surrender and returned west. There, he ordered a full evacuation of Luefmort, instructing all citizens to meet at the South Hold or to make for the north. The Shingal were offered Luefmort as an apology for the misadventure and they accepted the piece of land without any further retaliation.

Some in Broadheim saw this act as a display of weakness, but the king at the time chose to push through his own stubbornness; pride would not defeat power and there was no need to look for more lands. He believed what they already possessed was more than sufficient and adopted the idea that peace was the only thing that could bring prosperity, so he struck diplomatic and trade relations with the Shingally's in an effort to further ease the tensions.

It was commonly thought that the reason Luefmort was so sparsely protected was because the Shingally Empire did not see Broadheim as a threat after the surrender.

As they approached the walls of the town, Ogulf noticed that there were men patrolling on the battlements. A group of armour-clad men with smaller versions of the same hawk emblazoned on their breastplates stood near a wide entryway, talking calmly amongst themselves. Their heels clicked shut and their chests puffed out as they came to attention when they noticed the group approaching the gate. Two sizeable wooden doors opened wide for the travellers to enter the city. The rider who had spoken when they first found the travellers dismounted his horse and began to speak with

Rowden. Ogulf motioned for Melcun to follow him and they sped up to the front. He didn't want to miss anything important.

'Yes, your people will be taken to the temple. There is space there for them to rest and there will be plenty of food and water,' the rider said.

'Thank you,' Rowden said just as Melcun and Ogulf got close to him. Prundan was standing nearby, listening. The rider waved towards some soldiers at the town gates.

'Take these people to the Northern Temple. Make sure they are looked after,' he said.

Ogulf saw apprehension creep into the expressions on his peoples' faces; they wouldn't want to be separated from their leader at a time like this. If things were different, Ogulf would have volunteered to go with them, but he needed to be with his father now. The next few hours would be crucial.

'Now, if you would like to follow me, Earl Hanrik awaits you,' the rider said.

Prundan grabbed his arm. 'What about Runa?'

'She is still resting so it would be best for me to take you to see her tomorrow. For now, there are some pressing matters Lord Hanrik must discuss with Earl Harlsbane.'

'Very well, but my captains will come with me. That includes you now, Melcun, and Cohl... Cohl, with us if you will,' Rowden said. Ogulf watched the colour drain from Melcun's already pasty face while a beaming smile crept on to that of the young butcher.

'Of course. If you would all please come with me,' the rider said.

He took off his helmet to reveal a complexion of youth. Ogulf couldn't believe this rider was younger than him. His long, blond hair was well kept, it looked like silk – the kind of hair girls in Broadheim would kill their mothers for. Strands of his hair clung damply to his forehead. Pools of sweat from the heat of the ride gathered above his eyebrows. His face bore no blemishes, marks, or scars, and had a lovely brown hue as if he'd been kissed by the sun. He had the eyes of a knight from the fables; hard, stern, and most of all, trustworthy.

Ogulf was surprised at how quiet the streets of Luefmort were. Of the few people he saw weaving around and between them as they walked, none of them paid much attention to the strangers walking through their streets. He assumed they were used to seeing people they didn't recognise wandering around; this was a large trading town, so strangers would be common.

As Rowden and his captains made their way through the narrow streets, the rider glanced back occasionally to make sure they were keeping up.

Eventually, the streets opened up to a large square, which was decorated with intricate carvings and marble statues. In the centre of the area was a large, cubic building, which Ogulf assumed was the brutal blemish of a palace that he'd noticed on the approach to the town. He could make out two floors, both with tall windows that were evenly wrapped around the building, and above the marble frame of the main doorway was a small balcony. The building was an intimidating and perfectly placed assembly of perfectly speckled rock and smooth stone with edges, ledges, and corners that looked sharp enough to cut.

Carved into the stone above the main doorway were the words of the Shingal. Ogulf had heard them often, and knew that what they stood for had been a decisive factor in his father's decision to lead their people south. He read the words quietly to himself as he approached them – *With Peace We Shall Stand, With Peace We Shall Prosper.* Chiselled above the words, he saw the same hawk with the same crown from the riders' armour. Ogulf found himself mesmerised by how smooth the wings looked; they were textured to perfection. Even from this distance he could tell, he had never seen craftsmanship like it.

As they walked through the doors, they were met on the other side by a short man. He was athletic in build and wore a thin linen robe with some kind of tunic underneath. With every step, his sandals slapped against the marble floor. His hair was slicked back behind his ears with oil or wax, and a short, neat beard covered the lower half of his face.

'Earl Harlsbane, it is an honour,' the man said. 'I am Lord Hanrik Vranton, and I want to welcome you to Luefmort. I have just come from my guest chamber, where Runa is resting. I expect she should be able to see you all in the morning. For now, please follow me, I have a feast prepared for you.'

'Thank you, my lord,' Rowden said. Though an earl and a lord were much the same rank, a lord in Luefmort was a member of the Assembly, which meant they had personal dealings with the royal family and could actually influence the way the Empire of Shingal was run. This was very different to the meetings in Broadheim, where the earls and chieftains congregated to hear the king or the princes speak at them for hours, which often only served to annoy all those who were in attendance. Rowden motioned for Ogulf and the rest of the captains to follow. 'We are very grateful for you taking us in like this. The journey wasn't easy.'

The group walked into a dining hall where a long, sprawling table was filled with bread and fruits. Ogulf felt his stomach rumble as his eyes scanned the baskets of green and purple grapes; succulent-looking red apples; peaches; pears; and what looked like an orange, something he had never tried before. He felt himself salivating but tried his best not to show his hunger.

A candelabra hung from the ceiling, its golden rim encrusted with shimmering gems. Ogulf walked past the table and ran his hands along the complex wood carvings on the guest chairs. He had never been interested in carpentry or woodwork, but the detail and precision in the wares here had certainly caught his attention.

'Yes, I expect the mountain pass was very treacherous,' Lord Hanrik said. 'Did you lose many?'

'Quite a few at the peak, and even more when we were attacked,' Rowden said. As Lord Hanrik approached the top chair at the table, he spun round to face Rowden in shock. The lord sat himself down dramatically and quickly crossed his legs before slumping into the padded chair.

'Attacked?' Lord Hanrik said. 'Bandits on the pass – I have never heard of such a thing.'

'Not bandits, my lord. They were organised forces. I am not sure if you're aware, but we believe Broadheim is being invaded, and it would seem that those who attacked us on the pass are linked to that army which is swarming the country. I can't believe they made it that far south that quickly. They must have something otherworldly in their steps.' Rowden and the rest of the captains took their seats at the table. The only other Shingally present, other than the servers, was the young rider. 'They've taken Jargmire, Tran, the North Hold – '

'–Don't forget the East Hold,' Prundan Marsk interrupted.

'Yes, the East Hold also. Last we heard, they were as far south as Port Saker.'

Hanrik shot a glance at his comrade at the other end of the table. 'Danrin, could this be what our sea scouts noticed?'

The young rider cleared his throat. 'Yes, father. Two ships anchored in the Blades reported that an army was stationed at Port Saker. We presumed it was just a build-up of Broad-heim's forces.'

'When did this report come in, again?' Hanrik said.

'Two days ago, father. A substantial army there, thou-sands – maybe tens of thousands – with more gathering by the day. The distance hindered just how much the scouts could see, but there was no mistake, their numbers are vast. Are you certain Jargmire has fallen?'

'Yes,' Rowden replied, defeated. 'Certain. When did you last hear from your diplomats there?'

'We moved them out when the cold came. Planned to send them back when it passed. So, officially, we have had no word from any of your citadels in almost a year,' Danrin said.

'And unofficially?' Prundan asked.

'You hear musings. Tavern stories. Rumours,' Danrin answered. 'Nothing solid, but all that made its way to my ears suggested it was getting bad up there. If Jargmire has fallen, then this means all of Broadheim will fall, is that right?'

Rowden nodded. 'I believe you could argue that it already has.' His lips were pursed as if it pained him to admit this was the case.

Ogulf watched the tint of tan in Lord Hanrik's face slip away, and be replaced by a mask of shocking white. He was glad his father did not continue, but in a way, he wished he had. If this man was shocked about the fall of Jargmire, Tran, and the rest of Broadheim, he would be even more shocked to know the invaders were leaving no one alive in the places they attacked. *Organised barbarians*, Ogulf thought. *What a terrifying thought.*

'Do we know their motive?' Hanrik asked. 'Broadheim has been quiet for the better part of a year because of the cold, but has there been a war with the North? Anything?'

The servers began to bring more food to the table. Despite the seriousness of the conversation, Ogulf couldn't help but stare at the dishes in front of him: pork ribs, chicken, beef, potatoes, and roasted carrots, foods he hadn't seen prepared in such a vast array in years. Melcun was staring at the food like Ogulf was, Rowden paid it no attention.

Hanrik noticed them staring longingly at the dishes, as steam rose from the serving bowls and wafted the aroma of warm, fresh food all around the room. 'Please, eat while we talk. We can't come up with a solution on empty bellies, now, can we?'

With ferocious politeness, Ogulf and the other captains all reached for the food. Rowden and Hanrik continued to talk while Hanrik sipped on some wine. Danrin looked on in bemusement at the frenzy of strangers taking anything they could reach from the table. Melcun smiled at him. 'We're very civilised, just a little hungry,' he said with a laugh.

'No motive we can think of, my lord. We had the scholars try to figure out what it could be, and the only two credible options seem to be an invasion from Visser or a horde trying to fulfil an old prophecy,' Rowden said. Ogulf wished his father wouldn't call them a horde – they were an army, an organised, mobilised force with a tactical purpose and enough power to overthrow a developed nation. *Yes, organised barbarians,* Ogulf thought.

'Or a mixture of both. Yadlin did say this prophecy would return Visser to power, did he not?' Ogulf asked. 'The prophecy had something to do with onyx.'

'I will have my advisors look into this immediately. Danrin, go to Master Amryn and ask him about this. Perhaps fetch Tra- no, Amryn will do,' Hanrik said. The young man at the opposite end rose and gave a short, curt bow, then he left. 'The Onyxborn Prophecy,' Hanrik said aloud to no one in particular before taking a long drink from his wine glass and motioning to a server to refill the cup. 'Do you think they will make their way further south?'

'It's hard to tell, but if they're lining up on your shores ready and strengthening their numbers, I can only assume the worst,' Rowden said.

'They won't be using the pass anytime soon, though,' Cohl said as he bit down on a chicken leg. Ogulf and Rowden both shot him a warning glance.

'What do you mean?' Hanrik said.

'Well, my lord,' Cohl said as he chewed. 'Our sorcerer destroyed the Eternal Pass. Didn't you, Melcun?'

The room looked at Melcun as he glanced up from his plate. Ogulf fought an urge to defend his friend as Melcun was met with so many faces staring at him. He wiped crumbs from his lip and gulped under the strain of all that scrutiny.

'A mage from Broadheim. My, my, your kind have certainly changed your views,' Hanrik said with a chuckle.

'Actually, it was my first ... experience, my lord,' Melcun said, embarrassed.

'Well, that is something. They always say a mage is at their best in a time of great need, and happenings like this only add weight to such theories. You should spend some time with my niece while you are here – not Runa, but my other niece. She is a sorceress and is on leave here from her studies at the Tawrawth. She is fascinated by new mages.'

Prundan grunted towards Melcun, which was all he had to do to convey his feelings. Ogulf offered his friend a slight smile. He was just happy Melcun wasn't being ridiculed or threatened by their host. It wouldn't change the fact that Melcun was shaken by what had happened, but Ogulf hoped it would help him to understand that he wasn't a freak or burden in their new setting.

'Thank you, my lord,' Melcun said. Then he looked straight at Prundan with no fear or embarrassment visible in his expression this time. 'I would like that.'

Lord Hanrik continued to ask questions about Broadheim and how things had changed since the cold came. He was particularly interested in an inn in Jargmire known as The Sweetest Spice. His question drew sniggers from the captains, Ogulf included; that such a high standing lord should be worried about the fate of a pleasure house in the slums was an amusing, unexpected twist.

Once the plates were covered in bare bones and tiny crumbs, and the jugs of wine and ale had run dry, it came time for the group to part ways for the evening. A server led Ogulf to a small bed chamber with two comfy looking beds in it. He longed to wash the murk of death and dirt from his skin, but he was too exhausted to make it to the bowl on the nightstand, so he just kicked off his boots and collapsed on top of the closest mattress with a groan.

He was pleased to be sharing a room with Melcun; they hadn't had the privacy to talk properly since leaving Keltbran, and they had much to discuss. He had so much he wanted to ask Melcun, so many thoughts he needed opinions on, but after sinking into the soft comfort of the bed and letting the fresh smell waft from the sheets, he chose to save those conversations for another day. Wriggling to find a comfortable position that caused the smallest number of his bones to ache, he settled.

'Tomorrow, we need to find out whatever we can about Feda,' Ogulf said. He turned to engage with Melcun, but he was met by the light snoring of his friend, who was already peacefully asleep. Choosing to let him rest after his tumultuous journey, he licked his thumb and forefinger and pinched the lit wick of the candle next to him, plunging the room into darkness.

Chapter 12

Terror-filled screams wormed their way into Yadlin's dreams, causing him to waken, his body trembling in the cold and miserable air of the night. It took the old priest a moment or two to realise that the screams were still occurring, this time slithering into his eardrums and causing his guts to rumble with every piercing shriek. There was no doubt these howls were real, and they were coming from the east.

Yadlin rose gracelessly from his ragged bed roll, knocking over a log he'd used to prop up his tent cover, and the thick cloth covering landed on him, turning his already dark surroundings to an impenetrable void of black. His blankets began to slide off him as he fumbled with the heavy cover. Exposed areas of his skin were bitten by the cold, which had been trying all night to find a way through to him. As he shook himself free of the canopy, he reached for his over cloak, which was hanging from a branch nearby. Sliding his arms into the jacket's cold sleeves was like a form of torture. Another scream filled the air.

This time, though, it didn't just come from one source but echoed in a chilling chorus of terror from multiple crying throats. As Yadlin turned towards the source of the noise, he saw something he had not expected. The dark night sky to the east was tinged with an orange glow. Yadlin knew it could only be one thing: fire, and lots of it.

He hurried to the east as quickly as his old bones would carry him, and he felt his left knee clicking in an all too familiar rhythm as he planted it to take the next step. *Damn these old bones, wasn't I worthy of the ability to move freely when I pleased. After all I did you for you bastard gods?* he thought.

The forest of dead trees he called his camp thinned out as Yadlin stopped on top of a hill. The hill wasn't steep, and it opened into a long field with empty hay spools and broken fences, which cast menacing, flickering shadows in the glowing orange light. Yadlin's palms began to sweat profusely as he looked on. He could see the fire now – there was a perfect contrast between the black outline of the buildings and the raging inferno that was consuming them.

In between the static shapes, he could make out figures moving hurriedly, silhouettes of all sizes moving at different paces to the order of chaos with kicks, sword swings, axe chops, and torch hurling. Keltbran was in flames and its people were being slaughtered.

Fear swelled in Yadlin's belly as he took in the scene. The biggest flames rose from the Temple of Huntsun. The great towering spire of the House of The Guided stood out a harsh black amongst the orange, and the flames danced towards the skies as they crept up the structure.

Before the fear turned to panic, Yadlin forced himself to move closer. The sights may have rattled his resolve, but he was not a coward; he wanted to see who was doing this to the town. His town. Rowden's town. Yadlin's worst fear had been confirmed: invaders were here.

Yadlin's knee clicked as he crouched slightly to run, using the dirt mounds and the empty hay spools as cover as he weaved his way closer. The smoke made his eyes blurry, leaving him with only the outlines and silhouettes even this close. Still, he did not need to see their pure form to understand the barbaric nature of their actions. He edged as close as he could, now panting clouds of steam into the air as his heart and lungs pounded. With every advancement, he saw fresh, horrifying details that made him want to turn back and make for the hill or the shore or even the ends of the world. Anywhere away from this wickedness.

Not far from his position, he saw three hulking figures with long blades in their hands. The steel of each sword had been bent into an unnatural curve which had other, smaller blades sprouting from it. The group waded through the streets, seemingly unfazed by the flames around them. They cut down anyone who got in their way with a ferocious intent, even the ones trying to run.

Yadlin watched the group. They looked important. On the path they walked down, he noticed a man begging on his knees next to the angry fires of a building. The man was clearly asking for mercy as the three soldiers passed him. One approached the kneeling man and sheathed his sword. *Perhaps they seek prisoners*, Yadlin thought.

With no effort at all, the soldier hoisted the man from his knees by the scruff of his neck and hurled him into the burning building he was kneeling in front of. A new scream, one of pure agony, drowned out all of the sounds around Yadlin as he watched the attackers walk on like nothing had happened, while all around them, other soldiers all around them ransacking the buildings remained standing, and set them alight with torches when they were done.

Yadlin covered his mouth to stifle a sob and began to whimper. Began to pray. *Ignore my frustrations and curses, come to me and my people in our time of need,* he begged with his eyes shut tight. The situation was so dire he even found himself asking the gods to give strength to the Guided.

Then he saw the giant spire fall and heard another bout of screams. The House of the Guided was destroyed, the gods had no power here, this was a chasm of evil.

The adrenaline coursing through him slowly started to lose its fight against the fear that itched to take over as Yadlin accepted that there was nothing that he or anyone else could do. He must get away from here and make for the coast as quickly as possible, then he could find a way to get word of this to Rowden. He cursed himself for not leaving the area earlier or going with the group and taking his chances on the Trail.

He looked again at the carnage in the town and noticed more of the patrolling savages, their dark red armour, glimmering in the lights cast by so many fires. These men were no savages; this was an army. This was an army full of malicious intent.

All of the buildings were engulfed now, so the marauding band of soldiers in red focused on the petrified citizens of Keltbran, cutting them down as they fled, their blades making short work of the townsfolk who were mostly unarmed. Brief sword fights took place as some of the Keltbran tried to defend themselves, but they were no match for the hulking warriors bearing down on them.

Just as Yadlin steadied himself to leave, something caught his eye; walking in amongst a group of red-clad warriors was a face he recognised. One of the new acolytes who had served under Grolan. She was not under duress, she was not being attacked, she was being escorted. On her face there was an expression he had never seen from her before. The young priestess was smiling.

He began to hear the shouts of a single, booming voice, muffled at first, but gradually becoming clearer as its owner drew nearer.

'Burn it. In Loken's name, burn it to the ground. We have found her; we have found the Onyxborn.'

The men in armour cheered and thrust their weapons into the air. Accompanied by the roar of the raging fires and the screams of their victims, this was a deafening ensemble of death.

Yadlin's eyes went wide as he rose from behind a dirt mound and made to run back to his campsite. The cold had begun to sink into him again now that he had lost the internal battle to control his own fear. He moved as quickly as his old bones would allow him, his knee creaking like an old hinge with every step. He didn't care if he was seen now, he had to take a chance on getting away. He was at the bottom of the hillside and about to take his first step up the slope when a tremendous thud jarred him from behind.

He looked down at his chest and, protruding through his skin and garments just below his left collarbone, was what resembled a javelin – only it was the width of a log and its pointed end was barbed. With a crunching thud, he dropped to one knee, wheezing as his throat began to fill with blood. He tried to get to his feet again, but the effort was pointless and agonising, the weight of this projectile causing the real problem.

Yadlin gave up as blood splattered onto his chin and the warm liquid began to stream from his mouth. The weight of the javelin pulled him back to his final resting place, his head tilted back, forcing his eyes skyward. The sky was clear, full of calm and glistening stars. Their infinite sprawl across the canvas of black made him consider the power of the gods one final time. He let out a final, spluttering breath. The warm specks of blood landed on his cheeks as he accepted this as his end.

Chapter 13

Sunrise was already in full bloom when Ogulf awoke the next morning. He'd gone to bed with every intention of resting his aches for as long as he could, but no matter how much he tried, his body and mind worked in tandem to keep him from a real sleep. He guessed he'd managed two hours at most, and even then, those hours had been broken and troubled.

Wincing and clutching his side with one hand as he sat, he rubbed his weary eyes with the other. His ribs had gotten worse – he assumed there must be a break there somewhere. Nothing could be done for injuries like this, and thankfully, the gash on his shoulder wasn't giving him too much trouble.

As he began to dress, Ogulf was interrupted by an older maid who informed him that a bath had been drawn for him. Despite knowing he had a busy and intense day ahead of him, Ogulf chose to take the bath, mainly hoping that the warmth would take away some of the gnawing pain from his injuries.

Steam rushed out of the door as Ogulf pulled it open. His nose was filled with hot, clearing air, and the stone walls in the room dripped and glistened with a moist blanket of warmth. The only light in the room was the bright beam which burst through a small, stained-glass window to Ogulf's left. He moved into the room, breathing deeply. In there, Ogulf felt more relaxed than he had done in weeks, or maybe even months. There was some kind of salt in the water that made it smell fresh and welcoming – the kind he hadn't seen since bathing in the pleasure houses in Jargmire when the notion took him. He'd forgotten how much warmth could change your entire outlook. Here, they had it in abundance.

Every inch of his skin tangled as he lowered himself into the steaming water. His mind was calm. Must be the salt. He began to think about how Luefmort wasn't even that far from Keltbran, yet because of the cold, it was like another world. Broadheim had been like this years ago, at least, it had in the citadels – that would never be the same again, though. Letting the searing water go to work, Ogulf felt some of his tensions slowly dissipate and the tension in his ribs began to loosen.

He used the time of relaxation to cast his mind back to conversations he'd had with Wildar, thinking of all the trips they had taken or the times they spent days in the brush on hunts. *Had he mentioned a Feda before?* Ogulf couldn't remember for certain.

The heat from the water transferred to Ogulf as he lay in the bath. He wasn't sure how much time had passed, but the water was beginning to cool, which made him think it must have been a while. Now his thoughts began to shift towards Runa. If anyone knew who Feda was or how she could save them, it would be her; Wildar had told her everything.

Pain filled his body again as Ogulf got out of the bath and began to towel himself down. The rough fabric of the drying rag rubbing against his skin made him feel sick. As he got ready, a familiar tone crept out from a room nearby. There were two voices, one which he knew to be Melcun's and another, which was female. It must be Runa, she was awake. He hurried the rest of his clothes on and tied his mother's gem necklace around his neck, letting the black stone dangle proudly over the top of his shirt.

He followed the sound with giddy footsteps, excited to see Runa and make sure she was all right. With each step, the voices became louder. Ogulf knew Melcun's tones from a fair distance, and now he could tell that the female voice did not belong to Runa at all. Clearing the doorway into the room in which he had slept, he came to a sudden halt as he was greeted by the soft eyes of the woman Melcun was speaking with.

'Ogulf,' Melcun said. Ogulf didn't look at him, but out of the corner of his eye, he could see just how excited Melcun appeared to be. Ogulf moved further into the room and he was awestruck by her beauty; she was dark-haired, had intriguing dark eyes, wore black clothing, and had a deep tan. She wore no expression, but still her face conveyed so much. 'Ogulf,' Melcun repeated to get his attention. 'This is Crindasa, the Lord Hanrik's niece.'

'Nice to meet you, Ogulf,' the woman said. Her accent was unlike anything he had ever heard before – soft, foreign, and intriguing.

'And you,' Ogulf said, putting his hand out to greet her with a polite nod. Crindasa turned to Melcun and smiled.

'Melcun was just telling me about what happened at the bridge on the Trail. It's quite extraordinary. Normally, it would take a novice years to conjure that level of power. And even then, it would require extensive education and help at one of the colleges.' She turned to Melcun, picking up the thread of the conversation from where Ogulf had interrupted them. 'You said you have felt stronger the further south you have gone?'

Melcun nodded enthusiastically. 'Yes, I said this to Ogulf. It was like the further south we got, well, the further we got from the cold really, that I could feel an energy inside me. Even now, I know it's there, and if I wanted to, I feel like I could conjure it again with no trouble at all.' Ogulf felt his muscles tighten as his eyes darted straight to Melcun's palm. He expected to see it glowing like it had done before, but this time, much to his relief, his hand was perfectly normal.

Crindasa gave a slight chuckle at the statement and smiled at him again. 'You truly do not know why?' She didn't wait for an answer. 'You've spent all of your life in Broadheim, yes?'

Melcun nodded again, this time also glancing at Ogulf.

'Well then, you've never been close to an active Peak of Influence before,' Crindasa said. Ogulf and Melcun gazed back at the woman, hanging on her next words. 'Do they not teach you anything about magic in Broadheim?'

'No, it just isn't seen as important,' Ogulf said. His statement drew the first change in Crindasa's expression; she looked offended. 'I mean, that's not my view,' he added quickly, stuttering slightly in his haste to get the words out. 'It's just that it's frowned upon to be interested in such things in Broadheim, so no one really looks to educate themselves on it. If this had happened in Broadheim, and we hadn't been looking for shelter or refuge, Melcun might've been killed by now.'

'I still might be if Prundan has anything to do with it,' Melcun said, looking at Ogulf worriedly.

'They do that to keep you ignorant. If you're uneducated, then you look at magic as a negative, when in actual fact, the vast majority of mages, sorcerers, and practitioners of the arcane use their talents for peaceful and helpful purposes. Now that they know what you can do, are your people scared of you?' Crindasa asked him.

'I can see it in their eyes. I knew this day would come, but I never thought it would be as bad as this. That made me keep it to myself, for fear of judgement, threats of violence or banishment – I only ever told Ogulf about it,' Melcun said as he cracked his knuckles. 'I should have left Keltbran. I should have learnt about this. Learnt to control it. Maybe then Wildar wouldn't have died …'

'No. Then I would've died on that bridge and only the gods know how many of your people would have been killed when those men and whatever was behind them made it over the Eternal Pass.' Ogulf wanted to reassure his friend, he had to resign himself to the notion that it would take Melcun some time to accept that his actions were justified and that Ogulf and the people who cared about Melcun knew that he never meant for anything bad to happen to Wildar. Ogulf liked to think that, even now, Wildar would be looking down on them from the afterlife, understanding of what had transpired at the bridge, and willing the people of Keltbran onto a prosperous future, all while drinking deep from cups of fine ale and sharing stories with the gods.

'There is still time, Melcun,' Crindasa said. 'Perhaps, if you plan to stay a while, I could teach you some of the basics, give you an insight into the world you're a part of?'

'We won't be staying long, so I am not sure I can,' Melcun said as he looked at Ogulf. Crindasa's soft face changed again, and this time, her expression was full of disappointment. Ogulf could tell she really was fascinated by those new to her craft.

'A few days,' Ogulf said.

'What?' said Melcun.

'We're here for a few days. That should give you enough time to grasp the basics and learn what you can from Crindasa. I think it will help you, and all of us, in the long run if you know more about what you're capable of.'

'But what abou–' Melcun began.

'–I'll keep the other captains at bay. All you need to do is let me help you,' Ogulf said to Melcun before he turned to the dark-haired woman, whose bright smile was brimming. 'Crindasa, if the offer still stands, I would like to accept on my friend's behalf.'

She smiled and nodded at Ogulf, then turned to Melcun, her eyes filled with excitement. 'My uncle has a feast prepared for your people this evening. I will come and find you at dusk so that we can speak for an hour before we are due there,' she said. Giving a slight curtsy, she was just about to make her way out of the room when she stopped and turned to Ogulf. 'Your necklace – pure onyx! I have never seen one like it.' Before she could finish the first step towards Ogulf, a man came crashing into the room, bumping into Crindasa and dashing the young sorceress to the floor. It was Cohl, the butcher.

'Gods, lass, I am so sorry,' he said, while Ogulf and Melcun darted forwards to help Crindasa to her feet. 'Ogulf, you need to come with me. I think we may have worked out why Broadheim was invaded.'

Chapter 14

Ogulf followed Cohl through the long, elegant corridors of Lord Hanrik's home, and Melcun's heavy steps echoed a few paces behind them as they marched. Cohl had seemed nervous and was still uttering apologies to Crindasa despite the fact she had not come with them. The butcher's shovel-like hands were shaking, and a butcher's hand should never shake.

Their journey ended in a large room with an incredibly high ceiling that defied the height of the building. At the back of the room was a window almost as tall as the walls. The sun shone through the window, flooding the long, oak table in the centre of the room with light and making the room comfortably warm without the need for a firepit. Ogulf noticed his father chatting with Lord Hanrik beside the table at the other end of the room. Hanrik's son, Danrin, was standing tall next to his father, holding his helm under his arm. Ogulf was surprised to see that there was no sign of Prundan.

Stooped next to Lord Hanrik was a very slight man. His long overshirt was riddled with holes. His grey hair was lank, and he was missing some teeth, leaving the two at the top front looking prominent and rat-like. Of all the people Ogulf had met so far in Luefmort, this man was the first that he had seen who was not well groomed. Something about him filled Ogulf with intrigue; his eyes were mysterious, full of wonder, like the real him lived inside them in a world of his own. Ogulf knew that, regardless of what this man looked like, he must have been important, otherwise why would he have been in the lord's own chambers?

The small, skinny man dropped a large tome down on the table, causing a whirl of dust to erupt from its pages. It landed with a thud in the centre of a ring of already opened books. With frenzied looks and fingertip touches, the slight man scanned each book and then went back to the dirty book he'd just thrown down.

'Ah, yes,' the man said, speeding through the tight lines of text. He gave himself a slight slap on the forehead as if he had realised something obvious.

'Trayvan, are you all right?' Hanrik asked. The old man continued his mutterings, and then, with a clap, he gave a yell of triumph.

'Maledict. Evil. Bad. Not nice. From the north. The far north. A prophecy. A promised one,' he said, and with every word, he pointed to a different book for reference. He spoke incredibly fast, which made the words inaudible at times. 'Prath.'

'Prath?' Rowden said. 'Visser?'

Trayvan let out a wild howl of laughter. 'Yes. Yes, that's the one. The wilds of Visser. That's the home. The home of bad. The home of the Order.'

'Trayvan, slow down, and please, try to explain. This is a grave situation,' Lord Hanrik said, clasping the tiny man's shoulder and looking him in the eyes. 'Danrin, fetch some of that harsh spirit he likes, perhaps it will help to calm him.'

Danrin bowed and hurried out of the room. The old man moved away from Hanrik's grasp and continued to ramble, then he let out another howl, occasionally snapping his fingers. Ogulf watched on, mesmerised, as the man cycled through a series of words and phrases, some that Ogulf recognised and others that he didn't. 'Yes. Peak of Influence. Ridmir. No more power.'

'I'm sorry, Rowden, he gets like this sometimes. His mind is ... affected. Years of drinking whatever he could get his hands on has left him like this.' Lord Hanrik turned to Trayvan. 'We try to keep him away from it, but sometimes he needs it if we want him to make any sense. Believe it or not, you're looking at the strongest mind in all of Shingal; this man was the very first Sage.'

Cohl looked on in distress at the dithering man and addressed Lord Hanrik. 'This man was a Sage?' he asked. 'One of the All Knowing?'

'Yes. He founded The School of the Learned before becoming Sage of the All Knowing. Accolades like you wouldn't believe, he truly was the smartest man in the known world – in fact, I would go as far as to say he was the smartest man in the unknown world as well. There wasn't a mind that could keep up with him. He almost united Gelenea,' Lord Hanrik said. 'Now, though, he is a troubled man. He came to Luefmort from Shingal city, looking for respite from his problems. We took him in, and he has been with us ever since. You still see glimmers of his greatness from time to time, it's all in there somewhere.' He continued talking as if Trayvan wasn't there.

Soon Danrin appeared with a flagon and filled a large cup with a red substance before handing it to Trayvan with a slight, sympathetic smile. Ogulf watched the old man go from his shuffling, senseless ramble to something entirely different; he stopped moving, his spine straightened, and he looked at the cup with caution in his eyes. The former Sage's eyes went wide and he looked at Lord Hanrik, eagerness eclipsing his distrust as he hunched again closer to the cup, this time sniffing at it mindfully.

'For me, my lord?' he said. His eyes bulged from his head.

'Yes, Trayvan. Please, drink deep, calm your hands and that mind of yours. I need your assistance, old friend.'

Trayvan snatched the cup from Danrin and began to gulp the liquid down greedily. There must have been at least a pint of whatever it was in a cup that size, but it was empty in seconds. Ogulf watched on in disbelief; he had never seen a drink go down that quickly in all of his years, not even in the roughest taverns in Broadheim. Trayvan's hands seemed to stop shaking as he placed the cup on the table in a soft and controlled manner. Ogulf watched the man open and close his mouth to savour the taste.

'Oh, how I have missed the taste of those berries,' Trayvan said. His voice was clear, now, and his words were concise. 'Apologies, welcomed guests. My mind betrays me at times.'

Ogulf tried to remain indifferent out of politeness, but he was completely perplexed; the frenzy of this man had disappeared, and now he was acting and speaking with more clarity than anyone else in the room. Trayvan's clothes were still ragged, though it didn't seem to bother him much as he began carefully scanning the texts in front of him, now with an occasional sound as he found his train of thought. His fingers moved elegantly across the pages of the open books. Before, he had run them down the pages roughly, but now he traced over them like they were precious, delicate things.

'The Order of Maledict. They are dangerous, or they were, books say that the last of them were burned at the stake half a millennium ago. Anyone who believes that is a fool,' Trayvan began. 'They ruled all of Visser. Truly, that country never recovered after their last attempt at a power grab, though this would be common knowledge in Broadheim, I assume?'

'No, I had never heard of them before now,' Rowden said. 'We haven't had proper dealings with Visser since well before my birth.'

'Understandable. What they did to the people of Broadheim was atrocious. It is no surprise all mentions of the Order were struck from your history books,' Trayvan said, looking up from the books at Rowden, and then turning to Ogulf. 'You know of The Chasm and The Throws?'

'Of course,' Rowden said.

'The original Order was headed by a horrible man named Medin. He was a mage who ruled Visser for many years. He pulled power from the Peak of Influence there, and did everything he could to strengthen his hold on his lands. He relied on the power from the Peak to create a huge army – strong beyond measure, with numbers so vast they were truly unthinkable at the time. As the story goes, he wanted to fulfil an ancient prophecy. He even thought he was the one who was promised, and the people of Visser believed him. It took years of planning, but eventually, he set off with his army and took the North of Broadheim with ease. At this time, he was still drawing from the Peak in Visser and using it to fuel his efforts – but, unbeknownst to him, or anyone else back then, the power given by the Peak was not infinite.'

Cohl nodded. 'I've heard of this. The peak in Visser was Mount Ridmir.'

'Not just a simple butcher, then, are you, Cohl?' Ogulf said in disbelief as a boyish smile filled Cohl's chubby cheeks.

'Yes, that's right,' Trayvan said, pointing and smiling at Cohl. 'Visser was one of the only known places to have just one Peak of Influence in those times. So, eventually, Medin used all of the power it was able to give. He did it too quickly, so he wore it out and it gave no more. It never recovered, and that left him panicked, in need of a new source to continue the march of his forces. Medin hurried from the northern front of his invasion back to Visser, leaving his army behind to protect the lands they had taken; he was eager to pick up where he had been forced to leave off as soon as the power returned. Medin tried and tried with all of his abilities to keep drawing from the Peak, but to no avail. All the while, his army was left resourceless in the damning cold of the mountains, without orders, with less faith in their leader, and without the magical power that had been keeping them warm and strong.

'Medin wouldn't stop trying to pull power from the Peak, and eventually, Mount Ridmir exploded. Whether that was coincidence or consequence no one knows,' Trayvan continued. 'The eruption was huge and coated the northern edges of the world in a thick, black dust. This blanket kept the sun and the warmth from reaching the soil and pushed some regions into the worst winter known at the time. Medin perished in the explosion. Most of his directionless army died in the cold of the plains as the unexpected winter gripped the region. Some members of his cause made it back to Visser, but those suspected of being high ranking affiliates of the Order of Maledict were burnt alive. Their name and support for their ideals were outlawed, punishable by death. Most of the people of Visser were supportive of this and looked to repair the damaged ties with their neighbours. But some stayed loyal to their dead ruler – and more importantly, loyal to his cause, but kept their support hidden.'

The old man looked up at Rowden and then at Lord Hanrik, his eyes and voice as clear as they could be. 'I suspect that those invading Broadheim now may follow the same cause – they look to fulfil this prophecy and return dark magic to prominence. They will seek a source of power like the one Medin had. Only with the power of those Peaks can they obtain what they want.'

Ogulf was confused. 'If that's the case, then why attack Broadheim? We're not a magical country by any means. We don't even have a Peak of Influence.'

Trayvan let out a laugh, but unlike the howl before, this one was somewhat normal. This distressed Ogulf, irking him because this was not a laughing matter.

'You know of the Long Peaks?' Trayvan asked. Ogulf looked at his father before nodding at the old sage. 'What about the Short Peaks?' Again, Ogulf nodded. 'Falvail Peak? The Widow's Trail?'

Ogulf and Melcun exchanged confused looks then looked back to Trayvan.

'They were all Peaks of Influence. At one time, Broadheim was the strongest country in all the realm when it came to magicka and all things arcane. But when Medin tried to invade, they used the collective powers of all the Peaks in Broadheim to create The Chasm and the great expanse of The Throws. They intentionally drained all the life of their Peaks in the hope that doing so would keep any further invaders from the north at bay.'

This time, Melcun attempted to cut in. 'But why wou–'

'–Fear. Peace had held the realms together for so long, and then magic, from the Peaks in particular, became a commodity some sought in an effort to break that peace. Without these resources, and with some way to deter invaders, your leaders at the time must have thought this made them less of a target,' Trayvan said, going back to his books.

'I mean no disrespect, but this is all told in tales and fables where we come from,' Ogulf said. 'Do you know anything about this?' he asked Rowden.

'Nothing. History was never a focus of mine. Like you said, this is only mentioned in tales, and those same tales were laced with goblins and men that could fly, so I always assumed they were just that – tales, fables, stories. Even at council meetings in Tran, when they still happened, not one word was said about any Peak of Influence. Was it common knowledge here, Lord Hanrik?'

'Perhaps to Sages and masters of knowledge like Trayvan here, but not in the minds of the wider populace. Myths, musings, legends, yes, those stories are well known, but like you said, they're thought of as nothing more than bedtime stories,' Hanrik said. 'We know of our own Peaks of Influence, everyone in the Shingal does, but we use them for peaceful means, to support the people who reside here. It's in our code not to use them for anything else, that has always been the way.'

'Well, this story of Medin is fact. And this is why I think there is a resurgence. This is a new version of the Order of Maledict, which exists for only one reason: to fulfil the prophecy and use magic for the means of evil. I can see no other reason why they would want to invade the South,' Trayvan said. 'The army they bring, it is vast, yes?'

Ogulf looked on at Rowden, expecting him to speak, but his father was propped against the table, stroking his beard, apparently lost in his thoughts.

'Immense,' Ogulf said. 'Broadheim has fallen without so much as a fight. Even in a winter this cold, I still would have expected some kind of resistance, but the fact they've taken it so quickly, it's like there was no one there to oppose them. I can't fathom how powerful an army like that must be.'

'Too powerful,' Melcun said. 'To pass through The Throws with those numbers, make it that far south in a harsh winter, and to take the citadels the way they did – that can't be normal, can it?'

'Very good, young man,' Trayvan said, glancing at Melcun with a wicked smile and pointing his finger at him. 'Something must be aiding them. Something very powerful indeed.'

'What is this prophecy?' Ogulf asked.

'It is the prophecy of the Onyxborn, the one born to inherit Loken's powers and lead the armies of the Order of Maledict to the domination of the world.'

'That's what Yadlin mentioned. Is it possible they could have fulfilled the prophecy already, and that's how they took Broadheim so easily?'

'Oh no, my boy, that's what makes this all the more frightening. They have gotten as far as they have with the might of swords, and possibly some magic, but nothing on the level of power that the Onyxborn would bring them. If they had that then we would know about it; the world would be in darkness and hope would be lost. They seek to capture the Stone of the Night, a Peak that's long lain dormant but is said to have been crafted by Cormag's own hand. It is said that the Peak will come back to life when touched by Loken's heir, so they will fight to the last man to get into the old Altar Loken built to house it. The Esselonians have defences in place to deter people from trying – the Altar entrance was collapsed years ago, and a range of Peaks flank Cormag's dead stone; they fuel powerful enchantments to keep people away from it.'

'Esselonia?' Ogulf said, the hairs on the back of his neck standing up at the utterance of the word. He turned to his father. 'That's where Wildar wanted to go.'

'I wouldn't advise it; they're in the middle of a civil war,' Danrin said.

'Yes. Terrible news. I don't think Feda Essel will be able to hold onto power much longer, the way things are going. The South has all the gold, and rumour has it, they have paid for mercenaries to back up their already large force.' Lord Hanrik said. Ogulf glanced at his father, looking for some kind of reaction at the mention of the name Feda. It was the name Wildar used before he fell, and Ogulf had a feeling it could be the same person.

'Who is Feda Essel?' Rowden curiously asked, still stroking his beard. 'She is the rebel leader?'

'No. In fact, she is the Princess of Esselonia, the daughter of the recently deceased king. Her uncle challenges her claim to the crown, so you could say he is leading the rebellion. She has the support of the North. He has wealth and support from the South. It's a very messy affair and we are trying to remain somewhat neutral.'

'This Feda, is she–'

Rowden interrupted his son before he could get the rest of the question out. '–We have more important things to discuss than the internal wars of foreigners, Ogulf. For now, we focus on the matter at hand, which is a war of sorts that we are in the middle of,' he said, giving a subtle shake of his head.

'Lord Hanrik, this has been very helpful. I would ask for a couple of days more of your hospitality while we regroup.'

His father was stalling, and this worked to Ogulf's advantage; after all, he had promised Melcun a few days to allow him to learn from Crindasa and now he wouldn't have to make a case for it. As much as he wanted to press to know more about Feda, he stifled the urge. For now, he would focus on helping his father organise the safety of their people, but he accepted that there was no harm in finding out more about her in unofficial settings like this. Danrin seemed to be the right person to ask, so Ogulf would just have to wait for an opportunity to speak with him alone.

While the conversations around him dissolved into Trayvan pointing out paragraphs in texts for Lord Hanrik and Rowden to read, Ogulf's mind began to wander. *If this was the same Feda, the one that Wildar was sure could save his people, how could she do so in the middle of her own civil war?*

By the sounds of things, she was royalty, but she was losing a war, so she may not be royalty for long. The whole situation was daunting to say the least, especially given that it was dunked into a cauldron of already boiling soup with a vast list of ingredients that had only served to complicate Ogulf's life thus far. Ogulf was beginning to rethink his view of the gods, but he couldn't decipher if he was in their favour or at their mercy.

'Of course. This appears to be a daunting time for us all. We will offer you whatever we can, and you're welcome to stay as long as you need to. Trayvan, can you–' Lord Hanrik turned to the sage and his mouth fell agape. The gazes of the rest of those in the room followed. In a silent flurry of madness, Trayvan was flicking through the books again, carelessly pulling at their pages; the concoction had clearly worn off.

'Medin. Bad. Visser. South. Onyxborn. Lightwielders.'

'Apologies. I think we must let Trayvan rest. And you all need to see Runa – she should be well enough to see you now,' Hanrik said. 'Danrin, please take them to see her, and pass her my best wishes. We truly thought we would lose her when we first got her through the gates.'

With the same curt nod to his father as before, the lord's son motioned for them to follow him. Ogulf, Melcun, Rowden, and Cohl paced behind the young Shingally knight through the luxurious halls of the palace.

Chapter 15

The room they were led to was tranquil. A thin curtain blocked out some of the brightness from outside but left plenty for the group to see Runa, who was propped up on a large bed in the centre of the room. She was wearing an elegant night dress, something Ogulf thought she wouldn't be too happy about. Her eyes looked weary and her matted hair was tangled around her plump cheeks and scarred jaw. Ogulf could see no visible injuries on her, but something about her posture or maybe her aura told him that she was hurting.

'I'll let you all have a moment,' Danrin said, before turning on his heels to leave.

'Cohl, I need you to go to the temple and check on the people there. Gather Evy, the Bharra twins, and Sadie, and keep them with you until I get back. We need to promote a few more captains to keep everyone safe,' Rowden said.

Cohl looked sad, most likely because he wouldn't be able to see Runa properly, but he hardened his face, nodded at

Rowden, and headed away from them, leaving only a few steps behind Danrin.

'Runa,' Rowden said, walking over and gently embracing the woman, who smiled as he comforted her. Ogulf couldn't ever remember seeing Runa look so vulnerable. He wanted to reach out to her, though he feared his touch might cause her pain, so he just smiled and nodded and hoped that she knew he was glad to see her awake. 'What happened to you?' Rowden asked.

'You all made it. Thank the gods you're here and safe.' She looked at them all up and down, lingering on limbs as if to check they were whole. 'Where is everyone? How many came?' She rose up from a slumped position, eyes wide in anxious anticipation of the answer. The sharp straightening of her upper body made her wince. She yelped and doubled over again, clutching her abdomen.

'Slow down, Runa,' Rowden said. Melcun walked closer and laid a hand on her arm, but Ogulf kept his distance, not wanting to crowd her. 'We will get to that. But first, tell us what happened to you.'

Ogulf felt a wave of nausea flood him. Soon they would have to tell Runa about Wildar, and as much as he would rather be anywhere else right now, he wanted to be there for all three of the people around him, especially Melcun.

'Bandits, I think,' Runa said, eyes falling to the bed and away from her visitors. 'I remember passing the Trail, the three of us, then I remember waking up on the road on the other side and it was only me. Someone was carrying me.' She looked out towards the doorway with suspicion in her eyes. 'A man. He carried me. Left me nearby and then made a strange call, some kind of whistle or maybe a horn?' she said, as if asking herself the question. Ogulf watched as she closed her eyes and wondered if she was retracing her steps in her mind.

'Then the Shingal found me and brought me here. Somehow, I managed to tell them about you coming. I must have mentioned Lord Hanrik being my cousin, and for whatever reason, they must have believed me. Now I am awake, and you are here,' she said, her forehead creased, but whether it was in pain or consternation, Ogulf could not tell.

'What happened to you on the road, Runa?' Ogulf asked.

'I can't remember. Zemin, Pelta, and I were walking and talking about the weather. It was warmer than anything we could remember. We were excited, and then it all went- I don't know, I don't know where it went. I can't fault them, though they kept me going on that pass with their stories. Did you know Pelta won the Bronze Bow at the last Harvest Games before the cold? Anyway, I haven't seen them since I arrived. Truth be told, I haven't seen anyone. Where is that old lump Wildar?'

Ogulf exchanged glances with Melcun and Rowden. The calm atmosphere in the room disappeared, replaced by the kind of tense silence that makes people fidget. Ogulf knew this moment had been inevitable, but with every passing second, his palms got sweatier and his neck began to stiffen. Runa was the strongest woman any of them knew but this type of loss had potential to break her. Not only that, but Ogulf didn't want to cause her any more distress given the strain of her journey and nip of her injuries.

'He... He didn't make it, Runa,' Rowden said. Ogulf watched as his father tried to keep his eyes on Runa's, but he couldn't; they fell as his words did and dropped to stare at the ground. Tears began to flow down his cheeks before disappearing into the rough of his beard.

'What?' Runa asked, her eyes scrunching in disbelief as she clutched at her chest.

'He died. On the pass.'

'That's- that's not possible,' Runa reached up to cover her mouth. Her hands were shaking vigorously and Ogulf noticed all of the colour had drained from her face. 'He- Wildar- He wouldn't die on the pass. He's a chieftain and he is the strongest of all of us.' Runa's sentence faded into a disbelieving ramble.

Ogulf moved towards her as if to calm her and took one of her hands in his. 'I'm sorry, Runa.'

'How?' Runa said, breaking into a sob. 'How did this happen?'

Ogulf looked at his father and then at Melcun. He didn't want Runa to know the truth yet; she wouldn't understand. If they tried to explain what Melcun had done, she would probably react the same way that Prundan had earlier, not because she would believe Melcun meant to harm Wildar, but in her emotionally charged condition, Ogulf expected her to react negatively. This was not something he wanted, not for Runa and certainly not for Melcun.

An unanticipated wave of hatred coursed through him, spiking like a hot, flaming spear deep in Ogulf's belly. As he scanned the room and saw the devastation in everyone's faces, he vowed to himself he would get revenge for each of them, and most of all for Wildar. For now, though, he had to calm Runa and support her. Before Ogulf could interject and try again to calm her, however, he heard Melcun clear his throat.

'It was my fault, Runa. I am so sorry, I know he was like a father to you, I didn't mean for it to happen. I was trying to save him,' Melcun said.

Runa looked up at Melcun as tears continued to roll down her cheeks. She gasped and then forced her words through clenched teeth. 'What happened, Melcun?'

Ogulf watched his friend's eyes well with tears as he felt Runa's grip on his hand tighten to a vice like hold.

'They were being chased,' Melcun said, motioning towards Ogulf with a nod. 'They were sprinting across the bridge. I thought for a minute they would make it back and we could fight off the pricks in that bloody red armour, but they got so close, and one of them was about to reach Wildar, so I panicked.'

Ogulf watched Runa's face turn to a puzzled frown as Melcun continued his story. Even though Ogulf knew how the rest had transpired, he wasn't sure how Melcun could frame this to Runa to make her understand. Rowden looked on from the other side of the bed with a sombre calmness, stroking his beard.

'I had to stop them. The next thing I know, I am holding a ball of ... fire ... energy ... *something*, in my hands,' Melcun said. His fingers were spread wide and his palms were facing each other as if he was holding a large rock. Ogulf said another internal prayer to the gods. *Please don't let him demonstrate.* 'I knew I had to throw it and stop them from grabbing Wildar and Ogulf, but I have never done anything like it before. Hurling it was easy and I thought I had timed it perfectly to just about damage the bridge and slow them down – it's supposed to be an indestructible bloody bridge,' he said defiantly. 'But it just destroyed the whole far side. It sent the whole thing plummeting while they were still crossing. Ogulf made it over and clung to the edge. Wildar was just below him. We tried to help him up, but he fell.' Melcun's sob made the last few words trail off slightly, and he hunched over, causing his tears to drip straight onto the bedsheets he sat on. He coughed, spluttered, and snorted as he let it all out. 'I'm so sorry Runa, I never meant for this to happen. I was trying to help him ...'

Runa's hardened expression softened and Ogulf felt the agonising grip on his hand loosen. For a second he felt guilty just for making it out of the situation alive.

'Oh, Melcun, I know you didn't. You tried to save him. I know that, and for now, that's all that matters,' Runa said, through sobs. 'Come here.' She opened her arms, gesturing for Melcun to embrace her, which he did, and they wept in unison.

Ogulf gave a surprised smile to his father, making sure that neither Runa nor Melcun could see him. This was what was needed. He knew it would do Melcun the world of good to know that Runa held no ill will towards him. One thing that caught Ogulf off guard was Runa's lack of comment on Melcun's use of sorcery. Then again, in amongst the other parts of his story, it was barely even important. He was sure the two may revisit the topic at a later date, but if he knew Runa as well as he thought he did, he expected that she would be accepting of Melcun for who he was and encourage others to do the same.

Such feelings could be greatly beneficial; Runa was held in high regard among their people, and if she could forgive what happened to Wildar, then there was a high chance that others would also. And right now, the more people willing to accept Melcun for who he was and what he could do was incredibly important, especially as people like Prundan sought to tarnish Melcun's name.

Over the next hour or so, the group spoke a lot about Wildar and shared their many memories of him with one another; they seemed to go from joyful stories to tears, to tales of battles he spoke about, and then on to frustration at his stubbornness, all in the blink of an eye. It was the closest thing they could get to a funeral, and Ogulf found some solace in the discussions.

'He handed me this,' Ogulf said, pointing to Wildar's axe as it hung in his belt. He slid the axe up by the pommel and handed it to Runa, handle first, with a bowed head.

As she took the weapon, Runa seemed to stifle the flow of more emotion just before it escaped, her breath catching it just in time. She turned the axe over in her hands and smiled.

'You know, in all the years I've known the man, I never once saw him sharpen the blade of this axe. I've seen him cut down men and trees with it, but never once have I seen a chip come out of it or even so much as a blemish on the steel. An axe like this shouldn't be on a wall. I think you should have the axe, Ogulf; it's what he would have wanted.'

Ogulf looked at the gilded handle as Runa presented it back to him. He hadn't seen Wildar sharpen it either, and yet it always looked pristine and deadly, especially when it was compared to the weapons the other Keltbran had. With a gentle smile towards Runa, he accepted the axe.

'The thing is, he asked me to take it to someone. Someone named Feda. He said that she would need this axe to stop a prophecy.'

'What?' Runa tilted her head to the side and narrowed her eyes.

'I was hoping you might know more, maybe who Feda was and if Wildar had ever mentioned a prophecy or even anything about the axe?' Ogulf said, turning the axe to study it.

'Wildar said this?' Runa said. 'Are you sure?' She looked at the others, who nodded. 'I have no idea what any of this is about; I don't know anyone named Feda and he never mentioned a prophecy. As far as I was aware, the axe was just ... Wildar's axe?'

'It seems there is a princess in Esselonia named Feda, does that help?'

'By the gods I swear it, he never mentioned anything like this to me.'

'I think we have some questions we need to find answers to,' Rowden said.

'I'll find them,' Ogulf said, suddenly sure of himself.

'I know you will,' Rowden replied.

'Just when we thought we knew everything about him,' Runa said, laughing lightly in disbelief.

'It would seem there is a lot more to learn,' Ogulf said.

Once they had all said their piece, the three men agreed to leave Runa for a time to allow her to rest. Ogulf tried to convince her to come to the feast, but she declined the invitation, saying she had already informed Lord Hanrik that she had planned to rest, and this was before she had even learned of Wildar's passing, so now she needed to use the time to come to terms with that as well. Ogulf had been reluctant to leave his friend in that room all alone, but he respected her wishes and departed with his father and Melcun.

That afternoon, Ogulf decided to venture out of the palace and into the square; the sunlight had crept into the rooms he was in, but he longed to feel the true warmth of the world rush over his skin. As he emerged into the courtyard outside the palace, he looked upon his pale white skin as the sun began to warm it. A pleasant feeling of elation came as the beams kissed his forearms, and he let himself sink into that feeling. A feeling of hope.

He paid little attention to the people around him as they manoeuvred through their activities. There were guards jovially conversing with traders, older women in silken gowns testing the ripeness of fruits picked from the back of a cart… A strong smell of dried meat floated past Ogulf's nostrils. The people smiled here, and all of this mixed together filled him with an inner peace he hadn't felt in some time.

The gods came into his thoughts; he wondered if they had willed this, willed every hard step on the journey that had brought Ogulf and his people here. If this truly was the path they sought for him, he was being rewarded in warmth, in hope, in life, and in peace. The very idea rattled him to his core. If that was the case, then the gods were mocking him in his current tranquillity, because they would know he longed to follow the path Wildar had mentioned. He wanted to find

Feda, learn more about the prophecy, and save his people, but he had no idea how to do that. He sank back into the respite he had found in this moment in the square in Luefmort.

In truth, he was scared. He felt like he didn't know where his next steps would take him, and in his fear, he begged the gods to give him guidance. Regardless of outcome, he was willing to submit himself to their mercy and take the path they would choose. He knew this warmth, this happiness he was basking in, was temporary. Death was chasing them now; the cold had been mobilised into an army of blades and malevolence that had stolen his lands and slaughtered his people. He prayed to them as the sun kissed his skin in the square of a foreign land, asking for guidance and hoping wildly to see some kind of sign that they'd heard him.

Allowing himself to come out of his daze, the scene around him returned. The happiness of the people here was undeniable. Ogulf wondered if it could last. What if the armies of the Order of Maledict got here? The smiles would be cries, the smell of meat would be replaced by the metallic tones of human blood, and the ripe fruits in the carts would be swapped for the brutalised bodies of the silken maids who squeezed them.

Ogulf sat on the short wall which was wrapped around an ornate sculpture a few paces from the palace door and submitted himself to the next steps of his journey. The hope he found here would be replaced by a hope with no destination or understanding of how long it would take him to reach it.

In doing this, he gave himself as a vessel for something entirely different; he had no other choice.

He let the searing sun burn away his fear and rested on the wall, finding as much comfort as he could in the warm stone underneath him. It was amazing how different this world was to the one he left behind, and soon he would have to leave this one too.

Chapter 16

Melcun splashed the cold water from the tin pail onto his face. His cheeks hurt and his throat was raw from the crying and the laughing that had been brought on by the conversation with Runa. His whole body ached but his head pounded worst of all; his temples throbbed with every thud of his heart and nothing would stop it. He had hoped that speaking with Runa would ease the tension and the pain, but it hadn't – if anything, he thought it had actually made it worse.

As Melcun towelled down his face, he felt excitement building inside of him as he towelled down his face. He was to spend some time with Crindasa before the feast. His stomach was in knots, partly because Crindasa made his heart flutter, but mostly, he told himself sternly, because he was finally about to find out more about his abilities, and that made him nervous. He ran through all of the questions he had for Crindasa, feeling embarrassed because each one of them sounded equally as stupid as the one that had occurred to him before it. He felt like a child again, in equal parts eager and terrified for the first day of lessons. If only it could be an old bag of bones like Yadlin delivering the lesson today, then perhaps, his armpits wouldn't be great puddles of sweat like this. But no, it was Crindasa who would teach him, and she was the most beautiful girl Melcun had ever seen.

As Melcun made his way through the lord's residence, his body felt uncomfortably warm despite the airy breeze rolling through the stone corridors. He turned into his destination, which was the same room where the Sage, Trayvan, had given him and the others a scrambled history of the Order of Maledict, Peaks of Influence, the prophecy, and what the motives of the invasion might have been. The room had been stuffy, and in his current flustered condition, Melcun couldn't bear the idea of being trapped inside the sweltering room.

This time, the light was distributed more evenly in the room. No longer was there a harsh ray of sunlight focused on the long table, of now, in the more evenly apportioned radiance of the afternoon, Melcun was able to see the space in all of its glory – much to his relief, the thick, warm air had faded, leaving behind a pleasant temperature.

Earlier, the room had been cast in shadows which hid away the huge walls and made Melcun overlook the tightly packed shelves while he was engrossed in Trayvan's antics. He could see them now, bookcases that ran from floor to ceiling and were neatly stuffed with leather-bound books of varying shades. Most of the spines were worn and frayed. Melcun let his eyes devour the room in all of its wonder; he had never seen anything like this before.

Moving closer to one of the shelves, Melcun tilted his head to the side to read the markings that were pressed into the spines of each book. None of them had titles he recognised and only some were written in his language. Melcun was fascinated by the books in other languages; he longed to understand the meaning of the intricate carvings and maze-like patterns. He expected the books to smell old and sour, but they didn't. Despite their wear, they carried a musty smell that was familiar and comforting.

'Ah,' Crindasa said from behind him, interrupting his wonder. 'You've found my uncle's famous library.' She brushed her hand down the spines of the books as she spoke. 'It is envied across the kingdom – he likes to tell everyone that. He has written a few somewhere in here, and he likes to tell everyone that as well. Can you believe that he can point to every one of his own books with the precision of the realm's best bowman, but when tasked with knowing even what section any of the other texts are in, he would be looking for days? If you ask me, these are all for show, the kind of possessions that demand wonder and convey knowledge.' The woman moved closer to Melcun and smiled at him. 'Shall we begin?'

Melcun sat at the long oak table in the centre of the room, where marked out in the dust, was the outline of the five books Trayvan had splayed out earlier. Behind him, Crindasa whirled around the room, picking up books as she went. Melcun turned to catch a glance at the woman, her arms filled with volumes of text. He watched as she put a finger to her bottom lip and scanned the shelf she was staring at before her eyes illuminated and she snatched the book from its place with joy.

'What do you know of the foundations of magicka, Melcun?' she asked him, still staring at the endless rows of text, arm unwavering beneath the weight of several broad titles which rested on her forearm.

'Nothing. Nothing at all,' he said, embarrassed.

'In that case,' she said, dropping the pile she was holding to the floor and moved around the table to sit opposite him, 'Reading can wait. You need to understand where this–' She motioned to his hands. '–All comes from, before you can try to harness it.'

Melcun nodded, unsure of how else to react. He had to resist the urge to pick the books from the floor; it wasn't particularly dirty, but they still shouldn't be down there.

'The reason you feel strong is because you're closer to active Peaks of Influence than you have ever been before. Broadheim's are all dormant, but the ones here in Shingal, and the ones across the sea in Esselonia, are strong, and they will be pushing their power towards you, feeding your ability and making you feel the way you do. The peaks in Esselonia are perhaps the strongest in the known world. The last

Sage seemed to think it was because they run in a range of mountains while most others are huge, single peaks. I think a good place for me to start would be the first time you used your powers; do you remember when that was?' Crindasa asked.

Melcun shifted in his seat. His discomfort had disappeared just minutes ago but now it returned with a vengeance in the form of what felt like puddles in his palms. He couldn't remember exactly, but he was sure it had been when he was around eight or nine years old that he first noticed himself doing something he couldn't explain.

'Ogulf and I got lost in the woods, I think,' Melcun said. 'It was the dead of winter and we only had our thin furs, I don't think I've ever been so cold in all of my life – not even when the ice swept over Broadheim. Ogulf tried to start a fire and it wouldn't catch light. He was always better at that kind of thing than me, but he just couldn't seem to get a fire going that night. We both got frustrated, I started picking up sticks and snapping them, and then all of a sudden, two turned to fire in my hands. No pain, no anything, I didn't even feel it, they just turned to fire. I couldn't explain it, and for a moment I thought Ogulf was going to scream. Ever since, I have been trying to understand it. It came and went, and I was too scared to really try to find it in case I was banished. Then I found it one day and I managed to do it again. I couldn't call on it when I wanted but I could definitely... feel it. Does that make sense?'

Crindasa nodded. 'There must have been remnants somewhere you were drawing from, somewhere near where you lived – that's the only way a mage can keep the ability without having a Peak near them.'

'Trayvan said that there were some old Peaks in Broadheim. Some were not far from Keltbran. One of them, perhaps?'

'I doubt it, but really I can't think of any other sources that would be strong enough to support you for all of that time. Before you came south, what could you do?' she asked.

Melcun looked at her with a furrowed brow. 'Occasionally, I could light a fire. Well, before the cold came in, then it got harder. Sometimes …' Melcun paused. He wasn't sure he wanted to say the next part as it played to the idea that his abilities were a burden. '... Sometimes, when I would get angry or scared, I would feel that emotion building into a flame in my hand. Nothing substantial really, just the heat, maybe a spark, but I always forced it away.'

Melcun watched the young sorceress' dark eyes filling with excitement. 'Let's just say that is a normal reaction – when your brain thinks you're in danger, it wants to use what it can to allow you to protect yourself. Which leads me to my next point: I have to teach you how to Harness. If you can learn this, then you can wield and control your abilities at your own will, which is quite exciting really. It also means you won't just overreact and set things on fire,' Crindasa said with a playful giggle.

Melcun smiled at Crindasa. 'We can do this now?'

'Well, we can certainly try. We don't usually cram this kind of exercise into a few days under normal circumstances, but let's go ahead with optimism and see what we can do given the situation we're in. Before that, I would like to give you an insight into the origins of our world and the magicka that lives and breathes around us, because only then can you truly understand just how important, precious, and sensitive your abilities are, Melcun. I prefer to be blunt, the arcane did not come from admirable beginnings and it would be wrong of me to let you think that it did,' Crindasa said. She rose and made her way to a small table near the door, poured them both a glass of what looked like wine, and then sat back down. Melcun watched every step, the way her hips hinged when she sat and how her light touch transported the goblets from one surface to another. Each motion was graceful and strong at the same time. Crindasa reminded Melcun of a slightly softer version of Runa.

'No one really knows who the first mage in Gelenea was, but the old texts say it was Loken. He was born among the very first of our kind in the Farlands of Kostis more than a millennium ago. Notes in the scripture tell of him being banished on pain of death from Kostis. Now, the translations in those texts aren't the best, but the reason he was banished is deplorable whatever way you read it; either he murdered every female child he fathered or he murdered every wife who did not bear him a son, depending on which version you consult,' Crindasa said.

Melcun shifted from his slouched position in his chair to one that was more upright. He was hanging on every word Crindasa said. He leaned closer to her over the table, completely ignoring the wine beside him despite the way its tempting scent hovered near his nostrils.

'He managed to get on a boat heading north, and it wasn't long before he got to Esselonia. It's said that, when he got there, he spent the first few months entranced by everything he found – he called it a paradise, the land like no other, the home of hope, and most notably, he called it the spring of life. Among his favourite things to do in his newfound home was to trek along the foothills of the Grendspire Peaks.' She paused to sip her wine. 'The stories say that the serenity of his surroundings made Loken consider changing his ways to live as normal a life as a man of his power could, in hopes that, if he proved he could change, he would be able to rescue his family. It is said that he disregarded the darkness and looked to turn his back on all of his abilities. He found a cosy little shack in Radsbach and purchased it from the earl of the town using the last of his money from his homeland. There, in the shadow of his favourite peak in all the Grendspires, he decided to start a new chapter with the time he had left in this world, to right his wrongs and do some good in his life. What a fool he was.'

Melcun listened intently. He could feel his eyes widen as he listened to Crindasa. Her lips curled into a slight smile that showed her dimpled cheeks.

'After a few months in Esselonia, it is said Loken began to hear voices calling out to him from deep within the mountains. He searched and searched for the source but found nothing, and as the taunts became more and more vile, a bout of madness started to take a hold of him. Months passed without a hint of the origin of the voices from the mountains. Loken even tried to saw one of his ears off in an effort to make them stop, but they grew louder and mocked him even more,' she said, telling the story with such ease that Melcun was bringing it all to life in his head. It reminded him of the fables that Wildar had told him when he was a boy.

'The voices intensified, and eventually, Loken found a cave which led into the depths of a great black peak in Radsbach. He followed it as deep as it would go until it came to a dead end, but the voices didn't stop. If anything, they got louder, driving him closer to insanity. At his wits' end, he started digging into the mountains in search of the source, deeper and deeper over weeks, months, and years with fingers, pickaxes, and shovels, before finally, he came to a cavern where the voices stopped.'

'Who- Um, what was it?' Melcun asked. He was taken aback by the fact Crindasa didn't smile this time.

'In the cavern, there was a huge onyx gemstone rooted into the wall. The Stone of the Night,' she said. 'The voices stopped and the horror they caused Loken was replaced by an infatuation with the gem. It gave off a welcoming dark shimmer, inviting in a way that made Loken want it. He became obsessed and began to notice a surge in his powers whenever he was close to it. It is said that he gazed into it for days at a time, lost in its depth and letting its darkness slip into even the lightest parts of his soul. People say a man like that is easily corrupted but I say a man like that is already evil, and to make a man like that even more deplorable is like creating the end of the world in human form. Anyway, he spent years hiring stonemasons from the nearby towns, promising them payment when the job was done. They excavated the cavern and turned the space into an altar with the giant hunk of glittering black as the centrepiece. He even had a throne carved from the stone directly beneath the hanging monolith of onyx.'

'Why was he so obsessed with the gem, was it cursed?'

'Good question. Many believe the gem was crafted by Cormag's own hand, a counter against the other Peaks of Influence to aid his cause against the gods. But whatever it was, it latched onto the deplorable soul that found it – its power transferred to Loken, offering him a near infinite source of strength. We also must acknowledge that Loken was the most advanced mage in all the world *before* he got his hands on this source of power. This was a man who could turn towns to ash with the wave of a hand, a man who didn't need an army to fight for him. He was the most powerful man in the world before he was banished. Loken didn't know it then, but he stumbled across the corrupted remnants of the first ever Peak of Influence.'

'If he was so powerful, why did he accept his banishment?'

'It may be hard to believe, but the downfall of Loken came from love. He had many wives, but only one that he loved, and one daughter that he cherished – her name was Eesabella. The prince in the Far Isles captured Loken's wife and daughter, promising that if Loken harmed another citizen, his family would be burned alive. When he tried to get them back from that kingdom, the prince sent Loken his wife's ear and two of his daughter's severed fingers as a warning. Loken left and never returned; he couldn't face being the reason for their pain.'

She took a deep drink from her goblet of wine.

Melcun seized the opportunity to ask a question, one which he had carefully selected from the growing catalogue of queries accumulating in his head. 'Who created the Peaks of Influence, Crindasa?'

'The gods would be the wise answer, but the realistic answer is, no one really knows. Scholars I trust, the ones who taught me all I know of this world, believe the first one, this one Loken found was created by Cormag himself before he was cast away.' She took another sip of her wine. 'But let's go back to Loken for a moment. His obsession with the gemstone and the power that if offered never faltered and soon he let it envelop him; he dressed all in black, wore onyx jewellery, and prayed under the gemstone three times a day for his chance at revenge. Around this time, he began to craft horrible enchantments which sucked life from all around the altar and the forest that encircled the cave entrance, causing everything – all of the people, animals and life near Radsbach – to die.'

She paused. Melcun didn't feel like this was for dramatic effect. Recounting the story was clearly captivating her too.

'That was until Loken offered to share his knowledge. He began to teach those working for very unfavourable people in the hope that he could enlist an army to take over the world. Have you heard of Vantrim Norandholm?'

Melcun scoffed at the comment. 'His story is a myth, is it not? The kind of tale told to warn children from going into the depths of the forests, that kind of thing.'

'I assure you he was very much real, Melcun. And savage isn't even on a level close to how evil that man was. Loken turned him into something demonic, something so dark and consumed by power that many believed Vantrim would destroy the whole world. Loken called Vantrim the Onyxborn, the one true vessel of the dark powers of magic who would come to the world in a time of need and rid it of the bleeding hearts who took our world from strong to weak. Though he was an atrocious understudy and magnified all of Loken's horrible traits, Vantrim was not the one who was promised and so Loken cast him aside in the knowledge that, one day, the true Onyxborn would come to our lands and fulfil his wishes of retaking all the known world with the true power of dark magic.'

'Loken lived until he was one hundred and twenty-three years old, much longer than any man before him. He spent his days longing for his promised Onyxborn to come to him, but time passed, and then, so did Loken. Before he passed, he made sure to equip wicked men and women with his knowledge, arming them and instructing them to pass the teachings down until it came time to fulfil the Onyxborn prophecy. He turned the altar and the Stone of the Night into a temple – an assembly point, if you will, for the members of his organisation. They would come from far and wide to pray and give sermons under the jet black, nightmarish stone in Loken's name. They were called the Order of Maledict. They're not as brazen now as they once were, but it is believed their influence still reaches the highest echelons of our society, though they are incredibly skilled at staying hidden.'

'I have heard of that!' exclaimed Melcun, coming to life when he saw an opening to interject. 'Trayvan was telling us about them earlier today.'

'Ah, wise old Trayvan.' The corners of Crindasa's lips turned upwards into a slight smile. 'Some members of the Order have been linked to royal bloodlines, they have been generals in great armies, ambassadors to great nations – these are learned people, Melcun, and while their practices might be secretive, their intent is far from it,' Crindasa said.

Melcun felt embarrassed; they were only scratching the surface of his new world and already it was so complicated. 'When Loken died, the Order destroyed the entrance to his temple and his disciples were told to spread far and wide so as to make sure his teachings would touch all the known world. They had the entrance to the temple collapsed on the promise that one day the gemstone would speak to a powerful young mage who would find it and take over the Order and lead Loken's followers to greatness. A few have tried to claim the title of Onyxborn but none have actually managed to accomplish the prophecy,' Crindasa said.

She continued talking after taking a larger gulp of wine. 'Around the same time as Loken's death, mages all across the known world started discovering mountains which bathed them in vast amounts of energy that strengthened their abilities. We know them as Peaks of Influence, and luckily, many of the people who came across these peaks were not evil or wicked like Loken. For that reason, they fell into the control of peaceful nations and were treated and studied by educated sorcerers who sought to use them for good.'

'The peak in Esselonia, is it still corrupted?' Melcun asked.

'In a way, yes. The peak near Radsbach is no longer used and many think it's dormant now, but I've never believed that. The colleges sent archmages to Radsbach years ago to put enchantments all around the peak; they wanted to stop members of the Order getting anywhere near that gemstone. Personally, I don't know why they wouldn't just go into that cave and destroy it.'

Melcun nodded. He felt like his head was going to explode with all the information Crindasa was filling it with, so he finally took a sip of his wine, the explosion of fruity tones in his mouth taking him away from the cluster of information for a brief second. *It tastes as good as it smells,* Melcun thought before gulping down another mouthful. 'I feel like we've only just touched the tip of what we're going to try and cover.'

'You would need ten lifetimes to truly understand all that there is to know about our world and our abilities, Melcun, and even then, you would still have things to learn,' Crindasa said with a smile. 'There is one thing that is worth noting now, though, and that is, I have no doubts in my mind that, if an army comes from Visser like they have, with numbers like they have, they think they've found the Onyxborn.'

'So, you think Trayvan's theory about their motives are true and they want to take back the power of the Stone of the Night?'

'Absolutely. The altar at Radsbach is the only place the prophecy can be fulfilled, and the fact that they have already gotten much further than Medin's forces tells me that we should not sit by idle while this army tries to get to Esselonia. If only I could get my uncle to listen to me, he can influence the council and the prince, but I fear my pleas will fall on deaf ears.'

She took a long gulp of her wine and Melcun did the same.

'Enough history for now,' she said, clunking her cup down on the hard table. 'Let me begin your practical training by showing you the basics of Harness.'

Chapter 17

As he sat in a grand hall in the palace, Ogulf was surrounded by the smells of wine, bread, meat, and fruit, and the sweet scent of a woman's perfume. He took a deep breath, filling his lungs to the brim with them, and tried his best to relax. From floor to ceiling, this room was extravagantly decorated with detailed paintings and fantastically woven carvings of metal and wood. One particular piece had caught Ogulf's attention, a huge shield suspended on the wall, split into four equal sections in the shape of a cross of purple and yellow. He didn't understand the words emblazoned on it, but he couldn't take his eyes off them either.

Ogulf thought the feast seemed unusual given the circumstances. On one hand, the lord of a Shingally town had thrown a lavish dinner party for a bunch of refugees, and on the other, a dinner party didn't seem like the forum to tell your people about the invasion of the lands of your closest neighbour. Ogulf wondered what the sentiment would be – *would these Shingally's care?* Sure, their motto was to strive for peace, but would they defend the peace of another country at the risk of their own?

More bread began to appear from the kitchen on long silver platters, stealing Ogulf's attention away from the shield on the wall. The rapping of Prundan's knuckles on the smooth wood in front of him brought him back to tension that was seeping out of the group around him. At his table were Melcun, Prundan, Cohl, and Sadie, the innkeeper who was now a captain. To anyone else, this might have seemed like a strange appointment, but the Keltbran knew the Sadie that they needed – the tough woman who was a champion with a broadsword, the woman whose battle cry could reduce even the hardiest of men to puddles of piss in an instant, and the woman who had cut down more men in the Summer of Rebellion than any other Keltbran. Ogulf liked seeing her like this; she excelled when she could be herself. Her family broadsword was hanging from a scabbard on her back.

Conversation didn't flow like Ogulf hoped it would. He had been looking forward to the chance to speak with people he was familiar with, and had hoped that it would provide a sense of normality, but given the occurrences of the last few days, this was not the case. Ogulf was acutely aware of the tension between Melcun and Prundan, which had intensified despite the fact the two had spent some time apart since arriving in Luefmort. Ogulf looked at Prundan. The dark bruise on his eye was now turning yellow at the edges. He hated to admit this even to himself, but Ogulf was proud of that punch. Years of watching Prundan mock and tease Melcun had built up in Ogulf and that strike was an effort to rid himself of that build up in defence of his friend.

Ogulf shifted uncomfortably. The soft silk of his trousers was clinging to his legs. Lord Hanrik had organised for a new pair of trousers and overshirt to be presented to all of the Keltbran captains and their men for the feast. Despite his discomfort, Ogulf was thankful for this; the trek had left his clothes with a sharp odour and the handmaid had taken them away to wash them.

Hanrik's generous deeds didn't stop there. He had organised for the rest of the Keltbran to be treated to a banquet of their own at the temple, and that was to be coupled with entertainment to help raise their spirits. Ogulf had taken a liking to this man but there was something about him he was unsure of, something so small that he couldn't quite put his finger on it.

When Ogulf and the other captains arrived, there were already three full flagons of ale and two different types of wine waiting for them on the table. Within moments, Prundan had claimed a full flagon of ale for himself, and now the rest were working their way through the others, sharing them all evenly except for the light wine, which no one was fond of.

'Evening,' Danrin said as he sat himself down at the end of the table of captains. He was smiling and had brought with him his own cup of what Ogulf assumed was probably ale. He was sure of himself, Ogulf thought. Confident, though not to a fault. 'I asked to be seated with you all, and I hope it's not too much to ask, but I wanted to ask you about the invasion. If not, I understand, and I will leave you to enjoy the feast.'

Ogulf looked towards Danrin and smiled at the young Shingally Knight, though he thought he heard a scoff from Prundan.

'We don't know much,' Prundan said, not looking up from his flagon. 'Other than Ogulf and Melcun's – what would you call it? – encounter? – we have never had any contact with them. We have only heard the words of others, which in all instances, must be treated sceptically.'

'You're right. Too often, these stories become so far removed from the truth that they lose their roots. But I must ask, is it true what they say about Jargmire and Tran?' Danrin asked.

'And what would that be?' Prundan said defensively, still staring at his flagon of ale.

'Well, they said that Jargmire was impenetrable and they said the number of men at Tran made it impossible to defeat, let alone capture,' Danrin elaborated. 'So, if they've fallen, then surely–'

Prundan tutted loudly, cutting Danrin off. Ogulf turned to look at Prundan. The scout's eyes were narrowed, and he was looking at Danrin with disdain. 'Aye, that's how equipped they were, so that doesn't say much for the small walls of your city, now, does it?' he said, gesturing around with one hand. The other remained firmly on the handle of his flagon. 'If this horde or army of whatever whore's son makes it this far, you won't stand a chance.'

'Apologies, I wasn't meaning to provoke you,' Danrin said. 'I just meant that an army like that must be far more advanced than anything anyone in Gelenea has faced if they can take such incredible citadels with ease.' Ogulf liked Danrin's attempt at a flattering compliment in the last part of his statement. The young knight wielded diplomacy as if it were a weapon. 'If they are to come further south and try to attack Luefmort, then I will be responsible for the defence of the city,' Danrin said. 'And if I can, I would like to be prepared for such a fight. Well, as prepared as I can be, anyway. So please, don't mistake my questions for insults, we're on the same side after all.'

'You, defend the city?' Prundan let out a loud and obnoxious howl of laughter. Ogulf noticed others peering over from their tables, searching for its source. 'How old are you, lad? I reckon twenty years is all you've seen at the very most. How can you be defending a city?' Ogulf winced as the jibe left Prundan's lips, but Danrin did not react. Before Danrin could respond, Melcun jumped into the conversation, just as Prundan was in the middle of taking a long gulp of ale directly from the flagon.

'Why do you always have to be so disrespectful, Prundan?' Melcun said. 'This man is on our side and seeks only advice. Not to mention his father and their whole town have welcomed us with open arms, giving us food, shelter, and clothing. You should be grateful, but once again, here you are, full of fury, irritable, and looking to set your wrath upon whoever you can. You should be ashamed. And if this army does come further south, if they attack Luefmort while you're sheltered behind their *small walls,* wouldn't you rather have helped?'

'Oh, piss off, sorcerer,' Prundan said. 'Always trying to be so virtuous. I'd had enough of you before we all found out you were a freak, even when you were just the town orphan who sought pity at every turn. How I wish I had left you in the forest all those years ago. You're the reason the gods curse us, and you're lucky you're nestled nice and tight under our earl's wing, because if you weren't ...'

As Prundan trailed off, both men exchanged looks of pure hatred. The same look that Melcun had worn he almost re-acted to Prundan's aggression the night before the groups left for the Trail was stuck to his face like a mask. The tension in the air was unbearable. The time ticked by like years even though only a few seconds had passed.

Ogulf hoped Melcun would backtrack or dispute the statement, but he knew his friend and accepted that this was not going to happen. Melcun stood from his chair and Prundan did the same. The room suddenly became eerily quiet as if the harsh scraping of the chairs had been a booming call for silence. Ogulf looked at his two fellow captains eyeing one another over the table; both looked like they itched to make the first move, to deliver the initial strike that would plunge the next moments into chaos. Ogulf gulped as he watched, reluctant to call out or even move in case his actions were enough for either man to attempt a blow. His eyes darted to Melcun's hand. Luckily, it was closed in a fist and there were no sparks or flames to be seen.

'Go on, sorcerer,' Prundan said as all eyes in the room turned expectantly towards their table. 'Do to me what you did to Wildar. Go on, do it.'

Just when it looked like Melcun would give in to the temptation of landing the first blow, Rowden appeared in between the two men at the end of the table. Ogulf breathed out a sigh of relief; he didn't think he'd ever been so glad to see his father before in his life.

'Both of you, sit,' Rowden said. Neither man moved. '*Now,*' he hissed through his teeth. The men glanced at Rowden. Their steely looks did not falter, but they both sat down.

'This isn't over, sorcerer,' Prundan said.

'Oh, I know it isn't,' Melcun replied with a deep breath and a sip of his wine as Rowden made his way towards the head table.

***

The tension dissipated slightly when the Lord of Luef-mort stood up at the high table and cleared his throat. Sat alongside Lord Hanrik was Rowden Harlsbane, and a number of men Ogulf did not recognise, but he assumed they were people of importance here in Luefmort.

'Honoured guests, fellow Shingally, please accept our welcome to this feast,' Hanrik said. Turning to Rowden, he continued with, 'I am glad you found your way to the safety of our walls. The stories you and your people have shared with me are truly harrowing. You have witnessed the types of horrors I wouldn't wish on my worst enemy, much less my closest ally. So, I feel an appropriate place to begin the festivities is with a piece of good news which will no doubt be welcomed by all.'

Lord Hanrik's voice dwarfed his stature. Ogulf wasn't sure how such a commanding and confident voice could come from such a frame. He spoke with purpose and authority in a way that displayed his caring nature while giving off hints of his charming charisma. *He's a man seemingly full of good qualities*, Ogulf thought.

One thing that bothered Ogulf as he watched Lord Hanrik speak was that the man had never been tested. His confidence was based on a life lived without challenge or conflict; he had likely never felt struggle or known hard times. The lord most likely thought this whole escapade with the Kelt-bran and the invasion would blow over before it got too serious or that the Shingally army would run over their attackers if they were brazen enough to approach their shores.

'We will accept all Keltbran people, and any others who make it from Broadheim, and give them shelter in our city until their struggle is over. It is the way of our people to offer help to those who need it and it's safe to say–" Lord Hanrik looked down at Rowden next to him. '–You are in need.'

Ogulf thought Lord Hanrik said this in a compassionate way. He was not trying to belittle Rowden or the Keltbran people. Rowden offered him a thankful nod. Hanrik raised a glass to toast and those in the room did the same. Prundan was the only person in Ogulf's line of sight who never matched the gesture.

'What I will say, though, is that this is not the only news I must share today,' the lord continued. This time his tone changed, and Ogulf thought he heard a slight wobble in Hanrik's voice for the first time since meeting him. 'The reason we must open our doors to our friends from the North is because a great danger is moving towards us.'

The room was eerily quiet now and Ogulf noticed the looks on some of the Luefmortians' faces change from comfort to confusion. Their smiles turned to scrunched, puzzled expressions as Lord Hanrik let his words hang in the stillness.

'Broadheim has been invaded by an army from far beyond The Chasm and The Throws. The army who swarmed our neighbours' lands do so in the name of a terrible cause, one that threatens our very existence. And while this army is advanced in capabilities, they are also of a savage mindset. They took Broadheim and slaughtered all those who stood in their way, swept aside great citadels with barely an ounce of effort. And now–' He took a sip of his wine. '–Now they are just a short journey across the Sea of Blades from our shores.'

The room was so quiet Ogulf thought he could hear someone anxiously tapping their fingers on the thick wood of their table at least halfway across the hall. The tense atmosphere was confusing Ogulf's senses; the hairs on his neck were standing upright and his stomach was churning, but at the same time, his nose was being lulled by the gentle scents of the cooking meat from the kitchen.

Though none of what Lord Hanrik was saying was news to him, even Ogulf felt his chest tighten as he listened to the man speaking. Hanrik's words were clear and concise. Ogulf felt the lord was making an effort not to rush his statement as he paused often as if to let his audience digest each piece of new information before burdening them with another. Despite his efforts, it was plain for Ogulf to see that this was causing his guests a lot of distress.

'There is nothing to suggest they have immediate plans to continue towards our borders, but if they do, we must be prepared.'

'What do they want?' The voice came from a table behind Ogulf.

Lord Hanrik hadn't expected the interruption, that much was clear from the way his eyes bulged wide and darted to the direction of where the sound came from, heading moving from side to side as his senses searched for the correct source.

'It seems they seek to control the Peaks of Influence across our realm and fulfil an ancient prophecy set by the founder of their cause,' Hanrik said, forcing himself to calm somewhat by taking a long, deep breath. 'For this reason, I have dispatched riders to all the major citadels in Shingal to alert them, and I am telling you now because we must have a plan prepared in case these forces move towards our empire. Our scouts say they have no ships, but they are stationed at Port Saker, where their numbers continue to grow, and so, we will monitor them while they are there. We will also be sending a force to garrison the old South Hold fort near the Broadheim border to slow down anyone who tries to reach us through the Widow's Trail.

'Now it is our time to fight. Sometimes peace can only be achieved with power. To maintain peace, we must use that power. This is what we have prepared for in our glorious kingdom, and with the prince by our side, we will meet these savages in the field and run them into the ground with the full might of the kingdom's army.'

The lord's resolve seemed to harden again – untested or not, Ogulf felt like the lord was sure about his cause; he wanted to protect his people.

'I understand this will have stifled your appetite somewhat, so I apologise for ruining your feast. But it would have been wrong of me not to address this as soon as possible. For those who wish to leave, please do so and tell your subordinates of this news in an orderly manner – I do not need panic flooding our streets in a time when we must come together. Right now, we need resolve. We need to be Shingally. For those who wish to stay and enjoy the meal, please have your fill.'

With a clap from Hanrik, the room became a swirl of bodies as servers made their way into the hall to begin serving food. At the same time, some hefty men in armour made for the exits, orderly like Lord Hanrik requested, but there was no hiding the concern in their expressions as their heavy boots clanked towards the doors. Others, some in armour and some in plainclothes, moved towards the top table, hoping to catch Hanrik's attention while the servers frantically flowed around them, trying to protect the trays of food they carried.

'Bugger this, I'm not hungry,' Prundan said, standing from the table and sending his chair tumbling to the floor behind him. 'And I can't say I'm too fond of the company either,' he added, staring at Melcun's bowed head. He left the table with his fist wrapped tightly around the handle of the flagon he'd claimed earlier.

Sadie beckoned for Cohl to join her, and together, they shuffled away towards the top table towards Rowden.

'The relationship between you and your captains is strange,' Danrin said, taking a slice of meat from a platter on the table.

'I can't argue with that,' Ogulf said. 'I have a question for you, Danrin, since you were looking to discuss matters of war and invasion.'

'I'm all ears,' Danrin said.

'Shingal has always had a huge army, unrivalled numbers. Is this still the case?' Ogulf asked. Melcun dragged his gaze from the table to look up at Danrin. Like Ogulf, he appeared to be eagerly awaiting an answer. 'The reason I ask is, if this army comes South, and I believe that they will, do you have the numbers to stave them off?'

'It's a good question. The short and most accurate answer is no.' Danrin took small bites of the meat as he spoke. 'Not here and now anyway. Peace is our motto and it always has been, but it's weakened us, that much is undeniable. My father is a leader, that is certain, but I don't think he's ever held a sword when it mattered. I'd be surprised if he's ever been in a physical fight of any means in all his years, so he doesn't understand combat, he doesn't understand war, and he doesn't understand weakness,' Danrin continued, looking up from his plate to meet Ogulf's eyes. 'All because we were never threatened. We gained peace through power and then diplomacy, but now we are a nation built on the strength of ancestors who are nothing but dust. Our enemies don't fear the dead. I feel he might want to change this stance now that we are in peril, but I don't know if he can do so fast enough. We've just grown lazy and careless.'

'You said you were in charge of this earlier, can't you make some suggestions?' Melcun asked.

'Yes, and I am lucky to have the backing of a few of our generals, who will help. Even though war has never been the Shingally way, we do have warriors here, and if we have the time to prepare, then we can defend our land–' He chewed his meat for a few seconds. '–From anyone.'

'This army is different, Danrin,' Ogulf said. 'Even you were shocked to learn of Tran and Jargmire falling.'

'I know, but I plan to use the time I have wisely. And I have to be optimistic about the chances I have to defend my own homeland,' Danrin said, before taking a large swig of ale from his cup. 'Wouldn't you agree?'

Ogulf couldn't argue with that. Many factors could have played into the downfall of the citadels in Broadheim – the cold, the lack of food, the element of surprise, to name just a few. So, Danrin was right; if the Shingal could prepare, they would have a better chance of survival or possibly even a victory, though the latter seemed too difficult to consider for now.

The mood in the room stayed busy as more people joined the ensemble of yapping guests all trying to get Lord Hanrik's attention. A handful of others stayed at their own tables and ate the food brought to them. Sadie was standing behind Rowden, talking while the Keltbran leader picked at a tray of cured meat and nodded along. Ogulf looked at his father, knowing all too well he would be taking Sadie's council on something important.

'I have an idea,' Danrin said. 'I know a place that serves the best mead in all of Western Shingal. Why don't I take you there?'

Chapter 18

The place Danrin had led Ogulf and Melcun to was no bigger than the house that Ogulf had grown up in. Every seat in the place was filled with happy people drinking from mugs of ale and goblets of wine. Along the walls was a border of colourful shields, all of which were different shapes and sizes, none quite as ornate as the one in the feasting hall at the palace, but these were different; the scuff marks on them suggested to Ogulf that they had been used in tournament or combat. None was the same as the others around it and they wrapped around the walls of the room perfectly.

Many of the patrons stopped to give Danrin a handshake or a pat on the back as he moved through. Some of the greeters even extended arms to Ogulf and Melcun. Too polite to offend, they offered them confused smiles as they returned the gestures.

Danrin led them to a table in the far corner where three men offered to vacate their seats for the group in a gesture of respect. They smiled at Danrin and shook his hand as he accepted with thanks. Ogulf watched as the young knight looked around the room, faces beaming at him as he motioned to one of the serving girls to come to their table.

'Liesa, could you bring us three mugs of Krutmere mead please?' he asked politely.

'Absolutely, Danrin. Lovely to see you here again after so long. Your father- Well, let's just say all of us are so glad to have you back,' she replied, leaving the table with a flirtatious smile. Ogulf couldn't help but smile at the exchange; it was nice to see things like this happen regardless of what was happening in the world around them.

'You've been away from Luefmort?' Melcun asked as the three men sat down and settled themselves into the comforts of the booth they occupied. It was comfortably warm in here, the kind of warm that Ogulf could cope with. All around them were laughs, happiness, and signs of inebriated banter. From the mood in the room, Ogulf assumed the news of Lord Hanrik's statement had not yet reached the patrons here.

'Yes. I only got back a few days ago and it's been a bit of a whirlwind since then.'

'Where were you?' Ogulf asked. Just as he did, their mead was placed in front of them and a strong essence of honey came from the mugs as they swished from being placed down. The same serving girl had brought them and she came and left with the same lingering look at Danrin.

'I was studying in the capital,' Danrin said. He closed his eyes as he started to gulp his mead. As he brought the mug down, Ogulf noticed a thin line of froth across his top lip which Danrin quickly brushed away with the back of his hand as he, letting out an exaggerated breath as he did so. 'I missed the taste of a good mead. The capital is more famous for wines and I myself am not a fan of wines, sweet or otherwise.'

'Lucky that. We've been stuck with whatever we could ferment for the last two years. It's not been pleasant, but occasionally someone would find a cask of only the gods know what and break it for the town to try. The taste was almost always vile, but by that point, we weren't drinking for the taste. So, a tavern with options is a blessing,' Melcun said with a smile to Danrin.

'Do you mind me asking what you were studying, Danrin? I can't imagine it was politics when you're walking around with a sword like that on your waist,' Ogulf said.

The sword on Danrin's hip was indeed substantial, the kind any warrior would be envious of. Even Ogulf, who preferred an axe, was eyeing it desirously. It was long and broad, and Ogulf didn't have to see the blade out of its scabbard to know that it would be made from wickedly sharp steel of the highest quality. The hilt of the sword had a symbol on it, a circle with a single line running through it, which Ogulf had not noticed anywhere else here. None of the other warriors had it on their armour.

'A few things. I was training with the School of Swords to become one of The Fated Few. I studied war, military tactics, swordsmanship, and the importance of building diplomatic relations.'

'In that order?' Ogulf asked with a chuckle. Danrin and Melcun laughed.

'You could say that. These are apparently all of the things you need if you are to be what the kingdom classes as an elite knight,' Danrin said. 'I was accepted into the Fated Few after my first year training at the school. Forgive me, you probably don't know, The Fated Few are the custodians of the Kingdom of Shingal, and since Holatris himself, there has been at least one in every major citadel. I was lucky enough to be selected to represent and defend Luefmort.'

'So, you're a general?' Ogulf asked, tilting his head to the side. He had heard of the Fated Few, but only in passing.

'Of sorts. The strange thing is, I actually outrank a lot of the generals stationed here, which I struggle with at times, given that some of them practically raised me. They don't seem to mind, though; I am not precious about the title, because at the end of the day, a leader is only as good as the warriors around him, so I still listen to their counsel,' Danrin said.

'Ha, if only Prundan knew that after what he said at the feast,' Melcun said.

'So, the peaceful ideology in Shingal, is it going to change?' Ogulf asked. As much as he longed for the sweet taste of the mead, he still hadn't touched it. His eyes scanned the bubbled patterns in the frothy top layer.

'Not at all, but in order to keep peace, we must at least make ourselves formidable,' Danrin said, brushing his long hair behind his ears. 'My father is of the older ilk, the kind who come from much more traditional roots, a time when peace was unquestioned, but now – and this was true even before the rise of this army who took your lands – there are threats and threats are not something we are used to, so change is necessary. Otherwise, someone will see our weakness and strike. The gods know there are rebel bands in the Southfields, none of substantial numbers or prowess by any means, but if you let them prosper–' He sipped his mead, eyes closed again. '–If you allow their cause to grow, then who knows what they could do if they really took the time to rally a cause.'

'Sounds like things are changing here, then. You said some were of an older ilk, do they feel the same about the need to do so?' Ogulf asked, finally taking a drink of his mead, though he was careful to only have a sip. He let the mellifluous tones wash over his taste buds and the familiar feeling of calm brought on by cold liquids pulled the tension from his shoulders.

'Some of them do, but not all of them. Prince Zickari is the driving force for change in the capital. As much as he is not yet king, the whole world knows he is in charge. His mother may have the title of queen and the comfort of the throne, but every major decision that affects our country is decided on by Zickari.

The boy is wise beyond his years,' Danrin said. Ogulf squinted slightly when Danrin called the prince a boy given that the young Shingally knight was barely a man himself. 'Zickari wants to change tact and stance to one of strength in the hope that those who perceive us to be weak are less likely to try us. As soon as he is king, which I think will be soon, he will put the plan in motion, but as long as his mother is on the throne, there will be people at court trying to slow him down.'

'So, he is a kind of reformist – not what I expected from the Shingal; your ways seemed set for eternity. One thing I have been meaning to ask, do you think someone like the prince could have had advanced warning of a force planning to invade Broadheim? Could that be why he wants to change?' Ogulf asked.

'No, I don't think he would have, and if he had, he would have sent word to warn your people. If anything, I think his decision to strengthen ourselves stems from what is happening in Esselonia. The war there has torn the country apart, and the struggles have come from the inside. I mean, that's an understatement; the struggles have come from the same family there.'

Danrin went on to tell Ogulf and Melcun about the power struggle between Feda Essel and her uncle, Eryc. It seemed from reports that Feda remained in control of the North half of the Isle, propped up by the populace who were loyal to her father, while her uncle had control over the Southern territories where most of the wealthiest members of the Esselonian society resided.

'The news of the war sent the capital into a frenzy when I was there; Esselonia is a key trading partner of ours and always has been. When the war started, the ships stopped. Most fisherman, merchants, and sailor folk decided against venturing out onto the Sea of Lost Souls for fear of being caught up in a naval scuffle or preyed on by the bands of marauders taking advantage of the situation.'

'What an ominous name for a body of water,' Melcun said. 'Whose side did the Shingal take?'

'None. Well, I say none officially.' Danrin sipped his mead, cautiously glancing to his left and right. 'But given I am surrounded by the ears of men who wouldn't bother their backsides about this, I can tell you both that we have been sending supplies to the north of the island. Feda is up against a tough opponent, one with money, an army, and the backing of influential people who would see his succession come to pass. We support Feda because we couldn't have the same relationship with a money-hungry elitist like Eryc, not now and not ever.'

'He sounds like a tyrant. How do you send the supplies if the seas are so dangerous?' Ogulf asked.

'We have our ways. Once a week, we send one ship from Duchan and one from Luefmort. We use a certain type of courier, connected and respected on both sides. A shipment left the day you arrived, and they are due back into port here within the next few hours,' Danrin said. 'When we were in the palace, you mentioned Esselonia, did you have plans to go there?'

Ogulf glanced at Melcun, and was met with a shrug from his friend.

'Not us, our chieftain, the one we lost on the Trail, he wanted to go there. He knew of it and thought it could be the perfect place for us to seek refuge.' Ogulf took a deep breath in before forcing the air back out through his nostrils. 'But his plans were met with a lot of resistance.'

'I mean, he wasn't wrong,' Danrin said. Ogulf gave the young knight a strange look. 'It was a paradise, a place of true prosperity, and a place where people could thrive. Things change, though. It will be chaos now.'

'The thing is,' Ogulf said. 'I feel like there may have been another reason he wanted to go to Esselonia.'

Ogulf felt a sharp pain in his ankle. He looked over at Melcun. 'Ogulf. Do you think it's wise to burden Danrin with such *things*?' He was speaking through gritted teeth.

Ogulf didn't expect this, it wasn't like Melcun to be this cautious, so he did stop to think for a second before he decided to reveal anything about what Wildar had said to him before he fell. For a moment, he thought he was being too quick to trust Danrin, but at the same time, he didn't want to waste any more time avoiding something he considered urgent.

'Our friend here has confided in us, Melcun. I think it's only fair that we do the same. Do you want answers or not?' Ogulf said in an attempt to force Melcun's hand.

Ogulf watched the puzzled expression work its way from Danrin's eyes to his brows and finally into the squinted purse of his lips. He leant over, closer to the Shingally knight, and lowered his voice without compromising the seriousness in his tone.

'Before he died, our chieftain told me that a woman named Feda was the key to all of this. He said that she was our only hope for survival. He told me to take this axe to her, that she would need it to save us and stop a prophecy. I rarely gamble, but I would bet my life on the Feda that he mentioned being that same one fighting for her crown in Esselonia.' Ogulf took a deep breath and a big gulp of his mead before he continued. 'Our problem is that we have no ties to the Esselonians. We have no idea how Feda is supposed to help us. And with her current situation, how can she be in a place to help anyone?'

Danrin looked confused and began to stroke the blonde stubble visible on his chin as the candlelight around the room caught the angles of his jaw. He took a long, drawn out drink of his mead before the hollow cup echoed as he thudded it down onto the table. He waved over the serving girl, Liesa, and requested another round of drinks.

'I can't say I know of any other Feda's, and I know this one is important, very important, but you're right... I imagine *she* needs help right now, and it's not like she commands the type of army that could stand a chance against a force that took your lands the way it did anyway,' Danrin said. 'Perhaps you should send word to her, see if she knows more about what your chieftain said?'

'That seems like a weak option,' Ogulf said.

'Falling short of us going ourselves, what other option do we have, Ogulf?' Melcun asked.

Ogulf smiled. There was no other viable option in his mind; he wouldn't trust a letter or the word of someone he didn't know if they returned with a message. What he would trust would be an audience with Feda, one where he could find out once and for all if she could help them, and if she couldn't or she refused, then that would be the end of it. He felt foolish as he thought about what he was considering as these ideas raced through his mind, this was madness, but surely Wildar wouldn't send them on a Brait's quest for nothing. He didn't need it, but he wanted his father's blessing for the journey. Leaving Rowden now was not something Ogulf wanted to do; he wanted to be there while his father found his feet.

'You're right, Melcun, we will need to go ourselves,' Ogulf said. 'We will seek out Feda in Wildar's name and ask for her help.'

'And supposing she says, '*I'm so sorry, but I am in the middle of a war and can't possibly spare a soul for your cause*',' Melcun said, putting on a mocking feminine voice which made Danrin smirk but only irritated Ogulf.

'Now isn't the time to joke, Melcun,' Ogulf said. 'Broadheim is likely in ashes, only the gods know how many of our people have died, and Wildar's last words before plunging to his death were that this woman could save us all. I think we should seek some answers.'

'It seems your chieftain knew more than he was letting on,' Danrin said.

'Exactly,' Ogulf said, feeling the need to be blunt. He had made his mind up and there was no use trying to will himself toward another path. 'Danrin, can you get us to Esselonia?'

Ogulf sipped at the fresh mug of mead placed in front of him, savouring the flavour even more with this mouthful. Waiting in Luefmort would get them nowhere, this wasn't the path he needed to take. It wasn't really a path at all, it was staying still and waiting for fate to take its course without his input. But by going there, seeking Feda and seeing if there was truth in Wildar's words, words that Ogulf had trusted his whole life, then perhaps a new fate would await them. The refuge offered by the walls of Luefmort wouldn't last forever – eventually the people of Keltbran would have to choose their own way, so now Ogulf would take the first step on that path, even if he wasn't certain that something beyond him was guiding his steps.

'It will be difficult,' Danrin said, his face full of contemplation. He looked at Ogulf and Melcun, absorbed in thought as he continued to thumb his stubble. 'But I can have that arranged.'

Chapter 19

Ogulf was pleased with Danrin's proposal. Ogulf had originally been reluctant to involve anyone else in the process but caved to Danrin's pleas that they inform Lord Hanrik of the plans. The young knight had not wanted to keep his father in the dark about such things at such a sensitive time. Danrin wanted to ensure that Hanrik understood the true nature of the journey and its purpose, that this was not a pleasant trip or an adventure, but would be a perilous mission, one that could be beneficial to all involved in the long run.

Before they could move forward, Ogulf would also have to seek support from his own father. Ogulf felt like his father would endorse their plans, but at the same time he knew Rowden would wish to keep his son close and understood that no father would comfortably send their child to a foreign land being ripped apart by internal warfare. At the same time, they needed to seek answers to the riddle that Wildar had left. If it had been anyone else but Wildar who had tasked Ogulf with this then Rowden would likely have refused to support Ogulf on his journey.

After a few more mugs of mead, the three men left the tavern and made for the palace to retire for the evening. Ogulf felt that they had struck a bond of sorts with Danrin, as they were now entrusted with each other's secrets; Danrin had shared his worries about the contented stance of his homeland, and in return, Ogulf had told the young knight about Wildar's last words. Maybe they were not the kinds of secrets that wars are fought over, but they were secrets all the same.

They had not drunk anywhere near enough for it to be the kind of friendship struck in mead-fuelled camaraderie. He liked the Fated Knight and he couldn't quite put his finger on a reason why, so he decided he didn't need a reason at all.

Danrin bid them both a good evening as they tiptoed through the corridors. Ogulf wasn't sure of the time, but the silence in the palace suggested most others here were asleep. As Ogulf and Melcun navigated their way through the palace, they were occasionally nodded at by one of the mute Shingally guards on watch.

'I am not sure it was wise to tell Danrin about what Wildar said. We don't understand any of this,' Melcun said.

'You'll be surprised to hear I agree with you. I'm not sure it was the smartest option either,' Ogulf conceded. 'But what choice do we have? The more I think about what Wildar said, the more it just frustrates me. It's like a cruel puzzle, and I can't keep myself from trying to solve it. If only he said a few more words, maybe then we would know exactly what we needed to do.'

'Hard to get words out when you're dangling over your own death,' Melcun said. 'Do you trust Danrin?'

'I do. I don't know why, but I do,' Ogulf said as they turned into their guestroom. 'Melcun, I have to ask, when we were at the feast and Prundan squared off with you, you didn't seem as ... tempered as you would have been in the past?'

'You mean that you didn't see any sparks in my hand this time?' Melcun said, uttering a light laugh.

'Well, yes,' Ogulf said. 'You've always had tension with Prundan, and a few days ago, something far less serious almost tipped you over the edge. I was worried you would do something in that room tonight, though, to be honest I wouldn't have blamed you if you did. His tongue is sharper than his axe.'

'I don't think that kind of thing should be an issue anymore,' Melcun said. 'Crindasa taught me how to Harness.'

Melcun said this as if Ogulf would know what he was talking about. Rather than say anything, he let his weary expression fill with confusion as Melcun turned to look at him.

'Sorry, basically, she taught me how to control my power.' He held up his palms so that they were facing towards Ogulf. 'It was fairly simple, she just showed me how to disassociate it from my emotions. So that means, if I am in a situation where I feel threatened or angry, I won't reach for my ability without realising. Even I was surprised that I got it to work so quickly,' Melcun said. 'Crindasa said it's something they teach to a mage as soon as they show signs of having powers, so most learn when they are children. She said it would be much harder for someone my age to use without previous experience, so you could say I am a natural.'

'That's fantastic,' Ogulf said, genuinely relieved that he might not have to anticipate Melcun's every move in fear from now on, whenever they got into precarious positions. 'You'll be glad we have a few more days for lessons then, don't need you turning everyone in Esselonia to piles of ash.'

'Oh, piss off,' Melcun said, crossing his arms and falling onto the bed with his eyes fixed on the ceiling as Ogulf let out a laugh he tried and failed to suppress. 'It got me thinking. Your father said he knew what I could do since I was a boy. Do you think that's why he didn't let me fight much during the Rebellion, in case I used it?'

'Perhaps. How do you suppose you didn't use it when you did get to fight?' Ogulf said. 'I mean, I watched you take some amount of punishment during the skirmish at Glandown and there wasn't so much as a spark.'

'I've never really thought about it that day, might have been too scared to really comprehend it. I'll never forget the sound of that shield cracking when that big lad's greataxe hit it; I called out to the gods for help with a mouthful of splinters,' Melcun said. 'You had all been in battle by then, but it was my first taste of that kind of combat, and it was hard to feel frightened or anything, really, when your father made me stay with all the older lot in the rear guard. It was embarrassing. I think that was the first time Prundan mocked me, he called me a–'

'–Craven orphan of a whore,' Ogulf finished. 'I remember, but you weren't afraid, you were just being obedient.' Ogulf had had to tell Melcun this numerous times before; no one really thought Melcun was a coward, but Prundan made sure to fan the flames in an effort to mock Melcun.

Both men removed their new Shingally clothes and got into bed. Melcun was snoring within minutes but Ogulf lay awake, powerless to grab hold of the sleep that was evading him. He didn't mind much – he had things he needed to think about, whole scenarios he would play out in his head over and over while trying to piece together the best way to approach them.

The first was speaking with his father, but he was content with the plan for that. Then there was getting to Esselonia. This part bothered Ogulf because he didn't have control, so ideas sprawled out like tentacles in his mind, each one leading to a different outcome which then did the same, and so on until he was forced to abandon that line of thought amidst its endless maze of possibilities.

The scenario he dedicated most of his sleepless night to was how he would approach meeting Feda. He wasn't a diplomat by any means, but he also wasn't a fool. He had to get an audience with her himself. Even when his mind trailed slightly, warning him that the path to Feda was a dangerous one, he forced the notion aside and accepted that this was how things had to be; this was his will, and maybe even a renewed will bestowed by the gods. Perhaps they wanted to save him and his people after all.

***

The next morning, Ogulf went to visit his father with Melcun. Straight away, he told him of Danrin's plan to get the pair to Esselonia – time was not something they had a lot of and Ogulf wasn't one for mincing words.

The plan wasn't perfect, but Ogulf thought it would be sufficient. A supply shipment would be leaving for North Esselonia the next evening from a port not far from Luef-mort. It would be sailing under cover of darkness to a trading harbour in the Esselonian town of Vargholme. The captain of the ship was a friend of Danrin's, so the young Shingally knight would organise passage for both men. He said the captain owed him a favour.

Danrin was to tell Lord Hanrik of the plan. He warned Ogulf that he expected some resistance but would not go ahead with the plan without the blessing of his father.

'I think it is a good idea,' Rowden said. He was sitting at a table in the banquet hall, listening to the Ogulf as he explained the plan. Melcun sat next to him, facing Ogulf, who was on the other side of the table. With only the three of them in the room, the feast hall seemed much larger than it had done before, and Ogulf noticed a slight change in the decor of the space. Now the only ornaments he could see, other than the large shield which had caught his eye the night before, were all made of brass. Each piece was polished and gave off a dull glow. 'If it means we can get some answers, then I think it will be worth it. Even if the answer is, 'sod off, I'm fighting a war,' it's preferable to having to wait here and hope for the best. Lord Hanrik's son, does he seem trustworthy?'

'Yes,' Ogulf said, slightly surprised he had not met more resistance from his father at this stage. He opted to accept Rowden's position, though; any prodding or challenging could lead to him becoming less supportive of the plan. 'I trust him, and he is invested in this as much as we are – he wants to protect his lands and is willing to help us explore any ways that help him do that.'

'Even though I still don't understand it all, Wildar obviously did,' Rowden said. 'But giving you my blessing to do something like this is not easy, Ogulf,' he added, stroking his beard. 'There is no way Wildar would ask this of you unless he felt it was absolutely necessary. And though he might not have told us everything he knew, there must be a reason for that. I think he knew more about the invasion than he was letting on. Especially when you take time to think about the counsel we have received from Lord Hanrik and Trayvan since we arrived. This invasion will come here, the Shingally's need to find a way to stop it. We must get Lord Hanrik to prepare. Otherwise I fear the gate to the Shingally Empire will fall like Broadheim.'

'Danrin is worried about the same thing, so he is going to speak to Lord Hanrik,' Ogulf said. It satisfied him to hear Rowden speaking this way. 'Perhaps it's worth you offering to help with the preparations while Melcun and I are gone. I'm sure any help would be appreciated.'

'I'm not sure they would listen. The Shingally's have their ways, they have generals here and a military council.'

'I think a fresh perspective could be useful. And don't be so hard on yourself, you know as well as I do what that mind and that axe hand are capable of. They would be lucky to have you. It will keep our people busy, too – well, the ones who are willing to fight, at least.'

Rowden stroked his beard again. 'I suppose you're right. I just feel lost in a way. I am the earl of a pile of ash with only half my townsfolk, no chieftain, and a butcher, farmers, and an innkeeper for captains.'

'I bet you wouldn't say that to Sadie's face. She was the best swordswoman in all of Broadheim in her day,' Ogulf said in an attempt to lighten the mood. 'You're still our leader. We need you now, more than ever. This will be good for all of us.'

Rowden nodded. His eyes told Ogulf that he was still guarded about this idea, but willing to see what it could lead to.

'I'll discuss it with Danrin,' Ogulf said.

'Do you think they've gone through Broadheim yet, the army?' Melcun asked.

'Yes,' Rowden said. 'I can only assume it's ash and bone now. Just thinking about it turns my blood to ice, my heart to stone. I can't accept that any miracles or wonders from the gods could have stopped such an onslaught; the gods have forgotten about Broadheim now.'

'Maybe we should as well,' Melcun said.

Before Ogulf could say anything, they all heard the sound of light footsteps echoing up the corridor that led towards the room. Ogulf stiffened and tried to peer over Rowden's shoulder to see who was coming in. His stomach flooded with joy when he saw it was Runa. She was walking slowly, every step seemed full of pain, but she fought through it to show a half smile when she saw Ogulf looking at her.

'Thought I would come and see you all, sitting in that room is torture,' she said, sitting down gingerly next to Ogulf.

Ogulf exchanged a glance with his father as Runa shifted to find a comfortable position in her chair. As if he knew what his son was thinking, Rowden looked at Ogulf and gave him a reassuring nod.

'Runa, Melcun and I are going to Esselonia,' Ogulf said.

'Ogulf, please. I have something I need to tell you.'

For the first time he could remember, Runa looked vulnerable. It wasn't because of her injuries; it was obvious to Ogulf that she knew something that she didn't necessarily want to share. As much as Ogulf didn't want to cause his friend any distress in her current state, he had to know what this was.

'It's difficult to say out loud. I only found out late last night, and by the time I wanted to come and tell you all, everyone seemed to be drunk or asleep.' Runa bit her lip then looked to Rowden as if she was searching for protection or reassurance from the earl. The cracking pops of her knuckles told Ogulf just how anxious she was.

'I asked Lord Hanrik for a book on Esselonia. The one he gave me chronicled everything about the place from its founding and runs right up to about ten years ago. I was searching in it for anything about an axe or a prophecy, but I couldn't see anything.' She paused and took a breath. She pulled the book from a pocket in her gown and opened it at a pre-marked page. The text was miniscule, so much so that Runa was hunching over the table to read it. The text was split into two long columns on each page.

'I found this section. It's a history of the royal family on the island, and it states that the last monarch was Kelan Essel. It actually lists him as currently reigning king in this edition, but I can only assume this is the recently deceased king. It mentioned a daughter, Feda, and a son, Elundar.'

'We know that Feda's a princess, she's trying to stop her uncle from taking her crown,' Ogulf said.

'That's not all,' Runa said, scratching at her throat nervously.

'What do you mean?' Rowden said.

'The king had a brother. One that appears in this text as presumed dead for over twenty years. Not a word is written about him other than that and his name.' She closed her eyes and took a long breath through her nose. 'His name was Wildar.'

'What?' Rowden said, his voice sounding noticeably higher pitched than usual.

'But it said that Wildar died,' Melcun said.

'No, it said it is presumed he died. Not confirmed.'

'But he's from Paleways. He's not from Esselonia,' Melcun said.

'That's what I thought too, but this is all too specific. He wanted to go to Esselonia, he needed you to get to Feda, and he needed you to take his axe to her to stop a prophecy that he never mentioned to any of us before he was about to fall to his death.'

'Are you saying you think Wildar was related to Feda?' Ogulf asked.

'That's exactly what I am saying. There is no way this can all be coincidence, Ogulf,' Runa said. 'Wildar was Feda's uncle.'

'Impossible. That man was Broadheim to the bone,' Ogulf said.

'Do you know if he was born on Paleways?' Runa said. 'He came to Keltbran when you were a boy, only the gods know where he was before that. Or should I say, who he was.'

'If he had a history like this, he would have told us!' Ogulf said. 'He was one of us.'

'It looks like he was, and at the same time, he wasn't,' Runa said. 'And don't think for a second it doesn't pain me to learn of this.' She pointed a finger towards Ogulf but grimaced and jolted in pain as she did.

'Enough. This isn't a development we should be arguing about. If anything, perhaps it makes your journey a little easier, Ogulf.'

Ogulf couldn't hide his confusion. *How could this make things any easier?* If anything, this made everything more complicated.

'If you can prove you're a friend of Wildar's, perhaps it will be easier to get an audience with the princess,' Runa said. Rowden looked at her and nodded, then glanced back to Ogulf.

'And what proof do I have exactly?' Ogulf asked, standing up from the table and cracking his neck as he felt tension run up his spine.

'Well, you've got that for starters,' Runa said, motioning toward Wildar's axe as it hung from Ogulf's hip. 'Didn't he say she would need that if she was to stop this prophecy?'

'He did,' Ogulf said, nodding absently and replaying Wildar's final moments in his mind again.

The four sat silent for a few moments. Rowden tapped his fingers lightly on the table and Melcun just stared ahead blankly.

'Okay. So, it's settled that we're going then,' Ogulf said. 'I don't want it to look like we're just abandoning everyone, though, so how should we explain this to the rest of the captains?'

'Leave that part to me,' Rowden said. 'Let's hope Lord Hanrik is supportive of this and let's keep all of this between the four of us for now. You two,' he said, looking at Ogulf and Melcun. 'Do you think we should tell the Shingal about Wildar being related to Feda? Perhaps they might be able to shed some more light on this.'

All three nodded in agreement, then they sat in silence in the banquet hall for quite some time.

Chapter 20

After leaving Runa, Melcun, and Rowden in the palace, Ogulf began to wrestle with his feelings. Losing Wildar was affecting him more than he would care to admit. Dying was accepted as a normal passage in Ogulf's culture. Lingering on a lost loved one was normal, but he didn't have time for such emotions if he was to stay focused on what he had to do. If only he hadn't lost Wildar so suddenly, maybe then it wouldn't have hurt so much. But he could still see Wildar's body plunging into the Banespit whenever he closed his eyes, that was a sight he would never get rid of.

Ogulf thought about the other Keltbran who had died on the pass. He didn't see their deaths when he closed his eyes, but it didn't mean that he didn't mourn for them. If anything, the number of them only fuelled his want for retribution. Vengeance was not a feeling he was familiar with and it wasn't one that sat well with him. It felt like an uncomfortable rock in the depths of his stomach, one that wouldn't move for anything, the kind that decided to shake slightly whenever it sensed your happiness just to remind you that you still had something to take care of. Ogulf had accepted that that revenge, which he hoped would someday chip away at this boulder of discomfort, would not be achievable for some time to come.

Another feeling that he couldn't quite shake was an overwhelming sense of guilt. This guilt was stemming from his reluctance to leave his father and his people; it didn't seem like the right thing for him to do as a Captain of Keltbran, one that could potentially lead their people one day. But he was the son of their founder, a tested fighter in battle, and determined to do the best for his people, so he chose to accept the guilt for now.

He even considered not going to Esselonia at all, instead wondering if it would be best to remain and help his father. Thankfully, that thought had all but disappeared since he'd spoken to Rowden and received his blessing – plus, if he didn't seek out Feda, then he might not have people to return to at all. The invaders were expected to journey further south, but they had yet to make a move from their camp in Port Saker. Shingally scouts on the Sea of Blades had informed Lord Hanrik and his generals that the army in Port Saker was getting larger by the day, and from what they could tell, they were mounting men and arms before preparing to move towards the Kingdom of Shingal. Just like his mind, Ogulf's reality was also a war.

He let his strides shorten and his steps slow as he wandered through the square in Luefmort. It was bustling with life, which offered Ogulf a welcome distraction from the disruption in his head.

Positioned on the parameters of the square were carts large and small. Next to some of them were the horses that had pulled them, while others appeared to be hand drawn. There didn't appear to be a theme to this market, each stall had different wares – Ogulf could see a wine merchant; a jeweller; some kind of armourer dealing in ornate knives; and a man with a grand selection of colourful fruits amongst many others. Ogulf had next to no coin but he was excited to browse what was for sale; he hadn't seen a real market in a long time and this one had sounds, smells, sights, and other new and exciting things which could distract him from himself for a while.

The people of Luefmort were all polite and smiled at him as he made his way from stall to stall. Something was bothering Ogulf as he looked at them, their smiles were missing the true light of a smile, as if their toothy grins were coated in fear. He assumed this meant that word had trickled down from Lord Hanrik's announcement the night before and had worked its way into the fearful guts of its citizens. Despite the masked politeness, the smiles and the nods, there was a distinctly different mood in the air now – pressure from all sides like the walls were closing in, inch by inch, and minute by minute, as the invaders readied their attack just across the Sea of Blades.

He stopped himself from bargaining with the merchant at the stall with the ornate knives; he didn't have the coin or enough understanding of the haggling system here to get a deal, so he moved onto the next booth. It was surrounded by people.

As he tried to tiptoe to see what the stall was selling, he heard a harsh thud come from the canopied counter. He still couldn't see, so he slowly waded through the gathered crowd and was surprised to see a very short, muscular man. He had tightly cropped hair and Ogulf immediately noticed he only had one eye. His hands moved fast as they cut pieces from a hunk of marbled red meat in front of him. He did this with a grace similar to that of a noble dance.

In sharp, whipping motions, he slung small slices of meat into the hands of those in front of him. Ogulf watched as the ravenous band of customers bit into the succulent chunks of meat with pleasure painted on their faces.

'Full steaks available now. Best beef in all of the Shingal – better yet, best in all the world. Have it salted, have it charred, have it raw, have it your way. Five gold a round. Ten gold a loin,' the small man said. Ogulf noticed the people around him had their coins ready in their outstretched hands, some still chewing on their samples. 'See my men.'

The one-eyed man gave a gesture to the waiting crowd and they all flocked to the other side of the tent in an ordered frenzy, shouldering towards the front of the queue to exchange their coins with the two young boys on the other side of the stall. The boys waited eagerly with wrapped packs of meat in hand, swiftly dealing their wares to their keen customers. Ogulf didn't join the melee and was quickly the only person on his side of the stall.

'A people watcher?' the one-eyed man said.

'Not usually. I'm not from around here – don't get markets like this where I came from these days.'

'Ah, a wanderer like me. Where might you be from, my friend?' the man asked.

'Broadheim,' Ogulf said with a smile. 'Keltbran, to be exact.'

'Ah, Keltbran, I know it, I know it,' the small man said. He was still cutting meat, though not in as dramatic a fashion as he had been before. 'Used to stop at an inn there on my way to the big Jargmire festivals back when I had a boat. Long time ago that was, before the cold wrapped you lot up in that long winter. That's why you left then, searching for eternal summer like the rest of us?' He gestured up towards the striking blue skies with his hands.

'Not quite,' Ogulf said with a slightly awkward smile. 'Well, in a way yes. More of a forced search, though.'

'Ah, got too cold then?' the man said, holding out a sliver of meat towards Ogulf.

Ogulf smiled and accepted the gift. He hadn't eaten raw beef by choice before, but he was curious to try it like this given how much pleasure it had given the others. The cart owner joined him in eating a chunk himself. *It must be good if he's eating his own stock,* Ogulf thought. As he brought it to his lips, he felt the faint smell of blood coming from the smooth, cold meat. His teeth cut through it effortlessly and the succulent meat felt like it was melting in his mouth. It was delicious.

'You could say that. We waited it out as long as we could, but no use waiting for it to get any worse, is there? Where do you call home?' Ogulf asked, choosing not to bring up the invasion of Broadheim for now.

'Prath. I haven't been there in years, though. Went to see my mother after six years of trekking and found the place a wasteland, nothing like it used to be – it was coming back to prominence when I was a boy, you see. It might have looked something like this by now if it had.' The small man gestured around at the surrounding square. 'But it wasn't. It was dark. Desolate. Lots of shady folk going about their business, and the people there were just shells of what they used to be.'

Ogulf watched as the man gulped and looked skyward. Clouds filled his one remaining eye.

'My mother died while I was trekking, so I missed saying goodbye to her by three years. Hard stuff that,' the man said. 'She used to always say 'Sansul, you best come back to see me every harvest,' and how I wish I had or at least learned to write so I could have sent her a letter every now and then. I left Prath the next morning, got on a boat to the Shingal, and started working for an old butcher in the upper citadel in the capital. Used to serve slabs of marbled meat to the king himself before he died.'

Ogulf smiled as the man's demeanour brightened and his tone changed. His eye was back to normal and his words came out with a chipper lull that attached itself to his accent.

'You could say my home is the road,' Sansul said. 'Now at least, anyways. Me and my two lads–' He gestured at the two younger men still dealing out meat to anyone with coins. Ogulf noticed they were both head and shoulders taller than Sansul. '–We might settle down. Might head back to Prath one day, show them their roots and hope to the gods it's changed.'

Ogulf felt his smile crack slightly and hoped the meat vendor hadn't noticed. He couldn't and wouldn't mention the invaders to this man. Trayvan had said they could be from the vendor's homeland – maybe they were the types of shady characters Sansul had been referring to.

Just as Ogulf saw Sansul notice his change of expression, he heard a call come from behind him. The voice was familiar but new: Danrin's.

'Ogulf, come with me, I have news.' Danrin seemed composed and walked to Ogulf's side without looking at Sansul or the stall. The young knight smiled at Ogulf as he got closer. A gasp cut through the air and Ogulf turned to see the small man with his jaw dangling in shock, his working eye was wide and fixed on Danrin.

'My lord... My lord,' Sansul said. 'You're one of the Fated Few?' He pointed at the hilt of Danrin's sword. 'I mean, it's not a question, I always read a man by the hilt of his blade and I know that one well.'

Danrin smiled at the man, though Ogulf could tell that the lord's son was unsure of Sansul. The cart owner pushed his sons aside with ease and fetched a wrap of meat before returning and reaching over with an outstretched arm to hand the package to Danrin.

'A gift, my lord,' Sansul said. 'In thanks for all you and the Fated do for Shingal. The gods know I feel protected knowing we have your kind here. Gods fate it no one is stupid enough to test your skills.'

With a bow of his head, Danrin accepted the gift. 'Thank you, sir.'

Ogulf and Danrin walked back towards the palace. Ogulf looked over his shoulder as they did seeing Sansul staring on with admiration at the back of Danrin's head.

Just as they got near the palace doors, Danrin motioned for Ogulf to follow him through a gate to their left, which led to a different area on the outer wall of the palace grounds. The gate swung open to reveal an incredible garden filled with vines. Vibrant coloured petals were everywhere, and the perimeter was wrapped in a tall hedge that sprouted almost as high as the walls. In the middle of the garden was a circular marble fountain. Water coursed through it, creating an aquatic display of art.

Both men sat on a stone bench near the fountain and Ogulf watched as Danrin scanned the small garden. Ogulf couldn't quite understand why the Fated Knight did this; if there was anyone else in the garden, surely they would be clearly visible, but he did it anyway.

'My father has agreed to the plan,' Danrin said.

'Good, we'll be ready,' Ogulf said. 'I have something I need to share with you, but I need you to assure me it won't go any further for now.' Ogulf looked Danrin in the eyes and tried to be as stern as he could, and he intentionally paused after the statement to draw a response from Danrin.

'Of course. You have my word.'

'It came as a bit of a shock,' Ogulf said, taking a deep breath. 'But we recently found out that our chieftain, Wildar, could have been related to Feda.'

'Interesting, and definitely unexpected.' Danrin said. 'I wouldn't have thought Esselonian royalty would have third cousins scattered around the plains of Broadheim, but I suppose my very own cousin is effectively one of your own.'

'If the records in the book Runa read are right, Wildar was not a distant relative. Nor was he a third removed cousin. Wildar and Feda were of the same blood, he was a member of the Esselonian royal family, and he was Princess Feda's uncle.'

'You can't be serious?' Danrin said, his head craning forwards.

'It's a stretch, but given all that we know, and considering he has always been so eager to go there, I can't think of any other explanation. The book said he was presumed dead for over twenty years.'

'You might want to ask Trayvan about this,' Danrin said. 'If anyone knows more about that sort of thing, it will be the Sage.'

'There's no time. We need to press forward and get to Esselonia.'

'Very well, I will ask him if I can catch him at a moment of sense,' Danrin said. 'On the subject of your journey, my father requests one small favour of you – think of it as a payment of sorts for our agreement to help you reach Esselonia. Should you be granted an audience with Feda, please give her this.' Danrin handed Ogulf a wax sealed envelope. The emblem on the wax was the Shingally crest, the hawk holding the crown. 'To keep you from the temptation of opening it,' Danrin said with a playful smile. 'I will tell you what it says.'

Ogulf smiled at Danrin. He was now a little worried about accepting the man's word so easily, but a secret almost always bought another secret, which by Ogulf's count, made the two men even again.

'My father and some of the other lords in Western Shingal will pledge support for Feda's cause. For now, it will mainly be financial aid, but in the coming weeks, they expect the Crown Prince to offer his support officially, which may mean we can supplies, weapons, and who knows what else. They are hoping the coin will help strengthen her claim and perhaps purchase the help of some of the mercenaries to tide her over, but before we even get to that, we must wait on the formalities of The Wealth of the Empire to free up the funds.'

'Coins don't win wars, Danrin. You would be better off not giving her anything.' Ogulf took the note and chewed on the inside of his lip in an effort to stop himself from speaking. 'Why wouldn't Shingal support her with men to fight for her?'

'Haven't you learned anything about those in power here, Ogulf?' Danrin said. 'They don't want to fight, they never do. Centuries have gone by and not a single force has challenged us, so we have gotten used to being intimidating without even having to take to a field and fight. And now they may have an army of invaders regrouping on their doorstep, so of course they don't want to spare a single sword for someone else's cause when it looks like a war is coming for us. If the prince was the king, then perhaps we would send over droves of men to support Feda's cause, but he is not; he has a whole court of people who influence his decisions, and in order to protect his own kingdom, he has to work with them whether he likes it or not. This is the best we can get for now, and my father means to let Feda know that help is coming through this letter, so at this stage, it is all we have, and it is better than not helping at all.'

'I understand. I just wish I could say I understood any other parts of this mess,' Ogulf said. 'Getting an audience with a princess in the middle of a civil war is going to be difficult enough for starters. Then we have to give her a letter from a lord in a country we're not from. Then you consider we don't even know if she's still in control, let alone alive. And to top it off, we then have to tell her a now deceased family member of hers, whom she already thought was dead, told us she was the only person who could save us from a prophecy that will ravage our world. Oh, and also, she apparently needs this–' He pointed to Wildar's axe on his hip. '–To succeed in her efforts.'

Ogulf breathed quickly as the final few words flew from his mouth. It was everything that had been building up inside of him for days now, and as it all came out, he felt like a weight had dropped off his shoulders. He'd known all along that the task at hand was monumental but saying this out loud made him realise just how difficult it was going to be to achieve. He looked on as Danrin gave him a pitying smile.

Ogulf looked at the composure of the young Fated Knight. No doubt his thoughts were just as plagued by problems, but most likely thanks to his years of training, not a single crack showed in Danrin; he was solid and determined.

'I better get this inside before it spoils,' Danrin said, gesturing towards the wrapped beef. 'Come on.'

Just as they got up from the marble bench and made their first steps towards the side entrance to the palace, a near deafening crash echoed out from inside the building. Ogulf covered his ears. The sound had forced him to one knee, and he had to try and to stabilise himself while the sound rattled through his skull. He looked at Danrin, whose scrunched face suggested he was in pain, in less than a second, he had his Fated blade unsheathed and was scanning the gardens for signs of the source. What felt like small rocks hit the crown of Ogulf's head and he looked up to see pieces of glass raining down on them from a shattered window above. He exchanged a concerned look with Danrin and together, they ran inside to investigate as the glass continued to fall all around them.

Chapter 21

Luefmort was enveloped in alarm. A loud blast like that would have been heard across most of the city, and as Ogulf made his way through the palatial corridors trying to find the origins of the explosion, repetitive thudding of hurried feet echoing through the close walls of the passageways suggested that many others were on the lookout for the same thing.

Ogulf did his best to keep up with Danrin, but the man knew these corridors and moved through them effortlessly, cutting every corner and letting his hips snake past obstacles that were waist high while Ogulf's feet floundered. Eventually, after much weaving and some momentary confusion in the meeting points of the corridors, Danrin was at the front and up the stairs with Ogulf a few paces behind him, with the distant shuffle and clinking of armour from the corridor below them suggesting that some Shingally guards were jogging not far behind them.

'It's all right.' Ogulf heard the voice coming from within the doorway at the top of the stairs, and was relieved to find that he recognised it. 'It was an accident.'

Realising it was Crindasa, Ogulf began to push harder to take the remaining steps two at a time, keen to lay eyes on Melcun, as this was where he was supposed to be. Calm came over Ogulf as he caught a glimpse of his friend. Melcun was using a large painting to waft a dark haze of smoke out of a disfigured opening in the wall in front of him. Evidently, there had been a window there before, but now the hole was empty and the perfectly laid stones around it were misshapen. Melcun seemed unscathed but Ogulf could tell his friend was flustered.

'Crindasa. What in the name of the gods is going on?' Danrin asked. He had made it into the room, and was waving his hands to fan the smoke away from him.

'A slight... training accident,' Crindasa said, joining Melcun and Danrin in wafting the smoke from the room. The vapours were coming from the smouldering remains of a bookshelf on the wall to the right of the door. The books encased in it were black.

The slow clinking shuffled closer until five men emerged at the top of the stairs and crowded in the doorway. Ogulf looked at the men as they shuffled forwards, gawking in confusion at the mess. Most were unbothered, while others looked oafish at best as they scanned wreckage of the room without real care or concern. They all held long spears, but these were more decorative than deadly. There was no urgency in their movements. Now Ogulf knew what Danrin meant about the complacency.

'All of you, back to your stations,' Danrin said to the men behind him. They obeyed with a sudden sense of haste. 'The palace is no place for magic lessons, Crindasa,' Danrin reprimanded his cousin when they were gone.

'Are you all right?' Ogulf said to Melcun. His friend's eyes were wild and wide.

'I'm fine,' Melcun replied. His eyes seemed full of something, but Ogulf couldn't tell whether it was terror, disbelief, excitement, or a mixture of all three.

'I know that, Danrin. It's not like I expected this to happen. It was a mistake, everything is fine.'

'Everything is not fine. Half the windows on this wing of the palace are scattered across the gardens. My father will have to address the town about this.'

Crindasa looked at Danrin with a scowl that scrunched her eyebrows down towards her nose.

Ogulf thought they looked like a couple of bickering children and assumed this type of argument between the pair had taken place on more than occasion when they were growing up.

'Fine, I will go and explain this to Lord Hanrik myself.' Crindasa marched away and Danrin followed without a look at anyone else, his eyes focused on the back of Crindasa's head.

Scattered around the room were empty vases. The flowers they used to hold were also dotted around the room in jumbled piles of colour. A small puddle had formed at the bottom of the bookcase.

'What in the name of all the gods happened?' Ogulf asked.

'Well, I am not quite sure if I'm honest,' Melcun replied. He stopped fanning the smoke as it whittled down to no more than a few trails which floated their own way out the gaping hole. The look in Melcun's eye was the same as before.

'Okay, I'll try again. How did the window get blown out?'

Melcun looked at the window, and Ogulf noticed the way that look in his eyes changed slightly as he took in the shattered wall and empty window frame in front of him. He no longer looked stunned – now worry stretched his eyes wide and pulled the creases from his forehead. Ogulf watched as Melcun gulped and sweat began to bead on his brow.

'We were practicing Wield,' Melcun said, once again as if Ogulf was just supposed to know what he was talking about.

Ogulf looked at his friend, his face scrunched and his nose wrinkled. 'You're going to have to remember I know nothing about this kind of thing, Melcun. What is Wield exactly?'

'Oh, sorry. It's when you craft your power in your hands and hold onto it, then you control it until you wish to use it,' Melcun said. 'Think of it as drawing an arrow in a longbow and waiting to fire.'

Ogulf understood the analogy, and as simple as drawing a bow was, he couldn't imagine holding a spell or power was anywhere near as easy.

He looked around the room again, assessing the debris; a few paintings hung askew on the walls and there were large gaps present where others had fallen down. The squares and rectangles that they covered were a slightly different hue to the other areas. Above the charred bookshelf was a scorch mark that almost reached the ceiling. The room smelt like burnt bread.

'So, you fired... by accident?' Ogulf said.

'No, I just lost control,' Melcun replied. 'Crindasa wanted to see the type of power I could Wield, and at first it was easy to keep hold of. She thought I would find it too difficult, but I got the hang of it fairly quickly, so Crindasa asked me to keep summoning the energy and it just kept coming and coming. She was staring at me – she looked amazed. I looked at her for too long and my focus broke; the fireball came flying out of my hands and into the bookshelf.' Melcun looked at the bookshelf. His eyes lingered there as he evaluated the damage, seemingly taking in every splinter, crack, and shard. 'I am never going to get this right, am I?'

'You will. It's only been two days. Some of these mages go to schools for years to hone their abilities – Crindasa herself studied at the Tawrawth for six years, Lord Hanrik told me that himself. Now she's one of the best young mages in the realm. So just be patient,' Ogulf said, knowing full well that patience was not a trait that Melcun was well versed in. 'One piece of advice, though – I would be prepared to grovel a bit to Lord Hanrik; I can't imagine he will be happy about this.'

'I know, and I don't want Crindasa to take the blame either. It wasn't her fault,' Melcun said.

Ogulf wanted to disagree but he stopped himself just in time. This had been Crindasa's fault, and while she wouldn't have meant for such an outcome, she should have done a better job of supervising Melcun – he was her student, after all. Melcun didn't need to hear that right now, though, and Ogulf didn't want to put him on a defensive footing before their trip.

'I do have good news amongst all of this,' Ogulf said, trying to change the subject. 'Danrin managed to get Lord Hanrik to approve our journey, so we're going to Esselonia tomorrow.'

Ogulf chose not to mention the note to Melcun at this time – mentioning it in the palace seemed reckless, so he would tell Melcun when they were on the ship instead.

'Ah, good news indeed,' Melcun said. 'I would rather not spend too much time around Hanrik if I can't help it after this.' He motioned with open arms and glanced around the room.

Over the next hour or so, while the sun set beyond the empty window frame, the two friends attempted to fix as much of the damage in the room as they could. Crindasa came to check on Melcun and apologised to him, embarrassment written all over her face as she fumbled with her words. Before departing, Crindasa gave Melcun a leather-bound book, leaving it on the table in the room in front of him. Ogulf couldn't see any markings on the book but the cover was dark enough that, at first, he mistook it for one of the books that had been burnt.

'I heard you were leaving, but this should help. Read at least one Cast a night,' Crindasa said. 'We don't want to focus too much on what you can already do, and you'll have plenty of time to learn more on your journey, so I've marked the page of the first ability I want you to learn.'

She gave him a very awkward bow and an even more awkward smile, and left the room with a quick twist of her heels. Ogulf had only known the girl for a few days but he had never seen her manner change like this, she was flustered and let out an agitated breath as she made her way down the stairs. Perhaps Lord Hanrik had given her a dressing down over the damage, but Ogulf thought it was more likely that a bond of sorts was growing between Crindasa and Melcun and she was keen to help him understand his powers more before they had to part ways.

Eventually Danrin returned with some Luefmortian soldiers and a large, round-bellied man in elegant clothing. This man's face was over-scored by wrinkles, hard lines caused by years of frowning ran across his forehead, and his eyes looked as joyless as the depths of the Banespit.

'Master Drunos, this is the window in need of fixing.'

'I can see that,' the man replied, glancing around the room. His disgust was evident in the tight purse of his lips. 'I shall arrange it, though it will be a hefty price to fix.'

'Understood. Just let me know what you need,' Danrin said. 'Ogulf, Melcun, please come with me.'

As the three of them left the battered room, the large man gave a tut and shot a look full of loathing at Ogulf and his friend. This was the first experience of rudeness or disdain Ogulf had experienced since coming here. Melcun turned back to grab the book Crindasa had left for him and had to hurry to catch up.

'Ignore Master Drunos,' Danrin said when he was sure they were out of earshot. He must have heard the tut. 'Most people do, he's an exceptionally bad Shingally – gluttonous, hateful, greedy. I wouldn't be surprised if he turned out to be from the Wide Isles or another land of indulgence.'

Ogulf had never heard of the Wide Isles.

'Did you seek us for a reason, Danrin?' Melcun asked. His voice wavered slightly as if he thought it might involve an audience with Lord Hanrik.

'Yes, but don't worry too much, Melcun,' Danrin said, clearly noticing the panic-stricken paleness of Melcun's face. Ogulf couldn't help but laugh. 'Crindasa took the blame for the incident, and given that she is one of my father's favourite nieces, that seemed to be enough discussion on the matter. That, and she promised not to do any further teachings with you or anyone else on palace grounds.'

'Makes sense,' Ogulf said.

'The other reason is to ensure you're prepared for your journey,' Danrin said.

Ogulf followed as Danrin continued to lead them down from the ground floor of the palace to the basement. The walls down here were different. Gone was the warm marble and the stone carvings; they were replaced by brick, cold, and darkness. For the first time since passing the Trail, Ogulf felt himself shiver. He wasn't fond of it.

The three men made their way to an open space that, in any other place in the world, could have been a dungeon. But here in Shingal, they wouldn't have something like that under the grounds of a lord's palace. Where Ogulf would have expected to see wall shackles and cages, there were storage barrels and crates, some filled with candles, others full to the brim with heavy blankets. On the other side, there were sacks of grain and huge, empty jugs. The cavernous space was lit by torches and a single firepit in the centre of the room.

'This cellar was full before your people arrived. I am just glad all of the supplies went to good use, we normally have to discard them if they sit down here for too long.' Danrin led the pair to a table near the back of the room where there were two packs laid out. 'These should hold enough food to last you at least a week – it won't be much, but if you ration it, it should keep you moving. Hopefully by then, you will have made some contact with Feda, and be in her good graces enough to earn a meal. Or at least in a cell in one of the citadels, eating scraps of stale bread,' Danrin joked. Ogulf could tell from the delivery of this attempted jibe that Danrin wasn't one to make jokes often. 'There are also some other clothes and bed rolls in case you have to camp. You'll also find some flint, and most importantly, some coins.'

'Thank you, Danrin,' Ogulf said. 'We really appreciate this and all you've done for us so far.'

'You're welcome,' Danrin said. 'This seems like a time when we should all band together given your enemy now seems to be gearing up to attack us as well. So, if we can help find out why Feda Essel is the key to all of this, then we must lend a hand.'

All three men exchanged smiles. Then Ogulf remembered something, something he had to raise with Danrin. He bit his lip as he tried to find the right words; he needed to make sure whichever ones came out would not cause offence. The Fated Knight began to move towards the packs he'd organised for Ogulf and Melcun. He started testing the straps and patting them down.

'Danrin,' Ogulf said, and Danrin turned round to face him. 'When your soldiers reacted to the incident earlier, something was amiss. There was no urgency. Even when it was clear that something serious was happening.'

Danrin sighed. 'What are you trying to say, Ogulf?'

'I'm just worried that if this army makes it this far south, and if they mean to attack Luefmort, then those men will not stand a chance, not like that,' Ogulf said. 'If that army can ravage Broadheim – a land of men and women raised being taught how to fight – that easily, then they will do the same, or worse, in a land built on peace with an army that rests on its laurels.' Before Danrin could protest, Ogulf cut in again. 'I know what you will say. You have the numbers. But one hundred soldiers with no real fight in them are not worth ten who have malevolent intentions. Sure, they have discipline, but a lot of the ones I saw today seem meek. And a meek man on a battlefield is as good as dead before the first blood spills,' Ogulf continued. 'I know I am not Shingally. I respect you and your people for the support you've given mine, but I felt the need to be honest with you.'

Danrin's eyes fell to the floor as he nodded. 'I know. By the gods, I know. This is the kind of thing that plagues my nightmares. I can be frank with both of you – since I've returned, I've been petrified. We are strong in numbers, but weak in just about everything else. My grandmother could best most of the men who watch our walls. Worse still, I have no confidence in them being able to protect my home, not without a new way, a way without peace at the heart but instead with peace as the goal. Peace requires strength, courage, and a will. Too long have the men who patrol Luefmort – gods, all of the empire – been untested. I need to make sure we're prepared.' He looked up from the floor at Ogulf. 'I appreciate your honesty.'

'Perhaps you could ask for my father's help, Danrin,' Ogulf said. 'I'm sure him and some of his captains could lend a hand in sparring and the like, give your men some new types of opponents to fight.'

'He was a warrior?' Danrin asked.

'Not in the traditional sense of the word, but you could say we're all warriors in Broadheim, really. You're born, you learn to fight, hunt, and fend for yourself, and then you're left to find your path with those skills as a foundation should you need to call on them in life. And peace between countries doesn't always mean there will be peace *within* those countries. So, we've had a few occasions where we had to fight, and my father was the best man we had,' Ogulf said.

'You and your people fought during the Summer of Rebellion?' Danrin asked.

'Yes,' Ogulf said.

Though Ogulf had fought that summer, he did not consider himself a fighter on the same level as his father or Wildar. They'd had the advantage of experience, and while he was more than capable of fighting with an axe or a blade, his real skill in combat was his tactical mind. This was a trait ingrained in him by Wildar and his father, one that the two older men had drilled into him since he was a boy. 'War is about strategy first, bloodshed later,' they used to say, and Rowden was of a firm belief that the tactical mind Ogulf possessed was far superior to his own. His father always said Ogulf could have been the king's own chieftain if he wanted. He had never wanted that though.

Rowden, on the other hand, was a warrior unlike any other in all of Keltbran, and some would argue, the whole of Broadheim. On the battlefield, he was unmatched when it came to sword fighting, and the tactics he employed could pick apart a force of vastly higher numbers with ease. He was always able to find a way to turn the tide in his favour.

Ogulf recalled the first time he saw his father fight. It had been over some words a man in Jargmire had uttered about Ogulf's mother. She had recently passed and the man had mentioned something about her upbringing, something Ogulf never heard properly and his father would never repeat.

The problem was, this wasn't just a man, this was an appointed member of the King's Guard; a man of stature, title, and talent with a blade. Ogulf had only been twelve years old and was only allowed in the tavern that day because the owner knew he had nowhere else to go whilst Rowden drank his fill. The word the man said had been whispered, the only thing that suggested to Ogulf it had been a slight was the way life returned to Rowden's eyes, life Ogulf hadn't seen since before his mother died.

He calmly stood from his chair at the table, slowly moving his body so as not to touch the knight as he did. Without a word, he drew his sword and made his way outside. He didn't even look at Ogulf as he did it, but the whole tavern followed the men into the rain, the innkeeper pleading with Rowden all the while not to fight the King's protector, saying that Ogulf would be orphaned. It didn't change Rowden's decision.

As if at a tourney, both men lined up five paces apart and presented their blades to one another. Ogulf remembered the raindrops falling in the narrow street; it wasn't cobbled, so the ground was soft and unsure. He worried for his father in that moment as he looked at him, but there was no fear in Rowden Harlsbane that day. Ogulf wondered if this was him giving up, broken by the loss of his wife and ready to meet her in the afterlife. But that wasn't to be.

From the first action, Rowden was in control of his opponent, moving with a style about his blade that would have better fit the man in the carefully crafted armour. He spun away from swings, parried slashes, and outmatched the knight in a way that left the gathered crowd dumbfounded.

Before long, the knight was panting, his once shining silver armour now caked in mud from his falls into the ruined ground below him. He made one final flurry with his sword towards Rowden, hacking downwards, searching through the haze of the raindrops for a killing blow. With minimal effort, Rowden blocked the first three shots, and then, with a whipping motion of his sword hand, he disarmed the knight and gracefully swept his legs from under him, causing the knight to crash to the ground and sending muddy specks up towards Ogulf's face.

'I yield,' the knight said, his hands open for Rowden and the waiting crowd to see. Ogulf couldn't believe his father had not only disarmed but embarrassed a knight of the King's Guard; they were supposed to be the most elite fighters in all of Broadheim, and Rowden Harlsbane had left one red-faced in a puddle of mud while drunk.

Ogulf had never forgotten that day, and he never wanted to. Another reason he hadn't forgotten that day, was because it had been the last day Ogulf had seen that side of his father. He had seen flickers during the Summer of Rebellion, and he had even seen some recently, but nothing like the eyes Rowden Harlsbane had when he was at his best. Ogulf knew it was about time that those eyes were seen again.

'Very well – I will speak with your father,' Danrin said. 'Any help at this stage would be welcome, and perhaps he could show my men a thing or two... I've heard stories about the way your people fight.'

Smiling at Danrin, Ogulf made his way closer to his pack, standing next to Melcun. He began to take out each item and examine it. For the first time in as long as he could remember, Ogulf was beginning to feel excited, and even a little hopeful. The hope that was supposed to be here in Luefmort was nowhere to be found, but hope had a new destination, one that he would be heading towards tomorrow.

Ogulf watched Melcun place the book Crindasa had given him in his pack as the pit of his stomach started bubbling skittishly, creating a cocktail of all of his feelings with the giant boulder in his gut serving as a yearning for revenge. He needed to be on his guard; the time to leave for Esselonia approached.

Chapter 22

Night began to fall in Luefmort. The sun lingered on the horizon, glowing bright orange as the light to the west faded into a peaceful darkness in the east in a soft and perfect gradient.

Just like it had been for the past few evenings, the area near the palace was bustling with life. Beyond the palatial square was a busy street filled with taverns, inns, and pleasure houses. Danrin had asked Ogulf and Melcun to meet him in one of the taverns known as The Old Bricks, and he had also arranged for their packs to be taken to the supply ship ahead of them.

'A bit too conspicuous, wouldn't you say, Danrin?' Melcun said. The three men were sitting at a high table with tall stools, each cradling a bone-carved mug full of mead.

'You could say that. But better than trying to sneak you through a city and having to explain that to one of your captains if we crossed their path, wouldn't you agree? Don't worry, I have a plan,' Danrin said.

For the first time since meeting the young Fated Knight, Ogulf felt nervous. It wasn't that he didn't trust Danrin, he just didn't like the idea of not knowing exactly what was coming next.

'A plan you might care to share?' Ogulf asked quietly. The room didn't care much for them or their conversation, they were seemingly just another table, though this didn't put Ogulf any more at ease.

'No need, just trust me. I have told the man who will take you to Esselonia that you are official messengers travelling on behalf of the Shingally Empire. That is the story you should stick to until you get off his boat, and then you can be whoever you need to be to get to Feda,' Danrin said. 'I see no need to tell him anything else.'

Now a certain element of the plan made sense. Ogulf and Melcun had been given thick leather armour, new trousers, and leather-wrapped boots before they left. The leathers and armour were black and bore no Shingally markings, which was a relief. Though sturdy, the main body of the armour was very light and allowed Ogulf to move as if it were not there. The Shingally armorers had always been world-renowned, but Ogulf only truly appreciated why now that he had experienced their wares for himself.

Ogulf was also wearing another new piece of armour, a shoulder pauldron that was attached to his existing axe sheath that wrapped around his back. The steel covering had been given to him by his father. On it, etched, then painted with perfect white paint, was the outline of his mother's tree. He knew it would be his one day, he just hadn't expected that it would be given to him while Rowden was still alive. They hadn't shared many words when Rowden handed him the piece, just a look. One that was full of understanding, acceptance, and thanks from both men. It sat across his right shoulder. The unfamiliar weight was something he would need to get used to.

Along with the addition of the pauldron, he had also fastened a new loop to his axe sheath, so that he could carry Wildar's axe and his own on the journey.

Ogulf and Melcun sat with their backs to the door, sipping on their mead as they awaited Danrin's next instruction. The Fated Knight looked calm, but every so often, whenever the door creaked open, his eyes darted over the heads of Melcun and Ogulf towards the entrance. Most times, there was no further reaction, but on the next slow grinding of metal hinges, there was undoubtedly a flicker in Danrin's eye. Ogulf stopped himself from turning to see what had caught the young knight's attention.

'Ah, Aylan, my old friend, how are you?' Danrin said, smiling over Ogulf's right shoulder.

'Danrin, you little sod, how the bleeding oars are you? The capital treated you well, I see. Left a boy and returned a man,' a man said. His voice was light, and he gave a heartfelt chuckle with every few words. He embraced Danrin, dwarfing him.

It took Ogulf a second to realise the enormity of the man. His barrelled chest and muscular arms were trophies of hard work. He was a head bigger than Danrin, who was already quite tall. The orange hue of the candlelight in the inn bounced brightly off of the man's bald head. He had a chin that looked like it could take a direct impact from a war-hammer and do more damage to the weapon. He wore a light, sun-bleached shirt, black trousers, and boots that appeared to be made of animal scales. After embracing Danrin, he extended a slab-sized palm towards Ogulf.

'And these must be my travelling companions,' Aylan said. Ogulf met his hand first. The handshake was firm, but not crushing like he'd expected. 'Not often I have the pleasure of transporting those on official business, but when a man like Danrin needs me, the gods know I'll be there to lend a hand, or a boat in this case.' The hulking man's chest rose and fell as he chuckled.

'You flatter me, Aylan,' Danrin said, smiling as Aylan tried to fit his broad frame onto the wooden chair next to the Shingally Knight. The stool groaned under his weight as he shuffled to find comfort. 'These are our messengers, Ogulf and Melcun. They have a hefty task on their shoulders, but we need to do our part in an effort to broker peace in the war. We're hoping their counsel might be enough to start some kind of dialogue to lead us towards peace between the Northern and Southern armies.'

'Here's hoping they can do just that; this war has been terrible for business. I haven't sailed to the South of Esselonia for over half a year now. They have a blockade near the Red Isles and the bleeding fools won't even let my ship pass when I am carrying aid for *their* people. Curse the bloody rich,' Aylan said. 'Anyway, it's a pleasure to meet you both.'

'Aylan is captain of The Gwentar – you won't find a better man on all the seas. Consider the debt paid, and now the favour is mine to return whenever you need it,' Danrin said.

Ogulf had hoped that Danrin would have told the ones responsible for their transport the true nature of the journey. He didn't like the idea of a facade, but it seemed the only way now, and posing as messengers didn't bear too much responsibility. In essence, it wasn't even a lie, given that Lord Hanrik had tasked them with delivering a letter to Feda.

Melcun had seemed relieved when Ogulf told him of the letter; having something like that would not only help get them an audience with the princess, but it would let her know that they were associated with people who wanted to help her – people who were alive, at least.

'There is no such thing as favours amongst friends, Danrin. Do you have time for an ale before we set off?' Aylan asked.

Danrin nodded and Aylan summoned a server to fetch them four mugs of ale. Ogulf would have protested if he had the chance but he didn't want to cause offence. Aylan and Danrin began to catch up, and before long, the ales arrived and were drunk. Ogulf forced his down without enjoying a drop of the bitter liquid Aylan had chosen.

'We best be off; the boat won't steer itself. Tides be good to you until I see you again, Danrin,' Aylan said. All four men rose from their seats.

'Yes, understood,' Danrin said. 'It was a pleasure as always, Aylan. Next time, let's ensure the meeting is not so brief.' He turned to Ogulf and Melcun. 'The kingdom thanks you for this. I'll await your news. Pass the regards of the kingdom to both North and South Esselonia – we can't be looking to take sides. And most of all,' he said, looking at them sincerely. 'Be careful.'

Ogulf and Melcun departed the tavern with Aylan, and they followed him through the streets at a leisurely pace. They were headed for the southern entrance of the city, where there was a road that would lead them directly to the port nearby. As they approached it, Ogulf noticed it was far less fortified or guarded than the entrance they used when they arrived. Some of the men on watch nodded at Aylan as he made his way through the streets. The large man returned the nods. As they got to the outer walls, the gates began to open for them.

'You seem popular,' Ogulf said to Aylan.

'How's that?' the sea captain said, turning with a slight smile.

'Everyone seems to know you here,' Ogulf said.

'Aye, that's true, I know most of them. I've been in and out of Luefmort for years and many a man will buy a sailor an ale and listen to his stories,' Aylan said. 'Many a man will also ask if the spoils of the sea could fall off a cart for a small purse of gold every now and again. Don't worry, not Danrin, he's too noble for that, but others will hand over good coin for a case of Esselonian wine to charm their wives with once and turn a blind eye to my moves forevermore. So, knowing people certainly has its benefits, much like right now.'

Ogulf wasn't sure what Aylan meant, and that must have shown on his face because next Aylan said, 'Don't worry, Danrin hasn't said anything, and nor will I. Official messengers don't take night vessels to the ports of a country at war. Not unless they're on unofficial business,' Aylan said with a smirk, and as they walked, he continued to wave at the passing guards. 'My lips have been sealed by the coins I've received. In truth, whatever your plans are I hope they help end this bleeding war.'

Ogulf didn't want to divulge anything to Aylan; he was content in knowing that while Aylan had doubts about the official nature of their travels, he didn't seem to question their position as Shingally's. Either that or he didn't care. Ogulf assumed the latter.

'Going through official channels, like sending Lord Hanrik or another member of the Shingally council, was too much of a risk,' Ogulf said, unsure of where these lies were coming from, though a twist from his stomach suggested that the increasingly familiar iffy feeling in his gut was the most likely source. 'Regardless of the type of endeavour we're on, I am sure you'll understand we must be vigilant, the circumstances being what they are.'

'Aye, can't argue with that. Right, here we are,' Aylan said, pointing them towards a horse-drawn cart. Already on the cart was a small boy who sat upright and eager and seemed to relax when he saw Aylan. The horse at the front had a perfect coat of smooth brown hair, it looked almost statuesque as it waited to move again. 'No problems then, m'boy?'

The boy on the cart shook his head, his smile beaming like a beacon in the night.

'This is my lad, Emren.' The boy scooted over in the front seat of the cart and Aylan climbed on with notable ease for a man of his size. The cart sloped to one side slightly. 'Hop on,' he said, motioning to the back of the cart. Ogulf noticed the two packs Danrin had put together were already in the cart. He watched as Melcun patted his down and only stopped when he ran his hands over a certain part of the bag, checking for the book Crindasa had given him.

Ogulf and Melcun did as they were told, and as soon as they were seated, Aylan cracked a short whip and the horse began to move.

'Won't be long till we get to the docks,' Aylan said as the cart creaked and jolted along the rugged path. Turning back,

Ogulf watched the walls of Luefmort slowly shrink away as Aylan steered the cart onto a narrow road which was lit only by the vivid white of the moonlight.

Chapter 23

The ship was a sight to behold. Even in the dark, it was mesmerising. Light crept from candles in the cabin and the hold. Men of all shapes and sizes hurried aboard with crates and then busied themselves with tasks on the ship. They moved in a methodical way, like this was the thousandth time they had performed this same routine. On the top deck was a huge ship's wheel that looked too big to be real – it looked more like the centrepiece of a windmill, given how broad it was.

On board The Gwentar, Ogulf and Melcun were shown to an area in the upper hold where they could stay until the boat reached Esselonia. The wood wailed and creaked with each step as they were led to a dark corner of the space where two empty hammocks swung gently between two beams. Encased candles were attached to some of the wooden supports to illuminate the place. Between them rested a large crate and two smaller ones which Ogulf assumed were to act as a makeshift table and chairs.

Aylan grunted as he looked at the hammocks and put his weight on each of them to test their durability. Then he turned to Ogulf and Melcun, his previously sun-kissed complexion now resembled something closer to the snows of winter.

'I'm sorry about this, I know it's not much or very comfortable,' Aylan apologised. 'I asked some of the cabin boys to fix this up. You can have my quarters for the evening if you would prefer?'

'This is fine for us,' Ogulf said.

'We don't have too many passenger types on our vessel, and I wouldn't like to put you with my crew in the lower hold – there's more dirt and dust on them than you would find in all the alleys in the Shingal. You're sure this is okay?' Aylan asked. 'I wouldn't want to offend Danrin.'

'Please, Aylan, it is more than fine. Danrin will know we were treated well and travelled comfortably,' Ogulf said, trying to calm the man who was clearly keen to stay in Danrin's good graces.

'Aye, okay,' Aylan said, the colour in his face returning to its normal, light brown shade. 'We'll be setting off soon, just a few more things to sort. If you wouldn't mind staying down here until we're out of the port – it can get a bit lively up there when we're getting this old dear going – but once we're on the open, feel free to come up. There's not much to see at night other than the stars, but being on the waves is certainly good for the soul. Either that or get some sleep. I'll make sure no one disturbs you too much. If the seas are good to us, we will be in Esselonia around high sun tomorrow. The port we will be headed for is Vargholme. From there, passage to Delfmarc will be easy enough to find.'

Delfmarc. Danrin said that was where they would have the best chance of finding Feda. He said it was considered the capital of North Esselonia, and would be her seat until she could return to the island's official capital in Catermort, and retrieve her throne from her Uncle Eryc.

'Thank you, Aylan,' Ogulf said with a smile.

'I'll send one of the lads up with some water and some bread for your supper,' Aylan said as he departed.

The vessel rocked ever so slightly as it sat in the port. The wood shrieked and the wooden beams above Ogulf bent slightly as the crew of the Gwentar made their final preparations for departure. Curiosity got the better of Ogulf as he began to look through some of the supplies in the hold near their hammocks.

There were copious amounts of food in most of the crates – so much, in fact, that the contents towered above the edges of the containers. In another, Ogulf saw what looked like arrowheads. And then there were three filled with what resembled leather armour, not quite as protective as the ones given to Ogulf and Melcun, but certainly sturdy enough. It looked like the supplies going to Esselonia weren't as innocent as Lord Hanrik had made out. The assortment of smells from the crates suddenly hit Ogulf; leather, fruit, fresh meat, and steel mixed with the damp of the air in the hold made for an unpleasant collection of scents.

'Not too bad, all things considered. I mean, I would rather be sleeping in the palace but at least it's not too cold. And I never thought I would say this, but the idea of bread for supper isn't all that bad,' Melcun said.

'You're right,' Ogulf said, sitting on his hammock with his feet still firmly on the floor. It swung slightly beneath him. 'Danrin said Delfmarc was a day's ride from the coast, maybe two. How far do you think the messenger facade will get us?'

'It will be risky. I don't like the idea of having to keep the lie going any longer than we need to. And it's not like Aylan even believes it's true, not all of it anyway,' Melcun said, sitting on his own hammock. He swung his legs round and now lay prone, wrapped in the netting of the suspended bed.

'The old way,' Ogulf said. 'That might be easier – especially getting into the city.' Ogulf had thought about this for most of the day. Once they reached Esselonia, there would be no one but themselves to determine their path, and he relished the idea of being in control of his own will once more. He had come to the conclusion that acting as regular travellers would go against them; they had no idea who was and was not a threat to them by sight alone, so avoiding contact or confrontation would be key.

If they were smart, they could find their way to Delfmarc without placing themselves in any precarious positions. The closer they could get to Feda before they were intercepted the better it would be, given that there was no guarantee she would even be at Delfmarc – but where else would the princess of a nation at war be than inside the safety of one of her fortresses? The only problem he could see, aside from the obvious ones, was finding out how to get to Delfmarc without wasting valuable time.

Ogulf and Melcun exchanged thoughtful glances.

'It could work. I mean, it will be hard without knowing the lay of the land, and it might take us a while longer, but I think it's better than risking any other way,' Melcun said.

'All we need to do is work out how to get to Delfmarc. I want to ask Aylan. Perhaps I could say we had a map, but we lost it,' Ogulf said. Saying it out loud made him feel stupid; he knew it wouldn't work for the simple reason that Aylan would wonder why they wouldn't be paying coin to be taken to Delfmarc by cart.

It surprised Ogulf even more that the captain of The Gwentar had not asked why there were no accompanying soldiers or protectors with the two messengers, but Aylan knew more than he let on and asked no questions, just as he was supposed to, so dwelling on that now was not necessary.

Worse still, if they went around the port in Esselonia asking how to get to Delfmarc like a pair of babbling wanderers, then the suspicions of the locals were likely to be raised. No one would want to answer the questions of strangers, especially not during a war.

After a short while, the boat began its journey, pulling out of the choppy waters in the dock near Luefmort. The shouts and bustle of the task grew loud for a few minutes as Aylan, his ship mates, and the cabin boys all called out instructions, then the noise stopped, and was replaced by the calm whistle of the wind. Melcun was lying in his hammock while Ogulf was perched on one of the smaller crates beside his own swinging bunk. Both men were busy; Ogulf was going through his pack while Melcun was engrossed in the book Crindasa had given him. Melcun was mouthing something over and over and then he looked at his hands. He was pinching his forefinger close to his thumb and holding a tiny ball of what looked like water. Drops from the ceiling fell and latched onto the perfect liquid circle as Melcun looked on at it, smiling. Ogulf observed his friend, suddenly feeling a sense of pride as he watched him learning.

'Well, at least now if you set something on fire you can put it out,' Ogulf said. Melcun didn't look away from the slowly growing orb but he smiled and shook his head at the joke.

The creaking of the stairs from above pulled Ogulf away from the magic in front of him and caused Melcun to lose control of his ball of water. He let out a sigh as it dripped to the floor beneath him.

Ogulf looked up to see the descending frame of a thin man, with matted grey hair. His muscles were taut with years of use and malnourishment. His scraggly beard and moustache were so long they hid where Ogulf assumed his mouth would be. A baggy overshirt with ripped sleeves was draped on his near skeletal figure. His rough, battered feet looked like leather, and he had no need for shoes.

'Ah, Shingally messengers,' the man said. 'Aylan sent me down with this.' He placed a circular tray on the large crate between the two hammocks in a very ungainly manner. On the tray, there were four mugs and a bowl. 'Two waters, two ales, bowl of olives and bread,' the man said. 'Should you be needing anything else I would prefer you didn't ask as we don't have anything.'

Ogulf tried not to laugh but Melcun couldn't hold back his cackle. The noises coming from the lean man were appearing from behind the thick wall of hair on his face which made the exchange all the more comical.

'Something funny?' the man said.

'No. Apologies, my friend,' Ogulf said as Melcun stifled his laugh. 'We have had one too many ales with your captain before leaving Luefmort. That and the sea air must have gone to our heads.'

'Ah yes, fond of that stuff whenever he hits land is our captain. We don't get none of that on the ships and barely get time these days to make trips to a good tavern when we're in port,' the man said.

'Sit with us if you would like. I've had my fill of ale, so you are welcome to mine,' Ogulf said, gesturing to the man. Melcun looked on, perplexed.

'Don't suppose anyone will miss me much up there,' the man said, sitting down on the other crate between the two men. 'They get on at me a fair bit for being slow. Can't help it now, can I? Time takes us all. It's just taking me a bit slower than I would like,' the man said morbidly. He took the mug of ale from the tray and drank deep from it, gulping.

'What's your name, friend?' Ogulf asked.

'I'm Greth,' he said, pausing only to answer and then taking another greedy drink from the large mug.

'I am Ogulf and this is Melcun.'

Greth looked at both men and gave a slight nod. The moisture from the ale had soaked into his moustache; tiny droplets dangled from the longer hairs until his tongue appeared through the barrier of hair to lick them away.

'Do you know much about Esselonia?' Ogulf asked. Greth seemed like the perfect person to ask about how to get to Delfmarc, and Ogulf was sure the ale would help loosen his lips. 'The war won't stop us trying some of the fine delicacies and fermented treats this place has to offer.'

Greth looked as if he was pondering as he sat there with both hands clasped around the mug of ale, protecting it like it was a precious gem, then he took another mouthful.

'Depends. South Esselonia is where you'll go if you have expensive tastes. That applies to everything you could spend your gold on, like wines, meats, and women. But if you want to experience the real Esselonian spirit, you can't go wrong with the taverns in Fenrach. It's on the other coast of the island,' Greth said, squinting his eyes as if trying to make sense of his own statement. When he did this, his eyes disappeared behind wiry eyebrows and lank hair to make his whole face look like a mask of grey, straw-like locks. Ogulf stifled a laugh once more.

'How might we get to Fenrach? Is it close to Delfmarc?' Ogulf asked. Melcun turned slightly, leaning in closer to hear their conversation.

'Not close as such, but if you follow the Mule Road all the way north from Delfmarc, you'll find yourself in Fenrach.'

'The Mule Road,' Ogulf said, repeating this to himself to take note of it and to make sure Melcun heard him. He wanted to keep the conversation light, so he decided not to pry his source too heavily. 'We shall look for it once our business is done.'

'Oh, you won't need to look. The road runs from Vargholme all the way up to the Far Spire. It can be treacherous, make no mistakes about it, those long stretches between towns are bandit country – bushes full of thieves and forests packed with evil – so make sure whatever cart driver you use has some men to protect you.'

'Duly noted,' Ogulf said. 'Though I was under the impression that Esselonia was a peaceful place, idyllic even.'

'Heh, and which goat pissing fool told you that?' Greth said. With another swallow, he drained the mug and thudded it down on the large crate in a routine manor.

Ogulf didn't want to say it was Wildar; it wouldn't make a difference to the conversation. He took a sip of the water Greth had brought and then held the mug in his hands.

'A friend,' Ogulf said instead. 'It must have changed since he was last there.'

'Aye, that it has. It used to be the liveliest place in all the seas. A good place – pure, hardy, exciting, and what have you. It had its rough edges even then, but overall, it was a wonderful place. Since all these disputes came around, it's just like anywhere else. Hope you don't mind me saying but it will be like that in Shingal before you know it.'

Ogulf wasn't offended by the statement; the Empire of Shingal was not his homeland. More to the point, he knew what Greth meant; peace couldn't last forever, and whether it was the invasion or something else, there would always be someone who opposed the current norm. He thought about Broadheim and how the people left there would be fairing now. *Will there be a resistance yet?* he wondered.

Likely, though, this wouldn't be the case. Most people had flocked to the citadels when the cold came, so the chance of an uprising or counterattack from the villages of the plains was slim at best, and all information suggested that the invading army left no one alive.

'Here's hoping the peace in Shingal stays intact,' Ogulf said, looking Greth in the eyes and giving him a thoughtful smile.

'Aye, agreed. That will keep me on the seas, which is all I ask of the gods these days. Aylan fancies that port. Him and his chiselled jaw say we've never had it better. Your masters give us heavy bags of coin, we do their bidding. Occasionally, we have to transport a few of your types across the sea and keep quiet about it,' Greth said, throwing a look in either direction as if realising that he wasn't exactly keeping quiet. 'So, the longer peace in the Shingal stays, the better.' The hairy man toasted the air with his empty mug of ale.

'Feel free to use mine,' Melcun said. 'No use toasting without a mouthful of ale.'

Greth's face contorted into what Ogulf thought was a smile, but it was hidden by the mask of hair again. The old man smiled over his shoulder at Melcun and nodded. He took the other mug, choosing to sip this drink rather than guzzle it down like the last one.

'When was the last time you had a Shingally on board going to Esselonia?' Ogulf said. He glanced at Melcun, meeting his eyes to make sure he was paying attention. Melcun raised his eyebrows at Ogulf from behind Greth. Ogulf let the question linger as he watched the shipmate thinking. His eyes were fixed on the roof of the deck, making them properly visible for the first time, and his tongue crept out and hung to the left side of his mouth as he continued to think. 'It would be good to know if some of our colleagues are still over there,' Ogulf continued.

Greth was still staring at the underside of the top deck. His fingers opened from his fist as he counted in an odd fashion – thumb, then pinky, and then ring. The way the hairs on his face danced suggested he mouthed the numbers as he counted.

'Last one was a Tongueless,' Greth said quietly, almost to himself. 'Before that, there were two traders from Shingal proper, but we brought them back. Then, before that, there was that old, fat whore keeper looking for new girls, but we brought all of them back. Heh.'

Greth was still talking. He took another savouring swig of ale after a couple of words, then spoke, then drank again.

'We haven't taken any that we didn't bring back, so by my count, you two will be the only Shingally's on the island that I know of,' Greth said.

'You said something else, a … Tongueless?' Ogulf asked.

'Aye, one of them silent messenger types,' Greth said. 'Only a couple of days back, we took him from Luefmort to Vargholme. He paid double, said nothing, ate nothing, drank nothing, and caused us no troubles other than making our pockets a bit heavier.'

Ogulf had no idea what Greth was talking about. Ogulf had never heard of a Tongueless, and given the profile of the other passengers, Ogulf could only assume that this silent traveller was not a desirable type. Ogulf smiled as he realised this was now the company that they kept as well – he and Melcun were just as questionable as the rest with their false messenger personas.

A shout came from the main deck of the ship and called out to Greth by name. His stunning green eyes widened at the sound, and for a moment, they brought a bit of colour to his otherwise grey face. Greedily, he guzzled down the ale, causing some of it to spill out of the sides and down his cheeks, and then hurried up the stairs.

'Thank you, my friends,' Greth said as he climbed the steps two at a time disappearing into the dark of night on the ship's deck.

'Is it me, or are people getting more and more strange the further south we go?' Melcun said. He shimmied down and got comfortable in his hammock, opening Crindasa's book again.

'This coming from a sorcerer,' Ogulf said, smiling at his friend. Melcun rolled his eyes. 'There is some truth in it though, and the next few days are going to make it even more strange.' Melcun's expression changed to one of concern. 'What's on your mind?'

'Supposing the Order of Maledict is trying to fulfil this prophecy, the one about the Onyxborn, how do you think we stop it?'

'I have no idea. Wildar obviously did, so I can only hope that our meeting with Feda sheds a bit more light on all of this. What else did Crindasa say about the prophecy?'

'She said that it was the only thing that would motivate an army like that to come south the way they did,' Melcun said. 'Their initial goal will be to take some of the Peaks of Influence to weaken the mages protecting Gelenea and then to get the Onyxborn to Esselonia to perform some kind of ritual under the Stone of The Night at the altar of Loken.' Melcun looked up at Ogulf. 'If the fulfil that, if the Onyxborn can latch onto Loken's power, then there will be no going back. If they make it to the altar, then all that is good in the world will be lost.'

'If this was any other time, I would be laughing at you. This magic and prophecies and the promise of dark times, they come from our stories, not our real world,' Ogulf said. 'But after seeing Broadheim fall the way it did, nothing seems impossible anymore.'

'When we meet Feda, do you think she will laugh at us when we mention the prophecy?'

'Gods, I hope not. Being branded a fool would be more than I could take. I just wish Wildar was here,' Ogulf said. 'Leaving us with a riddle like this is torture, and if he was here, he would know exactly what we need to do.'

'Well, he's not,' Melcun said. 'And we do know exactly what to do.'

'I suppose you're right. One day at a time, I suppose.'

'One day at a time,' Melcun said

Ogulf got into his hammock in a slow, controlled manner to make sure it didn't falter underneath him. When he finally got comfortable, he shut his eyes and tried to drift off. He wasn't confident he would get a wink of sleep, but before long, the light sloshing of the waves put his mind to rest and he slipped away to a peaceful slumber.

Chapter 24

The bobbing of the ship woke Ogulf gently. Next to him, Melcun was slumbering in his hammock. It swung softly as it cradled the young mage while he snored peacefully with the book from Crindasa lying open against his chest, his arms wrapped tightly around it. Light crept to the corner of the deck they slept in and the caw of gulls pushed their way through the thick wooden planks to his ears.

Though the hammock was not as comfortable as the palatial guest room in Luefmort had been, it had provided Ogulf with a peaceful enough sleep for a few hours. As long as he was rested enough to make it through the day ahead, it didn't really matter to him where he laid his head.

As he made his way up the damp, rotted steps to the main deck of the ship, he screwed up his eyes against the bright sunlight. The noises coming from the softened wood underfoot were squelchy and unpleasant; he was surprised the stairs still remained intact. There was warmth in the air which was dulled slightly by the breeze of the sea. He still wasn't used to having the weight of two axes on his back. Wildar's blade was far superior to his own, but it was only half as heavy. From the gilded hilt to the long, curved blade with the wicked edge, it was simple and beautiful at the same time, and made his old axe look primitive or ordinary at best.

He moved towards the side of the ship and looked up admiringly at its huge sail. He had never seen anything like it in all his years. Most of the boats he had seen were powered by rowing men, and the ones that did have sails were much smaller than this one. The sail was bright red and it was pulled into a long arc as it filled with the air that propelled the vessel forwards.

Around him, Ogulf noticed a few deckhands milling around. He recognised Aylan's son, the boy from the cart; he was perched in the crow's nest at the top of the ship. He had a long-glass and was scanning around the seas. The waves, just like the mood on the boat, were calm.

'Morning, friend, did you sleep well?' Aylan asked. Ogulf turned to face the hulking man with a smile. Steam trickled up from a mug he was holding and Ogulf watched it rise longingly.

'Yes, thank you,' Ogulf said. 'How long until we make landfall?'

'Not long. Two hours at most. I've asked one of the lads to fetch you some mutton. We can't have you leaving The Gwentar with an empty belly,' Aylan said.

Ogulf wanted to protest; the thought of mutton made him feel nauseous, but he was keen not to offend.

'Thank you. When we get to port, will it be as simple as us walking out from the ship and being on our way?' Ogulf asked, 'silly question perhaps, but given the Esselonians are at war, I thought it best to ask. I wouldn't want to cause you any issues.'

'I appreciate that.' Aylan said sincerely. 'That answer depends, though. So, if you don't mind remaining on the ship until I fetch you, that would be best. I'll go ashore and see if there are any... problems, so to speak,' Aylan said before loudly slurping from his mug.

'What does it depend on?'

'Well, actually, nothing, if I'm honest, but it would be wise to be cautious. That's the problem with civil wars, it's so hard to work out who to trust. One trip it might be this or that group, the next, they might be dead or changed sides. Very complex situations,' Aylan said, his tone suddenly stern. He placed his mug down in the same manner Greth had done the night before and whipped an apple from his pocket before cutting thin slices from it with a rusty blade. 'Esselonia is getting more unstable every time we visit, so I need to make sure I don't piss off the wrong people. I don't envy your position much, though – wading through this mess isn't going to be easy. And I don't mean to speak out of turn here, but it won't do any good, regardless of what that message you carry says,' Aylan said before biting a slice of apple straight off the edge of the dark grey blade.

Ogulf waited for a second to think of the best way to respond. He tapped his finger on the side of the ship, and before he could find the words, Aylan had continued. 'All I mean is, what do you think you can achieve, realistically?' he said. 'Do you think the Shingal can bring peace to a blood feud, a family at war?'

His point struck home with Ogulf, but only in relation to the role he was playing as a Shingally messenger. His main focus for now was trying to find out what Wildar meant about Feda and the axe and to understand more about his ties to Esselonia.

'I wish I knew what we were capable of, Aylan,' Ogulf said. 'This does seem like a risky endeavour, but what else can we do?' He was getting tired of pretending, but this, at least, was the truth in terms of his actual purpose.

Aylan gave Ogulf a sympathetic smile and made his way below deck.

Ogulf watched the horizon as the waves caused the boat to bounce up and down. The waters were choppier than before, but not so much that it made the sail unpleasant, and the wind continued to aid them on their course.

Ogulf had never been on the seas. Not like this, anyway. This journey reminded him of his first experience of the open water, when he and his father made their way to The Paleways, a small island territory off the coast of the mainland of Broadheim. They travelled there in a small rowing boat with the intention of striking up a new supply route for the grain produced in Keltbran.

The seas were not kind that day and the boat sloshed from side to side, sometimes violently, and without a sail to carry them, the wind became a villain. Ogulf remembered cowering into his father for what felt like the whole journey. He dreaded that trip, but his father wouldn't entertain the idea of him not going. He'd said it would help shape and strengthen him, and between the waves and the freezing cold nights of camping before they got to shore, it had certainly had an effect on Ogulf.

It was on that trip that Rowden met Wildar for the first time. Wildar was a captain of the Paleways clan who ruled the islands and was keen to develop relationships with people from the mainland, especially those with valuable goods to trade like the Keltbran. Rowden and Wildar struck up an immediate bond, they had a lot in common, so Rowden invited his new acquaintance to Keltbran at his earliest convenience to show him the town and the offerings of the mainland properly.

Half a year passed and then Wildar appeared. He was welcomed with open arms, though he'd only planned to stay a few days, those days soon turned into a week, and that week into a month. Then he sent a letter home to Paleways to say he would be remaining in Keltbran. Soon he became one of their people, and everyone took to him.

Reminiscing made Ogulf shudder; he could still feel a tinge of the queasiness he felt in that rowboat that day. Ogulf thought this journey on the seas would terrify him given the previous experience, but if anything, this was the most peace he had felt in days. Staring at the waves seemed to cleanse his mind and wash away some of the feelings of guilt, grief, and distress that had clung to him since the events on the Trail. He thought it was something about being in between destinations – the waves weren't like a road or a path, they felt freer. The air was different too. Ogulf breathed deep and often, savouring the feeling of the sea air as it rushed his lungs.

As he stared out at the waves, he noticed something different on the horizon now. They were approaching land, and lots of it at that.

**

Ogulf found his patience wearing thin as he and Melcun waited aboard The Gwentar for the signal to disembark.

Ogulf wasn't as nervous as he'd expected to be at the prospect of setting out on the next leg of his journey. Trust didn't come easily to him, but he had thrust himself into the hands of others to get this far, and soon he would be in control again – or, at least, whatever was guiding him would be.

Aylan had asked Ogulf and Melcun to remain below deck, but Melcun politely protested and Aylan conceded.

Ogulf hadn't tried to stop Melcun from his effort; he was just as eager as his friend to get off the ship and find the Mule Road.

Ogulf had spent most of his time waiting scanning the buildings that lined the road which connected to the dock where the ship was moored. The row of red bricked establishments looked like they might have been inns or taverns, and the streets in front of them were teaming with people making their way through Vargholme.

The docks were busy as well – cargo large and small was being moved around by men, women, and children of all shapes, sizes, and creeds. A lot of them were calling out in accents Ogulf had never heard, while some made wild but calculated hand gestures. At first, Ogulf thought those people were mad, but upon closer inspection, he saw they were using the signals as some kind of communication which was being reciprocated by another on the dock. Like most ports, this one reeked of fish. It was jarring when compared to the pleasant scents of the open sea.

One thing that surprised Ogulf was the lack of soldiers in the port. Since arriving here, he had spent a significant amount of his waning patience searching the crowd for a helmet, armour, a weapon, or any other sign of authority, but there was none. All of the warnings from the last few days didn't seem to have been about the place they were in – this port in Vargholme certainly didn't seem like it was situated on the coast of a country at war.

Five minutes passed. This quickly turned to ten, and then dragged on to fifteen. Ogulf kept his eyes trained on the boardwalk that led to the ship. Aylan would have to come back that way to reach the boat and he would stand out by a mile compared to those around him.

Eventually he returned, wading his way in careful haste, showing a nimbleness that defied his size as he sidestepped through the crowd. He stood at the foot of the ship's gang-plank, looking around, and Ogulf saw caution in the captain's eyes as he finally relented and summoned his two passengers down with a wave.

'I just checked in with my man at the inn there.' He pointed to the one in the centre of the row of buildings in front of the dock. The sign above the door read, The Baron's Boots. 'He tells me there isn't much to report here. Some of the cart drivers in town have made their way to Delfmarc already, but there are a few still available, and if you like, he can arrange passage for you. You'll have to pay a hefty coin, but he'll make sure you get there safe.'

Ogulf had no intention of taking a cart as passage to Delfmarc. Despite this, he took in Aylan's every word and nodded along.

'One thing of note. There's usually heaps of soldiers patrolling here. I've only seen a few since we docked. The innkeeper said something about a calling of banners, telling all fighting men to head to Delfmarc. Sounds to me like Feda is expecting a battle,' Aylan said. He turned back to the busy streets and tiptoed to look around as if searching for any sign of a soldier or town watch. The act in itself was ridiculous, given that Aylan was already a whole head and shoulders taller than most of the people moving around him.

'A mass change of guard maybe?' Melcun said.

'Not something that would happen during a war,' Ogulf said. 'But I am sure it will be fine all the same. We will make contact with the cart driver and then make our way to meet the North Esselonian delegation in Delfmarc. I am not sure when we will be making the return journey, but we will wait in one of the inns until you come back.'

'Very well. I'll be sure to let Danrin know of your safe arrival, and if the supplies keep moving the way they are in Luefmort, then we will be in and out of port here every three days or so,' Aylan said. 'If you're going to stay in an inn, I would opt for The Baron's Boots – you won't find a better lamb roast in all of the world. I'm sure Blinda will throw in a free one with the stay if you tell her I sent you and if you tell her that her hair looks pretty.'

'Perfect. Thanks again, Aylan,' Melcun said. The large man gave them another smile, a slight dip of the head, and then walked back up the gangplank onto the boat. The rope-bound planks bent like a bow under his weight as he made his way onto the ship.

Ogulf turned into the dock and looked towards what appeared to be the rest of the town. Everyone around them was caught up in their own tasks, so Ogulf decided they should do the same. Together, they began to walk towards the row of red brick inns.

'I say we get on that road as soon as possible,' Melcun said. He clutched onto the strap of his supply bag as it draped over his shoulder. 'We can make good ground if we press on today.'

'Agreed, plenty of daylight left and it gives us time to work out how in the name of the gods we are going to get an audience with a princess. I have a few ideas, none are simple. Do you think we can just wander into Delfmarc and ask to see Feda?' Ogulf said. He was half joking and hoped Melcun would notice.

'I think that is our only option,' Melcun said.

'So do I. Don't you think it sounds too simple and yet far too risky, though?' Ogulf said. 'One thing troubling me is that I'm not sure Wildar's name alone will be enough to get us an audience.'

'I know we said we would drop the facade, but do you think we should keep up the messenger act in case it gets us further with less questions?' Melcun said.

'It might leave us in trouble once we lift the veil, though. I can't see them being too warm to us when we tell them we were lying.' Ogulf said. 'Regardless of our intentions, I am beginning to think honesty is the smartest option – it makes for less complicated outcomes.'

'You're right. Perhaps the cart would be worth consider-ing, then, since we do have the coin?' Melcun said. 'And at least we will be on the right path then. Not to mention it will be quicker.' Ogulf shook his head, the less contact they had with people the better.

The two men pushed through the crowds near the port to quieter areas of Vargholme. They stopped to ask a trader in Vargholme how they could get to the Mule Road. The man was wearing lavish clothes of soft looking silk, everything from his small hat to his slippers were gorgeous, but his stall had only ragged items for sale, which Ogulf found odd. He told them Delfmarc was a full day's walk from Vargholme, and if they started now and made the most of the daylight, they could be there by tomorrow evening, so they made for the Mule Road without delay.

The road was easy to follow even if it was not consistently paved. Some parts were inlaid with evenly spread stones, while other parts were missing stones, and some parts were not paved or marked at all. Sights like this made Ogulf glad they opted against a cart in the end. He didn't doubt that it would have been the more comfortable option, but some of the holes in the road looked deep enough to render a cart useless if they hit them.

The two men walked for the rest of the daylight hours, in all that time, they saw no signs of the war battered country they had been expecting to find. They passed sun-kissed fields, thick forests, and the occasional farmhouse with livestock outside; this place seemed quaint and idyllic, just like how Wildar said it would be.

By the time they decided to make camp for the night, Ogulf was already pleased with their progress. They set up their bed rolls near the road, at the bottom of a short embankment with enough cover to give Ogulf peace of mind that they wouldn't be too easy to spot from the main path.

The area they had chosen was flat and cordoned by high reeds that kept them out of view from the Mule Road. Reverting back to his old habits, Ogulf had scouted around the area before they settled in their position for no other reason than to listen to the sounds, take in the smells, and look at the new land he now found himself in. There was something familiar and calming about this place as he moved through the tall grass, even as the scorched edges of the brush rubbed harshly against the soft skin on the back of his hands. He felt like this was where he was supposed to be – he was finding his path just like he had hoped. When he returned from his brief recce, he found Melcun was already making a circle of stones to prepare a fire.

'I know it's not cold, I just thought it would be nice to have some light,' Melcun said as he placed dry branches within the circle. 'I reckon it makes us look less suspicious if we act like your ordinary travellers.'

Melcun had a point. The fire would also let the two relax a little, and the setting reminded Ogulf so much of treasured memories hunting in the forests in Broadheim, only this time, there were no others with them. No Wildar or Rowden or even Cohl. Now it was just the two of them, and this wasn't Broadheim.

Melcun left to gather more firewood and Ogulf flattened his bedroll a few paces from the pit. For a while, he lay on his back atop his bedroll and stared at the dark sky. It was so vast and clear, it would take two lifetimes to count all of the stars that glistened in the perfect black canvas. Staring upwards, Ogulf felt more of his accumulated tensions slip away from his body. By now, his father must have told the captains where Ogulf and Melcun were, and in an effort to keep everyone happy, Rowden would have also told them why. He wondered if Prundan would have been supportive or if he might have been happy to see the back of the two younger captains.

Melcun disturbed his peaceful mood as he shuffled through the reeds and dropped a pile of dried sticks near the fire.

'You took your time,' Ogulf said. 'I almost came to find you.'

'Sorry, I got caught staring at things. Did you notice how much the lake looks like the Tuntrelin Deep? That sight, the open water like that, it's different from the sea, isn't it? It's suppressed and free at the same time,' Melcun said, placing more fuel on the fire before it began to peter out.

'This whole place is like the plains. It's no wonder Wildar wanted to come here,' Ogulf said, shifting onto his side to look at Melcun as he spoke. After refuelling the fire, Melcun was now lying on his back in his bedroll, eyes scanning the sky above him. 'I can't stop thinking about him.'

'Me neither. This journey feels off without him, given how much he wanted to come here.'

'No, not that. Why wouldn't he tell us he was related to a princess?'

'Maybe he couldn't. Or maybe he didn't know how to. It doesn't seem like the kind of thing someone would just bring up in conversation. Most likely, he didn't know how people would react,' Melcun said, without looking down.

Ogulf waited a second before replying, remembering that his father had said something similar.

'I just find it strange that he longed to come to this land for as long as I can remember while not telling any of us that he had ties here,' Ogulf said. 'It seems selfish and misleading. And neither of these are things that I associate with the Wildar we knew.'

'What about the Wildar we didn't?' Melcun said, turning on to his side to face Ogulf.

Words failed Ogulf as Melcun's valid point hit home. It was obvious to Ogulf that the wise and noble Wildar hid some things from the people closest to him. Wildar could have told him anything, anything at all, and he would have understood. The key question now was, why was he hiding things from those who would do anything for him? The only thing that made Ogulf feel better about the situation was

there would be a reason why Wildar kept this from him –
there had to be.

Silence between the two lingered, and eventually, the
only sounds were those of the bugs in the reeds and the
crackling of the fire as Ogulf drifted off to sleep.

Chapter 25

Danrin rose earlier than usual the next morning, to find sunlight flooding in through the open curtains in his bedchamber. The air in the room smelt like sour sweat. It felt like someone was trying to hammer their way out of his skull from the inside – probably thanks to the ale or the mead or the whisky, or a combination of all three, from last night. He gorged himself with water to wash away the horrible taste in his mouth and to relieve it from its desert-like state. Today he would begin a hard task and one that he would have preferred to approach without feeling the way he did.

He found further relief in the cold stone floor and the way it turned the soles of his feet to ice; he always loved the feeling of anything cold when he was suffering from the consequences of an overindulgent evening in a tavern. A groan startled him as he turned to see the girl he had spent the night with was still sleeping lightly, clutching at the now empty space where Danrin had been lying moments ago. He couldn't even remember her name; her warmth was all he had needed.

He looked at the clothes in his dresser and decided against wearing armour. In his fragile state, surely he was better to favour comfort?

As he dressed, he looked in the mirror at his tired eyes. He looked like a man of thirty, not twenty. His long hair was dry, and he desperately needed a shave. He pulled his neck to either side until it clicked. He was becoming just as complacent and comfortable as the men at his disposal, something that would have to stop. Luxuries wouldn't be accessible in the battles to come.

The palatial corridors were quiet, just like Danrin had expected, given that it was just past sunrise. The young knight made his way to the opulent gardens and sat by the fountain in the same spot he had sat in the previous day with Ogulf. Glancing up, he noticed the remnants of the window that Melcun had damaged and laughed. Doing so hurt his already thudding head. Only Crindasa could get out of such a calamity like she had. His eyes were drawn from the window as hurried footsteps approached the gardens from the outer walls – at least ten paces away, but in the quiet of the morning, clear for Danrin to hear. He was expecting someone, but not from that direction.

Instinctively, his hand went to his upper thigh, not far from the handle of his sword. That was a technique taught in the academy during his Fated Few training. Near the hilt is prepared, on the hilt meant you weren't fit to have a Fated blade. Danrin thought it right to employ the same tactics with his own men after the comment Ogulf made about their readiness... or lack thereof, for war.

The haste in the footsteps eased as they got closer. Danrin then noticed a man in Shingally armour turn into the stone gateway to face him.

'Captain Richel,' Danrin said, smiling at the man. He was big and broad. A short, thick beard coated his jaw. His cropped hair was receding slightly, and the sunlight turned the beads of sweat on his forehead into glistening gems.

'I have word from the port, sire,' he said. 'Our messengers have made it to Esselonia safely. Words from Aylan of The Gwentar himself. He told me to tell you at once.'

Danrin had requested that, as soon as Aylan returned to port in Shingal, he would send word via the highest-ranking officer available on watch. It wasn't ideal that this was a man like Richel, who was not fond of Danrin or his father. Richel had expected to be in charge of the armies of Luefmort by now, but had instead been rendered a captain for longer than he had planned, due in part to his brash nature, but also due to a severe dislike for him in the capital. When he learned of Danrin's ascension to becoming one of the Fated Few, it only furthered his animosity toward him.

Like the rest of the Luefmortian forces, Richel hadn't been aware that messengers had been sent from the Shingal. Equally, he was unaware that they had not been Shingally messengers at all. Lord Hanrik had wanted to be sure that Ogulf and Melcun made it to Esselonia safely before telling others about the plan, and all involved had agreed.

'Very good. Thank you, captain,' Danrin said. He watched as the man lingered, his eyes locked on those of the young Fated Knight. The captain was clearly eager to say something. 'Is there anything else?' Captain Richel's lips pursed slightly as if he was at war with his own want to speak out. Danrin could practically see the bitterness oozing from his pores. 'Speak freely,' he finished firmly.

'Your being back does not mean the men will follow you,' Richel said, and Danrin wondered if the cocksure captain cared that he was speaking out of turn. 'A boy cannot lead an army, much less defend a city. Your father will lose Luefmort for the kingdom if he allows you to act as our protector.'

'I suppose this is a role you would like to be tasked with instead, Richel?' Danrin said.

'Perhaps. And perhaps I will have the chance. Being Fated means you're handy with a blade, and that you know something about the tactics of warfare, but that doesn't mean anything when you're actually on the battlefield,' Richel said.

Danrin couldn't deny that Richel was a hardened warrior – his efforts had been instrumental in the Coastal Struggles, when bands of marauding sea clans had tried to storm the Southern Shingally shores. His heroics in that campaign helped him get to the rank of captain, but they'd also filled his head with bluster as he began to believe his own myth.

'Be that as it may, captain, do not forget your place,' Danrin said, letting out feelings that had harboured inside him for a long time. 'Giving you the chance to speak freely does not mean you should speak mindlessly. I know you have issues with me – my age, my position, my family ties. The last thing I want to do is question your loyalty to the kingdom, but how can I not, given your stance towards the man you're supposed to serve under?'

Danrin knew he had struck a nerve as Richel squirmed and his mouth tightened.

More footsteps came, this time from the direction he was expecting. Rowden emerged from the side door of the palace. He gave Danrin a nod, then turned to Captain Richel, who was staring straight at him with a sour look on his face.

'Thank you, Captain Richel, that will be all,' Danrin said. The captain gave him a slight bow and turned to leave the gardens, his footsteps thudding disdainfully away into the distance. 'Please, sit,' Danrin said, motioning to Rowden. Once he was sure that they were the only ones in the walled green grounds, he smiled at Rowden.

'Ogulf and Melcun have made it safely to Esselonia,' Danrin said.

'I knew they would get there just fine,' Rowden said, also smiling. 'Now comes the hard part for them and for me. The other captains are breathing down my neck. Prundan was asking where they were this morning.'

'When will you tell them?' Danrin asked.

'Today. I assume you called me here for more reason than just to tell me of the safety of our travellers, though,' Rowden said. Danrin admired the way Rowden always seemed to want to get to the point; it was hard to find people like that these days.

'Yes. I know you've been through a lot, but I need your help,' Danrin said. Rowden cocked his head to the side, listening intently. 'Luefmort is not a city built to take an attack or a siege. The walls aren't tall. To be blunt, we are vulnerable, and though we have strength in numbers, we need to reassess how we protect ourselves.'

Rowden nodded.

'If this army is intending to make it this far south, if their ultimate goal is to fulfil a prophecy and sweep the realm by force, then if we do not prepare, we will lose Luefmort and give them a base to stage further attacks across the Shingal. We will put up a fight, I know that much. However, I can't see how we can stop them. Ogulf mentioned your prowess, and he suggested you might be willing to help me prepare Luefmort for an attack.'

A silence held in the air for a few seconds longer than Danrin would have liked.

'What did you have in mind?' Rowden said.

'Helping me prepare my men or having some of your fighting men train the younger soldiers in our ranks. A lot of them, and the men who trained them, have never seen battle before. Above all, I think a fresh perspective to combat would be beneficial to them. Not only that, but we need to prepare the lands around Luefmort – I need to turn them into a weapon, and ... you can help with this, can't you?'

Rowden stroked his beard and chewed on his lower lip. His eyes went up to the empty blue skies.

'Do you think your father will agree to this?' Rowden asked.

'Yes, he will,' Danrin said confidently. 'Once I convince him that we need to rethink our positioning, he will understand.'

'Jargmire, Tran, all of Broadheim fell. And the tactics they used are the same ones me and my people know ...' Rowden said.

Danrin conceded with a slight nod. 'I accept that, but this time it will be different, because we have more time to prepare. And correct me if I am wrong, Rowden, but aren't you the only man who managed to get his people to safety?' He didn't wait on an answer. 'I would bet that you can do more to help than you think. In fact, I would wager my world on it.'

Chapter 26

As they traipsed along the Mule Road, the warm sun beat down and baked Ogulf in his armour. He could feel beads of sweat trickling down his spine every minute or so before they pooled at the small of his back. When he longed for the heat of the sun on all the cold winter days in Keltbran, he never wanted this type of warmth, the kind that made him feel sticky and uncomfortable, the kind he hadn't missed in the slightest.

Walking along the ragged road, the two friends spoke about Keltbran and about Broadheim. They had started moving as soon as the sun came up and now they were making good time as it reached its highest point. So far, the journey to Delfmarc had been full of reminders of home, which had both calmed and discomforted Ogulf; the soothing feelings were chased away by the aching reminder that the memories he had and the places he called home would never be the same again.

The road itself was dusty now and the huge potholes and uneven paving slabs were nowhere to be seen. Instead, they had been replaced by a straight, dirt road that went on and on in a bumpy line. A stream ran adjacent to the path for a small time as it weaved through a thicket of trees. Birds chirped from the vast tangle of branches in the trees they sporadically passed.

Ogulf looked at his surroundings often. He seemed to linger most often on the incredible outlines of the colossal mountain range to their left. He took this to be the Grendspire Peaks that Trayvan the Sage had mentioned. The range went on for as far as the eye could see, their sheer enormity making Ogulf stagger slightly as ran his gaze along their length. He turned to Melcun to see that his friend's eyes were wide, staring at the snow-touched peaks of the mountains.

'They make the Widows Trail look like a foothill,' Melcun said. 'How do you reckon people scale that?'

'I don't think they do,' Ogulf said. 'I should have asked, is Crindasa's book helpful?' Melcun's cheeks turned bright red and Ogulf couldn't help but smile.

'Yes, it's definitely useful,' Melcun said. 'She left other notes in pages I should focus on. She said I should treat this time as an opportunity to understand more about the fundamentals of sorcery, so that when we return to Luefmort, I can work with her on the practical elements to gain more experience. I think I've learned a new ability – well, in theory, at least.' Ogulf watched as Melcun's eyes dropped to his feet as he kicked dirt on the path. 'Ogulf, do you think I could go to the Tawrawth one day?'

'The mage school?' Ogulf responded. Melcun nodded. 'Perhaps one day. I mean, I don't see why you wouldn't be able to.'

Melcun smiled. 'There are drawings of it in here. It looks incredible. I've never seen anything like it.'

The road bent in a harsh corner not far from where they were, and what lay beyond the turn was hidden by the remnants of an old wall which ran down either side of the Mule Road. One part had a large chunk of bricks missing.

Ogulf heard the creaking and scraping of a wagon's wheels. He grabbed a hold of Melcun and pulled him behind a part of the wall to their left. Both men ducked, mostly hidden by the wall and shadow it was casting.

The wheels trundled closer. From the scuffing in the dirt, Ogulf could tell that there was a cart of sorts being pulled by one horse coming towards them. He slowly raised his head over the beaten barrier to get a look.

Rumbling down the path at a steady pace was a single horse pulling a large cart. In the front seat was a man with an obnoxiously large smile on his face. He gently shook the reins to will his steed forward. The horse cantered along further and Ogulf saw a second man sitting on the back of the cart. His legs dangled down to a foot from the ground, and in his hands, he carried a crossbow. Both men wore ragged, light leather armour.

The main body of the cart was more like a cage. Light shone into small circular holes which were dotted all over the squared body of the hold. Thanks to the angle of the sun, Ogulf could see into it. He could just about make out the shape of someone inside and there was a large iron padlock affixed to the outside door.

Ogulf cowered down again as the cart got closer and gestured to Melcun to stay low. The wall was high enough to keep them concealed as the wagon screeched towards them.

'How much you reckon we will get for this one, Sindred?' the voice closest to them said. It sounded gruff. 'I'm going to say we barter for at least five hundred gold.'

'Heh, is that all? For a man like this, I reckon a thousand gold would be about right. These Southerners have the coin so we should take them for all we can.' The man on the back of the cart said. His voice was boyish. The horse's canter continued until the cart was only a few paces from where Ogulf and Melcun hid.

'If he really is one of Feda's wretches then we will make sure we get all we can. One thousand would be nice. It would get us lots of ale, lots of weapons. Means we might be able to take Vargholme before the king's forces come north,' the man said, shouting over his shoulder to his companion at the back of the cart.

'Think of the favour we'd have with the king if we presented him with the port when he finally gets here. You'll be made a knight, Dronal,' the younger man said. His eyes were fixed on his crossbow, which he was struggling to re-load as they spoke.

As the pair passed, Ogulf managed to catch a proper glimpse of the riders. The man at the front was wearing light grey armour, the front of which was splashed with blood. His hands were covered in thick metal gauntlets, their neutral steel colouring washed with a light coating of crimson. The man's face was a collection of scars. One particular disfigurement was an inch across at its widest and ran from his jawline to just above his ear in a clean, chunky line.

The man on the back was younger than Ogulf, and he was so small in frame that his armour sagged on him. He wore no gauntlets and there was no blood to be seen on his clothing. His hair stuck up in uneven tufts, leaving his remarkably fresh face looking out of sorts with the rest of him. If it were not for the dark shadows drooping from his eyes, Ogulf would have thought this man a boy. With a loud click, the small man managed to pull the crossbow wire all the way back, then slotted a bolt into it.

The only person Ogulf couldn't see was the person inside the cage. It was too dark in the hold of the cart for Ogulf to see anything other than an occasional outline. The cart gently bumped down the road and towards the enclosed forest that Ogulf and Melcun had just come through.

'Melcun, follow me,' Ogulf said as he darted away from the road. He cast a glance at the younger man on the back of the cart, but his attention was still focused on his now-loaded crossbow. Keeping low to the ground, and with Melcun behind him, Ogulf made a looping motion to reach the cover of a small ridge.

Ogulf had decided he was going to stop the cart. Without ample protection, it would be easy enough for him and Melcun to overpower the driver and his companion, especially if they kept the element of surprise. And if in doing so they made contact with someone loyal to Feda, that could undoubtedly be advantageous. Ogulf instructed Melcun to stop the cart, making sure to let his friend know he could do so by any means necessary; at this stage, his powers could be another element that could sway the outcome in their favour.

Both men dumped their packs at the ridge and Ogulf watched as Melcun made his way into the dark of the forest.

Ogulf edged in towards the rear of the cart, moving through the forest at a controlled pace and using the cover of the large trees to conceal himself. He thought he would be out of practice, he was naturally light on his feet and that meant he was able to move between the trees with more stealth than he had anticipated. The cart was still rolling along and now the rider at the back was scanning his surroundings with his loaded crossbow on his lap.

Ogulf sucked his stomach in and pulled his arms and shoulders tight as he leant on the nearest tree. Even the keenest eye wouldn't see him in this light-starved wood.

All of a sudden, a light entered the darkened forest. Ogulf peered out to see that Melcun had blocked the road with fire, just as Ogulf thought he would. The horse reared up and kicked violently, and Ogulf watched as the driver's mouth flapped in soundless movement, words muted by the screeching whinny of the horse.

In an agile flash, the young boy at the back of the cart was standing on the rear seat and now looking forward at the blocked road using the cage as cover, his crossbow trained on the flames as if it were a physical enemy.

Ogulf seized his opportunity as the panicked noises became a whirlpool of confusion that had consumed his target. He darted through the trees, which got thinner the closer he got to the road. He slid Wildar's axe from its sheath on his back. He'd meant to take his own, but it was too late now. The axe was so much lighter, it felt like it wasn't even there.

Ogulf watched as the flames licked higher and created a perfect wall of oranges and yellows in front of the horse, completely preventing the cart from moving forward unless it attempted the swampy mess on either side of the road. The younger man's crossbow was still aimed forward as he carefully scanned the fire, searching in vain for its source. The horse calmed slightly, its hooves flicking anxiously in the dust, and it backed a few paces away from Melcun's block-ade.

The cart jutted back violently, causing the man on the rear to lose his balance. Seeing this, Ogulf made his final sprint for the main part of the road from his position among the trees. Ogulf skirted the rear of the cart as it manoeuvred backwards in an ugly fashion. Without force, he traced the blade of the axe along the backs of the knees of the man with the crossbow, just above where his leather boots stopped.

Though he had done this before – it was a good way to eliminate an enemy without killing them – the blade had never gone through the flesh and muscle as smoothly as it did this time. The skyward sound of the crossbow being fired, and the shrieking groans of the man, were enough to tell Ogulf that he had immobilised him for now as he made for the cover of the trees on the other side of the cart.

The man at the front of the cart must have realised his companion was injured because he abandoned the driver's seat to go and investigate. As he stepped down, he pulled a greatsword from the seat underneath him. His abandoning of the reins caused the horse to panic as it tried to free itself from the harness of the cart. The man with the crossbow had been crouched on the rear seat, wincing as he held on to his gushing wounds. As the horse thrashed wildly to break away, it threw the smaller man from the cart and he landed with a thud on the dirt of the road, still groaning as blood poured from his calves.

The horse escaped from its bindings, and in doing so, it flipped the cart onto its side. Narrowly missing the prone form of the bleeding man on the ground, it galloped fiercely into the forest, its mane was getting tangled in low hanging branches as it passed.

The driver was calmly scanning the forest with his broadsword in his hand, using the wall of fire to cover his rear. Ogulf was waiting by the side of the road, peering through the bush he was using to conceal his body.

'Show yourselves, you shit eating bastards!' the cart driver shouted. Though his words were bold, his movements were still calm. The groans from his ally had faded.

A dull crack sounded, and the man fell to one knee, a rock the size of an apple landing heavily beside him. The man's eyes filled with wrath and a light trickling of blood ran down his cheek. Clearly stunned, he wobbled and used his sword to push himself to his feet and turned in the direction of where the rock had come from.

The driver had his back to Ogulf as he sprang from the bush. Normally, he would throw his axe in a situation like this, but Wildar's was lighter and he didn't want to miss or overthrow. Relying on his light footing, he sprinted towards the dazed man, who swivelled to face him just as Ogulf got close.

Ogulf was mid-swing with his axe when the man turned and clumsily blocked Ogulf's strike at his lower half. As if recharged, the man went on the offensive, swinging strong, controlled strikes that Ogulf parried or dodged.

Ogulf wondered where Melcun was; he could use his help right now. The two men were moving around the cart in a dance of blades, the cart driver's relentless swings at Ogulf did not seem to tire him. The blade cut through the air with a menacing whistle when suddenly the man stumbled and looked at his foot.

Protruding from one of the holes of the tipped cage carriage was the arm of the prisoner. It was clinging tightly to the driver's ankle, causing him to stop for a brief moment. The driver swung down gracelessly and managed to nick the prisoner's hand with his blade, causing it to retract inside the carriage.

Ogulf grasped the opportune moment of the hesitation from his opponent; he took a mighty swing with his axe and caught the man in his ribs. The blow struck true and sunk into the man, much deeper than Ogulf expected. As if he still had fight in him, the driver made to raise his weapon to strike Ogulf, but his effort failed almost immediately as life escaped him. He slumped to the floor, letting out a final, rasping breath as blood surged from his side.

Melcun appeared a few seconds later, panting slightly as he took in the scene. 'Sorry, conjuring that wall took it out of me a little.'

The driver was in a prone position and the man with the crossbow was lying on his side, clutching his calves. They were both clearly dead, which had not been Ogulf's intention; he wanted to question them. The fact that they were still in the North of Esselonia and had already encountered fighters who opposed Feda was disheartening. She was supposed to be supported here.

Curses came from the tipped cart and Ogulf climbed onto it so that he was standing over the padlocked door, which was upturned towards the sky. With a hard swing of Wildar's axe, he managed to burst the lock on the door without chipping or even scratching the elegant blade of the weapon. He found himself growing fonder of it with every swing and wishing that he didn't have to give it away to anyone else.

As soon as the door opened, he extended an arm to the captive. The hand that came from the darkness was wet with blood and pulling the person out was a slippery struggle. Eventually, the man emerged, stumbling slightly due to the chains around his feet. He was older than Ogulf, his eyes glistened with the wonder of distress, and his hair flowed to his shoulders. Dark stubble coated his soft jaw and he had a gash in his lip that looked like it was in the first phase of healing. Ogulf and the man eyed one another, the liberated man clutching his injured hand to his chest.

'You serve Feda?' he asked.

'No, actually, we don't,' Ogulf said. 'We're not from around here, but we do *seek* Feda.' The injured man startled slightly. 'No, not like that, we're not an enemy. We're messengers from abroad and mean you no harm.'

The man had uttered thanks at least one hundred times in the five minutes that had passed since Ogulf and Melcun had freed him. After rummaging through the pockets of the dead driver, they found a key that would release the shackles around the captive's ankles, and the man used his first chainless steps to walk to the other man, snatch his drinking skin, drain most of it, and then pour the rest over his head and face.

'Why did those men have you captive?' Ogulf asked the man, who turned to glance at his liberators with droplets of water running down his cheeks.

'They captured me near the Grendspires. Swarms of them. Militias working for the Southern forces,' he said, rubbing the back of his neck. 'One of them, who I can only assume was a bloody defector, recognised me – said he'd seen me win a tourney before the war and give a token to Feda. I thought they would shackle all of us, but they slaughtered every one of my men and their horses, only taking me in the end. They were going to sell me to the turncoat Southerners in the Red Isles. First thing they do to a new prisoner there is lop off their thumbs,' the man said, staring at his hands.

'So, you're of worth?' Melcun asked. Ogulf shot him a look of warning.

'What my friend means to ask is, you've served Feda directly?' Ogulf asked. 'Don't worry, I can assure you we mean you no harm. My name is Ogulf, and this is Melcun.'

'My name is Vellan. And yes, I served the princess. I was in her High Guard and we were... betrothed.'

Ogulf's eyes opened wide and he thought he heard Melcun sucking in a sharp breath. It had been some time since he had felt like this, like something or someone was encouraging him in a direction and aligning his fate. For now, they were serving him well. He prayed they didn't stop anytime soon.

Chapter 27

The tent was large and circular. A long narrow pole in the centre raised its textile ceiling at least fifteen feet high. Other, smaller poles encircled the outer rims of the space, breaking the constant slope from the top of the tent to create more room to move around inside it.

Despite the space available, this tent had only one bed inside. On it were numerous layers of furs and blankets. The pillows looked soft and their silken covers gleamed in the firelight. The firepit was modest and sat just next to the centre pole, above which was a smoke hole where the dark fumes gently floated as the wood crackled and burned in the grated structure.

At the back of the tent stood the ruler of Visser, King Nadreth Olenihan. He was leaning over a large table. His fingers ran across a piece of parchment that covered almost half of the surface, and occasionally, his eyes meandered to another flattened scroll to its left. One was a declaration of sorts, the other was a map. His long, slender fingers traced along a coastline slowly, and he hummed and muttered to himself as they did.

The North Hold had fallen easily. Too easily for his liking, he would have relished a challenge on the mountains. Then Jargmire, the impregnable city, fell to his forces. He remembered the fear on the faces of those on the wall when the doors fractured, sheer disbelief laced with terror. He was at least two hundred yards from the walls of the citadel when the offensive was in full swing, but he could still hear the citizens of Jargmire screaming as they died. He replayed the sound in his mind as if it were a harmonious chorus of victory.

His favourite take of all had been Tran. His advisor said the forces there would be too many, that the attack there would result in a possible stalemate and weakening of his forces. Nadreth had no time for recreants; he put them to his executioner's blade before launching his invasion of Broadheim. Otherwise, he would have had to listen to their snivelling cowardice for the whole journey South. Yes, in Tran they had vast numbers, but they didn't have the power or ferocity to match his men. They launched the attack at dawn, and by sundown, the heart of Broadheim was a mess of blood and flames. The stench of death that came afterwards had lingered in his nostrils for the best part of a week.

All of this effort had led them to the real prize – a tiny town placed in the vast, empty expanse of the plains of the country. A town that may as well have not existed. As far as importance went, places like Keltbran were on the lowest rung in normal circumstances. But in recent times, the place had piqued his interest because of a rumour he heard.

It involved a young sorceress who was too young to know her worth and not old enough to be unshielded. She was from the Throws – the wasteland in the Frigid Valley. Only hardy people and those who were not sound of mind were able to survive in a place like the Throws. But this girl was different, she was said to wield immense power, the type that only comes around once in an age.

Stories about her had trickled north. It was said that she was involved in an incident when a raiding party attacked her village. She was a child at the time – a real child, not a teenager. Somehow, she used her abilities to kill all the members of the raiding party. No definitive numbers ever surfaced but most tales set it at over twenty men. All of them dead, and not a single blade wound on them – all bludgeoned.

It was said that she tried to wake her mother and some of the other villagers, but they were all dead too, hacked and slashed to bits by the savages who ransacked her village. Realising she was on her own, the child walked and walked as far as she could. Fate took her South and she was found, cared for, and protected.

That had been over five years ago now, and by the time the stories had trickled up to the High Domains of the King of Visser, they had grown arms, legs, and other intrinsically linked parts which caught the man's attention.

The tales made him think of a prophecy that had always fascinated him. An ancient promise he was determined to fulfil. He sent scouts to Broadheim and began to learn as much as he could about this young sorceress. While that was happening, he called in his banners and aligned his people under the campaign of a new, commonly sought glory – the return of arcana and power to the great people of Visser, and the resumption of their dominance of the known world in Loken's name.

Support came as easily as the sun rose in the mornings. Every man willing and able accepted the call to arms and placed themselves at the behest of the king's mighty forces. Years of preparation were painstaking as they eagerly awaited their chance to pursue their destined glory. And then it came, the time came, and the march South began. They had been prepared for the cold and the treacherous terrains thanks to enhanced armour and they were ready to take the fight to the defenders of the once great nation of Broadheim. They were steady and sure, and they would fulfil the prophecy of the Onyxborn.

The march had lasted over four months now. The hardest part was not the battles in Broadheim but the scaling of the Frigid Valley, the stubborn and treacherous border between the Far North and Broadheim. The armour each man wore staved off the cold, but it did little to stop the ground from moving or the hills from sending a wave of rocks at them from height. That place was ungodly – even the dark gods wouldn't lay claim to such a wasteland.

Here in Port Saker, the King of Visser was awaiting his meeting with the girl who would lead them to greatness, the Onyxborn herself.

The flaps of the tent opened, and he turned to face the sound. Coming through the door was a small hooded figure who moved gracefully into the room. She carefully pulled her hood down. Her eyes were striking – they were dark and light at the same time. Her complexion was pale, and despite the freezing cold of the outside, there was not a single red blemish from the bite of it on her skin.

Her hair was a perfect mix of silver and grey. It looked like pure silk. She could be no older than seventeen. She looked confidently at the man as he turned to greet her. She was the first person in as long as he could remember to seem calm when meeting him for the first time. More often than not, those who had audiences with the king turned to puddles of piss in front of his eyes before he even uttered a greeting.

'Nevea, we meet at last, my dear,' the man said, smiling at his guest.

Nevea's only reply was a bow.

'Even when a day is promised, it does not fully prepare a man for the true feelings that destiny being fulfilled can bring,' the man said. He placed his hands behind his back and casually moved around the room with wide steps. He was tall and thin. Long black hair crept from the high peaks of his forehead and was tucked neatly behind his ears, dropping just past his shoulders. He was not young, but he didn't look his age; if it wasn't for his withered hands, you could mistake him for a man of forty. 'You will be pleased to know that the whole of Broadheim is finally under our control. We can now move to the second part of our plan and look to fulfil Loken's prophecy,' the man continued. 'You will be kept here at Port Saker until we have taken control of enough of the Shingal and we have word from Esselonia that we can advance there. It is my duty to ensure that the prophecy is fulfilled, and for that to happen, your safety is my priority.'

'Thank you, sire,' Nevea said. 'I must say, the prophecy in itself is not something I am too familiar with; I would appreciate it if you could teach me more. And if I can be of any help in doing *his* work, then please do not hesitate to call on me.'

The man smiled at his young guest. She was enthusiastic. 'That is what was promised, my dear, that a child of humble beginnings would be born under the black and that they would possess a trait, a skill if you will from Cormag himself. They would rise from arduous depths and restore power – unmatched power – to the ones who fulfil the prophecy. You will resurrect the soul of our great master and embody Loken's powers to lead us to victory. We will reclaim the altar, summon the power of the Stone of The Night, and we will do this all in the name of the Order of Maledict.'

He licked his lips as he considered the possibility of getting the Onyxborn in front of his fighting men. It would be a boost of morale that could be beaten only by the fulfilment of the prophecy itself. They had just taken an entire nation with ease, so their spirits were high, but unveiling The Onyxborn would inspire them onto further victories, of that he was sure. And they would need it; Shingal was not Broadheim.

'And you think this is me?' Nevea said.

'I don't *think* it is you, my dear, I know it is. You were promised to us, and I was fated to find you. I'm just glad we found you when we did. Time is of the essence.' Nadreth moved back to the table and he heard Nevea's soft footsteps follow him towards it. 'This is it – this is the prophecy in Loken's own words. This is your destiny, Nevea.'

Nadreth watched the young girl tilt her head sideways and take in the words on the scroll. They were written in a common tongue and the letters were written in a thick and bold manner. The scroll itself was over fifteen hundred years old, and while it was weathered and slightly frayed, it was otherwise in immaculate condition.

'Read it aloud. Feel the words, and let Loken hear you say them,' Nadreth said.

Nevea gulped and clutched a hand to her chest. She cleared her throat and began to read from the scroll. 'Born under the dark of Onyx, this one will inherit my power. They will lead our cause to victory in the fields, destroy the weak, and restore glory to the Order. Let it be known that the one who brings this promised one to power will rule the world beside them. Eternal life awaits the one born beneath the black. Eternal power will belong to them. Weakness will be cast to the fire. The power of Loken will return, and a new age will begin.'

'You will wield a great power, Nevea. Together you and I will rule this world in his name.'

A broad-shouldered man in glistening red armour made his way into the tent. From his belt there hung a razor-sharp blade, one side of which was jagged, while the other was smooth. His armour clanked as he walked in before standing stiff and to attention, awaiting a signal to speak. With a sigh, the man nodded to the armour-clad soldier.

'King Nadreth. The number of ships in the Sea of Blades has doubled, my lord,' the soldier said. Then he looked at the young woman in the king's tent, before his eyes darted back to the king.

'The Shingally's are far more aware of their borders than those in Broadheim were, it would seem. Challenging, for now. How long until we can have ships to meet them?' King Nadreth asked.

'One week, my king. Perhaps two,' the soldier said. The king's hands went behind his back as he began to pace the room again, slowly.

'Make it a week, General Hassit. We must make sure the path to the Shingal is clear. The sea offensive first, and then the transport of our troops – and find a way of getting word to them. The blockade is one thing, but I want the fear to seep into every crack in the citadels before we get there. Remember, general, fear spreads like fire and does just as much damage.'

'Yes, my king,' General Hassit said.

'And what news of our excursion to the Widows Trail?' King Nadreth asked the man.

'Positive outcome, my lord,' he said. The king squinted at him, intrigued by the vagueness of his answer. This caused the general to straighten. He cleared his throat and continued, 'The chieftain, Wildar Paleways, is dead, my lord.'

'Good,' the king said simply. 'And the axe?'

'Nowhere to be found, my lord. Must have plunged with Paleways into the Banespit,' the general said.

'And you have men looking for it?' King Nadreth said.

'With respect, lord,' the general said, then he gulped. 'The Banespit is said to descend for miles, it would be impossible to send men down there. Much less possible to retrieve them.'

'No harm in trying, general. Just make sure to use a long rope,' the king said with a sadistic smile. His annoyance was something he struggled to contain at times but Nadreth found himself trying even harder in the presence of Nevea.

'Yes, my lord. I will see it done.' The general gulped again.

The girl stirred from her prone position next to the general when he stopped speaking and moved towards the table. King Nadreth watched as she scanned the map, her head moving slowly from side to side.

As she scanned, she tapped her fingers on the map. Her pale face lit up as she smiled, her lips curling in an act of wickedness.

'I never believed in destiny, though I always knew I would do great things – something inside me told me that. I felt powerless in Keltbran, anchored by the flaws of the fragile minds around me. I thought I was to be a priestess of the gods, to worship silently and watch as heretics called for divinity and salvation forever without a sign of intervention. I only stayed for the food and the shelter. I think that's why I smiled when your men found me. Even when I was walking past corpses and burning houses, I smiled. Ever since that day in the Throws, when I murdered all of those men, I knew I was different. But I hid it. In Broadheim, they strike down anyone suspected of sorcery; a young girl seeking refuge like me would have been swinging from the rope before I could say a word in my defence, even if it wasn't always easy to call upon my power. In his name, I wish I hadn't hidden it.'

'But you had to, my dear. This is all part of your destiny,' Nadreth said.

'Only now do I truly feel like I understand what different really is, and I am ready to serve him and understand my role in this world. If power is everything and the feeble should be washed away, then I can play a part in that.' Her eyes returned to the map, she drew a circle with her fingertip right over the Sea of Blades. 'My lord, I have a proposal.'

Chapter 28

The addition of Vellan made Ogulf and Melcun's journey much easier. Despite being battered and bruised, the young man was still able to move well. The cut on his hand was well wrapped and he acquired the broadsword from the dead cart driver. Luckily, it was not his sword hand which was injured.

They still had a few hours of sunlight as they made their way towards Delfmarc. Vellan's knowledge of the area meant that they could move towards the city without being on the Mule Road – a development that Ogulf and Melcun welcomed. The way now was marred with jagged bushes and unsure footing, but it was much better than being visible on the road. Vellan had told the pair how he was due to be taken to the Bloomsunk Fortress, a militia-held outpost near the Eastern Coast of the island. Once they realised that two of their men and a valuable prisoner were not back by nightfall, they would surely send a party out to investigate.

'How did you end up getting captured, Vellan?' Ogulf asked.

The Esselonian man sighed. 'Where to begin,' he said. 'Feda had sent me to a town at the foot of the Grendspires to seek news about her brother, Elundar's, whereabouts. He's not been seen since the war started but word had trickled to Delfmarc that he was camped near Kerstal. He was nowhere to be found and the locals hadn't seen him, so we scouted the forests. That's where we were ambushed. At first, some of my men thought it was Elundar's forces, perhaps not recognising us, but it wasn't. It was a bastard Blackbloom militia. At least sixty of them. Killed all of my men then surrounded me – giving up my sword was the only way to stay alive and to get back to Feda if I could.' As he walked Ogulf noticed him balling his uninjured hand into a tight fist by his side.

'People think these militias are pitchfork carrying halfwits, but they're not. They are deserters and bandits all coming together to put up resistance to Feda's cause in the North,' Vellan said, spitting at the ground. 'They think the Southerners will pay them handsomely for their so-called loyalty when this is all over. The cretins won't get so much as a silver coin.'

'Sounds to me like you were deceived,' Ogulf said, aware of the thin line he was treading with such a statement. The words clearly struck a nerve as he saw Vellan's posture stiffen.

'Oh, I know,' Vellan said with a slightly sadistic chuckle. 'I realised this when I was surrounded. All those swords pointing at me, not one of them man enough to move forward and take a swing, right then I knew I'd been had.' He cleared his throat and sighed. 'This message you have for Feda, could it help her turn the tide of this war?'

'Are Feda's forces losing?' Ogulf asked.

'We're certainly up against it. I expect the forces in the South to make a march on the North within the coming weeks, so we've called in our banners to rally and meet them in the field. It will be a hard-fought battle and we'll need all the strength we have to win it,' Vellan said. 'I tell you these things in the hope that you will share news of aid coming to us, from Shingal or anywhere else. So, I expect an element of openness in return.'

Ogulf understood, though he was not willing to give information on the letter from Shingal – that was not his to pass on to anyone other than Feda.

'Fair is fair,' Ogulf responded. 'We do not bring aid. In fact, we come looking for aid.' Vellan scoffed in disbelief. 'I know. It seems humorous given you're in the middle of a war. But while your war is confined to your island, another war is coming. Broadheim has fallen to an incredible army. If our theory is accurate, the power they desire most is here in Esselonia. They washed over Broadheim with next to no resistance and they have the Shingally's in their sights now. If the Shingal falls, then all that stands between you and their army full of evil is the short trip over the Sea of Lost Souls. We have come to seek Feda's help and to warn her that no matter who wins this war, the North or the South, an enemy is coming for all of us.'

Vellan raised his eyebrows. 'Another cult trying to fulfil the Onyxborn prophecy?' He laughed off the end of his sentence as if dismissing everything Ogulf had said.

'Didn't you hear the part about Broadheim falling?' Melcun butted in, his face screwed up in disbelief.

'I heard,' Vellan said, throwing his eyes towards Melcun. 'Though, in truth, I have believed Broadheim to be weak for years now. First the rebellion, and then the cold, you were vulnerable – it's no wonder they took your lands that easily.' Ogulf knew that Vellan didn't mean this mockingly, but the harsh tone in which it was delivered left a sting in Ogulf's gut. 'And while we have a war here in Esselonia, I couldn't give a toss about foreign wars or another cult trying then failing fulfil a prophecy, and I would like to think Feda will feel the same,' Vellan said. 'I will take you to her, though. And I will see to it that you get an audience with her. I owe you that much for saving me. After that, you're both on your own.'

Choosing to take the conversation no further, Ogulf nodded at Vellan. It seemed like a fair trade, and this way they would get their audience with the princess.

Following the truths that Vellan presented, Ogulf grew more puzzled with every step. How could he possibly ask

Feda for help? And if he did, would he be met with the same retort he just suffered from Vellan? She seemed to be on the losing side of a civil war. It would have been hard enough to convince her if she had been on the winning side. Nonetheless, Ogulf knew he had to at least try to gain her help – or her understanding of the situation, at the very least – before returning to his people.

The three men were now wading through a shallow marsh as they spoke. Insects buzzed past them as they pulled their boots out of the thick, black mud and waded towards a dense forest. It was black as night beyond the trees, much darker and far denser than the one they had passed through previously. This one was also substantially larger. The flat ground leading up to it hid its true size, so Ogulf didn't know how long it went on for, he could only assume it would be quite the trek.

Following Vellan, they pushed through the forest boundary and into the dark thicket. The treetops hugged one another, starving the moist ground of light. It looked like midnight on a moonlit evening, when in actual fact, beyond the trees, it was still a sunny afternoon. Ogulf could not imagine how to navigate such a place, but Vellan moved through the space effortlessly.

'You know where you're going?' Ogulf asked Vellan, trying to mimic the positioning of his steps.

'Sort of. I have travelled through these woods many times,' Vellan said, striking at a cluster of branches in his path with the stolen broadsword. 'The only thing is, these woods are said to be haunted.' He swung again, shattering a branch, then moved forward. 'So, they change. They have a mind of their own. One minute you think you're on the right path, the next, you're lost. The key, I've found, is to just keep pushing through.'

'And this will lead us to Delfmarc?' Melcun asked.

'Yes. If – and I mean if – we're lucky, we should get out just at the cusp of the Dail Valley, which leads right to Delfmarc.'

Ogulf hoped that Vellan was right. If what he said was true and the forces from the South were looking to make a march on the North, then the sooner they got to Delfmarc, the better. Ogulf would prefer to be behind the walls of a city if a battle was going to take place.

Eventually they made it to a part of the forest which seemed impassable. Rising up from the moist soil for at least two metres, the branches and vines intertwined to create a wall. It went on and on for as long as Ogulf could see in either direction. Some parts were wide enough for a hand to go through, maybe, but there were no gaps big enough for any of the men to squeeze through. Vellan hacked at it with his sword and Ogulf chopped at with his new axe, but the same blade that had effortlessly cut through the two cart riders was now rendered useless by the branches.

'Let me try something,' Melcun said. 'Don't worry, it's not fire.'

Ogulf noticed Melcun standing to his left. He was flexing his fingers and staring intently at the wall of wood. He began to move his hands as if he were prying open a door, pulling it open from the centre. Ogulf couldn't believe his eyes as the thick branches began to bend, splinter, then snap into tiny wooden shards. Melcun's fingers began to tremble as his power bent the awkwardly wrapped limbs to create an opening. Ogulf looked over Melcun's shoulder to see through. It was still the same dense forest, but it looked like they could get through the gap and make some more progress. Ogulf turned to Vellan. His eyes were bulging, and his head reared back slightly.

'So that explains the fire when you rescued me,' Vellan said, to which Melcun just smiled and nodded.

Melcun just looked at the pair, extremely pleased with himself. Ogulf was just relieved that whatever Melcun had done had worked.

The three men pushed through the gap. They had to put their packs through first to fit. On the other side, they were met with a horrid, nauseating stench that was pungent enough to make Ogulf wretch. It smelt like decomposing leaves mixed with the rotting remains of a dead animal.

'I think we may have stumbled on Petunia's Graveyard,' Vellan said. 'Not to worry, though; that means we're on the right path. Now move with me, quickly.'

Ogulf and Melcun followed his lead as he moved more swiftly through the woods. For every thick tree stump, there were at least ten thinner ones around it, but these ones were easier to pass than they had been on the other side of the branch wall. Ogulf assumed that, beyond the canopy of darkness created by the trees, the rest of the world still basked in daylight. The men must have been pushing through this forest for at least two hours now, but the covering created by the towering trees prevented him from being sure.

The thick trunks became stumps as they moved through the forest. This area was almost clear but for a few huge trees which provided the roof of the world they found themselves in. Their trunks were broad and looked as solid as steel.

In the middle of the clearing was an immaculate hut made of thick circular logs. A candle shone bright in a small window on the side of the cabin. The hut looked out of place in such a setting. Its peaceful and quaint aura didn't belong in a place with such a stench. It stood out like a radiant, warm ruby on a bed of dead fish.

Vellan had noticed the cabin just as Ogulf had. The Esselonian stopped and turned, motioning for the other two to halt. The look on Vellan's face was not worry but real fear. Just as he quietly began to turn back the other way, they heard a harsh, dull thud nearby.

As they all turned towards the noise, they were met with a frightening sight. An old, haggard woman, hunched over in an unimaginably crooked way. Her eyes were shut tight and her mouth hung slightly open as if her jaws were unhinged. Her clothes were ripped, they looked hundreds of years old, some parts connected only by single lines of thread. Since she had appeared, the horrible aroma in the air had been replaced by one far more unpleasant – the sour smell of rotting human flesh.

'I see you stumbled upon my humble abode,' the woman said. Her voice was shrill and full of anguish. 'Despite my best efforts to prevent exactly that. Heh.' She didn't look at them, just spoke in their direction. The closer Ogulf looked, it was clear that her eyelids had been sewn shut, thread crudely lacing them together through folds of crusted green skin.

'Who are you?' Melcun asked, covering his nose.

'You dare to dwell in my lands and yet have the insolence to not know my name?' The shrill voice cut through Ogulf like a blade. His body shivered. 'I am Lady Petunia Canlan. I need not ask who you are – or should I say, what you are.'

Melcun threw a confused frown at Ogulf and pushed through to get closer to the old woman. 'What is that supposed to mean?'

'You are impure. I can sense it. You've been on your way to me for days, but they're coming back and it won't be long before you and all your evil lot join them.' She took a feeble step forwards and hobbled between Melcun and Vellan towards Ogulf who was at the rear of the three, standing at the end of their short, staggered line.

'Forgive me,' Melcun said, taking his hand from his face. 'I am not who you think I am. We wish only to pass through the forest to meet our friends in Delfmarc.'

'You do not fool me. Evil courses through you, the same evil that used to course through me. What will you do? Will you turn away from it or embrace it? You darken the world even now. This place strengthens you and it will give you further power.' She turned to look straight at Melcun. This time her eyes were wide open and shone a powerful, scintillating blue, as the rough threading that was keeping her eyes shut split. 'Power you could never have dreamed of until now. Never would you have been able to grasp it in Broadheim.'

Melcun took a step back, as did Ogulf. It was a combination of seeing the woman's eyes shine like they had and the mention of their homeland. Ogulf couldn't comprehend how the woman could have known such things, but the accuracy of her statement sent a sudden and overwhelming feeling of dread through every fibre of his body.

Melcun moved towards the old woman aggressively. Suddenly, she straightened from her crumpled posture and pushed her hand out in Melcun's direction. With her palm wide open and pointed in Melcun's direction, he stopped in his tracks, held back by something as he tried to fight forward.

'No. This is not how it will be. I can die now knowing the prophecy will come to pass. But it will not be your hand. Leave my lands, all of you.'

Vellan and Ogulf were rooted to the spot. Lady Petunia lowered her hand and Melcun was no longer prevented from moving. He paused when he realised this before thundering forward toward the old woman at a sprint.

As she saw this, her eyes lit bright again. 'Leave at once!' she screamed in a grating shrill, throwing her arms wide. A force came from her that sent all three men tumbling backwards. The force created a whirlwind which danced around the clearing. It howled through the trees, causing the candle in the hut to gutter and die. With another tremendous thud, it was over, and Petunia Canlan was nowhere to be seen. Her moth-eaten clothes lay empty in a pile in front of them.

As Ogulf stood and realised that she had vanished, he gazed at Melcun and then Vellan. Vellan's eyes were still wrought with terror but he was on his feet. Ogulf's eyes were drawn to the immaculate hut. Vellan led the way as they moved through the forest with fear in their footsteps.

A few minutes passed in silence as they made their way away from the woodland hut.

'What did she mean by that?' Melcun asked Vellan. He didn't stop, so Melcun grabbed his arm and turned him to ask him again.

As Vellan turned to meet his gaze, his nostrils flared. 'That is not for me to say.'

Chapter 29

The air felt less stale as the trees began to thin, and Ogulf breathed a sigh of relief, still reeling slightly after their encounter with Lady Petunia. In all his years scouting and travelling, he had never seen anything like her; the way her body was folded like an accordion one minute and then as straight and strong as the trees around her the next was worse than even the most unpleasant scenes of his nightmares. He kept thinking about her eyes and the vile thread that clamped them shut.

In the last week, Ogulf had already had more dealings with magic than he had in all of his previous years put together. He chose not to count Melcun's occasional flare or spark in their youth as the same kind of magic he had seen since venturing South for the same reason he wouldn't hold a pebble and arrow in the same mind, even if they had the same purpose when used as projectiles. This no longer felt like his world – it was different, frightening, intriguing, and exciting all at once.

'Why won't you tell me what she meant, Vellan?' Melcun asked. He had been asking the Esselonian variations of the same question for the last hour. Ogulf watched Melcun's routine of frustrations when he would ask the question, get frustrated with the lack of an answer, push the urge to enquire again to the bottom of his stomach, then when it rose in him again, minutes later, he nervously cracked his joints before trying a different combination of the same words in the hopes that, this time, Vellan would relent.

'I've told you. It's not my place to say. She thinks you practice dark magic. It's the kind of conversation to have with a Thinker or a priest,' Vellan said at last.

'A priest?' Melcun said, stopping in his tracks in front of Ogulf as Vellan kept walking. They were nearing the edge of the forest. 'What in the name of all the gods would a priest do? Are you trying to say I am cursed?'

'Something like that,' Vellan said, finally giving in to Melcun's onslaught of questioning. 'It's said that dark magicians have a different aura, like they're marked as an evil person, but that's as much as I'll say, so save your breath, because it's not something I understand.'

'And who in the gods was that crazy old woman?'

'Petunia Canlan, former Overseer of the Order of Mages in Esselonia, cast out and left to decay for practicing dark magic. She believed she was Cormag's very own daughter at one point. She's an imbecile of the highest order, so I wouldn't take what she says too seriously.'

'Gods, just as I am getting used to not hiding my abilities, I get called a dark one. I thought magic was accepted here?' Melcun said.

'Not all magic,' Vellan said.

Vellan made it past the tree line and disappeared from the dark of the forest into the harsh light outside it. The perfect wall of white burned Ogulf's eyes as he made his way closer.

His eyes began to adjust as he passed through the invisible boundary and emerged onto a grassy knoll. Not just warmth but real, prickling heat washed over his body, like he was surrounded by the lick of ten fire pits. He had not felt the sun so powerfully since the morning after the Battle of Mrandbrog Gorge during the rebellion and he had greatly missed its touch.

That day it was like the sun gave out its very own reward to the Keltbran people and members of the Ravgrin clan. They had successfully held off the rebel advance while waiting for the King of Broadheim and his forces to arrive. Outnumbered five to one, they managed to almost even the odds before the heavy charge of the king's cavalry finished off the fighting men of the revolt.

As his vision returned to normal, Ogulf noticed the long grass field sloping down from the edge of the forest. Vellan was already bounding down it with a spring in his step, and Ogulf could see why; visible in the distance was a huge mound of rock which could only be Delfmarc. It was even more stunning than any citadel Ogulf had seen in all of his life. Its sprawling perimeters almost made Jargmire look small.

The outer walls of the city were massive and were protectively wrapped around a mount encircled by a moat. The only visible crossing over the ring of water was a stone bridge which led to a huge gate. Dotted evenly around the top of the walls were huge battlements, the bricks of which were complexly twisted to look like flames of stone.

From his elevated position, he could see the roofs of buildings touching the same heights as the huge stone walls. In the middle of the outer walls sprung another walled circle with more of the flame-like battlements. Roofs and rising spires came up to the brim of the walls. In the centre of this district was a gargantuan squared tower with more fortified ramparts which looked more like diamonds than flames.

From the squared stronghold rose a huge spiralling keep surrounded by steeples. It towered for what looked like leagues into the air, and despite its obvious intricacy, it still appeared formidable. The top of the keep was a flattened-out battlement that would give a view for miles in all directions. Ogulf had never seen anything like Delfmarc. Melcun emerged from the tree line and stood by Ogulf's side, squinting at the incredible citadel.

'Have you ever seen anything like this?' Ogulf asked, rooted to the spot with wonder.

'Never. This is like something out of the old stories Wildar used to tell us. Remember when he told us of the clouds of Eskaine?'

Ogulf laughed lightly. His friend was right, this was like something Wildar spoke of in his fables. When he was full of wine, he had loved to talk about the gods and where they came from. Ogulf wondered if even the gods lived in a palace as amazing as this.

'This place certainly looks like it was carved by something otherworldly.' Ogulf's eyes were training up and down the city in front of him. 'You could fit over a hundred Keltbrans in there. I couldn't imagine living in a place like that.'

'It looks like an ant hill,' Melcun said.

Vellan had covered a few hundred yards in the time Ogulf and Melcun had been staring at the wondrous city. They paced fast to close the gap on the Esselonian Knight. Their eyes were still wide and mouths were still agape as they approached Delfmarc.

When they reached the bridge to the city, Vellan told them he wished to stop at the store of a friend on their way to the Keep in the Middle Circle. Vellan had told the pair that things were almost exactly how he left them, from the outside at least, which meant that there was no immediate sign of an attack from the Southerners.

The gate they headed to was smaller than the one Ogulf had seen from the hill – much smaller. He couldn't help but think it was more than impractical given the sheer size of the city it protected. He stared in bewilderment as they crossed the stone overpass.

'You look dumbfounded, Ogulf. You have truly never seen anything like this?' Vellan said as they approached the bolstered door. There was a small crowd waiting to gain entry. Upon closer inspection, Ogulf noticed just how reinforced the smaller door was; it looked like thick oak braced with solid steel near the edges, and well-set hinges were moulded deep into the wall around it. To the left of the door was a smaller opening manned by two guards.

'I haven't. Broadheim is not like this, even in our citadels. Until I saw this, I thought Jargmire was the biggest city in all the world. Before the invaders came, it was impressive, but it was never anything like this.'

They moved closer to the door, which was heavily guarded; ten men stood near the entrance with spears in their hands or fingers brushing the hilts of their swords. Ogulf and Melcun followed Vellan through the crowd until the guards stiffened as he tried to push past them, perhaps forgetting that he wasn't in his usual armour and that he had a bloodied broadsword on his belt.

The guard at the front was a brawny type and he stood forward to stop Vellan with a hand pushed towards the knight's chest. 'Where in the depths do you think you're going?'

'Stand down. My name is Vellan Strunheir, Captain of the Guard of the Princess.'

'Oh, is that right? Well, in that case, I'm Eryc himself. Piss off, peasant.' The soldier gave Vellan a heavy shove.

In a natural movement, Ogulf reached back for his axe, but before his hand got to it, Vellan motioned towards him to hold. The guards opposite them looked ready as they closed their fists around their spears and closed the gap on the group. They would be confident that they could subdue three travellers if they had to.

Suddenly, one of the men behind moved closer to the main guard and whispered something in his ear. The strapping man's initially confused look turned to dread; Ogulf noticed a bead of sweat run down the man's face. His eyes danced left to right as if looking for a solution. He broke to a firm attention, arms by his side, and his men did the same.

'Incredibly sorry, sir,' the man said, eyes towards the sky as more lines of sweat coursed down his cheeks. Ogulf wouldn't have been surprised if he saw a puddle of piss forming at the man's feet.

Vellan walked to the man. He could be no more than an inch from him when he looked him up and down. Then he moved past him and the rest of the guard, beckoning Ogulf and Melcun to follow.

'I thought he deserved at least a slap for that, Vellan,' Melcun said.

'He was being vigilant. Can't ask for much more, can you?' Vellan said confidently. 'Plus, now his loyalty will be tenfold. I haven't scolded or embarrassed him, he owes me, and I expect him to pay me handsomely when the Southerners get here.'

'How is this practical for a city this size?' Ogulf said, gesturing towards the door.

Vellan laughed and led the way into the tunnel that would transport them into the citadel. It was made of grey stone and lit by flaming torches secured in brackets on the walls. 'This is the Old Gate. When Delfmarc was first established, it was the only way for people to get in and out of the city. It used to be enough to service Delfmarc before the Mardrens ordered the expansion of the city a hundred years ago. This is more suited for small parties and quiet entrances now, while practicality is sought at the north entrance at Hayter's Gate.' At the other end of the passageway, two guards holding crossed spears blocked their path. A shout came from behind the trio and the spears were withdrawn, allowing them to pass through into a wide street bustling with people on the other side.

'Both of you, stay close.' Vellan stopped and turned as the crowd seemed to flow around him. The whole place was a wall of noise coming from street stalls and passers-by. Vellan began to weave through the crowd and Ogulf and Melcun had to duck and dive and stick their elbows out to make sure they didn't lose him in the crush. The buildings towered over them and the streets were growing narrower. A sweet smell filled the air – it was a mix of meats, fruit, wine, and some kind of incense. Ogulf felt his eyes and mind wandering as he tried to keep up with Vellan. 'Ogulf! Come.'

Ogulf pushed through a few bodies to make it into side street which was much calmer than the main road. 'Why is everyone so manic out there, Vellan?'

'Wartime is upon us. Everyone is looking for food and resources. This is only a slight frenzy compared to what it looks like sometimes,' Vellan said in a noticeably calm manner. 'Still, we are a few more scares away from a riot. We are heading to Rozmeer's bookstore, near the inner walls. I understand the scenery is somewhat mesmerising, but please keep your eyes on me,' Vellan said with a smile, prompting a nod from Ogulf.

By the time they reached the border of the Inner Circle, Ogulf was starting to feel tired. He was used to being physically active, but the incredible stimulation of this place and the journey from Vargholme was beginning to drain him. Nothing he had ever experienced had come close to what he had been through in the last two weeks.

The streets near the Inner Circle were much calmer than those closer to the entrance. The group came to a narrow passageway. A handful of carts lined the road leading to a dead end marked by a gleaming window. A sign above it read, 'Rozmeer's Goods'. Vellan bounded towards it and pushed straight through the door with Ogulf and Melcun in tow.

When they got through the door, they found the store-keeper. He was a short man who barely stood taller than the counter in front of him. The top of his head was bald, and around his ears, there was a perfectly groomed border of hair. His beard was thick but also very well combed. His eyes were a vibrant green and were chock-full of positivity, clearly visible through the lenses of his half-moon glasses. Ogulf couldn't see his whole outfit, but from what he could tell, the man's clothes were flamboyant and incredibly well designed.

'Vellan, my old friend, how are you?' the man said with a genuine warmth in his tone.

'Sparrin.' Vellan moved to greet the man with a hand-shake. The storekeeper reciprocated but had to extend to the tips of his toes to meet Vellan's hand over the counter. 'I've been better, but I am well. I come in need of a favour. My companion here–' He motioned towards Melcun. '–Is in need of a book. The kind of book I have a feeling I would only find here.'

'Must be a serious book then,' Sparrin said, moving round from behind the counter and looking Melcun up and down. 'No book dealers like me where you are from, my good man?' he said, trying and failing to hide the judge-mental look in his eyes as he took Melcun and Ogulf in.

'Nothing quite like this,' Melcun said, watching the small man skirt around him.

The wares in the store were interesting to say the least. Ogulf noticed some of the books were locked inside glass cabinets, and many of the ones on the shelves had wraps and padlocks on the front.

Sparrin scurried off past a number of high bookshelves, then he darted to the front door, locked the latch, and appeared back beside them in a showcase of speed that Ogulf never would have thought possible for such a small man.

'Just us,' Sparrin said. 'Vellan, I have warned you about visits like this. They do me no good. One of these days, someone will see you come in and notice the door locked, then questions will be asked, and answers will be demanded.'

'Don't worry, Sparrin. This is business on behalf of the princess.'

'Ah, so for the great of the realm I suppose,' the store-keeper said sarcastically, drawing a smirk from Vellan.

'I need you to help me. We have a new mage over here, one struggling to understand the comings and goings of good and bad magic. You've heard of dark magicians being marked or different, even if they don't realise it themselves?' Vellan asked.

'Only in the tales of dark sorcerers. Gibberish to some. Truth to others. That kind of accusation commands many pages in many books,' Sparrin replied. 'Mainly linked to the followers of Loken and those who commit their lives to his teachings and his prophecy.'

'I was hoping you would have one of these books that will help my friend here understand Loken and this prophecy; he's interested in it.'

'As it happens, I do,' Sparrin said, moving closer to a locked chest. He drew a key holder from his pocket, which must have had fifty keys attached to it. The small man flicked through them, shaking his head as he searched for the right one.

Vellan moved closer to Ogulf and Melcun. He began to whisper. 'You won't like what a priest tells you about this kind of thing, their view is lopsided. And an audience with a Thinker would be more difficult to arrange than an audience with a princess at the moment. So, consider this a beginning to your education, though don't take it personally – I don't believe what the old crone said.' He glanced at Sparrin who was still fingering through the keys. 'Two guards you saved me from means two debts are owed. So, consider this payment of the first.'

With a whoop of delight, Sparrin held a key aloft, looking at it as he turned it in the light. He busied himself with unlocking the huge trunk, which almost came up to his waist. He rummaged for a few seconds before pulling out a thick book with what looked like vines wrapped around its cover.

'The Paladins of the Blackened Gem,' he said, peering down at the book through his lenses, which were perched on the bridge of his nose. 'Here it is.' He turned around to face the others. 'A dark read, even when compared to the other volumes that grace my walls. The kind of title that will give you terrors in your dreams.'

'It focuses on the Onyxborn prophecy?' Vellan asked, reaching for the book.

Sparrin moved it from his grasp. 'Oh yes, among other things considered to sit within the darker realm of the powers bestowed by the gods. This is a most detailed account of the prophecy, its origins, and accounts of the ones who sought to fulfil it. I believe it to be one of three books of its kind in existence. Only one other is accounted for at the Tome Chamber at the Tawrawth in the Shingal. The other, I can only assume is lost.'

'How did you come to have such a book?' Melcun asked.

'I have my ways. And I have my interests,' Sparrin said. 'I cannot part ways with a book like this without adequate payment,' he turned and said to Vellan.

The Esselonian knight crossed his arms as the calm nature of their interaction now changed into the beginnings of a hard bargain.

'This is the princess' own task, Sparrin,' Vellan said. 'I'll pay you good coin but don't make a fool out of me when I'm on an errand like this. Two hundred gold is what I am permitted to offer.'

The small man scoffed and started tapping his foot. 'You ask me not to make a fool of you and then you mock me with that offer. Five hundred gold is the lowest I'll see it go for.'

Sparrin was driving a hard bargain and Ogulf couldn't fathom the thought of a book being so expensive. Five hundred gold was the type of coin that the Keltbran paid for a good lot of grain for a whole winter. Yet here in Esselonia, the same price was worthy of just one book.

'Three hundred,' Vellan answered.

'Four,' Sparrin replied.

'Three hundred and fifty and not a coin more,' Vellan said, opening his stance.

'Fine,' Sparrin said with a sigh. 'But only because I like you, Vellan you brazen sod. Let me assume since your garments are somewhat different to your usual attire that you do not have the gold on your person?' Sparrin was smiling now.

'You assume correctly. A hunting trip, and I couldn't wear my armour for the wolves, could I?' Vellan said.

Sparrin gave him a smiling nod, eyes bursting with disbelief. 'Very well. I will await the payment from the tower. More prompt than last time, if you will?'

'By noon tomorrow, you have my word,' Vellan said.

The men exchanged goodbyes and left the store. Vellan instructed Melcun to take great care of the book. The price he managed to haggle for was far less than it was worth – not to mention, a book like that would be valuable in the hands of someone with ill intentions, so he advised against making a show of having it.

Chapter 30

Vellan led Ogulf and Melcun to the gates of the Inner Circle of Delfmarc. The atmosphere here was different, and it was quieter, both in terms of audible noise and the number of people in the streets.

The citizens made their way through the streets here in a much calmer manner. No one seemed to be buying lots of anything in particular, and while some seemed to gravitate the more lavish stalls, the types that sell silk garments or ornaments or the like, the queues at the food stalls seemed normal. This was a world apart from the Outer Circle.

The journey to the Centre Circle holdfast was quick from here. Ogulf found it was easier to keep up with Vellan, especially when he concentrated on copying the man's steps as he they manoeuvred through the streets.

They approached the heavily fortified hold, which looked uninviting. It was brutally square and intimidating with arrow slits dotted around the walls. The only way in or out appeared to be a huge, heavy gate, which was currently raised.

What seemed like a whole battalion of guards were stationed around the gate. One of the men caught Ogulf's eye as he approached the group.

'Vellan, you bastard, where have you been?' The man's excitement alerted the guards around him and many turned and smiled. 'And what in the name of the gods are you wearing?'

'Rigin, my brother. A hunt gone wrong,' he said, embracing the man. 'Is the princess well?'

'She's been troubled since you didn't return, but I'm sure she will be much happier once she knows you are unharmed. I think General Cedryk had planned to send a full unit to look for you if you had not returned in the next few days, so as usual, your timing is impeccable. I am not sure we could have spared the men if I'm honest,' the man said, lips pursed. 'Hunt unsuccessful then?'

'In more ways than one,' Vellan said. He then turned to Ogulf and then Melcun. 'These men rescued me. That militia got me and my hunting party, and they were stupid enough to think they were going to sell me to the Red Isles.'

'Oh, well, at least you would've got a nice tan out there,' Rigin said, extending handshakes to Ogulf and Melcun. 'And you decided to file them into your ranks, did you?'

'Not quite. Fate seemed to bind us as they were already on their way here with a message for the princess when they managed to free me,' Vellan said, prompting a cautious look from his friend. 'Don't worry, I trust them, and I will escort them to see her myself.'

'Very well,' the man said, though he was clearly still cautious wary. 'I'll just ask that they go in unarmed.'

Vellan looked at his companions. 'Rigin, they are with me. You can keep your arms.' Ogulf nodded. He hadn't come this far to let a quarrel over him carrying a weapon be the thing that stopped him from meeting with Feda – especially not when he was supposed to be taking the axe to her.

'That's fine,' Rigin said to confirm. 'Incredible axe you have here,' he added, inspecting the weapon. 'Shingally steel I will bet.'

'Most likely. We hail from Broadheim so Shingally wares are easy to come by,' Ogulf said.

Rigin nodded and then motioned for the three of them to follow him beyond the gate and into the main holdfast of Delfmarc. The whole area was filled with soldiers. Ogulf noticed some sharpening blades, while others tended armour, and two were leading an archery lesson with what looked like younger recruits. Ogulf was relieved in a way; the men here looked ready to fight, not at all like the meek men in Luefmort. They looked hardened and battleworthy, the kind of soldiers who would take the fight to whoever they had to.

Soon the three were being waved through numerous doors and passageways as they climbed what seemed like an endless staircase. The steps started outside and then wound their way into an opening in the side of a tower, where they continued to spiral upwards. The air inside the tower was stifling and Ogulf was breathing heavily. For the first time in as long as he could remember, he found himself wishing for a breeze.

At the top of this tower, they were greeted by a smiling soldier. Unlike most of the others, he did not wear a helmet. His eyes were weary, and his short hair was straggly and flat. Some dried red stains were visible on his Esselonian armour.

'Paladin Vellan,' the man said, his eyes lighting up with relief. 'The princess will be eager to see you've returned.' He escorted them out of the doorway. Suddenly, they were no longer in the near infinite stairway; instead, they were outside, high above the city, on the top battlements that Ogulf noticed on his approach. He had never been so high, and the sight of the ground so far below made his stomach churn. Despite trying to stop them, his feet disobeyed him, and he took a few steps closer towards the edge of the wall to peer down.

To the west, he could see the Grendspires rising. They were as immense as the stories said they would be. The tips of the mountains were dusted with bright white snow.

'Ogulf, Melcun, with me please.' They followed Vellan and the other man up a set of stairs and through a door. Looking around, Ogulf noticed guards everywhere. There was no doubt in his mind he was about to meet with the princess – no one else would be in the tallest tower of a fortress like this with so many guards. His stomach fluttered the way it used to before a battle, during that tense moment ahead of a charge or an ambush. He had never had it in a situation like this, but he supposed that this was a battle of sorts. Or at least a fight. He would have to fight to get Feda to understand he needed her help. He couldn't grovel or beg; he must be strong.

They entered a large hall which was partially lit by the dwindling light of dusk and helped by four evenly spread out fire pits, one in each corner of the room. At the end of the room there was a grand chair, not quite as sumptuous as the throne in Jargmire, but a regal seat nonetheless. Standing in front of the chair was a woman.

Her hair was red, and her youthful face was sprinkled with freckles. She was pale, not quite pale in the way of people from Broadheim, but pale in comparison to a lot of the faces Ogulf had seen in Esselonia. She was athletically built and wore the most elegant and feminine armour Ogulf had ever seen; she looked every bit the warrior and the princess at the same time.

Leaning by her chair behind her was a longsword, crafted at the perfect mix between elegant and deadly. The blade itself must have been around the same height as her if you stood them side by side, but there was no doubt to Ogulf that this sword must have belonged to the princess.

The princess was bidding farewell to an elegantly dressed man who attempted to kiss the back of her hand as they parted. As he did, her eyes shot up and she noticed the odd people in the room. Drawn to Vellan, she pulled her hand away from the man and sprinted towards him, throwing her arms around his neck.

The man she was speaking with before looked on, evidently unsure of how to react. The clothes he wore were all in grey with tasselled shoulders – fashioned in a ceremonial design rather than armour for combat, Ogulf assumed. The man's features were sharp, his nose as straight as an arrow and pointed like one too. His intense eyes met Ogulf's and lingered. The muscles in his face were taut from decades of pursed lips and a jaw that may as well have been wired shut. Despite the severity of his features, he was a graceful man. He turned to leave the room, clearly realising his time with Feda had passed.

'I thought you were dead,' Feda said. The words tumbled out of her mouth as she looked Vellan up and down.

The elegant man walked towards the exit. Through his malice-carved features, he offered Ogulf a mouthy grin. The smile never reached his eyes, though; they remained unmoved and intense. Wildar had always said never to trust a man who didn't smile with his eyes and this man's eyes were all but dead. The door clicked shut with his departure.

'No. I was rescued,' Vellan said, extracting himself from the embrace of the princess.

Feda walked back to her throne and he followed a few steps behind. Betrothed or not, they were clearly used to sticking to chivalrous traditions until they were married.

'Why are there no guards in here, Feda?' Vellan asked, his eyes darting all around the dimming room.

'I asked them all to stay near the gate. We need to look like we have the numbers, it's good for morale,' Feda said, sitting on her throne gracefully. 'Besides, the meetings I have today are all with members of the council, so I didn't think them necessary.'

'Very well, Your Grace,' Vellan said, his face suggesting that his words were forced. Ogulf heard him take a sharp breath in. 'We couldn't find your brother. He wasn't in those forests. It seems like it was a trap set by one of the militias.' Feda reared slightly. Ogulf couldn't be sure if she was reacting to the first point or the second. 'I suspect we were deceived; the ambush was too precise for it to be a fluke. My whole unit was killed, and they took me. Their plan was to sell me to The Red Isles.'

'And you escaped?' she said. 'I assume this isn't some kind of barter with these two men behind you?'

'Yes, I escaped. Well, no, actually, that's not right – I was rescued by these two. They were travelling the Mule Road when they came across the cart I was being taken in and they saved me and rid the world of two traitors in the process.'

'Well, for that, the kingdom gives you thanks. And so do I,' Feda said. 'It's one thing to save a paladin but another thing entirely to save the one who I am promised to. I expect you brought them here to reward them?'

'You could say that, ac–'

'–Actually, Your Grace,' Ogulf interrupted and stepped forward from behind Vellan. The paladin sighed and Feda's eyes widened as they latched onto Ogulf's brazen breach of court etiquette. 'We were sent here to meet with you. I have travelled a long way to do so and to bring you a message.' He placed his hand in the inside breast pocket of his black armour, and took a fleeting moment to praise the Shingal for their ability to put such a thing in armour like this. He extracted Lord Hanrik's note and held it out, making sure to convey an expression of stern assertiveness.

Feda gestured for Vellan to take the note and bring it to her. Once he got close enough to hand it over, the princess looked hurt for a moment, then a hand went to cover her mouth as she noticed the bloodstained bandage around Vellan's hand. The fleeting moment passed, and her expression resumed its royal impassiveness as she turned her attention to the letter.

'You're Shingally?' she said in some kind of disbelief, flipping the letter over once and then again to inspect it. The lord's wax seal shimmered slightly as she did. 'We haven't seen an emissary from your country in months.'

'No, not Shingally,' Ogulf said. 'But please, open the letter. It is from Lord Hanrik Vranton in Luefmort.'

Vellan shot Ogulf a querying glance as he moved back to where he had been standing. 'You kept that quiet,' he whispered to Ogulf before he turned.

The princess was scanning the letter and nodding. She folded it and held on to it. 'You do bring good news. Though I am not sure their help will come quick enough. We are expecting an attack on Delfmarc by the South in the coming days. If we're lucky, some of us might survive to receive their aid,' the princess said, her tone flat, defeated. 'I will arrange for your safe passage across to the Shingal first thing tomorrow. We should have enough time to get you to the coast, and I'll see to it you get on a ship.'

'Your Grace, there is one more thing I need to bring to you,' Ogulf said. The statement drew ire from the eyes of the princess. 'I was promised an audience.'

'An audience to provide the message you were sent to deliver, which I believe you have done. I am not in the position to take requests right now. If it is gold you seek for your troubles and travels, then I will see to it that you are paid. Thank you.' Feda's eyes went back to the letter as she opened it again.

'With respect, Your Grace, I was promised an audience and I am not finished with my message,' Ogulf said. He wondered where the excited girl he had seen when Vellan entered the room had gone.

'He was, Your Grace. I promised him an audience with you for saving me,' Vellan said, eyes pointed downwards to avoid the glare of his betrothed. The princess sighed and raised a hand as if to allow Ogulf to begin.

Ogulf took a deep breath, 'I am not from Shingal,' Ogulf said. 'I have come from Broadheim. And as far as I am aware, the whole of my country is now overrun.' He looked at Feda, hoping for even the slightest of reactions, but she gave nothing away. 'All of it. Jargmire, Tran, Port Saker, all of the Holds, and even my town of Keltbran.' He thought he saw a twinge in her eyes at the mention. 'We were invaded by a force from the North. We think they come from Visser. They march in the name of a dark power looking to fulfil an ancient prophecy and obtain the powers of the Peaks of Influence across the world. If our interpretations are right …' His words were coming out too quickly. He took a second to breathe and focus, and then he said, 'Then, eventually, that war will come to Esselonia. To stop that from happening, I was told to bring you this.' He slowly unsheathed Wildar's axe from his back and displayed it to Feda across both of his hands. Feda sat up in her chair. She still wasn't giving much away, but the fact that she had not protested let Ogulf know he could continue. 'Before Esselonia, we expect they will make an attempt to invade the Shingally Empire,' Ogulf said. Feda didn't twitch but Vellan snickered slightly.

'Invade Shingal? They'll be quashed at the first battle,' Vellan said.

'I thought this too. But after spending time there, I wouldn't be so sure,' Ogulf said.

Feda interrupted the pair. 'Where did you get that weapon?' she asked. Ogulf looked to see the princess' eyes, they were wide with wonder and fixed on the gilded hilt of Wildar's weapon.

'It was given to me when we were fleeing the Order of Maledict in Broadheim – they are the ones who seek to fulfil the Onyxborn prophecy and return dark magic to prominence in the name of Loken.' Ogulf felt like a sage as the words tumbled out of his mouth.

'You didn't answer my question,' Feda said. 'Where did you get it?'

It was time.

'Your uncle gave it to me,' Ogulf said. Her eyes widened and she took a quick breath through her nose, making her back straighten. 'Wildar. He basically raised me. Showed me all the tricks with an axe, spear, and sword; taught me to hunt; protected my father; and looked after my people. He was one of the few people in this world I trusted. His dying words to me were that you–' He pointed at Feda. '–You, and only you, were the one who could save us all. And that I had to bring this to you. Now I am not one for prophecy or for destiny, at least I wasn't until recently, but Wildar–' Just as he hoped, she gave another involuntary twitch at the name. '–Said that you can help us. So, by all the gods, I believe it to be true.'

'He died?' Feda said, looking at the clasped hands on her lap. A tear streamed down her cheek.

'Yes. Fell in the Banespit when we were making the journey South, away from the members of the Order who were chasing us,' Ogulf said.

Feda stood from her chair and descended the two steps from its platform. She began pacing slowly back and forth across the floor.

'What else did he say?' she asked, not making eye contact.

'Just that you could save us. That you would need the axe to do so. Vague, I know,' Ogulf said.

'Of all the times this could land at my feet, it had to be now.'

'Wait, Feda, that isn't what I think it is, is it?' Vellan asked.

'It's exactly what you think it is, Vellan. That is Solsana.'

'Solsana?' Ogulf said.

'The Light of the World, The Guiding Light of Esselonia, a weapon of the Lightwielders, and one that can stop the powers of dark magic,' Vellan said. Ogulf looked at the axe in his hands – it was beautiful, powerful, and deadly, but it didn't look special. 'Feda, does this mean Wildar had this all along?' Vellan said.

'He must have, and here the world thought that it was nestled at the bottom of the ocean or gathering dust in some far away shack.' She let out a heavy sigh. 'I'm losing this war – how can I possibly lend a hand in another? The gods seem to hold me to a fate I cannot escape.'

Feda walked towards him and went to take the axe in her hands. Just as she was about to touch it, someone burst through the door behind them with vigour.

A man, who was actually more like two men across, strode in with a few armoured guards behind him. The big man's face was round and red, and his white sideburns wrapped around his cheeks, making his cropped hair look like a spiked helmet.

'Your Grace, there is a glow coming from the Old Stone. It means that the Solsana is near,' the man said.

'Yes, General Cedryk.' Feda chuckled in disbelief. 'It's right here.' She took it in her hand and spun around, letting the firelight dance off the blade as she showed him.

Chapter 31

The waves were choppy, much more so than Danrin had expected. It had been some time since he was on the waters of the Sea of Blades, and his other experiences of the seas came from near the capital in the Illindrian Ocean, where the waters were much calmer. Perhaps that was why these felt so rough, he just wasn't used to them anymore.

He was aboard a vessel which drifted halfway across the Sea of Blades. In the blurry distance, he could see the shoreline of Port Saker.

Men moved around the ship. They were waiting for more ships to join them in the blockade. Danrin wanted to get a closer look at the build-up of forces in Port Saker for himself – only then did he feel he could properly explain to his father the severity of the peril they faced.

Far in the distance, visible only through his long glass, Danrin could see the beachhead and the build-up of forces around it. Their numbers were incredible.

Danrin was at the edge of the blockade formation, and from his position, he could see the middle ship, The Prince's Peace, the grandest and most powerful ship in all of the fleet. Aboard would be Admiral Maitlund. He had been enforcing the blockade for days now and encouraged the prince to bolster the numbers as they waited for the next move from the Order of Maledict and their positions in Broadheim.

Danrin was becoming impatient as he looked through his long glass. He'd hoped to have been and gone from this part of his day by now, and he had seen all that he needed to, but he had to wait for the other blockade ships to arrive before he could return to Shingally shores and then back to Luefmort.

He glanced back towards the Shingally shoreline, hoping to see signs of the other ships, but there was nothing. When he returned his eyes to the other side of the Sea of Blades, he noticed a deep fog had begun to ride over the waves towards them. At first, Danrin thought it was a heavy rainstorm, but it was too thick to be that. Then it encroached the ship Danrin was on, plunging his surroundings into a grey haze. It was like a huge wall of swirling grey that went from the waves all the way to the very edges of the sky. Confused murmurs came from the sailors behind Danrin as they also noticed this incredible sight.

'Have any of you seen anything like this before?' Danrin called out, unable to see any of the men aboard the ship, although he was sure they had only been feet away moments ago.

'Nothing like this, sir,' a voice called back. Danrin heard unease in the words.

There was also a smell in the air. Not the salty scent of the sea but a dark smell – the smell of death.

***

In Port Saker, Nevea was standing on the coast and staring directly at the tiny ships bobbing on the horizon while Nadreth watched from a few paces behind her. They were Shingally. Yesterday there had been six and today there were ten. If King Nadreth and his advisors were correct, then before long, there would be a full fleet of them. The intention of the Shingally Empire was clearly to blockade the Sea of Blades to stop the advance of the king's army.

They were smart. Either they had been warned or the Shingally vigilance was just as committed as it always had been. The planners of the king's army had scratched their heads for days about how to tackle this problem, and they had had teams working to build ships as quickly as possible with the intention of attacking the Shingally fleet in the Blades. The daily increase in the numbers on the blockade had forced them to abandon this idea for the time being.

Building their own boats had also not been easy as not all of the wood in the areas around Port Saker was fit for purpose; most of it was dead or already chopped down to stumps.

When Nevea had first arrived in Port Saker, the king had planned to make a spectacle of her. He, Nadreth, Son of Tolqrana, blood descendant of the very first of the clan Maledict, had fulfilled his family's age-old promise. He had found the Onyxborn.

He wanted to have a rally of sorts, something good for the men to replenish them after their difficult march South. The taking of Broadheim had been much easier than expected, but the cold was beginning to take effect. The armour his men wore was specially designed to keep the cold at bay, but even though it didn't affect their bodies much, it had started to drain their minds.

Showcasing the Onyxborn and the saviour of their cause would bring them back to readiness before the offensive against the Shingal and the Southerlands began. It would let them see the power they had and hasten their steps to victory.

Nevea had another idea, though, a striking one that caught the king off guard. She wanted to deal with the fleet herself. At first, the King argued against it, saying she must save her strength for the battles to come, but the young sorceress had insisted. She told him she had been storing her powers for years in Broadheim and that she too wanted to show the men at the heart of their cause what she was capable of.

Unwilling to upset his prophesied sorceress, King Nadreth agreed to the idea.

The King watched as Nevea sauntered down the beach towards the shore a few more paces away, the waves rushing and retreating peacefully in the morning tide. She let her long-hooded robe fall to the floor, unveiling her dark red armour, the edged scales of which were menacing from the squared-off shoulders to the built-in bracers. On each of her delicate fingers, she wore one ring, and then two rings encircled each thumb. All of the rings were an opulent black. A sea breeze whirled around her as she walked, causing her flawless silver hair to flow like the waves of the Blades.

The king watched as the prophesied girl began creating a whipping, circular motion with her right hand. With that, she pulled a small cloud of smog from nowhere and let it hover above her outstretched palm. She uttered words to the mist in a whispery dark tongue, and then, with a strong breath, she blew the ball out of her hand and off towards the sea.

Nadreth watched her, mesmerised. She was calm, powerful, and elegant, everything that had been promised.

His eyes moved to the ball of smoke as it flowed towards the sea. Nadreth squinted. As it began to morph, he was sure it was getting larger. The ball went from the size of a fist when it left the sorceress's hand to something resembling a small boulder now, and with every inch that it progressed towards the sea line, it seemed to expand.

Once it began to hover over the Sea of Blades, there was no doubt in the king's mind that this plume was growing. Before long, it had enveloped the whole sea and stolen the horizon from Nadreth's own eyes. He turned to look at the men who gathered on the beach, and was met with a collected gathering of dumbfounded expressions as the waves disappeared in the fog.

'My king,' Nevea said. The king turned back to her. 'Would you like to see what happens next?' She beckoned the King forward with an outstretched hand.

As soon as he touched Nevea's hand, Nadreth felt something. Power. She looked out at the thick wall of smoke and so did the king.

The barrier of smog was no longer in front of him, now he was inside it. He was weaving through the cloud at pace, headfirst like he had been shot from a giant longbow. The thickness of the fog meant he could barely see his hands in front of him. As he focused, though, he realised these weren't his hands at all. Where his gauntlet-covered hand should have been was a monstrous fist, heavily scarred with chunks of bone missing from the walnut-sized knuckles. He glanced at the other one, only to find it was the same – a huge other-worldly hand. And, in this one, there was a rusty cleaver, its blade a horrible mix of silver, grey, brown, and red, but the edge of the weapon still looked sharp and sinister.

'You will see my power through my eyes, my king. I want to show you what I can do in his name.' It was Nevea's voice

inside his head. The control he had over the hideous hands had disappeared. Instead, he was viewing this creature's flight through the cloud from behind its eyes. Occasionally, an animalistic grunt was heard above the howling sound of the winds as they flew through the air, just above the waves.

Nadreth noticed something ahead as his feral vessel coursed through the fog. It was the bow of a ship, which for a second, Nadreth was sure they would crash into, but then with an upwards swoop and a stomach-turning drop, the creature landed hard on the deck of the boat. The king, still seeing the scene from the point of view of the creature, felt like he was standing twice as tall as usual as the men on the boat scattered in confusion like a pack of panicked children. The others on the boat must only be hearing the spooked screams of their comrades, unable to see what was going on due to the thick covering of fog.

With a roar, the beast began swinging his great cleaver at the men on the ship. Moving through them as they were nothing, it slashed at one, leaving a horrid gash in his throat, almost decapitating him with a single glancing blow. At the same time, it struck another in the chest with a closed fist. The hawk emblazoned on his victim's armour crumpled inwards, caving in his sternum.

With a suppleness that seemed to defy his brutal form, the beast moved along the ship, striking as he pleased. The fractured and slashed bodies of his enemies fell at his feet as he moved along the deck. Some of the Shingally sailors fired crossbows into the mist in desperation, still unable to see their target. All of their shots flew past the undeterred fiend.

The king watched on eagerly, unable to get enough of the brutality. He could feel himself willing the creature on, just like if he was watching a triumphant play in his court in Prath. But this was different, this was real. And this was power that was now at the disposal of his cause, destined to help him take the world in Loken's name.

Before moving on to the next ship, the beast made sure to light a fire, taking flint from his pocket and sparking it with the rusty cleaver. Within seconds, the wrapped sail of the ship was engulfed, the flames slowly creeping on to other areas of the boat, leaving a trail of charred black across the deck in its wake.

He pressed on to the next ship and found his enemies already alert. Nadreth thought this was probably due to the screams and the orange glow coming from their sister vessel. The beast moved through them with ease yet again. The king's bloodlust was still far from quenched. Another sail was set alight. Before jumping to the next boat, the creature stamped his foot down on the wounded body of one of his adversaries who was weakly attempting to pull himself away from the fire. With a horrible cracking sound, the king watched as the soldier's head turned to mush under the brute's heavy foot.

With a mighty roar, the beast jumped to the next ship. As he waded through the soldiers, punching and cleaving, the king watched on in delight. This creature was truly unstoppable. As if their minds were connected, both his and the creature's eyes found their next target at the same time. His garment was different to the others. The crest emblazoned on the chest was much larger, and rather than a short sword, he carried a huge broadsword. He readied himself as the beast walked towards him with calculated steps and sporadic grunts. The man did not flinch, rather he kept his posture tight and his sword high.

The king felt his excitement bloom into something entirely different. He wanted to see if the creature would be challenged. Then he could understand the true limits of its power.

The Shingally soldier swung the greatsword with the might of ten men, aiming to strike the creature between the ear and shoulder. The length of the weapon allowed him to do so despite the soldier being significantly shorter than his opponent. As if it were nothing, the beast caught the blade in its hand. The sword sunk into its fleshy palm, cutting at least an inch deep, without bothering the beast in the slightest. Blood poured out as the creature's fingers tightened around the blade, tight enough to wrench it from the hands of the soldier.

The sword must have weighed at least twenty pounds, but the beast hurled it into the sea as if it were a pebble. It was lost to the mist after a few feet and a distant splash was heard as the blade hit the water.

The soldier still didn't back down. He drew a short blade from behind his back and leapt at the creature. Using the same hand that it had caught the broadsword with, the creature grabbed the leaping man by the face, his palm covering the soldier's features like a mask of gore. A metallic thud rang out as the beast dropped the cleaver. He gripped the man's lower half with his now-free hand. Stretching the man briefly, there was a pop as the soldier's head parted from his body in a smattering of viscera.

Dropping the torso of the man to the deck of the ship, the creature looked into the still rolling eyes on the head of his victim. The king may as well have been jumping for joy. This was only the beginnings of the immeasurable power he was promised. He began to think of what this meant for when the prophecy was fulfilled once they reached Esselonia and Nevea touched the Stone of the Night. But that could wait. For right now, the King was finally seeing the yield of his influence with his own eyes. This was Cormag incarnate. This was the work of Loken's own hand.

The beast hurled the head to its left. There was a dull boom from not too far away, followed by the screams of multiple men. The king, in all of his time watching through the beast's eyes, had not been able to make out many of the words shouted by the soldiers succumbing to the monster's savage power, and then one was coming through as clear as crystal.

He couldn't see the other ships, but in the blood-curdled yell of such a word, he knew exactly what this show of strength had achieved. Without a single ship of their own sunk, without a single life lost, they had overcome the Shingally watch fleet on the Sea of Blades. He focused back on the perspective of the beast as it lit another piece of flint. This time, instead of using the sail to start the fire, the beast held it against the torso of his last rival until a flame flickered to life.

As quickly as he had been taken to the inside of the beast's eyes, he was back behind his own. Overwhelmed, he fell to one knee while still clutching Nevea's hand. He looked up at the beautiful young girl, whose eyes were bright with something he couldn't quite decipher, and she smiled at him.

Men rushed to his side to help him, but he fanned them away as Nevea's gaze turned to the Sea of Blades once more and the fog began to dissipate. Slowly at first, and then more rapidly, the King watched from the sands as it crept away from them, revealing more and more of the choppy waters.

The king's eyes were drawn directly ahead. In the retreating fog, there was a distinctly orange glows that were becoming more prevalent by the second. Like a sunrise waking up the world, it finally revealed what he had seen to the rest of his men: three huge longboats all ablaze on the horizon.

A near deafening cheer came from behind the king as the men noticed. Even General Hassit was roaring with triumph.

No other ships were visible as the fiery outlines of the three ships began to sink, swallowed by the Sea of Blades.

***

Danrin was covered in blood. Only seconds had passed since the severed head of Admiral Maitlund had landed at his feet, the eyes rolled back into the skull as if they were hiding from the horrors of the situation. Two glowing, flickering beacons stood out to his left, and one was coming from the very spot where The Prince's Peace should have been, if his bearings were correct.

All around him, men hurried and hid, blades drawn as they scanned the fog for any sign of a threat. Some had come to investigate the source of the thud that had sounded when the admiral's head landed on the deck; one younger soldier vomited when he saw the torn flesh.

Seconds turned to minutes as they waited for another sound or scream but all that was heard was the fan and crackle of a large fire taking hold. Danrin turned to see a third beacon now glowing in the mist and he had no other choice but to say a word he never expected to, not in his whole life. At first it was muttered, quiet and unsure, then it grew louder as he accepted that it was the right thing to do. Finally, he shouted it as if his life depended on it.

'Retreat. All men to the oars!' Danrin shouted. It felt like the words clawed their way out of his throat. 'Make for the Shingal! Retreat.'

Then he saw it start to dissipate and fall away from them towards the shore of Port Saker like a great grey curtain slowly unveiling more and more of the jagged waves. Danrin felt tension drip away from his neck and upper back. He had not even noticed it building until it vanished, but the feeling of relief was fleeting at best. His eyes jumped from ship to ship, looking for the cause of the fires.

Something was wrong, but there was no sign of an enemy.

In his panicked search for their attackers, he hadn't noticed just how badly the three ships in the blockade had been damaged – they were all ravaged by flames. They were all in the final part of their descent to the depths of the Sea of Blades. The parts still jutting from the water were wrapped with blazing fire. They looked like candles with an hour's life left in them. They had minutes or even seconds before they were submerged completely.

He tried to shout again, but as he watched The Prince's Peace, the pride of the fleet, sink into the Sea of Blades, the very waves where it was launched, he felt real fear for the first time in his life. 'Retreat. Back to shore. Retreat,' he said as he watched terrified men around him scurry to their stations.

Chapter 32

Night had fallen in Delfmarc, leaving the top tower throne room dark apart from the fire pits in each corner, which were now serving their true purpose. Ogulf rubbed his temples, trying to alleviate some of the tension that was building there. The large man who had rushed in was General Cedryk Mahran. He was the princess's top military advisor who had also served her father and grandfather before her. And since he'd arrived in the room, he had been accusing Ogulf of theft – the theft of the great axe, Solsana.

Feda was atop her throne at the end of the room. In front of her stood Vellan, Ogulf, Melcun, General Cedryk, and one of the general's guards.

Ogulf and Melcun were standing to the side of the room. It was as if they had been discarded as a fierce debate was raging in front of the throne. Feda rarely said a word other than trying to calm the participants. The melee was not what Ogulf expected at her court.

The general was brandishing Wildar's axe in his huge hand, and while Ogulf was sure he didn't mean it in a threatening manner, General Cedryk was waving the axe dangerously close to Vellan. He was questioning how it was possible that Ogulf and Melcun could be in possession of the weapon. Vellan confirmed they had it when he met them on the road and that he believed it was given to them by Wildar.

The bickering went on for a few moments more before the princess rose from her throne. She was much smaller than both men, but it was clear from her eyes she had had enough of the general's squabbling. She interrupted the man with a firm shout, and as she moved from her throne with authority in her steps to stand between the men, both took a pace back and assumed the straightened posture of their military positions.

'I will hear no more of this from either of you,' she said not, looking them in the eye. 'These men are not thieves, General Cedryk. And if you would remember your position long enough to listen to your princess, then I will explain why.' She looked at the man and paused. Once she was satisfied he wouldn't interrupt, Feda took the axe from the general. In her hands, it looked like a regular sized axe again.

'You said you were given this by my uncle?' she asked.

'Wildar handed me it before he fell into the Banespit, yes,' Ogulf said.

'Has he always had this?'

'As long as I've known him.'

'And how long had that been?' she asked, moving closer towards him.

'Wildar came to Keltbran fifteen years ago. You don't get axes like that where we come from, so it stood out. That axe was on his hip then, and it was there every day and night until he died.'

'How did you come to meet Wildar?'

'He came from Paleways. My father and Wildar organised trade routes between his town and mine. They became friends. He came to visit us for the hunting season one year and never left.'

'Paleways,' she said, turning to General Cedryk. 'The islands off the coast of Broadheim?'

'Yes, Your Grace.' He responded without looking at her. 'The islands your grandfather sent Wildar to when he was a boy.' The general looked like he wanted to continue but stopped himself at the last second, though he clearly had more to say.

'He actually did do it.' Feda laughed lightly before taking the axe from Cedryk. 'My father always said Wildar stole this. I always thought it was his way of pinning a crime on a sibling in a joking way, there was never any real conviction in his words. And then he would say how could a twelve-year-old boy steal one of the most protected weapons in all the realm? I didn't know the man other than through letters, but by the gods, I wish I had been given the chance. General

Cedryk, it looks like one of the greatest mysteries in the history of Esselonia has been solved.'

The princess turned to Ogulf again and walked towards him. She was looking at the blade. Gently, she ran her finger down the edge of it, creating a light scraping noise. She handed the weapon back to Ogulf.

'Your Grace, I must protest,' General Cedryk said. He broke from his stance and turned towards the princess. 'He is not of our blood.'

The princess held a hand up to silence her advisor as she looked at Ogulf. 'You're holding a relic, a weapon gifted by the gods to help us in our struggles against those who seek to cause us harm. This axe is called Solsana – it means dawn in the words of our ancestors. They say the first mages of this island carved that axe from the first metals they found, and gilded it to perfection over years of craft and spellbinding. It is to be called upon only when it is absolutely necessary, when we come up against a fight with pure evil.'

Ogulf looked at the axe. Given its perfect edge, glasswork in the blade and ornate pommel he had thought it was Shingally . It didn't look like anything more than a fancy blade, but he could find no reason to doubt what Feda was saying.

'We have been searching for this weapon since before I was born and here you are bringing it to us from the colds of Broadheim. Do you believe in the will of the gods, Ogulf?' Feda said with a smirk.

Ogulf was still staring at the axe. He didn't want to answer the question. Everything that had happened over the last few days had made him know there was something or someone guiding him. He felt like he was at the mercy of something entirely unworldly. It was liberating and terrifying at the same time.

Melcun cleared his throat. 'If your father thought Wildar had it, why didn't you check?'

Feda conceded the point with her eyes. 'No one ever took the idea seriously. My father always said it with humour in his tone, he never hinted that Wildar could actually be capable of such a thing. Was the idea ever investigated, general?'

'No. Our searches were focused on the Shingal and the pirate islands in the Southerlands. We had reason to believe Dibial cults had stolen the weapon. We searched for four years for that axe. One of the most precious relics in all of the world stolen by a wayward child and taken to that cesspit of an island.'

'The odd thing is, he wasn't one to keep secrets, and yet, on the day he died, he told us to find you and give you the axe without a mention of you or its importance before then. And there was never a single hint that he was of royal blood, he never even told us that part – we found out in a book and put the two together. It makes me wonder why he chose to leave?' Ogulf asked.

'The general can correct me, but I believe he was sent to Paleways for being a pain in the backside. In an effort to ground him and prepare him for life in a family like ours, my grandfather sent him away,' Feda said. 'He refused to fall in rank at the Academy of Swords. Instead, he was known for running beyond the walls of the capital, hiding in the forests, and hunting for himself for weeks on end. He had a knack for evading my grandfather's men, who were sent to bring him home.'

'Yes, that's right. It all became too much for your grandfather one time,' the general said. 'Your uncle made it as far as the shores of Hyl. Evaded us for three whole moons and crafted himself a raft. When we caught him, he said he wanted to sail to Red Isles and live in the woods near the old Vikesfort. We stopped him just as he was about to push that floating death trap into the sea. One of the paladins got a hold on him and Wildar hit him with a club. He bloodied him badly. The poor lad had only just graduated and he never quite recovered. This aggravated your grandfather. He was a patient man, but Wildar always seemed to seek the very limits of that patience. We all knew he would break it one day, but we never expected your grandfather to do what he did. Sending him to one of the old Guard Outposts in Paleways seemed like the best idea to him, but I knew it wouldn't work. The whole idea was something of a misfire – Wildar felt abandoned and shut himself off from the family. Eventually, the king grew tired of sending letters and messengers without a response, and he turned his back on Wildar. It pained him to do it – I remember his tears – but he didn't think he had any other choice than to let Wildar choose his own path.'

'After the king died, Feda's father took the throne. He was eager to bring his brother back to Esselonia; he wanted people he could trust on his counsel while he found his feet in his new role as ruler. He sent riders to find his brother on Paleways. They returned to tell the king that Wildar no longer called Paleways home and hadn't for some time. The townsfolk who knew him said he left one night and never returned. King Uthyn sent riders all over the known world searching for his brother, but none had ever heard of so much as a whisper about him in the citadels. He left it be, believing that Wildar did not want to be found – or worse, that he was dead.'

'You would have a hard time finding someone in a pocket like Keltbran,' Ogulf said.

'Aye. We never gave the smaller towns a chance. There were just too many of them and none of the riders or even Uthyn himself even knew what they were looking for. None of them had seen him since he was a boy,' General Cedryk said.

'I know he exchanged letters with Feda – how did you make contact with him in the end?' Ogulf asked.

'He contacted my father when he heard about the uprising in the South. He said he wanted to come back,' Feda said.

'But he was torn, he didn't want to abandon his people – your people in Keltbran, that is. He mentioned the cold, said it was harsher than any winter he had seen in all of his years, but he promised to come here when it passed. We kept exchanging letters. He told us how bad it had gotten in Broadheim, and equally, our messages were full of our own troubles – first the uprising grew, then I had to write to him to tell him my father was ill. That wasn't easy.' Feda took a deep breath to calm herself. 'His tone changed, and he seemed more determined to get to us after that. He started telling me he would help me defeat the uprising. I managed to get one final letter to Wildar when the uprising became a full revolt just after my father died. It also read that my Uncle Eryc had attached himself to the claim of the South. It was more of a desperate plea, really. His last letter to me arrived a few days ago. In it, he wrote that he was making the journey South and soon he would help me regain the throne. Some part of me really thought he would make it,' Feda said.

'Wait a second, how were you getting letters to Wildar?' Melcun asked.

'We have our ways,' she said, gesturing to the man behind Ogulf and Melcun. They had not paid him much attention before, believing him to be one of the general's guards. Upon glancing at him a little longer, they realised he was entirely different to anyone they had seen so far in Esselonia. His robust frame was similar to the general's. His armour was light, foreign, and had purple flashes on the shoulders and knees. His shoes were bulky and grooved in a way that Ogulf had never seen.

Ogulf recognised the man's jawline. He couldn't place his unwavering eyes, though. He scanned more of the man's features and his studious eyes were drawn to the man's wrists, where an angry red wound jogged Ogulf's memory. The mark was more defined now, the most artistic scar Ogulf had ever seen. It looked like it was beginning to heal but there was no doubt in Ogulf's mind that this was the same person. This was the man Ogulf saw in Keltbran the day before they left for the Trail. The man who had been leaving Wildar's home in a hurry.

'This is Acolyte Tiam of the Tongueless Brothers. He is my personal messenger.'

Ogulf looked at the man, feeling slightly uneasy at the idea of another one of Wildar's secrets being exposed.

'The cold was only half of our worries,' Ogulf said. 'When he wrote to you, did Wildar mention the invasion of Broadheim?' Feda shook her head. 'They were only a day at most from our town when he sent that last letter. If Wildar had your weapon and it could be called upon to defeat evil, then why didn't he use it to save Broadheim?'

'It doesn't work like that. It is paired with another, a mace our ancestors called Sursola,' Feda said. 'Their power must be called upon together in ceremony in order for it to be used. Without that ceremony, it is just an axe. But together, the weapons are bound to the fate of the holders; they become Lightwielders, the champions of our cause.'

'Why would Wildar take such a thing, then?' Ogulf asked.

General Cedryk cleared his throat, indicating he would like to speak. 'It was promised to him that, when he was of age, should there be a need for the weapon to be used, Wildar would bear the axe and Uthyn would wield the mace. He must have decided that he wanted what was promised to him, even if he was forced to leave.'

'He wasn't a thief,' Ogulf said.

'Evidently he was. Otherwise, how do you explain this axe being in his possession before it was handed to you?' the general said.

'You didn't know him, not like we did. He wouldn't have taken something like this without a reason,' Ogulf said.

'Well, regardless, the Old Stone has been sitting empty ever since,' Feda said. 'We need to ensure that no one sees it glowing now. Close off the chambers at the Morastram and make sure that the room there is guarded at all times. We don't need too many people knowing that Solsana is near its home stone. Not now, anyway. There are more important things to deal with.'

'Couldn't you call on the powers now, to win your war?' Melcun asked.

'No. This is not the right time for that. It serves a specific purpose and cannot be called upon until both bearers and weapons are present. I will keep Solsana with me at all times, which is why it is imperative that no one knows it is back on Esselonian soil for now. General, is that clear?'

'Yes, Your Grace. A wise decision,' the general said.

'Good. Which brings me to my next point,' Feda said, turning to Ogulf. 'While you are here, I would like to ask for your help. If you knew Wildar the way you say you did, then you could be useful in the fight which awaits us. Would you be willing to offer counsel in the way Wildar would have?' Feda said.

'Your Grace, again, I must protest. We do not know these men, what makes you think they have the skills to contribute?' General Cedryk said.

'Ogulf is a tactician. He picked apart a rebel army when he was outnumbered five to one. He could have been the King of Broadheim's own general if he wanted to be,' Melcun said, using Rowden's oft said claim.

'This is not a rebel army we are facing. And am I not right in saying Broadheim has fallen?' the general said. 'That doesn't say much for the military tacticians of your country.'

The general didn't seem like someone who could be convinced by words. He would need to show him what he was capable of.

'At this stage, I don't think there is any harm in including the eyes and opinions of others,' Feda said. 'If Wildar had been here, he would have been accepted into the fold of my protectors without question, and I had never met that man either. This is not the same, but I would be interested in your input – it might be similar enough to what Wildar would have offered.'

'It will be better,' Melcun said. Ogulf looked at his friend in disbelief. 'What? Wildar would have said it too.'

Feda smirked and turned away. 'Well, in any case, I expect you both to be fighting for my cause. Do this, and if we make it out alive, I will help you in the war to come. But don't forget, this war must be dealt with before I can move my focus elsewhere.'

'Understood.'

Not long after that, Ogulf and Melcun were excused by the princess. A member of her guard came, and they were taken from the main hold to a guest room. There was no lavish feast like there had been in Luefmort but there was bread and some meat brought to their small room.

Cold seeped from the rough stone wall and the blankets they were given were rough to touch. Ogulf could not find any comfort as he shifted on the bed. Melcun was across from him on his own bed, face buried in his book of spells once more.

'She seems confident,' Melcun said, not looking up from his open page.

'She's related to Wildar, it's no surprise,' Ogulf said.

'I know, but... the odds certainly seem stacked against her,' Melcun said, turning to face Ogulf.

'Well, think about if it had been us. If it had been during the Rebellion, what if we had just accepted death that day at the Battle of Mrandbrog? We wouldn't be here today. Five to one, they had the advantage on us, and we still beat them.'

'You beat them,' Melcun said.

Melcun was right in a way – his ideas, his tactics had helped crush a rebellion before. But Wildar had been there, and so had Rowden, which made a significant difference when it came to the actual fighting. He wondered if he could do it again without them. He weighed up the positives of the situation; this time he was in a fortress, rebel forces were usually less organised than proper armies, he had a few more years of experience since that summer, and lastly, from what he had seen, the forces in Delfmarc seemed prepared for a battle.

Then he allowed himself to process the negatives; he didn't know this citadel, General Cedryk clearly wasn't pleased at him being involved, he wouldn't be able to lead like he had before, he was there only to give advice.

When they left, Feda had mentioned that her riders were due back from the pass of the Grendspire Peaks any day now. They would have an update on the movements of the Southern forces, and once she had this, then she would call a meeting with her Honour Guard, the paladins, her generals, and her counsel, which now included Ogulf in Wildar's place. There they would devise a battle plan based on the information from the riders and begin to prepare measures for counterattacks and the rest of the campaign once her banners arrived.

This is where Ogulf could make a difference. He just had to do it in the right way. These people wouldn't trust him immediately. He accepted that. So, in order to get them on his side, he needed to find a way to make them believe in him, and the best way to do that was be the key to the defence of their city in the battle to come.

As Ogulf rolled around on the squishy mattress, trying to find comfort to sleep, he kicked the prickly covering off of his bed and closed his eyes, picturing his mother's tree.

Chapter 33

Danrin was kicking his horse harder than he ever had before, so much so that he felt pity for the animal. He had ridden through the night to reach Luefmort from the coast because he didn't want the story of what happened to come from anyone else but him.

He had seen the terrified faces of the men who were on the ships, the ones lucky enough to make it back across the Sea of Blades. He wondered if he looked as scared as they did. That wasn't what he wanted – he needed to be stern. Danrin was recounting his experience over and over. Even though he hadn't, surely one of his men would have noticed an assault from the enemy shore, but none of them had. Something was not right about the attack or the mist; it had not been natural.

Sinking his heels into the side of his horse again, he whispered to will it faster. Luefmort was only minutes away as he sped past the Vyne river, its sloshing waters weaving parallel to the road. The normal trickle of its flowing waters was accompanied by the dull cadence of the horse's rapid hooves against the dry path.

The doors were waved open as Danrin approached, and still atop his horse, he bounded through the entrance and into the walled city of Luefmort. The streets would normally be quiet at this time, but in the wake of his father's announcement about a threat to the kingdom, Danrin saw more men patrolling the walls today than ever before.

As he reached the main square before the palace, he slowed his horse down to navigate the narrow paths. Dismounting as he got closer, he ran his hands through his horse's mane and whispered thanks to her before instructing a man on guard there to fetch water for drinking and cooling his steed.

Bounding through the doors, sweat dripping down his cheeks, Danrin headed straight for his father's small study, which was where he had taken refuge since the incident in the library. This was a much more personal room, filled with Vranton family heirlooms. Turning into the room, Danrin saw the same face that always greeted him when he came here, a portrait of his grandfather surrounded by four ornate ceremonial knives. Below it was a huge great axe and the gilded skull of the first of their lineage, Raik Vranton. Danrin used to love spending time in this room as a boy, soaking up family histories through the stories of his father. To others, such things would be useless, but to Danrin, these were the most valuable possessions he could imagine, and one day they would all be his.

Behind a desk, eating his breakfast, was the Lord of Luefmort. In his hands were two frayed pieces of paper, and the yellow ribbon on the desk let Danrin know these letters were dispatch reports. Between mouthfuls of eggs, Lord Hanrik carefully reviewed each line of the note. Danrin felt like he managed to breathe for the first time in hours as he stopped in the doorway. The tightness in his chest might have eased, but his heart continued to thud.

'Danrin, are you all right?' Lord Hanrik asked, standing from his desk and moving towards his son. Danrin was trying to catch his breath. 'Danrin. Speak to me. What is wrong?'

'Three of our ships ... gone ...' He was trying to regulate his breathing. 'Three of them on the Blades ... The Prince's Peace and ... two others ...'

'The invaders have a fleet?' Hanrik said, his eyebrows contracting, until a deep line appeared between them.

'No. We don't know how they did it. There was an attack. I saw the ships sink with my own eyes and there were no boats, no nothing. But it was an attack.'

Danrin went on to tell his father his story. He watched on as his father's demeanour changed with every major turn in the story. He knew Hanrik would not be able to fully comprehend what had happened – Danrin couldn't even do that, and had been there – but he knew he needed to force the urgency of the situation on his father. They must begin to prepare, for now, there was no doubt that a war was coming.

'I must send word to the prince immediately,' Hanrik said.

'Yes. And riders to all of the citadels to let them know we have less time than we thought. Do you think the prince will send men to help us?'

'Yes. But the mobilisation of a force large enough to make a difference might take too long,' Hanrik said.

'You're right. In that case, we need to do everything we can to strengthen Luefmort. They will come straight for us when they land on our shore, so we must make every inch of our land, from the first grain on the shore to the first brick of our walls, an obstacle.'

Hanrik looked like he was pondering the idea. 'You think we should wait for a siege?'

'Broadheim was not prepared, that's why they took it so easily. We have time to be prepared, father. I saw the shores of Port Saker – the army the Order of Maledict brings is vast to say the least. I think if we meet them in the field, we will lose; they don't fear our numbers, and I can't believe I'm saying this, but I don't think they have to. By engaging them in combat, we would be needlessly sending men to slaughter, and then there would be nothing to stop them holding the key to our kingdom.'

'No force has ever defeated the Shingally army in open combat. The prince will want to fight that way, meet them head on.'

'I don't think he will. It's not wise, and they won't wait for him to arrive just so that he can have his battle. If anything, that will make them act quicker. Now that the enemy has seen us retreat, they will think we are vulnerable and expect Shingal to be theirs for the taking. We can use that to our advantage by preparing for them. We can slow them down, hurt them, and make them fear us without even swinging a sword. Please trust me, father.'

'This is the nonsense they fill your head with at the Academy of Swords?' Hanrik asked. 'You can't be taught such things. Fated or not, Danrin, combat should be fought properly.

'I don't think our enemies will be worrying about what is and isn't proper, so we shouldn't either. War is war, and this one will not be one of honour on any side.'

***

A short meeting was called to allow Danrin to tell his commanders about what had happened on the Sea of Blades. He told them that, over the next few days, preparations would be made to ensure that Luefmort was ready for any potential conflicts should the forces of the Order of Maledict make it to Shingal.

Danrin suggested that the fighting men from Keltbran be accepted into the towns forces as their own unit, a militia of sorts who would help in the effort of preparing for the siege. This notion was well received by most of the Shingally commanders.

Danrin had not been surprised, though, when he saw Captain Richel stand to argue a point. 'We should wait for the prince and then meet these heathens in the field. They will be backed against the Blades and we can slaughter them and end this,' he said. 'Not only that, I would like to take my chance with the floor to say I oppose the inclusion of foreign fighters being in our ranks. We don't know anything about them – they could be spies for all we do know.'

Danrin looked over at the table where Rowden and his captains sat. He watched on as none of them reacted to Richel's jibe, thankful for their lack of animation or emotion.

'Captain Richel, I won't justify the second part of your statement with an answer. As for the first, we do not have time to wait. Even if we did, this army that comes to our shores will not back away, not even if they are stared down by the might of every sword in our army. They have evil in their ranks, they have something driving them forwards, and retreat is not a word they are familiar with.'

'We weren't familiar with it either until you yelped it on the Blades, Danrin,' Richel said, his every word dripping with malice. 'News like that travels fast. What about the Shingal, eh?' Richel moved to the centre of the room and looked at the other commanders. 'What has happened to us? Cravens, all of us. You betray our lands and I am ashamed to call myself Shingally.'

His comments were met with jeers from his comrades, and eventually, unable to bear the brunt of the onslaught, he stormed out of the meeting. No one protested as he uttered a curse for every step until he vanished into the dark corridors of the palace.

After the meeting had finished, Danrin was walking through the palace when he heard someone call his name.

'Danrin,' Crindasa said, jogging lightly to catch him. 'I am sorry I missed the meeting.'

'No need to apologise. You didn't miss much, just war talk.'

'I was hoping to be there to let you know I want to contribute – if you need me to, that is. The academy has granted me a further three months leave, and they're keen to have at least one mage in every town, so I offered to stay here. The Assembly is concerned about everything that's happened in Broadheim and want to do all they can to stop it happening here.'

'It's not like the Tawrawth to get anxious about war,' Danrin said. 'What's changed?'

'I don't know. Principal Wallis has sent archmages to all of the citadels and authorised them to use force if they need to, as long as it is in the interest of defending the kingdom.'

In all of his years, Danrin had never heard of this happening. It was a troubling development.

'Could you try to find out why?' Danrin asked. 'I mean, I would rather not be blindsided by something if you already have connections who can give us the insight.'

'Of course,' Crindasa said. 'I have a feeling it's because of the ties to the prophecy. People have attached their name to it for years, but no one has ever made headway like this before. The fact Broadheim has fallen will have unnerved a lot of people across the kingdom.'

She was right. He thought back to the conversations he had with Ogulf and Melcun about Feda. This was all intertwined with the Onyxborn prophecy, and only now had Danrin truly linked it all up. Things seemed far graver now than they had done even moments before.

'Do you think there is truth in this prophecy?' he asked his cousin.

'As someone who practices magic, I can say that I never discredit anything I can't prove to be untrue. In this case, I can't say it is a falsehood. Not yet, at any rate.'

'And do you know much about it?'

'About the one who is promised?' she said. 'About the Onyxborn who is to take hold of all the power of the world and use it to give a ruler their platform for domination with dark magic? I know a little bit about it, yes,' Crindasa said with a wicked smile.

'I thought you might,' Danrin said, rolling his eyes. 'With all of these things there is a countermeasure, though. How do you stop it from coming to be?'

'What you are talking about now is another prophecy entirely. To beat back the darkness, you have to summon the Light of the World; only then can the battlefield be even. But both foretellings end in a gruesome battle to the death where the winner is also all but decimated, paying the price for their use of power with an outcome that is barely a victory.'

Danrin nodded, pondering what she said. 'A stalemate.'

'You could say that, but there will be a winner of sorts.'

'I have to check in with some of my men, but perhaps we could discuss this in more detail tomorrow?'

'Of course.' Crindasa smiled at Danrin. 'Oh, and my offer to help with the preparations… Consider it?'

'I will,' Danrin said as he turned to leave.

He walked through the palace doors and out towards the main square. He had not taken two steps outside when he noticed Captain Richel mounting a heavy bag onto a horse.

'I didn't think this would lead to you leaving,' Danrin said. 'What about defending your home?'

'Your father is sending me on urgent business to take a message to Drach,' Richel said. 'I just spoke with him in his chamber now and he agreed it would be best for me to take a few days to think about everything. The ride will do me good,' Richel said.

'You know we're on the same side, Richel?' Danrin said. 'All of the past grievances we've had are miniscule compared to this. You're a fierce warrior and good Shingally. I would prefer to have you here to contribute to the fight. So, hurry back.'

Danrin was being sincere. Every man counted now and Richel had his skills, that was undeniable. The defence of the city would benefit from having him present. His father asking Richel to leave made sense in a way – it removed him from the initial preparations and would let those who supported the plan focus on the details of the defence of Luefmort. Hopefully, it would also give Richel a chance to reassess his priorities.

'Perhaps when I am back, we can share an ale and bury the issues we have had. Better them in a grave than us, right?' Richel said, patting Danrin on the shoulder. 'I best be going; your father said this message was urgent.'

'Very well. Safe travels,' Danrin said.

Danrin began to walk through the square as he heard the clipping of Richel's horse going in the other direction. He liked the square after darkness had fallen. The only sounds crept from the inns and the taverns – inviting sounds of laughter, singing, and the familiar drone of collective conversation. It was quieter now, given the circumstances, but there were still the faint tones of happiness lingering in the narrow streets of Luefmort. The openness of the square along with the pleasant sounds made Danrin feel at peace. A complete contrast to the chaos he'd felt over the course of the last day. He had not had a moment like this since he returned from the capital, so he slowed his steps and savoured the walk.

His eyes found their way to his favourite inn, The Shattered Blade. He could see it not more than twenty paces away. The small window in the side of the building was open wide. As expected, the place was full of patrons. Its wooden door was light and welcoming, just like the colours that covered the building.

This was the place fighting men in Luefmort went to drink. It was also the friendliest tavern in all of the citadel. Danrin liked it for those reasons. There was no doubt that, by now, many of the patrons in The Shattered Blade would be aware of the plans and would be looking at tonight as the last opportunity for them to relax for the foreseeable future. Danrin was one of those men. With each step he took towards the tavern, he felt he could taste the mead more readily on his tongue.

Then he heard the bell, so faint at first he thought he was imagining it. Then there was another bell, its chime coming an instant after the first. This one was accompanied by shouts as the choir of bells swelled until every bell in the citadels began to sound.

Danrin spun around, listening and willing them to stop. The bells could mean only one thing at a time like this: an attack.

Danrin moved quickly through the square and the scabbard of his heavy Fated sword bounced off his right thigh as he ran. Just as he passed the palace, he heard a shout louder than all of the ringing.

'Danrin. In here!' It was Crindasa. She stood in the doorway, waving him forward.

'No, I need to go to the battlements,' he replied, slowing slightly, then stopping altogether as he realised she was crying.

'Danrin, you have to come with me,' she said, Danrin obliged, and before he knew it, he was darting through the palatial corridors, less than a pace behind her. Men running in the other direction became blurred figures, but he caught the eyes of one of them, and there was no doubt in his mind that the soldier was offering Danrin a sympathetic glance.

Crindasa led him to his father's study. Perhaps he wanted to give orders before Danrin did anything about the attack, given that they were not prepared for something like this. In reality, though, Danrin was not prepared for what had actually been the cause of the bell.

The first thing he noticed when he entered the room was the blood. The sight of the dark red puddle caused the life to go from his legs. He crumpled to his knees and looked at where it came from. His father was lying in the middle of the floor, a foot from Danrin, his pale hand clutched to his chest. Underneath his hand, his shirt was soaked crimson and his eyes were fixed on the ceiling. A trickle of blood was running from the corner of his mouth and down his cheek. Danrin's knees were wet. He was kneeling in a puddle of his father's blood.

Coherent thought evaded him as he tried to think of what to do next. He would take his horse and he would scour the forests for this coward who did this. Every time he tried to stand, though, his body refused to let him. He knelt there in the warm puddle of his father's blood and began to weep. Jarring sobs pushed their way out of his lungs, the kind that hurt your chest and steal your breath. His body wouldn't move. He felt utterly broken, and the battle hadn't even begun.

Chapter 34

Ogulf found himself suspended in the air once more, but this time, it was different. The last time this had happened, he had not been frightened straightaway. But now, as soon as he realised what was going on, every muscle in his body pulsed with terror.

The scenery had changed too. Before, he had been hovering high above the ground, looking at a mountainside citadel in all of its complex glory when flames had suddenly burst from every crevice and an army of dark red had amassed before the structure, watching on as it turned to ash. Now, he found himself hovering in a room. The stone reminded him of the basement in Luefmort, but the markings on them would not be markings found on the walls of a palace. They were primitive scrapes and scratches of symbols Ogulf didn't re-cognise. The room was lit only by the faint dash of moonlight which pushed its way through a small opening lined with iron bars. It was a cell of sorts.

Every time he turned to get a better look at the room, he found himself in pain. It shot through him like a thousand hot needles sinking into his flesh in a slow, sadistic manner. He was being tortured here.

'Worry not. No torture will take place, but please stay still. It makes my job easier and will keep you comfortable,' a voice said. It was female and coming from behind Ogulf. He recognised it instantly as the same one from the vision he'd had at his mother's tree. In spite of her warning, he tried to turn to see her and incurred the stinging wrath of the invisible needle. This time tens of thousands of them pierced every inch of his body.

'You have to listen, Ogulf. We do not have much time. Now that they have her, they will move faster. Support builds for them. They will move from the inside soon. The foundations of the prophecy are in place, and if you don't act quickly, there will be no saving him.'

'What in the name of the gods are you talking about? You speak in riddles,' Ogulf said. Even speaking caused him pain. 'Who are you?'

'It is not time for that. For now, I can only give you warnings, nothing more. Do with them what you will, but please, heed my words. Hurry.' The voice was getting quieter with every word.

'Wait, wait. Don't leave. I don't understand.'

'You're not supposed to. Just follow your path, Ogulf Harlsbane. Some of what you have seen has already come to

be. Let this warning hasten your steps,' the voice said in a whisper. The sound came from next to his left ear rather than behind him. Pushing through the pain he knew he would feel, he forced his neck left, but there was nothing there except the messy carving of a symbol on the wall. This one he recognised. He had seen it every day for the majority of his life and stared at it for hours on end trying to understand what the lines and corners of it meant. It was etched on his mother's gemstone.

As if a trapped door had opened up below him, the stone floor disappeared, and suddenly, Ogulf found himself plummeting through the darkness. At first, the rushing of the air past him was a welcome feeling, one far more pleasant than the searing needles he had felt before. This time, though, there was no ground coming towards him as he fell, only infinite darkness.

That was when he heard the shriek. It was so loud and sharp that it caused his head to throb. He was free to move and rolled in the air as he fell, looking for the source of the noise. He was expecting to see the same spectre in its crown of spikes, but he saw nothing as the shriek continued. It swept across his senses from left to right a few times before he finally felt it.

The flesh in his ribs was torn open. Something was grating across them slowly – it felt like the claws of an animal. The wound was deep, Ogulf knew that much as his body spun out of control in his freefall. Then there was another

413

shriek and something blunt hit Ogulf in the head, stupefying him and making him feel instantly groggy. He felt his eyes flicker as he continued his descent, wondering for a moment if this was how Wildar felt when he plummeted into the Banespit.

With a swinging of his arms, Ogulf forced himself awake. He greedily sucked in air like he had been submerged in water. His entire body was soaking, his undergarments were drenched, and when he looked at the sheet on the mattress, he saw that it was now stained wet with sweat.

Still gasping, he looked over to Melcun's bed, and was met only with the concerned grey eyes of his friend. Once he'd got his breathing under control, something else began to take a hold of his senses. A scorching pain across the right side of his ribcage. Looking down, he saw a line of four scars that hadn't been there when he got into bed.

'Are you all right?' Melcun asked, rubbing sleep from his tired eyes.

'I'm not sure.'

***

Ogulf had requested early that morning that he be shown the rest of the citadel. He wanted to do so for two reasons: first, he was keen to learn more about the layout of Delfmarc, he had to learn as much as he could to be able to lend a hand and contribute to its defence; and second, he wanted to keep his mind off of his vision. It was important, he knew that much, but right now, it wasn't his priority. Still, the feelings and sounds crept up on him when he tried to block them out, a nagging reminder that they were with him and wouldn't be disregarded so easily.

General Cedryk had been less than supportive of Ogulf's requested tour of the grounds, so he ordered one of his guard groups to accompany them to ensure they weren't doing anything untoward. Vellan had offered to guide them instead. Ogulf had been on that tour of the citadel with Vellan when they got news of the riders' return.

The war council that Feda had called for later that day was not going to plan. The first order of business was an update from the riders who had been sent to scout the passageway through Grendspires, the mountain range which connected the North and South of Esselonia. They were awaiting any sign of the advancing army from the South. The news they brought back to Delfmarc dampened the spirits of even the toughest men in Feda's ranks.

A sombre mood filled the room. The news was far worse than expected. A force of over seven thousand men marched through the flat relief in the mountain range and were heading straight for Delfmarc. Most were heavily armoured infantry, but there was also a host of mounted units, and Eryc himself had travelled for the battle.

And there was another piece of news, one that seemed to catch Feda by surprise. A wealthy family who were yet to declare their support for either side in the war had chosen not to involve themselves at all. The Urthdarks commanded a huge private army, one that had the potential to swing the war in favour of whomever they supported. Feda had seen hope in the fact they had not declared for the South, given the fact that the Urthdarks were Southerners, after all, and they had always aligned with Feda's father's ideals, so the princess had fully expected that they would eventually fight by her side. However, these new reports suggested that they had no intentions of declaring for either side. In fact, if the whispers were to be believed, they had called the war ludicrous and intimated that they would retreat to their private islands off the West Coast until Esselonia was at peace.

'Your uncle will try a full assault. He is too cavalier for anything other than a show of power,' General Cedryk said.

'The general is right, Your Grace,' Vellan said. 'My best advice would be to hunker down and rely on the walls, inflict casualties where we can, and delay the full assault for as long as we can. With the supplies and provisions, we can hold out for at least a year. How long until they arrive?'

'Two days at best, sir,' the rider said.

'How many men answered the banner call?' Feda asked.

'Not enough. We have two thousand fighting men at the most here,' Vellan said. Feda slammed her fist on the table and shook her head.

'We should call all of the people within the walls, arm every able-bodied person and make a stand,' Cedryk said.

'And delay an inevitable slaughter?' the princess asked. 'I am sick of being on the back foot. Everyone who is meant to come to my aid has abandoned me or died,' Feda said, presumably referring to her brother, Wildar, and now the Urthdarks. 'Is there no way we can win this battle? Is this it?' Ogulf watched as the princess seemed to process the statement, as if all she had been fighting for was for nothing. 'Maybe this cause was doomed from the start. But there must be something.

'General?' She looked at Cedryk, then turned to her betrothed. 'Vellan?'

'Short of a change in tone from the Urthdarks or aid from the Shingal, I cannot see how we can win this battle. But we can buy ourselves time in the hope that aid arrives,' Vellan said.

'Hope does not win battles,' Feda said, and with an exasperated sigh, she pounded her fist on the table again.

'Why don't we use his strength against him?' Ogulf said. He was seated at the bottom of the table in Feda's war room. He stood and moved closer to her at the other end. Near Feda and her main generals was a miniature carving of Delfmarc and its surrounding areas. Ogulf peered over people's shoulders as he tried to get a better look at it. 'What's this?' he said, pointing at part of the map.

'Hayter's gate,' Vellan said.

'And this?' Ogulf pointed at another.

'The Old Gate,' Vellan replied.

'These are the only two ways in and out of the citadel?' Ogulf asked. Vellan and General Cedryk both nodded. The latter looked displeased at Ogulf's interjection, though he had not stopped him because the princess was listening intently. 'Which is weakest?'

'This is a fortress; our walls can withstand months of siege and barrage,' Cedryk said.

'Yes, but which is weakest?'

'The Old Gate,' Vellan said. 'It's our secondary entrance, the same one I brought you in through.'

Ogulf remembered. The long narrow bridge over the moat and then the entrance. Four people wide at best. Not the kind of entrance an army would waste time getting through with the type of numbers expected from the South.

'Do they expect you to yield?' Ogulf asked, still scanning the map.

'Yes, either that or hold the siege for as long as we can,' Vellan said.

'They know you won't meet them in the field?' Ogulf said.

'Haven't we covered this already, Your Grace?' Cedryk said to the princess. She turned to look at Ogulf, impatience in her eyes.

'Get to the point, Ogulf,' the princess said, and in that moment, he was fond of her. She was sure of herself and to the point.

'We should let them into the citadel,' Ogulf said. The room erupted into noise as the Esselonian commanders voiced their vehement protests. Ogulf looked at Melcun for reassurance but his friend just stared back at him, confusion warping his furrowed brow.

'You believe we should give them the city? Surrender?' Feda said. 'I will tell you that, from all the bravado in my uncle's letters, I am disappointed to hear you tuck tail like that. Didn't you say you wanted to help? What exactly will giving them our walls do?'

Ogulf wanted this to happen. He wanted to lure these people into believing him foolish before he explained the rest of his plan. They thought him a babbling idiot. Even Feda did. But staring at this small carving of a city he had only spent a day in had already shown Ogulf exactly how they would win this battle.

'No. We let the enemy see an opportunity. But this is not one of chance. This is one we give them,' Ogulf said. A few people still uttered their disagreements. 'This gate, Hayter's Gate, is it hand powered or mechanical?' Ogulf asked.

'Mechanical,' Vellan said.

'Drop door or swing hinge?'

'Drop.'

Out of the corner of his eye, he could see the princess shifting uncomfortably in her seat, clearly questioning her decision to allow Ogulf to speak.

Ogulf smiled at her. 'Eryc is rash, yes?'

General Cedryk chuckled. 'Like even you wouldn't believe.'

'Well, in that case, consider this battle won.'

For the next hour, Ogulf spent his time talking with the various captains and commanders in Feda's guard about his proposed idea. Some points were met with backlash, but over the course of the conversation, the mood changed as Ogulf started to win them over with thorough explanations and solutions to their arguments.

At first, only Vellan saw potential in the idea. Then Feda had started to grasp the proposition and its benefits. After she fell in line, a string of others did too. As the meeting drew to a close, only General Cedryk was still opposed to the idea. That was when Ogulf revealed his final puzzle piece. General Cedryk stood and looked at the map, head tilting and mouth pursing from side to side. He traced his finger over a route through the tiny streets before nodding to himself.

'This just might work.'

Following the meeting, Princess Feda had requested a meeting with Ogulf alone. This time General Cedryk had not protested, though Ogulf was sure Vellan had looked bothered at the prospect.

The room felt different now that the tension had eased. Ogulf felt like he was about to experience the real Feda, not the princess, but the person – the one he'd seen a glimpse of when she first saw Vellan after he returned.

The four fire pits, one in each corner, lit the room and made it warm. The sun had shone brightly in Delfmarc today, but the evening was noticeably cooler, especially at the lofty heights of the princess's throne room at the top of the citadel. Ogulf was perched on the end of a bench in front of Feda's throne. She didn't sit there, though. Instead, she had placed herself on the bench across the table from Ogulf.

'Would Wildar think we could win this battle?' she asked, sipping on a cup of wine.

'Without a doubt. He taught me that you don't fight battles or wars you cannot win. If I didn't think we could win this then I wouldn't have offered my help.'

Feda laughed. 'You offered your help before you knew the odds of the fight.'

'I can win any fight,' Ogulf said. He did his best not to sound cocky because he meant what he was saying.

'Can you tell me about him? Not as a warrior, but as a person.'

The answer came easily. Of course he could talk about Wildar. He had endless stories of their time together – some good, some bad, and some not for the ears of a lady. But what didn't come easily was the horrible feeling he got in his stomach when he realised he would have to talk about him in front of Feda. He was still struggling with Wildar's death, unable to process it properly when everything else around him moved so fast. He swallowed the lump in his throat and took a deep breath.

'What would you like to know?'

'Was he a good man?' she asked.

'The best,' Ogulf responded, finding the lump lodged in his throat once more and feeling the sting of tears tease the corners of his eyes. They both looked at the table and then Ogulf began to laugh. 'There was one time we were hunting out on the plains. He was teaching Melcun and I how to use a short bow to kill a deer without ruining the meat. A thing you must understand about Wildar before I go further is that, when he hunted, he always made sure his waterskin was filled with wine, especially in the autumn and winter. He said it kept him warm. So, one time, he drinks far too much of his wine, finishing it just as we finally manage to track down a deer. He doesn't think that Melcun or I can hit this deer from the distance we were at, so he says he will show us how it's done.' Ogulf mimicked the motion of pulling back an arrow in a bow.

'He lined his shot at the deer. It hadn't noticed us as it was grazing, so we had it exactly where we wanted it. We all held our breaths as the string creaked tight, knowing this deer was going to be dinner for us and the captains. And then, just before he let that arrow go, he had the loudest hiccup I have ever heard; the arrow came off the bow at a weird angle and thudded into a tree. The deer startled and Melcun almost pissed himself with laughter. Wildar cursed and swayed the whole way home,' Ogulf said, beginning to laugh heartily. Feda offered him a sympathetic smile. 'Perhaps you had to be there,' Ogulf said, calming his laughter.

'Why are you helping me?' Feda asked.

'Because it is what Wildar wanted. That man would have done anything for me and my family, so I will do whatever I can for his.' Feda smiled. 'Do you mind if I ask you a question?'

'No, please go ahead.'

'This war. What is it all about?'

'The same thing any war is about. Power,' Feda said. 'The only difference is my Uncle Eryc seeks power to use against the people of this country, whereas what my father did and what I will do is make the people the power of our country. This isn't just my land. My title grants me leadership, but this land belongs to all of my people. Eryc wants gold, servants, castles, and enough influence to keep his rich friends happy. For him, it's about stifling the people just trying to get on with their lives.' Her eyes changed to anger. 'He wants to turn our land into a haven for him and the wealthy while the normal people suffer. He and his band of arseholes have always been like that.'

'He was Wildar's brother?' Ogulf couldn't imagine Wildar being cut from the same cloth as someone who would do this to their family.

'Oh, gods no, he wasn't an Essel. He was married to my Aunt Grayce, Wildar and my father's eldest sister. When he was wed into our family, everyone was overjoyed. Wildar would have still been here at the time. If I remember rightly, my father had a story about Wildar interrupting the ceremony in the Halls of the Gods in the capital. He started singing a particularly crude rhyme as the vows were being exchanged.' Feda laughed. 'Eryc comes from a line of Southerners who never quite accepted my family being in power. They masked it well, though, marrying off their eldest son to the daughter of the king. For a while, Eryc seemed like a true loyalist, the king's champion, but things changed after Grayce died. My father always said she kept Eryc where he needed to be and made him a better person.'

'Does Eryc blame your father for her death?'

'Not at all,' Feda said. 'A sweating sickness took her one winter, and ever since then, he has grown more and more hateful. It would be easy to say I have never liked him, but it would be a lie. There were times when I was fond of him and so was my father. However, like I said, things change.'

The two of them sat together for some time, regaling one another with stories. Feda told Ogulf about her losses in the South and why they happened. It was a land full of wealth and people looking to establish themselves in more lucrative positions. These people commanded private armies or had enough money to bribe formerly loyal soldiers to fight for their cause. Feda began to look tired as she began her story about the Urthdarks, promising to share it with Ogulf another time.

'I have something for you,' she said, rising from the bench and moving towards her throne. She opened a chest and pulled something out of it. 'It's not Solsana but it is the finest axe we have. It was my father's.'

Ogulf pulled the axe from the long velvet sack it was in. It wasn't as ornate as Solsana, but it looked just as deadly, and it was certainly far superior to his own axe. It was a relief to be given it to say the least. Ogulf had been worried about using his old axe in the battle. This would serve him better.

'I'm not deserving of this,' Ogulf said.

'You are. Besides, it's wasted here. Destined to be hung on a wall somewhere and stared at. I think it's got some use left in it and I have no use for it when I have a blade like that and Solsana at my disposal.' She motioned to the sword that sat by her throne.

'You will use it in the battle?' Ogulf said. 'Solsana, I mean?'

'No. It's not time for that yet. But I have a feeling it will be soon,' Feda said. 'Take care of your new axe.'

'I'll use it well. Thank you, Feda.'

'I bid you a good evening, Ogulf Harlsbane,' Feda said.

'Same to you, Your Grace,' Ogulf said, standing to leave. As he approached the door, he turned back to Feda, who was staring out of the window next to her throne. 'Feda.' She turned to look at him, an innocence and vulnerability in her eyes he had not seen before. 'Wildar would have loved you. In fact. I can say with the certainty of the sun rising tomorrow that he did love you. Goodnight.'

Ogulf left the room at the top of the long climb down to the main citadel. He didn't want to sleep, not yet, he wanted to smell the air before it changed tomorrow.

Chapter 35

Melcun was violently awoken by Ogulf shaking him by his shoulders.

'Get up. They've sounded the horn. Eryc is approaching.' Ogulf was already halfway dressed in his light Esselonian battle garb, his father's shoulder guard fastened securely and his two axes, the old and the new, hanging from the hooks on his back. Melcun rolled his neck and flexed his fingers while yawning. He pushed himself up on his elbows and his book slid down his chest. He had fallen asleep reading again. When Melcun began to realise this wasn't a dream, he sprung from the bed, causing Crindasa's book to slam on the floor.

'You need to get to Hayter's Gate. Vellan will meet you there,' Ogulf said before grabbing his axe and leaving the room.

Melcun was ready shortly after. He grabbed his own axe and placed the book on his dresser table before beginning a near sprint through the corridors and down the stairs into the square in the main holdfast of Delfmarc. Getting to Hayter's Gate would take some time, so he steadied his pace.

He had been told the horn meant only one thing – Eryc's army was near. With knowledge of the impending battle, he had not gotten much sleep, and his body still carried aches from yesterday's tireless tasks and his journey to get here.

He and Vellan had headed up a group of men in charge of destroying the bridge that lead up to the Old Gate, the secondary entrance into Delfmarc. Ogulf and General Cedryk eventually agreed that it would work in their favour not having the two gates vulnerable to storming, so they completely destroyed the bridge leading to the Old Gate, meaning that anyone who tried that way would need a boat and a very tall ladder to get close to scaling the walls. It also meant all defensive measures could be focused on the main entranceway at Hayter's Gate.

Ogulf made a joke about Melcun using fire again to see if his power only worked well on bridges. For a moment, he'd thought Ogulf was being serious until Cedryk had a man fetch combustibles. The bridge shattered into pieces, and the whole endeavour of destroying it took no longer than an hour.

Ogulf made a point of ensuring no one asked the citizens outside Hayter's Gate to flee into the citadel until they were instructed to do so. They were told the order would come from Vellan himself, and until he called them in, they were safe. To further quell these people, they were told there would be an attempt at a negotiation. Ogulf told Melcun he didn't want those outside the walls to know they were effectively bait. The decision wasn't weighing well on either of the men from Broadheim's consciences, but battles needed risks to reap reward.

The key to Ogulf's plan was to ensure that Eryc and his forces saw Hayter's Gate open when they approached. Ogulf wanted them to think that Delfmarc was not prepared and Cedryk advised the princess this was wise. The old general agreed the idea was dangerous beyond comprehension, but given the circumstances, and in line with the rest of the plan, it could work as a lure.

Melcun was pleased that the Esselonians had listened to Ogulf. If they had not, they would just have shut their doors and be waiting for starvation or a storming of the city walls by Eryc's forces, scenarios that would render Feda's cause as good as dead and buried.

Melcun was now approaching the gate of the Inner Circle. People were flooding through the entryway as he tried to push his way out. Already there were soldiers assembling around the gate. Ogulf would be here somewhere but Melcun didn't have time to find him.

Melcun reached the long causeway which ran from the gate of the Inner Circle all the way to Hayter's Gate in a near perfect straight line. It was wide, its sole purpose being to give the citizens enough room to hold their annual celebration to the gods. The festival was the only day such a wide space served a purpose, so when it wasn't being used, it was just an extended road with buildings on either side that led from the gatehouse entry to the inner walls of the citadel. Melcun jogged the half-mile to the gate with others streaming past him in the opposite direction.

As he passed through the throngs of people, still searching for a glimpse of Ogulf, he noticed that people were flooding through Hayter's Gate. Vellan must have given the signal already. Melcun quickened his pace to a sprint. He was late. People took up most of the causeway as they headed towards the Inner Circle. Not only the ones coming through the gate, but also the residents coming from the houses and buildings in the Outer Circle. They had all been instructed to abandon their homes and move to the protection of the interior fortifications.

Ogulf didn't want any innocent people being slaughtered when Eryc's forces eventually made it into the citadel and Princess Feda had agreed; she turned the request into a decree to make it enforceable.

Even though this chaos was intentional, it slowed Melcun down. He cursed Ogulf for having such a complex plan, then remembered what Wildar used to say, *battles and wars couldn't be won by men and women with simple minds.*

Eventually, he reached Hayter's Gate and scaled the ladder that was waiting for him. There were no stairs up to the battlements at the gate for safety reasons, a feature Melcun was sure had its benefits, but right now, as his arms and legs ached with every rung he gained, he found himself wishing desperately for stairs. The only way up was either the stairway on the opposite side of the citadel or by ladder. As he hoisted himself over the edge of the battlement, Vellan stretched out a hand to help him.

'I thought you had changed your mind, sorcerer,' Vellan said, smiling at him.

'I couldn't trust you with a task like this, now, could I, paladin?' Melcun said. Vellan wasn't like the other men in Feda's council, speaking with him made Melcun feel like he was at home.

The pair pulled the ladder up. It was much heavier than it looked. They might need it if they had to get down quickly and didn't have time to get around to the other side along the battlements.

Above the portcullis at Hayter's Gate was a stone gate tower where the lifting mechanism for the entrance was housed. It was dark, and other than the lever for the gate and three thick iron bars, there wasn't much else in the room. The only lighting was the sunshine which streamed in through the three turret windows, each a foot tall and a few inches across.

'They're here?' Melcun said, looking through one turret while Vellan watched through another.

'Oh, by the gods they are. Seven thousand of them at least. Mostly foot soldiers, some heavy horse,' Vellan said. Melcun could see some of them through the rectangular gap in the bricks. 'They're forming up. And as expected, the bastard himself has made the trip. Those knights all in black, then the one in silver near the back, that's Eryc and his guards.'

Melcun couldn't see everything through the opening, but what he could see made his skin prickle and his stomach churn. On the open field in front of Delfmarc, only two hundred or so yards away, were droves of fighting men. Behind the rows of infantry were four smaller columns of what looked like cavalry and then the king's guard. The men at the front formed a huge line that looked at least fifty bodies deep and well over two hundred wide. They stood perfectly still, sunlight glinting off their armour.

'They wait to see if we surrender,' Vellan said. 'Soon, if Eryc is still the overconfident weasel I remember, he will realise the gate has been open for too long.'

Melcun glanced down, seeing the last few citizens scrambling into the citadel, their screams audible as they passed underneath the gate tower. Ogulf had told Melcun and Vellan that this point was crucial. Eventually, the enemy would make a move, but it would take a showing from Melcun and Ogulf to draw them in.

'How long should we wait? We need to give them a chance to get inside the Inner Circle,' Melcun said as the slapping of footsteps passed underneath them in an anxious patter that was directed towards the citadel.

'They will finish forming up shortly, that should give enough time. Eryc will want to make a show of his numbers, he knows Feda is watching from somewhere,' Vellan said.

A tense minute passed. Despite remaining completely still, Melcun felt sweat drip down his face as he waited. The citizens should be through the Inner Gate and safe now. It was time. He took one last glance at the armies in the field beyond the walls before sighing and looking to Vellan.

'Let's see if this plan works, then, shall we?'

Both men stood near the wheel that held the gate. Vellan was staring at it, clearly unsure of how the next part would play out. Melcun gave him a nod and he unleashed the latch, causing the holding wheel for the gate to spin to life quickly, lowering the huge door of Hayter's Gate.

Pulling with everything he had, Melcun stopped the wheel with his power. It was unbelievably heavy. He clenched his jaw and tightened his core as he strained to hold it in place. While he was doing this, Vellan was in the process of slotting the huge iron bar in the rungs of the wheel to jam it. Once Melcun felt the bar taking some of the weight off of him, he gently eased it down to rest on the bar completely. It shifted slightly as it fitted into its resting place and then the wheel stayed steady.

'By the gods, please let that hold,' Melcun said.

'The gods can't help us now, Melcun; this is up to us.'

If they had done this properly, it would have meant that the gate stopped around halfway from the ground, leaving plenty of space for people to get under it. Both men glanced out of the turrets. The enemy had noticed what had happened and were looking at the gatehouse, glancing side to side as the opportunity became visible.

The next part seemed comical. Vellan and Melcun were to rattle the iron bars together. The loud noise would make it seem like they were trying to free the wheel and lower the gate. This would create a sense of urgency and make it look like a mistake. They got to work swinging the thick bars into one another, creating a clang that was deafening within the small walls of the gatehouse. To add to the effect, Vellan even shouted out, 'It's stuck, it's stuck!' followed by, 'Run!', before dropping the iron poles to create another metallic ringing. Such a parody didn't feel right in the tenseness of the moment, but it was necessary.

They couldn't show their faces at the turrets after that – it was an unnecessary risk to break their façade, which so far seemed to be working. All they had to do now was wait to see if Eryc's force took the bait.

There was a silence that felt like it lasted an age. The only sound was the chirping of birds nearby. It felt like all of Esselonia accompanied Melcun in holding its breath, waiting for someone to make the next move. At first there was a distant rumble, then it grew louder, and closer. Eventually, it was just over the stone bridge of Hayter's Gate. The sound then travelled underneath them, in and away from them as

Eryc's forces stormed the castle. They'd taken the bait – Ogulf's plan was working.

Melcun watched as Vellan scurried up and looked out of the window, keeping as much of himself hidden as possible.

'Eryc is too bold for his own good, that brazen nature will be the death of him, in this war or the next. Droves are coming through – not all of them, but a good amount. Let's just hope Ogulf is ready over there.'

Melcun went to the other side of the gatehouse. There was one turret there which faced into the city. He could see the mass of men running up the causeway towards the gate to the Inner Circle. They must have thought this was a route. More and more bodies were passing through Hayter's Gate, and eventually, the whole causeway all but disappeared with the sheer volume of the enemy coming through.

They were almost at the Inner Circle gate now. Melcun squinted as the sun's reflection bounced off something and distracted him. The group nearest the gate were holding metal coverings over their heads. They must have known they would meet some resistance. Melcun looked up, noticing that just as Eryc's forces reached the gate to the Inner Circle, Ogulf was signalling for the archers on the battlements above the causeway to fire their arrows.

Melcun tried to calm himself. This was only the beginning of what would undoubtedly be a battle to remember.

Chapter 36

Though it wasn't close to being breached, the fortifications around the main entrance to the Inner Circle of Delfmarc were being ferociously attacked by South Esselonian forces.

From the battlements, those loyal to Feda's cause rained arrows down on their attackers as they tried to break through the door. The arrows were rendered useless for the most part; the long sheets of thick metal Eryc's forces held over their heads deflected all but a few of the bolts and now the metal shields were littered with a layer of spent missiles.

Ogulf looked down from the battlements. His eyes crept towards the far reaches of the Outer Circle. Southern forces were still making their way onto the main causeway. In some ways, this was going to plan. In others, it wasn't. Fires were popping up all around the perimeter, but the huge door below him was staying true, even as the Southern forces battered it with whatever they had in their hands. From the dull thuds, Ogulf assumed they had some kind of battering ram.

Ogulf hadn't expected the coverings they used to protect themselves. He instructed the archers to keep firing, to find the gaps in the covering or focus their arrows on those still coming up the causeway.

He looked at the attackers. They all had uniform armour consisting of identical bracers, dark grey helmets that left only their eyes showing, leather gambesons and trousers, and grey plated boots. Each seemed to carry a different weapon – he saw maces, morning stars, swords, spears, and axes all made in the same dark grey hue of their armour.

He still had time to turn the tide of the battle back in the favour of Feda's forces, even as the ram thundered against the door below him. Ogulf turned to the other side of the battlement and glanced down at the calculated brutality lying in wait for whatever came through that huge door when it eventually gave way. Positioned in front of and to either flank of the huge door was a battalion of North Esselonian men.

Ogulf had seen his father use the same tactic during the Summer of Rebellion. It had not been on a scale like this, but its effectiveness made all the difference in the battle at the time. If it worked here, they could deal a significant blow to the power and numbers of Eryc's forces. More importantly, the sheer ferocity of it would hopefully rattle the resolve of the sieging forces.

After a few more thunderous cracks of the battering ram against the Inner Circle door, something finally gave way and there was a sudden surge from the South Esselonian warriors below as they managed to push through. Ogulf ran to the battlement with his hand raised, ready to give the signal. He was running from side to side on the battlement to glance at what was happening on either side, waiting for the perfect moment. His right hand staying high the whole time, willing his allies waiting in the square to hold.

The battalion of Feda's forces had the Inner Circle's entrance gate surrounded – now they would see if Ogulf's plan could work.

The first row of the battalion were manning siege weapons all diagonally pointed at the entrance gate. Each side was lined with three ballistas and two scorpions. The weapons had been crudely reworked to fire malicious projectiles over a short distance. Some were loaded with buckets full of metal shards, all twisted and sharp, while others were packed with stone or steel balls. Perhaps the most dangerous of all were the two scorpions closest to the gateway; they were going to fire pieces of discarded sword blades at the oncoming South Esselonians. All of the weapons were ready to fire as soon as Ogulf gave the signal.

Ogulf glanced around, looking for General Cedryk. His hand was high and his palm was open as he waited and waited. Cries came from below as some of the shots from the battlements struck true on those attacking the city. The metal coverings the attacking forces were utilising had become less of a priority as the Southern forces noticed how close they were to breaking through the huge door. The ram they concealed under the metal sheets was still pounding at the door, turning the splinters into a proper opening with their next few thrusts.

Down in the square, the first few warriors began to push into the opening. As they forced their way through, Ogulf watched their steps slow and postures change, their adrenaline seeming to turn to dread as they saw what awaited them. Some fanned out to the sides in defensive stances, glancing back eagerly over their shoulders, waiting for their comrades to join them. Some seemed to halt entirely, looking for a second like they might turn back.

Wanting to cause a choke and a panic, Ogulf and General Cedryk had made sure there was nowhere for them to turn but back the way they had come. To the immediate left and right of the door were sharpened wooden structures. Although they were not sharp enough to slice through skin on their own, they certainly looked menacing enough, and their jagged ends would cause wounding if someone were to be forced against them. They acted as a deterrent – and a good one at that. As the cautious attackers skirted around them, more bodies spilled through the gateway and into the square as the shattered holes in the door got larger.

The reluctance of those at the front of the gate had meant that only a trickle of South Esselonian warriors made it through at a time. They pushed past those in front before succumbing to the same realisation as the ones who already made it through. They were stared down by the loaded weapons and none seemed willing to charge forward. Some tried to call out to those behind to hold them, but the ruckus was too loud for the sound to travel.

Ogulf gave one more look to the outside of the gate. The metal shields were all but ineffective now as the South Esselonian forces surged towards the door all the way from the main entrance at Hayter's Gate. Ogulf could see a crush starting and he heard one of Feda's captains on the wall telling his archers to fire at will.

He darted back to the other side and made eye contact with General Cedryk down on the other side. He threw his hand down.

'Now!' he cried. He didn't think Cedryk would hear him, but he felt he had to cry out anyway. At the same time, he reached for a lit torch and began waving it to signal to Melcun. With an audible clang, Hayter's Gate slammed shut; Ogulf needed to have the attackers trapped if he wanted the next phase to work. He saw the huge entrance to the citadel crash from the position it was stuck in. Some of the attacking men trying to get in were turned to piles of gore after being caught under it as it fell.

The huge wooden door of the inner circle had intentionally been pulled inwards to allow for the opposing forces to get through. Ogulf had waited to give the signal until he was sure those trying to break through were on the verge of a crush, the attackers pushing through running into the backs of those struck with the projectiles. When the doors swung open, there was a chorus of metal crashing into metal as the surge pressure eased and the South Esselonians crashed into one another again.

Ogulf turned to see Cedryk call out to his men. The sound of his shout did not reach Ogulf, but the ferocity in Cedryk's eyes was clear to see. The clinking and mechanisms underneath Ogulf cut through the flurry of noise from the rest of the scene. He heard a bolt ricochet off of something, a chorus of gurgling screams, and cheers from the defending forces in the square.

Though he couldn't see it, Ogulf could hear the gasping cries of men underneath the battlement as they were crushed by their compatriots forcing their way through the gateway. The arrows from the battlements continued to rain down on the confused attackers as the bodies began to pile up – the crushed eventually being covered by the punctured. Ogulf gave orders for the men on the battlements to focus on the forces coming up the causeway now, hoping the arrows would slow them down enough for Cedryk's forces to deal with the ones close by and storming the now gaping entranceway.

On the other side of the battlements, in the square, General Cedryk's second group were waiting to fire their wave of missiles at the oncoming enemies. Ogulf looked down just in time to see the crude shards of death cutting the attacking men at the front of the warband to pieces. Some of the projectiles went through two or even three targets before coming to rest in the torn flesh of another.

The next row of the battalion now stepped forward – at least one hundred of them from the count of Ogulf's eye. They all had their bows drawn and trained sure-handedly on the entranceway, while some of the larger men had their spears shouldered and ready. The only sound that filled the air was the hiss of the arrows from the battlements. Ogulf made sure to tell them not to let up; they had to slow those coming up the causeway. He had two teams delivering staggered volleys of arrows to keep the constant stream of arrows raining down on the attackers.

General Cedryk gave another shout and the arrows and spears from his men were released with a high-pitched whistle at their targets in the entrance square with menacing precision. A group of simultaneous thuds followed as the weapons hit their marks. Ogulf glanced from one side to the other to make sure that the plan was still going as it should.

The initial wave force of the attackers had been all but decimated. They were now blocked into the citadel without a way of getting out. Phase three of Ogulf's plan was about to be tested as more Southern fighting men made their charge up the main causeway, bearing down on the gate to the Inner Circle. Their numbers meant that the constant peppering of arrows from the battlements didn't hinder all of the attacking forces bounding up the road. This was where the gamble had the worst odds.

A new shout came from behind Ogulf down in the Inner Circle. The last row of General Cedryk's battalion were charging at the rest of the attackers, bows no longer their weapons of choice. Now, each was armed with their blades and ready to fight to the death for Feda. Those attackers who were lucky enough to be missed by the arrows would be hacked down fiercely with axe and sword.

By now, some of the South Esselonian forces were moving back from the gate. Seeing no way to pass the mountain of bodies in their path, they looked to be regrouping, and some took hold of discarded metal coverings to use as protection from the onslaught of arrows still coming down from the battlements. Ogulf looked as a band of men, including General Cedryk, cut their way through the remaining attackers, climbing over battered, fractured, and carved up bodies as they did.

Despite some of the Southern forces turning back, there was still a large group pushing forward undeterred. The armour they wore was thicker than that of their compatriots. It was a gleaming black and looked like it swirled as the sunlight caught its edges. The man leading the group was filled with rage as he waded through those who fled.

'Cedryk!' he shouted. 'Cedryk, you old bastard, come and face me.'

The man's helmet was donned with the twisted horns of a ram. He did not slow as he walked through the chaotic melee. Arrows were landing not far from him, but his resolve never faltered. He let a long, wide blade hang in his left hand and a spiked club dangle from his right.

'Cedryk! Before this is over, I will have my chance to end you. No one touches Feda's pet before I have had my chance.'

Eventually, the man stopped just short of where the packed bodies were lying. Riddled with arrows from the battlements, the pile of corpses looked like a giant hedgehog. Ogulf saw General Cedryk approach, his long blade readied and already dripping with blood, the usual regal demeanour he possessed replaced with a scowl of bared teeth and malicious intent.

Ogulf noticed that Hayter's Gate was still shut. He could only imagine the confusion on the other side of it. He expected Vellan and Melcun to appear at the gate of the Inner Circle any moment – he just prayed they weren't cut off on the way back. Vellan said he could navigate the streets without being near the causeway and rendezvous with the main force to join the push back attack.

Watching the causeway, its wide road still full of enemies making their way towards the gate, Ogulf wavered slightly when he saw just how many men they were still up against. Cedryk, Vellan, Feda, and her advisors had not been wrong when they said Eryc would send his full might. By how little he could see of the wide causeway, Eryc had sent a minimum of three quarters of his entire army through the gates when he was presented with the opportunity to attack.

Because of that, the fight was much harder for the forces loyal to Feda. They would continue to tire as they chopped down enemies and made their stand, but fresh enemy warriors would be on top of them after every sword stroke.

Once again, he heard the man in black shouting for General Cedryk. He darted to the pathway of the battlement and down the stairs to the gateway. His foot plunged into a puddle of blood. He stumbled over the obliterated bodies and through the gateway towards the causeway. He had to scurry over a pile of men barely clinging to life. They groaned as he stepped on them.

As he got over the mound of fallen warriors, he saw that General Cedryk was already in combat with the man who called on him. The soldiers immediately around them were not fighting. They had encircled the two men and were cheering on their respective leader.

'Who is that man?' Ogulf asked, pulling on the shoulder of the nearest man loyal to Feda.

'That's the Grim Knight, Steryn Wyndmyre – Eryc's brother.'

Ogulf watched as the two men swung their blades at one another. Cedryk's broadsword moved through the air like it was a practice weapon. He moved with showings of grace and power that defied his age and had the Grim Knight on a back foot. The Grim Knight was a large man like Cedryk. His blade and spiked club were like extensions of his body as he spun, crouched, and parried away attacks from his older opponent.

Then, with a flurry of forward attacks, the younger man made a furious swing for General Cedryk. All of the shots were aimed at his face or neck. The general continued to sweep them out of the way with his sword until he missed one, but managed to parry it away with his fist, which was protected by a thick, metal gauntlet.

The Grim Knight backed away by a few paces and began to circle. His weapons now hung by his sides. Cedryk was breathing heavily as he reset his footing, holding his blade sideways in front of him with two hands, waiting on his opponent to move again.

'I made Eryc promise me I could have you,' the Grim Knight said, swirling the blade in his left hand as he moved. 'Twenty years I've waited for this. Twenty years I have promised my blade it could taste you.'

'You still hold me to blame for you not becoming a paladin?' Cedryk said. His blade stayed true across his body. 'You only have yourself to blame for that, Steryn.'

The Grim Knight aimed two savage swipes at the general. Both were parried with ease. The general pivoted and they separated again.

'Wrong, old man,' Steryn, the Grim Knight said. 'You sent me to the dungeons. You cast me to the pits and left me to rot.'

'Anyone would have after knowing what you did with your black magic. I knew it was a false promise you made when the king released you. I knew it all along. Your heart will always be black, Steryn – even after I rip it from you.' This time, Cedryk pressed forward to make an attack, which Steryn caught with his weapons crossed and swung away from his body. The flurry of blows continued as Cedryk moved towards his opponent who manoeuvred away from the heavy shots. Neither man was able to gain the upper hand in the fight.

Ogulf realised that some men around them had resumed fighting. The forces loyal to Feda were making ground against their opponents again, but they were tiring quickly, just as he expected. He decided to turn away from the single combat and unsheathed his new axe. He wasn't a fan of close quarters fighting but he moved through his opponents, trying to land a killing blow on at least every second one. Parrying with the axe he had been given by Feda had been much easier than it would have been with his old weapon. It wasn't Solsana, but this weapon was incredible.

As he swung the axe in the melee, he barely noticed it catching on the limbs of his opponents as it glided through their flesh. Another body crashed into his, sending him tumbling to the floor. As he rolled over, a heavy boot met his ribs, causing him to tumble again. His eyes went up, looking for the source, and cutting through the sun's outline, he saw a blade coming towards his face. It would surely split him in half. He tried to get his axe in front of him to parry, but the swing was coming down with such force, he wasn't sure it would work. He tried as best as he could not to close his eyes.

Then he heard the metallic crash blades make when they collide. He looked up to see Vellan blocking the shot from his adversary. Then it was Melcun's axe, swinging in from the right side, catching the attacker in the throat. Ogulf was helped to his feet, and when he regained them, he noticed that all of the men who had been firing arrows from the battlements had now moved down to join the fray in front of the entranceway. The numbers were still against them, but Ogulf was sure that seeing General Cedryk fighting one of the enemy commanders had rallied the men for now.

The next few minutes were a tiresome affair as Ogulf swung, stumbled, and sweated his way through the close combat. He had small cuts all over his body from where swords around him had caught him, nicking at his skin. He wasn't even the intended target of the strikes, and he was sure some of them were from fighters on his side. The whole top of the causeway was a sea of flailing weapons.

An armoured hand stuck Ogulf's nose. On impact, it cracked, and Ogulf felt it twist. Warm blood started to stream down his face as he spun, dazed from the blow.

Ogulf couldn't be sure, but he occasionally heard shouts which sounded like the Grim Knight and Cedryk, which meant their fight was still ongoing. Then he heard a cry that was definitely Vellan – he couldn't see the man, but the shout suggested he was close.

'Feda… Feda!' he heard Vellan shouting. At first, he assumed it was the dying cries of a man in love. Then he noticed Vellan standing on a cart next to the huge walls of the Inner Circle. His head was moving, his eyes following something. Ogulf turned to see what Vellan was focusing on and his heart sank when he realised.

Feda was sprinting along the battlements of the Outer Circle. She was far away, but between the flowing hair and the armour she wore, there could be no doubt as to who it was. She carried the sword in her hand as she ran and paid no mind to anything around her. She was covering the ground quickly, and the only place this led to was where the wall circled to meet Hayter's Gate at the main entrance to Delfmarc.

Vellan jumped down from the cart and Ogulf lost him in the mass of bodies. He could tell that Vellan was heading away from him, though, as the shouts of Feda's name got more and more distant.

Then he heard another barrage of noises. First a cheer, then an exhausted grunt. He didn't say a single word, but the grunt alone was enough to confirm this was Cedryk. Ogulf spotted a few men in enemy armour with their arms raised, cheering on their commander as he fought. The Northmen around them were too focused on fighting to keep their eyes on the showing of prowess from the two behemoths. Ogulf waded through the bodies, dodging a jutting spear and slicing at the kidneys of an opponent along the way.

'Are you tired now, Cedryk?' The Grim Knight was circling the older general, occasionally swinging light stabs or hacks with his sword, taunting his rival. 'I wish I got you in your prime. Doesn't feel right taking the life of someone so close to the grave, but I'll take the satisfaction it gives me. Come on, you old, fat shit.'

Cedryk was wheezing, outmanoeuvred by the Grim Knight, but still doing his best to fight on. Ogulf had so much admiration for the man. Even if, at first, he was less than pleasant, he was a man of valour. In one mind, Ogulf considered aiding the General and fighting the Grim Knight himself, but doing so would only taint Cedryk's honour.

'You son of a fool,' Cedryk said, spitting on the floor as he parried the tormenting attacks. 'I'd already be wiping your guts off my blade if I got you in my day. And even if it takes longer than I would like, I'll still be doing it today.'

With a burst of energy that seemed to explode from the balls of his feet, the general pushed forward, deflecting two of the shots from the Grim Knight with his shield which he held high as he rammed the chest of his enemy, causing him to stumble backwards. With a furious flurry of swings, Cedryk hacked at the flailing body of the Grim Knight as he tried to regain his footing. Ogulf watched as a lick of the general's blade left a huge gash that ran down his rivals forearm, and the Grim Knight cried out as the blade cut through his skin with ease.

Cedryk's onslaught continued as he swung at the Grim Knight, who had just recovered his position and was handling the shots with ease as blood trickled down his wrist. As if the general had used everything he had, he started to fade again, and the swings he tried became laboured and slow, meaning they were easier for his opponent to deal with. Eventually, they petered out until they were nothing more than empty attacks that wouldn't do more than graze the skin if they struck true.

'Oh, enough of this shit,' the Grim Knight said. With a downward swing, he sank his spiked club into the general's thigh. With a groan, Cedryk fell to one knee, the disgusting weapon still lodged deep in his leg. Ogulf fought against his urge to aid his ally as he watched him breathing heavily with tired eyes. His shield slipped from his grasp, though the fingers of his sword hand remained tightly wrapped around its handle.

Slowly and methodically, the Grim Knight took one step forward and slid the tip of his blade into Cedryk's throat. Almost instantly, the general began spouting blood like a tap from his mouth, a dribble first and then a flow of thick red liquid. His eyes still looked tired, even as the Grim Knight carefully slid the weapon deeper. Ogulf watched the Grim Knight staring down at Cedryk as if he wanted to see if he could see something change in the general when life finally left him. With a kick to Cedryk's chest, he slid his victim from his blade, spitting on the general's lifeless body as soon as it hit the ground.

Cedryk had fallen and the Grim Knight had won.

Spurred on by the victory, Eryc's forces began to hack down at their opponents, and within seconds, they had the advantage. Feda's forces were being driven back towards the pile of bodies in the gateway to the Inner Circle.

Ogulf looked up to the battlements at the side again and now he could see Vellan up there too. The man was quite a distance away from Feda, who had just reached the main fortified area of Hayter's Gate where the gate levers were. Suddenly the huge gate, its bottom covered in the smashed parts of the men it crushed, began to rise up, opening the entrance to Delfmarc.

Had she turned on them? Was she going to surrender the city? Had that always been her plan, to set up a slaughter of those loyal to her to hand her uncle the power on a platter? Ogulf felt sick as his mind raced through the possibilities. Had his tactics helped orchestrate the death of all of these men? He would surely die if that gate opened and the rest of Eryc's forces made their way through. So would Melcun. *Would Wildar have been so foolish?* It would have been worse if Wildar got here – more Keltbran would have followed him and been slaughtered for nothing. And he had given her the axe. She had Solsana.

Ogulf was parrying furious shots from opponents as he found Melcun, struggling to keep the brutal shots at bay and bleeding from a deep gash in his bicep. Ogulf gave a fleeting thought to the idea of asking Melcun to use his powers, but too many of their own forces would get caught in the fireball – most likely including Ogulf. It seemed far too reckless.

His eyes traced down the causeway as he tried to catch a glance of what was happening in front of them. The gate was pulled high, leaving the gaping entrance open for the rest of Eryc's battle-fresh forces to make their way in. Within seconds, the mouth of the gate was filled with shapes moving at an incredible pace. Eryc had sent his mounted forces in to finish the job. The battle would be over in minutes; Ogulf and those around him would be trampled into the stones of the citadel and crushed under the hooves of the dark mounts.

Some of Eryc's forces cheered as they noticed the reinforcements speeding towards them. Others didn't stop with their onslaught, already swinging their weapons, drunk on blood and ready for the killing spree that awaited them as they hacked and stabbed their way to victory.

Ogulf found himself standing on the mound of bodies from the initial assault as they were being pushed back. He noticed some of Eryc's forces falling to the ground as the mounted unit passed. Ogulf assumed they were accidents of war and a further confirmation that Eryc favoured brutal force over everything else as he let his forces trample their own men on the way to victory. But this kept happening, and as the horsemen got closer to them on the causeway, Ogulf noticed these forces were not accidentally striking at the men in front of them, they were doing it intentionally.

Confusion spread like wildfire in a dry brush. Those loyal to Eryc realised something was wrong as blood curdling screams came from behind them.

The men in front of Ogulf began to swing frantically, encouraged by the fear on the faces of their opponents. Ogulf joined them and began to hack at the enemy where he could.

One of the riders pushed through, close to the front of the gate to the Inner Circle. His horse was huge. He rained down shattering blows with a morning star. One swing caved in two enemy skulls, turning the first to pulp before it was embedded momentarily in another.

'It's the prince,' one of the men said as he punched his sword forward at his enemy. 'We are saved, the prince is here.'

'Keep fighting, we have reinforcements!' Ogulf said, his heart swelling with hope.

The men around Ogulf fought with a kind of might he had never seen before. It was as if they had rested and feasted for days in the seconds that had passed since they realised who had come to their aid. Ogulf himself felt rejuvenated, gaining more and more energy every time his axe sunk into the flesh of an adversary as if the weapon leeched the life of its victims.

He stepped back, letting the men of Esselonia finish the job as they gradually thinned the enemy line until it was nothing more than a twitching pile of flesh and bone.

His breath finally came back to him as he looked down the causeway and to the battlements at Hayter's Gate. There he saw Feda and Vellan both thrust their weapons into the air in triumph. As Eryc's forces scrambled and fell victim to the blades of her men the beautiful edge and glass of Solsana danced in the sunlight. Feda had not betrayed them. She had saved them. Her bravery to run round the battlements herself to ensure the battle was won reminded him of the type of courage Wildar showed. She had been cut from the same cloth as the old chieftain after all.

Chapter 37

Ogulf and Melcun sat on the battlements above the Inner Circle gateway, Ogulf's nose
was throbbing. They were both silently staring at the causeway as the citizens of Delfmarc began moving their dead. The streets were a horrible dark crimson, and the smell of death hung in air underneath the afternoon sun.

Ogulf ran his eyes along the Grendspires. The huge peaks were hidden slightly, the tips of the mountains wrapped snugly about with thick, grey clouds.

'Looks like rain,' Ogulf said, his eyes fixed and still on the swirling cloud.

'Might be a good thing, the streets could do with a cleanse,' Melcun said.

'I didn't think it would rain here,' Ogulf said.

'It rains everywhere. I know Wildar thought this was a paradise, but it's just like everywhere else, isn't it?'

A scream forced Ogulf's eyes away from the clouds and down to the causeway. There was a woman kneeling on the cobblestones, cradling the head of a fallen soldier on her thighs. One hand covered her horrified mouth, and with the other, she stroked his hair and tried to wipe the dried blood off his face. Ogulf looked on, just glad the dead man's eyes were shut.

'You're right. I don't think there is such a thing as a peaceful life.'

'Certainly not now, anyway. I just wish there was something I could do, this all feels ...' Melcun shook his head. Ogulf watched as his eyes were drawn to the weeping woman. '... Bigger than us.'

'I've felt that since before we left Broadheim, as if something was laying the path for me. Did you ever stop believing in the gods?'

'I don't think I stopped believing, but for a while, I didn't feel them close to me. I feel something now, though. It's different to what I felt before. It might just be a change as I learn more about what I can do,' Melcun said.

'It might be. I thought the gods abandoned me when I chose to leave Keltbran, but it's like they've found me again since.'

'Your father would be glad to hear you say that,' Melcun said.

'I know he will, and I can only hope he feels the same.'

'So, what now?' Melcun said, dusting his trousers down.

'Well, now we get Feda to save us somehow.'

'Still no idea how?' Melcun asked, pulling his lips to the side.

'Not in the slightest. But I am hoping she has some idea – and now that she has the axe, who knows what she has to do to call on its powers. I suppose we should start as soon as we can. And you, what's next, o wise sorcerer?' Ogulf did his best to let a jovial tone carry in his words but he knew deep down the words sounded as dead as the corpses below him looked.

'Find out how I get stronger to stop this–' He gestured towards the carnage of the causeway. '–From happening again.'

Just as Ogulf opened his mouth to speak, a call came from under them. It came from a young boy, who could have been no older than fifteen. His hair was stuck to his forehead and he had bloodstains on his cheeks. He was smiling. 'We've caught him. We've caught Eryc!' he shouted. 'Gods be good, we've caught the traitor.'

'Let's go to Feda,' Ogulf said. Melcun nodded.

Both men meandered down the steps. Ogulf felt his knee crack every time he moved it, and his blocked, broken nose was making it more difficult for him to breathe. He had missed the aches that followed a battle, that was something he wouldn't deny, but at the same time, he didn't hadn't felt the sting like this before; his body felt defeated, not victorious.

Wincing down the steps, he looked at the dead strewn across the cobbles at the Inner Circle gate. There would be many more scenes like this in the days, weeks, and months ahead. For now, he had to rest and focus on the most important part of the journey, finding out how to save the realm from the Onyxborn and the Order of Maledict.

Chapter 38

King Nadreth had not moved from Nevea's bedside for the last three days. Almost immediately after the incredible showing of strength on the beach of Port Saker, she had fallen into a deep sleep. The physicians had said she was stable, but Nadreth wanted to be around her, to ensure her safety and to pray to Loken that she would recover.

The men of Nadreth's army had still been cheering when the young sorceress fell to her knees. He had caught her and carried her to his tent. One of his confidants, an old mystic named Baliq, said this was commonplace for a mage to be weakened after a feat of strength like that. She didn't have a Peak of Influence to draw from, so her internal power had all but been expended. If she had used any more power, she might have died.

The king received regular updates from General Hassit while he kept vigil at Nevea's bedside. The production of the ships was moving faster than they had expected. The men were spurred on by the sorceress's sinking of the enemy boats on the Blades. More and more men had also found their way to Port Saker. Their full force had almost arrived and there were enough men to overthrow the world twice over. It would take a number of trips to transport them all to the Shingal, but that was a risk they would be willing to take.

Nadreth watched as Nevea's chest rose and fell slowly. What she had done had been truly incredible – it was more power than he could have dreamed of and it had not even been a slither of what she would be capable of once the prophecy was fulfilled.

The sound outside the tent was a mixture of hammer falls, shouts, and wind. The weather had been kind to them today, and though it was far from warm, the bite of the cold was nowhere to be felt. Breaking through the usual chorus of sounds, Nadreth heard footsteps pacing towards his tent from outside. He had held council with General Hassit no more than half an hour before and told his man not to disturb him unless absolutely necessary. Agitation grew inside Nadreth as the steps drew closer.

'My king.' It was General Hassit.

'I told you I was not to be disturbed.'

'Apologies, my king, but we have discovered a Shingally soldier. He has requested an audience with you.'

'Have they attempted to cross the Blades?'

'No, my lord, this one came alone on a rowboat.'

'Bring him in.'

Nadreth watched as the flaps of his tent opened and the man was dragged in, the arm of a brawny Order soldier hooked through each of his. The man's hands were tied with rope. He was unassuming, not tall and rather homely looking, but the size of the hawk emblem on his chest suggested he was an officer in the Shingally army. First, his eyes went to Nadreth, and then they went to Nevea, sleeping on the bed.

'You requested an audience with me. We are not accepting surrenders, so make this quick and I will request the same of my axeman. Waste my time, and I will see to it you die one month from now but feel pain every second until then,' Nadreth said. The man's eyes snapped back to the king's.

'I do not wish to surrender,' the man said.

'With that, you have earned yourself a quick death,' Nadreth said, turning back to Nevea. The men began to restrain him and turn him toward the flaps to leave the tent.

'My king.' He fought against the men trying to turn him away and to the outside. The king looked at the man, nodding slightly to indicate he would listen. The strong soldiers straightened the man in front of Nadreth. 'It is an honour to meet you. My name is Lixan Richel. I am a captain in the army of the Shingally Kingdom. I wish to defect and pledge allegiance to your cause.'

Acknowledgements

To my incredible wife - You read this novel even though you didn't have to, you supported me more than I can say and without you this would have never happened.

To my beta readers - Sean, Duncan, Callum and Simon. Thank you for helping me find the confidence in this story, for your suggestions on tweaks and for telling me the bits that were garbage. Oh, and don't forget pointing out all the typos.

To Duncan Fyfe - you helped me bring my world to life in one piece of art. Without you, characters like Ogulf and the Grim Knight wouldn't exist the way they do.

To my family - your encouragement means everything.

To my Papa Kenzie - Thanks for showing me just how great books can be.

To Scott - you helped me turn my life around, without those first steps I never would have come so far.

To Cherie - You took my baseless idea and turned it into the cover, I am eternally grateful.

To Kits - Thanks for making my words good and polishing what was definitely a turd.

To Jordan and Chris Byrne - Thanks for helping me get Gelenea on the map...

To Stu and Ryan - Your contributions and influences set the first flame.

To everyone else who has supported me, a man on a journey to write a story, thank you.

About D.W. Ross

I wish I could talk about my previous work or education in literature but in truth there is nothing to say on those fronts. I was simply a man with a vivid imagination who was plunged into the chaotic and exciting world of Dungeons and Dragons who let a character's backstory get out of hand.

Now, when not working my day job, I can be found...writing. The good news for anyone who enjoyed this story is that it is part one of a trilogy. Terrible news for anyone who hated every word and wishes I would stop.

On a serious note, I can be found spending time with my wife, watching wrestling, eating too much food, throwing weights around my garage or watching the Houston Texans as they break my heart over and over.

The Darkness of Dusk - An Onyxborn Chronicle will be out in 2021

Printed in Great Britain
by Amazon